THE COVE

THE FBI THRILLERS

THE COVE

AN FBI THRILLER

CATHERINE COULTER

G. P. PUTNAM'S SONS

NEW YORK

This is a work of fiction. Names, characters, places, and incidents either
are the product of the author's imagination or are used fictitiously, and
any resemblance to actual persons, living or dead, business
establishments, events, or locales is entirely coincidental.

G. P. Putnam's Sons
Publishers Since 1838
a member of
Penguin Group (USA) Inc.
375 Hudson Street
New York, NY 10014

PUBLISHING HISTORY
Jove paperback edition 1996
G. P. Putnam's Sons hardcover edition 2003

Library of Congress Cataloging-in-Publication Data

Coulter, Catherine.
The Cove : an FBI thriller / Catherine Coulter.
p.   cm.
ISBN 0-399-15086-2
1. United States, Federal Bureau of Investigation—Fiction.   2. Savich,
Dillon (Fictitious character)—Fiction.   3. Government investigators—
Fiction.   4. Oregon—Fiction.   I. Title.
PS3553.O843C68   2003   2003043156
813'.54—dc21

Printed in the United States of America
1   3   5   7   9   10   8   6   4   2

This book is printed on acid-free paper. ∞

Book design by Gretchen Achilles

TO MY CREATIVE AND TALENTED SISTER, Diane Coulter, who said to me, "Let me tell you about this little town on the coast of Oregon called The Cove." And thus *The Cove* was born.

To my assistant, Karen Evans, who snits without fear of death, and with charm.

And finally to my husband, Anton, partner and confidant, who manages to keep everything in proper perspective.

Dear Reader:

Thanks to your many requests, here is *The Cove* in hardcover. We kept the cover like the original so there wouldn't be any confusion.

The Cove, first out in paperback in 1996, is where the FBI series began, although at the time I had no idea that a suspense thriller series would spring from it. I'll never forget that after I sent *The Cove* to the publisher I thought to myself: Hmmm, what will I write next? Suddenly, there was this guy's deep sexy voice in my left ear saying, "What about me?" Dillon Savich asserted himself and the FBI series was born.

Serendipity is a wonderful thing. I hope all of you enjoy *The Cove* in hardcover.

CATHERINE COULTER

SOMEONE WAS WATCHING HER. She tugged on the black wig, flattening it against her ears, and quickly put on another coat of deep red lipstick, holding the mirror up so she could see behind her.

The young Marine saw her face in the mirror and grinned at her. She jumped as if she'd been shot. *Just stop it. He's harmless, he's just flirting.* He couldn't be more than eighteen, his head all shaved, his cheeks as smooth as hers. She tilted the mirror to see more. The woman sitting beside him was reading a Dick Francis novel. In the seat behind them a young couple were leaning into each other, asleep.

The seat in front of her was empty. The Greyhound driver was whistling Eric Clapton's "Tears in Heaven," a song that always twisted up her insides. The only one who seemed to notice her was that young Marine, who'd gotten on at the last stop in Portland. He was probably going home to see his eighteen-year-old girlfriend. He wasn't after her, surely, but someone was. She wouldn't be fooled again. They'd taught her so much. No, she'd never be fooled again.

She put the mirror back into her purse and fastened the flap. She stared at her fingers, at the white line where the wedding ring had been until three days ago. She'd tried to pull it off for the past six months but hadn't managed to do it. She had been too out of it even to fasten the Velcro on her sneakers—when they allowed her sneakers—much less work off a tight ring.

Soon, she thought, soon she would be safe. Her mother would be safe too. Oh, God, Noelle—sobbing in the middle of the night when she didn't know anyone could hear her. But without her there, they couldn't do a thing to Noelle. Odd how she rarely thought of Noelle as her mother anymore, not like she had ten years before, when Noelle had listened to all her teenage problems, taken her shopping, driven her to her soccer games. So much they'd done together. Before. Yes, before that night when she'd seen her father slam his fist into her mother's chest and she'd heard the cracking of ribs.

She'd run in, screaming at him to leave her mother alone, and jumped on his back. He was so surprised, so shocked, that he didn't strike her. He shook her off, turned, and shouted down at her, "Mind your own business, Susan! This doesn't concern you." She stared at him, all the fear and hatred she felt for him at that moment clear on her face.

"Doesn't concern me? She's my mother, you bastard. Don't you dare hit her again!"

He looked calm, but she wasn't fooled; she saw the pulse pounding madly in his neck. "It was her fault, Susan. Mind your own damned business. Do you hear me? It was her fault." He took a step toward her mother, his fist raised. She picked up the Waterford carafe off his desk, yelling, "Touch her and I'll bash your head in."

He was panting now, turning swiftly to face her again, no more calm expression to fool her. His face was distorted with rage. "Bitch! Damned interfering little bitch! I'll make you pay for this, Susan. No one goes against me, particularly a spoiled little girl who's never done a thing in her life except spend her father's money." He didn't hit Noelle again. He looked at both of them with naked fury, then strode out of the house, slamming the door behind him.

"Yeah, right," she said and very carefully and slowly set the Waterford carafe down before she dropped it.

She wanted to call an ambulance but her mother wouldn't allow it. "You can't," she said, her voice as cracked as her ribs. "You can't, Sally. Your father would be ruined if anyone believed us. I can't allow that to happen."

"He deserves to be ruined," Sally said, but she obeyed. She was only sixteen years old, home for the weekend from her private girls' school in Laurelberg, Virginia. Why wouldn't they be believed?

"No, dearest," her mother whispered, the pain bowing her in on herself. "No. Get me that blue bottle of pills in the medicine cabinet. Hurry, Sally. The blue bottle."

As she watched her mother swallow three of the pills, groaning as she did so, she realized the pills were there because her father had struck her mother before. Deep down, Sally knew it. She hated herself because she'd never asked, never said a word.

That night her mother became Noelle, and the next week Sally left her girls' school and moved back to her parents' home in Washington, D.C., in hopes of protecting her mother. She read everything she could find on abuse—not that it helped.

That was ten years ago, though sometimes it seemed like last week. Noelle had stayed with her husband, refusing to seek counseling, refusing to read any of the books Sally brought her. It made no sense to Sally, but she'd stayed as close as possible, until she'd met Scott Brainerd at the Whistler exhibition at the National Gallery of Art and married him two months later.

She didn't want to think about Scott or about her father now. Despite her vigilance, she knew her father had hit Noelle whenever she happened to be gone from the house. She'd seen the bruises her mother had tried to hide from her, seen her walking carefully, like an old woman. Once he broke her mother's arm, but Noelle refused to go to the hospital, to the doctor, and ordered Susan to keep quiet. Her father just looked at her, daring her, and she did nothing. Nothing.

Her fingers rubbed unconsciously over the white line where the ring had been. She could remember the past so clearly—her first day at school, when she was on the seesaw and a little boy pointed, laughing that he saw her panties.

It was just the past week that was a near blank in her mind. The week her father had been killed. The whole week was like a very long dream that had almost dissolved into nothing more than an occasional wisp of memory with the coming of the morning.

Sally knew she'd been at her parents' house that night, but she couldn't remember anything more, at least nothing she could grasp—

just vague shadows that blurred, then faded in and out. But they didn't know that. They wanted her badly, she'd realized that soon enough. If they couldn't use her to prove that Noelle had killed her husband, why, then they'd take her and prove that she'd killed her father. Why not? Other children had murdered their fathers. Although there were plenty of times she'd wanted to, she didn't believe she'd killed him.

On the other hand, she just didn't know. It was all a blank, locked tightly away in her brain. She knew she was capable of killing that bastard, but had she? There were many people who could have wanted her father dead. Perhaps they'd found out she'd been there after all. Yes, that was it. She'd been a witness and they knew it. She probably had been. She just didn't remember.

She had to stay focused on the present. She looked out the Greyhound window at the small town the bus was going through. Ugly gray exhaust spewed out the back of the bus. She bet the locals loved that.

They were driving along Highway 101 southwest. Just another half hour, she thought, just thirty more minutes, and she wouldn't have to worry anymore, at least for a while. She would take any safe time she could get. Soon she wouldn't have to be afraid of anyone who chanced to look at her. No one knew about her aunt, no one.

She was terrified that the young Marine would get off after her when she stepped down from the bus at the junction of highways 101 and 101A. But he didn't. No one did. She stood there with her one small bag, staring at the young Marine, who'd turned around in his seat and was looking back at her. She tamped down on her fear. He just wanted to flirt, not hurt her. She thought he had lousy taste in women. She watched for cars, but none were coming from either direction.

She walked west along Highway 101A to The Cove. Highway 101A didn't go east.

"YES?"

She stared at the woman she'd seen once in her life when she was no more than seven years old. She looked like a hippie, a colorful scarf wrapped around her long, curling, dark hair, huge gold hoops dangling from her ears, her skirt ankle-length and painted all in dark blues and browns. She was wearing blue sneakers. Her face was strong, her cheekbones high and prominent, her chin sharp, her eyes dark and intelligent. Actually, she was the most beautiful woman Sally had ever seen.

"Aunt Amabel?"

"What did you say?" Amabel stared at the young woman who stood on her front doorstep, a young woman who didn't look cheap with all that makeup she'd piled on her face, just exhausted and sickly pale. And frightened. Then, of course, she knew. She had known deep down that she would come. Yes, she'd known, but it still shook her.

"I'm Sally," she said and pulled off the black wig and took out half a dozen hairpins. Thick, waving dark blond hair tumbled down to her shoulders. "Maybe you called me Susan? Not many people do anymore."

The woman was shaking her head back and forth, those dazzling earrings slapping against her neck. "My God, it's really you, Sally?" She rocked back on her heels.

"Yes."

"Oh, my," Amabel said and quickly pulled her niece against her, hugged her tightly, then pushed her back to look at her. "Oh, my goodness. I've been so worried. I finally heard the news about your papa, but I didn't know if I should call Noelle. You know how she is. I was going to call her tonight when the rates go down, but you're here, Sally. I guess I hoped you'd come to me. What's happened? Is your mama all right?"

"Noelle is fine, I think," Sally said. "I didn't know where else to go, so I came here. Can I stay here, Aunt Amabel, just for a little while? Just until I can think of something, make some plans?"

"Of course you can. Look at that black wig and all that makeup on your face. Why, baby?"

The endearment undid her. She'd not cried, not once, until now, until this woman she didn't really know called her "baby." Her aunt's hands were stroking her back, her voice was low and soothing. "It's all right, lovey. I promise you, everything will be all right now. Come in, Sally, and I'll take care of you. That's what I told your mama when I first saw you. You were the cutest little thing, so skinny, your arms and legs wobbly like a colt's, and the biggest smile I'd ever seen. I wanted to take care of you then. You'll be safe here. Come on, baby."

The damnable tears wouldn't stop. They just kept dripping down her face, ruining the god-awful thick black mascara. She even tasted it, and when she swiped her hand over her face it came away with black streaks.

"I look like a circus clown," she said, swallowing hard to stop the tears, to smile, to make herself smile. She took out the green-colored contacts. With the crying, they hurt.

"No, you look like a little girl trying on her mama's makeup. That's right, take out those ugly contacts. Ah, now you've got your pretty blue eyes again. Come to the kitchen and I'll make you some tea. I always put a drop of brandy in mine. It wouldn't hurt you one little bit. How old are you now, Sally?"

"Twenty-six, I think."

"What do you mean, you think?" her aunt said, cocking her head to one side, making the gold hoop earring hang straight down almost to her shoulder.

Sally couldn't tell her that though she thought her birthday had come and gone in that place, she couldn't seem to see the day in her mind, couldn't dredge up anyone saying anything to her, not that she could imagine it anyway. She couldn't even remember if her father had been there. She prayed he hadn't. She couldn't tell Amabel about that, she just couldn't. She shook her head, smiled, and said, not lying well, "It was just a way of speaking, Aunt Amabel. I'd love some tea and a drop of brandy."

Amabel sat her niece down in the kitchen at her old pine table that had three magazines under one leg to keep it steady. At least she'd made cushions for the wooden seats, so they were comfortable. She put the kettle on the gas burner and turned it on. "There," she said. "That won't take too long."

Sally watched her put a Lipton tea bag into each cup and pour in the brandy. Amabel said, "I always pour the brandy in first. It soaks into the tea bag and makes the flavor stronger. Brandy's expensive and I've got to make it last. This bottle"—she lifted the Christian Brothers—"is going on its third month. Not bad. You'll see, you'll like it."

"No one followed me, Aunt Amabel. I was really careful. I imagine you know that everyone is after me. But I managed to get away. As far as I know, no one knows about you. Noelle never told a soul. Only Father knew about you, and he's dead."

Amabel just nodded. Sally sat quietly, watching Amabel move around her small kitchen, each action smooth and efficient. She was graceful, this aunt of hers in her hippie clothes. She looked at those strong hands, the long fingers, the short, buffed nails painted an awesome bright red. Amabel was an artist, she remembered that now. She couldn't see any resemblance at all to Noelle, Amabel's younger sister. Amabel was dark as a gypsy, while Noelle was blond and fair-complexioned, blue-eyed, and soft as a pillow.

Like me, Sally thought. But Sally wasn't soft anymore. She was hard as a brick.

She waited, expecting Amabel to whip out a deck of cards and tell her fortune. She wondered why none of Noelle's family ever spoke of Amabel. What had she done that was so terrible?

Her fingers rubbed over the white band where the ring had been. She said as she looked around the old kitchen with its ancient refrigerator and porcelain sink, "You don't mind that I'm here, Aunt Amabel?"

"Call me Amabel, honey, that'll be just fine. I don't mind at all. Both of us will protect your mama. As for you, why, I don't think you could hurt that little bug that's scurrying across the kitchen floor."

Sally shook her head, got out of her seat, and squashed the bug beneath her heel. She sat down again. "I just want you to see me as I really am," she said.

Amabel only shrugged, turned back to the stove when the teakettle whistled, and poured the water into the teacups. She said, not turning around, "Things happen to people, change them. Take your mama. Everyone always protected your mama, including me. Why wouldn't her daughter do the same? You are protecting her, aren't you, Sally?"

She handed Sally her cup of tea. She pulled the tea bag back and forth, making the tea darker and darker. Finally, she lifted the bag and placed it carefully on the saucer. She'd swished that tea bag just the way her mother always had when she'd been young. She took a drink, held the brandied tea in her mouth a moment, then swallowed. The tea was wonderful, thick, rich, and sinful. She felt less on edge almost immediately. That brandy was something. Surely she'd be safe here. Surely Amabel would take her in just for a little while until she figured out what to do.

She imagined her aunt wanted to hear everything, but she wasn't pushing. Sally was immensely grateful for that.

"I've often wondered what kind of woman you'd become," Amabel said. "Looks to me like you've become a fine one. This mess—and that's what it is—it will pass. Everything will be resolved, you'll see." She was silent a moment, remembering the affection she'd felt for the little girl, that bone-deep desire to keep her close, to hug her until she squeaked. It surprised her that it was still there. She didn't like it, nor did she want it.

"Careful of leaning on that end of the table, Sally. Purn Davies wanted to fix it for me, but I wouldn't let him." She knew Sally wasn't hearing her, but it didn't matter, Amabel was just making noise until Sally got some of that brandy in her belly.

"This tea's something else, Amabel. Strange, but good." She took another drink, then another. She felt warmth pooling in her stomach. She realized she hadn't felt this warm in more than five days.

"You might as well tell me now, Sally. You came here so you could protect your mama, didn't you, baby?"

Sally took another big drink of the tea. What could she say? She said nothing.

"Did your mama kill your papa?"

Sally set down her cup and stared into it, wishing she knew the truth of things, but that night was as murky in her mind as the tea in the bottom of her cup. "I don't know," she said finally. "I just don't know, but they think I do. They think I'm either protecting Noelle or running because I did it. They're trying to find me. I didn't want to take a chance, so that's why I'm here."

Was she lying? Amabel didn't say anything. She merely smiled at her niece, who looked exhausted, her face white and pinched, her lovely blue eyes as faded and worn as an old dress. She was too thin; her sweater and slacks hung on her. In that moment her niece looked very old, as if she had seen too much of the wicked side of life. Well, it was too bad, but there was more wickedness in the world than anyone cared to admit.

She said quietly as she stared down into her teacup, "If your mama did kill her husband, I'll bet the bastard deserved it."

SALLY NEARLY DROPPED her cup. She set it carefully down. "You knew?"

"Sure. All of us did. The first time I ever got to see you was when she brought you home. I was passing through. That's all our folks ever wanted me to do—pass through and not say much or show my face much, particularly to all their friends. Anyway, your mama showed up. She was running away from him, she said. She also said she'd never go back. She was bruised. She cried all the time.

"But her resolve didn't last long. He called her two nights later and she flew back home the next day, with you all wrapped in a blanket. You weren't even a year old then. She wouldn't talk about it to me. I never could understand why a woman would let herself be beaten whenever a man decided he wanted to do it."

"I couldn't either. I tried, Aunt Amabel. I really tried, but she wouldn't listen. What did my grandparents say?"

Amabel shrugged, thinking of her horrified father, staring at beautiful Noelle, wondering what the devil he would do if the press got wind of the juicy story that his son-in-law, Amory St. John, was a wife beater. And their mother, shrinking away from her daughter as if she had some sort of vile disease. She hadn't cared either. She just didn't want the press to find out because it would hurt the family's reputation.

"They aren't what you'd call real warm parents, Sally. They pretended not to believe that your papa beat your mama. They looked at Noelle, saw all those bruises, and denied all of it. They told her she shouldn't tell lies like that. Your mama was a real mess, arguing with them, pleading with them to help her.

"But then he called, and your mama acted like nothing had ever happened. You know what, Sally? My parents were mighty relieved when she left. She would have been a loser, a failure, a millstone around their necks if she'd left your father. She was special, a daughter to be proud of, when she was with him. Do you ever see your grandparents?"

"Three times a year. Oh, God, Aunt Amabel, I hated him. But now—"

"Now you're afraid the police are looking for you. Don't worry, baby. No one would know you in that disguise."

He would, Sally thought. In a flash. "I hope not," she said. "Do you think I should keep wearing the black wig here?"

"No, I wouldn't worry. You're my niece, nothing more, nothing less. No one watches TV except for Thelma Nettro, who owns the bed-and-breakfast, and she's so old I don't even know if she can see the screen. She can hear, though. I know that for a fact.

"No, don't bother with the wig—and leave those contacts in a drawer. Not to worry. We'll just use your married name. Here you'll be Sally Brainerd."

"I can't use that name anymore, Amabel."

"All right then. We'll use your maiden name—Sally St. John. No, don't worry that anyone would ever tie you to your dead papa. Like I said, no one here pays any attention to what goes on outside the town limits. As for anyone else, why, no one ever comes here—"

"Except for people who want to eat the World's Greatest Ice Cream. I like the sign out at the junction with that huge chocolate ice cream cone painted on it. You can see it a mile away, and by the time you get to it, your mouth is watering. You painted the sign, didn't you, Amabel?"

"I sure did. And you're right. People tell us they see that sign and by the time they get to the junction their car just turns toward The Cove. It's Helen Keaton's recipe, handed down from her granny. The ice cream shop used to be the chapel in the front of Ralph Keaton's mortuary. We all decided that since we have Reverend Vorhees's church, we didn't need Ralph's little chapel too." She paused, looking into a memory, and smiled. "In the beginning we stored the ice cream in caskets packed full of ice. It took every freezer in every refrigerator in this town to make that much ice."

"I can't wait to try it. Goodness, I remember when the town wasn't much of anything—back when I came here that one time. Do you remember? I was just a little kid."

"I remember. You were adorable."

Sally smiled, a very small smile, but it was a beginning. She just shook her head, saying, "I remember this place used to be so ramshackle and down at the heels—no paint on any of the houses, boards hanging off some of the buildings. And there were potholes in the street as deep as I was tall. But now the town looks wonderful, so charming and clean and pristine."

"Well, you're right. We've had lots of good changes. We all put our heads together, and that's when Helen Keaton spoke up about her granny's ice cream recipe. That Fourth of July—goodness, it will be four years this July—was when we opened the World's Greatest Ice Cream Shop. I'll never forget how the men all pooh-poohed the idea, said it wouldn't amount to anything. Well, we sure showed them."

"I'd say so. If the World's Greatest Ice Cream Shop is the reason the town's so beautiful now, maybe Helen Keaton should run for president."

"Maybe so. Would you like a ham sandwich, baby?"

A ham sandwich, Sally thought. "With mayonnaise? Real mayonnaise, not the fat-free stuff?"

"Real mayonnaise."

"White bread and not fourteen-vitamin seven-grain whole wheat?"

"Cheap white bread."

"That sounds wonderful, Amabel. You're sure no one will recognize me?"

"Not a soul."

They watched a small, very grainy black-and-white TV while Sally ate her sandwich. Within five minutes, the story was on the national news broadcast.

"Former Naval Commander Amory Davidson St. John was buried today at Arlington National Cemetery. His widow, Noelle St. John, was accompanied by her son-in-law, Scott Brainerd, a lawyer who had worked closely with Amory St. John, the senior legal counsel for TransCon International. Her daughter, Susan St. John Brainerd, was not present.

"We go now to Police Commissioner Howard Duzman, who is working closely with the FBI on this high-profile investigation."

Amabel didn't know much of anything about Scott Brainerd. She had never met him, had never spoken to him until she had called Noelle and he answered the phone, identified himself, and asked who she was. And she'd told him. Why not? She'd asked him to have Noelle call her back. But Noelle hadn't called her—not that Amabel had expected her to. If Noelle's life depended on it, well, that would be different. She would be on the phone like a shot. But she hadn't called her this time. Amabel wondered if Noelle would realize that Sally could be here. Would that make her call? She didn't know. Actually, now it didn't matter.

She reached out her hand and covered her niece's thin fingers with hers. She saw where there had once been a ring, but it was gone now, leaving just a pale white mark in its place. She wondered for just a moment if she should tell Sally that she'd spoken to her husband. No, not yet. Maybe never. Let the girl rest for a while. Hopefully there would be time, but Amabel didn't know. Actually, if she could, she would get rid of Sally this very minute, get her away from here before . . . No, she wouldn't think about that. She didn't really have a choice.

Everything would work out. Besides, what would it matter of Scott Brainerd did find out his wife was hiding out here? So she said nothing, just held Sally's hand in hers.

"I'm awfully tired, Amabel."

"I'll bet you are, baby. I'll just bet you are."

Amabel tucked her in like she was her little girl in the small second bedroom. The room was quiet, so very quiet. She was asleep within minutes. In a few more minutes she was twisted in the covers, moaning.

THERE WAS SO MUCH DAYLIGHT in that room, all of it pouring through the wide windows that gave onto an immaculate lawn stretching a good hundred yards to the edge of a copse of thick oak trees. The two men led her in, shoving her forward, nearly knocking her to her knees. They put their hands on her shoulders, forcing her to sit in front of his desk. He was smiling at her. He didn't say a word until they'd left, quietly closing the door behind them.

He steepled his fingers. "You look pathetic, Sally, in those gray sweats. And just look at your hair, all stringy, and no makeup on your face, not even a touch of lipstick in honor of coming to see me. Next time I'll have to ask them to do something with you before bringing you to me."

She heard every word, felt the hurt that every word intended, but the comprehension quickly died, and she only shrugged, a tiny movement because it was so much work to make her shoulders rise and fall to produce a shrug.

"You've been with me now for nearly a week and you're not a bit better, Sally. You're still delusional, paranoid. If you're too stupid to understand what those words mean, why, then, let me get more basic with you. You're crazy, Sally, just plain crazy, and you'll stay that way. No cure for you. Now, since I've got to look at you for a while longer, why don't you at least say something, maybe even sing a little song, maybe a song you used to sing in the shower. Yes, I know you always sang in the shower. How about it?"

Oddly, even though the comprehension didn't remain long in her brain, the viciousness of the words, the utter cruelty of them, hung on. She managed to rise, lean forward, and spit in his face.

He lunged around his desk as he swiped his hand over his face. He jerked her to her feet and slapped her hard, sending her reeling to the floor. The door to his office flew open, and the two men who'd brought her came banging through.

They were worried about him?

She heard him say, "She spit on me and then attacked me. Bring me three milligrams of Haldol. No pill this time. That should calm our poor little girl down."

No. She knew that if they gave her any more of that stuff she'd die. She knew it, knew it. She staggered to her feet. She ran to those wide windows. She heard shouts behind her. She dove through the glass. For an instant she was flying, white shards of glass falling from her, letting her soar higher and higher above that beautiful lawn, flying away from the horror of this place, the horror of him. Then she wasn't flying anymore. She heard screams and knew it was she who was screaming.

Then she felt the pain drag at her, pulling her down, down, until there was blackness and beautiful nothingness.

BUT THE SCREAMING WENT ON. That wasn't right. She was unconscious, no longer screaming.

Another scream jerked her awake. Sally reared up in bed, straining to hear those screams. They'd been here, in The Cove, in Amabel's house, not in her dream back there. She didn't move, just waited, waited. A cat? No, it was human, a cry of pain, she knew it was. God knew, she'd heard enough cries of pain in the last year.

Who? Amabel? She didn't want to move, but she made herself slip out from under the three blankets Amabel had piled on top of her at nine o'clock the previous evening. It was freezing in the small guest room and black as the bottom of a witch's cauldron. Sally didn't have a bathrobe, just her long Lanz flannel nightgown. Scott had hated her nightgowns, he hated . . . no, forget Scott. He truly didn't matter, hadn't mattered in a very long time.

The room was very dark. She made her way to the door and gently shoved it open. The narrow hallway was just as dark. She waited, waited longer, not wanting to hear that cry again, but knowing she would. It was a cry of pain. Perhaps there had been surprise in it. She couldn't be sure now. She waited. It was just a matter of time. She walked in her sock feet toward Amabel's bedroom.

She stumbled when she heard another cry, her hip hitting a table. This cry came from outside. She was sure of it. It wasn't Amabel; thank God, she was safe. Amabel would know what to do.

What was it? She rubbed her hip as she set the table against the wall again.

Suddenly Amabel's bedroom door flew open. "What's going on? Is that you, Sally?"

"Yes, Amabel," she whispered. "I heard someone cry out and thought it was you. What is it?"

"I didn't hear a thing," Amabel said. "Go back to bed, dear. You're exhausted. It's probably the leftovers of a bad dream. Just look at you, you're white as the woodwork. You did have a nightmare, didn't you?"

Sally nodded because it was the truth. But those screams had lasted, had gone on and on. They'd not been part of the dream, the dream that was a memory she hated, but that always came in her sleep when she was helpless against it.

"Go to bed. You poor baby, you're shivering like a leaf. Go back to bed. Hurry now."

"But I heard it twice, Amabel. I thought it was you, but it's not. It's coming from outside the house."

"No, baby, there's nothing out there. You're so tired, so much has happened in the past few days I'm surprised you haven't heard the Rolling Stones bawling at the top of their lungs. There's nothing, Sally. It was a nightmare, nothing more. Don't forget, this is The Cove, dear. Nothing ever happens here. If you did hear something, why, it was only the wind. The wind off the ocean can whine just like a person. You'll learn that soon enough. You didn't hear anything. Trust me. Go back to bed."

Sally went back to bed. She lay stiff and waiting, so cold she wondered whether the tears would freeze on her face if she cried. She could have sworn that she heard a door quietly open and close, but she didn't have the guts to go see.

She would relax, then stiffen again, waiting to hear that awful cry. But there weren't any more cries. Maybe Amabel was right. She was exhausted; she had been dreaming and it had been hideous and so very real. Maybe she was paranoid or psychotic or schizophrenic. They had called her all those things for six months. She wondered—if she saw the person actually cry out would that be a delusion? Just a fabrication of her mind? Probably. No, she wouldn't think about that time. It made her hurt too much. She fell asleep again near dawn.

It was a dreamless sleep this time.

JAMES RAILEY QUINLAN had more energy than he'd had just twenty minutes before. His body was humming with it. That was because she was here. He was sure of it now, he could feel her here. He'd always had these feelings—more than intuition. The feelings just came to him suddenly, and he had always followed them, ever since he was a kid. The time or two he hadn't, he'd gotten himself into deep shit. Now he was out on a very long limb, and if he was wrong he'd pay for it. But he wasn't wrong. He could feel her presence in this very charming and well-manicured little town.

Dreadful little place, he thought, so perfect, like a Hollywood set, just like Teresa's hometown. He remembered having the same reaction, feeling the same vague distaste when he'd traveled to that small town in Ohio to marry Teresa Raglan, daughter of the local judge.

He pulled his gray Buick Regal into a well-marked parking place in front of the World's Greatest Ice Cream Shop. There were two large plate-glass windows, painted all around with bright blue trim. He could see small circular tables inside, with old-fashioned white wrought-iron chairs. Behind the counter an older woman was talking to a man while she scooped chocolate ice cream out of a carton set down into the counter. The front of the shop was painted a pristine white. It was a quaint little place, just like the rest of the town, but for some reason he didn't like the looks of it.

He stepped out of the sedan and looked around. Next to the ice cream shop was a small general store with a sign out front in ornate type that could have come straight out of Victorian times: PURN DAVIES: YOU WANT IT—I SELL IT.

On the other side of the ice cream shop was a small clothing store that looked elegant and expensive, with that peculiar Carmel-like look that the rest of the buildings had. It was called Intimate Deceptions—a name that for James conjured up images of black lace against a white sheet or white skin.

The sidewalks looked brand new and the road was nicely black-topped. No ruts anywhere to hold rain puddles.

All the parking spots were marked with thick white lines. Not a faded line in the bunch. He'd seen newer houses on the drive in, apparently all built very recently. In town there was a hardware store, a small Safeway barely large enough to support the sign, a dry cleaners, a one-hour-photo place, a McDonald's with a very discreet golden arch.

A prosperous, quaint little town that was perfect.

He slipped his keys into his jacket pocket. First thing he needed was a place to stay. He spotted a sign reading THELMA'S BED AND BREAK-FAST right across the street. Nothing fancy about that sign or title. He pulled his black travel bag out of the back seat and walked over to Thelma's big white Victorian gingerbread house with its deep porch that encircled the entire house. He hoped he could get a room up in one of those circular towers.

For an old house, it was in immaculate shape. The white of the clapboard gleamed, and the pale blue and yellow trim around the windows and on cornices seemed to be fresh. The wide wooden porch planks didn't groan beneath his weight. The boards were new, the railing solid oak and sturdy.

He announced himself as James Quinlan to a smiling lady in her late fifties whom he found standing behind the antique walnut counter in the front hall. She was wearing an apron that had lots of flour on it. He explained he was looking for a room, preferably one in the tower. At the sound of an ancient cackle, he turned and saw a robust old lady rocking back and forth in an antique chair in the doorway of the huge living room. She was holding what appeared to be a diary in front of her nose with one hand, and in the other she held a fountain pen. Every few seconds she wet the tip of the fountain pen with her tongue, a habit that left her with a big black circle on the tip of her tongue.

"Ma'am," he said, and nodded toward the old lady. "I sure hope that ink isn't poisonous."

"It wouldn't kill her even if it was," the lady behind the counter said. "She's surely built up an immunity by now. Thelma's been at that diary of hers with that black ink on her tongue ever since she and her husband first moved to The Cove back in the 1940s."

The old lady cackled again, then called out, "I'm Thelma Nettro. You don't have a wife, boy?"

"That's a bold question, ma'am, even for an old lady."

Thelma ignored him. "So what are you doing in The Cove? You come here for the World's Greatest Ice Cream?"

"I saw that sign. I'll be sure to try it later."

"Have the peach. Helen just made it up last week. It's dandy. So if you aren't here for ice cream, then why are you here?"

Here goes, he thought. "I'm a private detective, ma'am. My client's parents disappeared around this area some three and a half years ago. The cops never got anywhere. The son hired me to find out what happened to them."

"Old folk?"

"Yeah, they'd been driving all over the U.S. in a Winnebago. The Winnebago was found in a used car lot up in Spokane. Looked to be foul play, but nobody could ever find anything out."

"So why are you here in The Cove? Nothing ever happens here, nothing at all. I remember telling my husband, Bobby—he died of pneumonia just after Eisenhower was reelected in 1956—that this little town had never known a heyday, but it just kept going anyhow. Do you know what happened then? Well, I'll tell you. This banker from Portland bought up lots of coastal land and built vacation cottages. He built the two-laner off Highway 101 and ran it right to the ocean." Thelma stopped, licked the end of her fountain pen, and sighed. "Then in the 1960s, everything began to fall apart, everyone just upped and left, got bored with our town, I suppose. So, you see, it doesn't make any sense for you to stay here."

"I'm using your town as a sort of central point. I'll search out from here. Perhaps you remember these old folk coming through, ma'am—"

"My name's Thelma, I told you that. There's lots of ma'ams in this world, but just one me, and I'm Thelma Nettro. Doc Spiver pronounced me deader than a bat some years ago, but he was wrong. Oh, Lordy, you should have seen the look on Ralph Keaton's face when he had me all ready to lay out in that funeral home of his. I near to scared the toenails off him when I sat up and asked him what the hell he was doing. Ah, yes, that was something. He was so scared he went shouting for Reverend Hal Vorhees to protect him. You can call me Thelma, boy."

"Maybe you remember these old folk, Thelma. The man was Harve Jensen, and his wife's name was Marge. A nice older couple, according to their son. The son did say they had a real fondness for ice cream." Why not, he thought. Stir the pot a bit. Be specific, it made you more believable. Besides, everyone liked ice cream. He'd have to try it.

"Harve and Marge Jensen," Thelma repeated, rocking harder now, her veined and spotted old hands clenching and unclenching on the arms of the chair. "Can't say I remember any old folk like that. Driving a Winnebago, you say? You go over and try one of Helen's peach ice cream cones."

"Soon I will. I like the sign out there at the junction of 101 and 101A. The artist really got that brown color to look just like rich chocolate ice cream. Yeah, they were driving a Winnebago."

"It's brought us lots of folk, that sign. The state bureaucrats wanted us to take it down, but one of our locals—Gus Eisner—knew the governor's cousin, and he fixed it. We pay the state three hundred dollars a year to keep the sign there. Amabel repaints it every year in July, sort of an anniversary, since that's when we first opened. Purn Davies told her the chocolate paint she used for the ice cream was too dark, but we all ignored him. He wanted to marry Amabel after her husband died, but she wouldn't have anything to do with him. He still isn't over it. Pretty tacky, huh?"

"I'd say so," Quinlan said.

"You tell Amabel that you think her chocolate is perfect. That'll please her."

Amabel, he thought. Amabel Perdy. She was her aunt.

The stocky gray-haired woman behind the counter cleared her throat. She smiled at him when he turned back to her.

"What did you say, Martha? Speak up. You know I can't hear you."

Like hell, James thought. The old relic probably heard everything within three miles of town.

"And stop fiddling with those pearls. You've already broken them more times than I can count."

Martha's pearls did look a bit ratty, he thought.

"Martha, what do you want?"

"I need to check Mr. Quinlan in, Thelma. And I've got to finish baking that chocolate decadence cake before I go to lunch with Mr. Drapper. But I want to get Mr. Quinlan settled first."

"Well, do it, don't just stand there wringing your hands. You watch yourself with Ed Drapper, Martha. He's a fast one, that boy is. I noticed just yesterday that you're getting liver spots, Martha. I heard you got liver spots if you'd had too much sex when you were younger. Yes, you watch what you do with Ed Drapper. Oh, yes, don't forget to put walnuts in that chocolate decadence cake. I love walnuts."

James turned to Martha, such a sweet-looking lady, with stiff gray hair and a buxom bosom and glasses perched on the end of her nose. She was tucking her hands in her pockets, hiding those liver spots.

James laughed and said, knowing the old lady was listening, "She's a terror, isn't she?"

"She's more than a terror, Mr. Quinlan," Martha said in a whisper. "She's a lot more. Poor Ed Drapper is sixty-three years old." She raised her voice. "No, Thelma, I won't forget the walnuts."

"A mere lad," James said and smiled at Martha, who didn't look as if she'd ever had any sex in her life. She was tugging on those pearls again.

When she left him in the tower room, which gave him a panoramic view of the ocean, he walked to the window and stared out, not at the ocean that gleamed like a brilliant blue jewel beneath the full afternoon sun but at the people below. Across the street, right in front of Purn Davies's store, he saw four old geezers pull out chairs and arrange them around an oak barrel that had to be as old as James's grandfather. One of the men pulled out a deck of cards. James had a feeling he was looking at a long-standing ritual. One of the men arranged his cards, then spat off the sidewalk. Another one hooked his gnarly old fingers beneath his suspenders and leaned back in the chair. Yes, James thought, a ritual of many years. He wondered if one of them was Purn Davies, the one who'd criticized Amabel's chocolate because she'd refused to marry him. Was one of them Reverend Hal Vorhees? No, surely a reverend wouldn't be sitting there spitting and playing cards.

It didn't matter. He'd find out soon enough who everybody was. So there'd be no doubt in anybody's mind about why he was here, he would talk to this group too about Harve and Marge Jensen. He'd talk to everyone he ran into. No one would suspect a thing.

He would bet his next paycheck that those old geezers saw just about everything that went on in this town, including a runaway woman who just happened to be the daughter of a big-time lawyer who had not only gotten himself murdered but who'd also been involved in some very bad business. A woman who also happened to be Amabel Perdy's niece.

James wished Amory St. John hadn't gotten himself knocked off, at least not until the FBI had finally nailed him for selling arms to terrorist nations.

He turned from the window and frowned. He realized he hadn't cared at all about Harve and Marge Jensen until ancient Thelma Nettro, who'd been pronounced dead by Doc Spiver but had risen from the table and scared Ralph Keaton shitless, had lied to him.

Investigating the fate of the Jensens had just been a cover that one of the assistants happened to find for him to use. It was a believable cover, she'd told him, because the couple really had mysteriously disappeared along a stretch of highway that included The Cove.

But why had the old lady lied? What reason could she possibly have? Now he was curious. Too bad he didn't have time. He thrived on mystery. And he was the best of the best, at least that was what Teresa had told him in bed time and again before she'd run away with a mail bomber he himself had hunted down and arrested, only to have her defend him and get him off on a technicality.

He hung up his slacks and his shirts, laid his underwear in the top drawer of the beautiful antique dresser. He walked into the bathroom to lay out his toiletries and was pleasantly surprised. It was huge, all pink-veined marble, and totally modernized, right down to the water-saver toilet. The tub was huge and was curtained off so he could take a shower if he preferred.

Old Thelma Nettro was obviously a hedonist. No claw-footed tubs for her. He wondered how the devil she could make enough money off this place to modernize the bathrooms like this. As far as he could tell, he was the only guest.

There was one restaurant in The Cove, a pretentious little cafe called the Hinterlands that had beautiful red and white tulips in its window boxes. Unlike the rest of the buildings that lined Main Street, the Hinterlands forked off to one side, faced the ocean, and looked painfully charming with its bricked walkway and gables, which, he was certain, had been added merely for decoration.

They served cod and bass. Nothing else, just cod and bass—fried, baked, poached, broiled. James hated all kinds of fish. He ate everything the small salad bar had to offer and knew he was going to have to live at the Safeway deli. But, hell, the Safeway was so small he doubted it even had a deli.

The waitress, an older woman decked out in a Swiss Miss outfit that laced up her chest and swept the floor, said, "Oh, it's fish this week. Zeke can't do more than one thing at a time. He says it confounds him.

Next Monday you come in and we'll have something else. How about some mashed potatoes with all those greens?"

He nodded to Martha and Ed Drapper, who were evidently enjoying their fried cod, cole slaw, and mashed potatoes. She gave him a brilliant smile. He wondered if she recognized him. She wasn't wearing her glasses. Her left hand was playing with her pearls.

After lunch, as James walked toward the four old men playing cards around the barrel, he saw at least half a dozen cars parked out in front of the World's Greatest Ice Cream Shop. Popular place. Had the place been here when Harve and Marge came through? Yeah, sure it had. That's when old Thelma's rheumy eyes had twitched and her old hands had clenched big time. He might as well get to know the locals before he tracked Susan St. John Brainerd down.

He wasn't quite certain yet just what he was going to do with her when he found her. The truth, he thought. All he wanted was the truth from her. And he'd get it. He usually did. Then maybe he'd work on the other mystery. If there was another mystery.

TEN MINUTES LATER James walked into the World's Greatest Ice Cream Shop thinking that those four old men weren't any better liars than Thelma Nettro. Unlike Thelma, they hadn't said a word, just shook their heads sorrowfully as they looked at each other. One of them had spat after he repeated Harve's name. That one was Purn Davies. The old man leaning back in the chair had said he'd always fancied having a Winnebago. His name was Gus Eisner. Another one of the men said Gus could fix anything on wheels and kept them all running. The other old man wouldn't meet his eyes. He couldn't remember the names of those last two.

It was telling, their behavior. Whatever had happened to Harve and Marge Jensen, everyone he'd met so far knew about it. He was looking forward to trying the World's Greatest Ice Cream.

The same older woman he'd seen upon his arrival was scooping up what looked to be peach ice cream for a family of tourists who'd probably seen that sign on the road and come west.

The kids were jumping and yelling. The boy wanted Cove Chocolate and the girl wanted Basque Vanilla.

"You've just got the six flavors?" the woman asked.

"Yes, just six. We vary them according to the season. We don't mass-produce anything."

The boy whined that now he wanted blueberry ice cream. The chocolate looked too dark.

The older woman behind the counter just smiled down at him and said, "You can't have it. Either pick another flavor or shut up."

The mother gasped and stared. "You can't act like that toward our son. Why, he's—"

The older woman smiled back, straightened her lacy white cap, and said, "He's what, ma'am?"

"He's a brat," the husband said. He turned to his son. "What do you want, Mickey? You see the six flavors. Pick one now or don't have any."

"I want Basque Vanilla," the girl said. "He can have worms."

"Now, Julie," the mother said, then licked the ice cream cone the woman handed her. "Oh, goodness, it's wonderful. Fresh peaches, Rick. Fresh peaches. It's great."

The woman behind the counter just smiled. The boy took a chocolate triple-dip cone.

James watched the family finally leave.

"Yes, can I help you?"

"I'd like a peach cone, please, ma'am."

"You're new to town," she said as she pulled the scoop through the big tub of ice cream. "You just traveling through?"

"No," James said, taking the cone. "I'll be here for a while. I'm trying to find Marge and Harve Jensen."

"Never heard of them."

James took a lick. He felt as though sweet peaches were sliding down his throat. The woman was a good liar. "The lady was right. This is delicious."

"Thank you. This Marge and Harve—"

James repeated the story he'd told to Thelma and Martha and the old men. When he finished, he stuck out his hand and said, "My name's James Quinlan. I'm a private investigator from Los Angeles."

"I'm Sherry Vorhees. My husband's the local preacher, Reverend Harold Vorhees. I have a four-hour shift here most days."

"A pleasure, ma'am. Can I treat you to an ice cream?"

"Oh, no, I have my iced tea," she said and sipped out of a large plastic tumbler. It was very pale iced tea.

"You know, I'd like some iced tea, if you don't mind," Quinlan said.

Sherry Vorhees winked at him. "Sorry, sir, but you don't want my kind of iced tea, and we don't have any of the other kind."

"Just ice cream, then. You've never heard of this Marge and Harve? You don't remember them coming through here some three years ago? In a Winnebago?"

Sherry thought he was handsome, just like that Englishman who'd played in two James Bond films, but this man was American and he was bigger, a lot taller. She really liked that dimple in his chin. She'd always wondered how men shaved in those tiny little holes. And now this lovely man wanted to know about these two old folk. He was standing right in front of her licking his peach ice cream cone.

"A lot of folk come to The Cove for the World's Greatest Ice Cream," she said, still smiling at him. "Too many to remember individuals. And three years ago . . . Why, at my age I can barely remember what I cooked Hal for dinner last Tuesday."

"Well, you think about it, please, Mrs. Vorhees. I'm staying at Thelma's Bed and Breakfast." He turned as the front doorbell jingled. A middle-aged woman came in. Unlike Martha, this one was dressed like a gypsy, a red scarf tied around her head, thick wool socks and Birkenstocks on her feet. She was wearing a long skirt that looked organic and a dark red wool jacket. Her eyes were dark and very beautiful. She had to be the youngest citizen in the town.

"Hello, Sherry," she said. "I'll relieve you now."

"Thanks, Amabel. Oh, this is James Quinlan. Mr. Quinlan, this is Amabel Perdy. He's a real private detective from Los Angeles, Amabel. He's here to try to find out what happened to an old couple who might have come through The Cove to buy ice cream. What was their name? Oh, yes, Harve and Marge."

Amabel raised her dark gypsy eyebrows at him. She was very still, didn't say anything, just looked at him, completely at ease.

So this was the aunt. How fortunate that she was here and not at home, where he hoped to find Sally Brainerd. Amabel Perdy, an artist, an old hippie, a former schoolteacher. He knew she was a widow, had been married to another artist she'd met in SoHo many decades ago. His art had never amounted to much. He'd died some seventeen years ago. James also knew now that she'd turned down Purn Davies. He noted she didn't look anything like her niece.

"I don't remember any old folk named Harve and Marge," Amabel said. "I'm going in the back to change now, Sherry. Ring out, okay?"

She was the best liar yet. He tamped down his dratted curiosity. It didn't matter. Sally Brainerd was the only thing that mattered.

"How's your little niece doing, Amabel?"

Amabel wished Sherry wouldn't drink so much iced tea. It made her run off at the mouth. But she said pleasantly, "She's doing better. She was just so exhausted from her trip."

"Yes, of course." Sherry Vorhees continued to sip out of that big plastic tumbler and smile at James. That English actor's name was Timothy Dalton. Beautiful man. She liked James Quinlan even better. "There's not much to do here in The Cove. I don't know if you'll last out the week."

"Who knows?" James said, tossed his napkin into the white trash bin, and left the ice cream shop.

His next stop was Amabel Perdy's house, the small white one on the corner of Main Street and Conroy Street. Time to get it done.

When he knocked on the trim white door, he heard a crash from inside. It sounded as though a piece of furniture had been knocked down. He knocked louder. He heard a woman's cry of terror.

He turned the knob, found the door was locked. Well, shit. He put his shoulder against the door and pushed really hard. The door burst inward.

He saw Susan St. John Brainerd on her knees on the floor, the telephone lying beside her. He could hear the buzz of the dial tone. Her fist was stuffed in her mouth. She'd probably terrified herself when she screamed—that or she was afraid someone would hear her. Well, he had, and here he was.

She stared at him as he flew into Amabel's small living room, huddled herself against the wall like he was going to shoot her, jerked her fist out of her mouth, and screamed again.

Really loud.

"STOP SCREAMING," he yelled at her. "What the hell's the matter? What happened?"

Sally knew this was it. She'd never seen him before. He wasn't old like everyone else in this town. He didn't belong here. He'd tracked her here. He was here to drag her back to Washington or force her to go back to that horrible place. Yes, he could work for Beadermeyer, he probably did. She couldn't go back there. She stared at the big man who was now standing over her, looking at her strangely, as if he was really concerned, but she knew he wasn't, he couldn't be, it was just a ruse. He was here to hurt her.

"The phone," she said, because she was going to die and it didn't matter what she said. "It was someone who called and he scared me."

As she spoke, she slowly rose and began backing away from him.

He wondered if she had a gun. He wondered if she'd turn and run to get that gun. He didn't want this to turn nasty. He lunged for her, grabbed her left arm as she cried out, twisted about, and tried to jerk away from him.

"I'm not going to hurt you, dammit."

"Go away! I won't go with you, I won't. Go away."

She was sobbing and panting, fighting him hard now, and he was impressed with the way she jabbed him with her knuckles just below his ribs where it hurt really good, then raised her leg to knee him.

He jerked her back against him, then wrapped his arms around her, holding her until she quieted. She had no leverage now, no chance to hurt him. She was a lightweight, but the place where she'd gotten him below his ribs really hurt.

"I'm not going to hurt you," he said again, his voice calm and low. He was one of the best interviewers in the FBI because he could modulate his voice just right, make it gentle and soothing, mean and vicious, whatever was necessary to get what he needed.

He said now, in his easy and soft tone, "I heard you cry out and thought someone was in here with you, attacking you. I was just trying to be a hero."

She stilled, just stood there, her back pressed against his chest. The only sound breaking the silence was the dial tone from the telephone.

"A hero?"

"Yeah, a hero. You okay now?"

She nodded. "You're really not here to hurt me?"

"Nope. I was just passing by when I heard you scream."

She sagged with relief. She believed him. What the hell should she do now?

He let her go and took a quick step back. He leaned down and picked up the telephone, dropped the receiver into the cradle, and set it back on the table.

"I'm sorry," she said, her arms wrapped around herself. She looked as white as a cleric's collar. "Who are you? Did you come to see Amabel?"

"No. Who was that on the phone? Was it an obscene caller?"

"It was my father."

He tried not to stare at her, not to start laughing at what she'd said. Her father? *Jesus, lady, they buried him two days ago, and it was very well attended. If the FBI weren't investigating him, even the president would have been there.* He made a decision and acted on it. "I take it that he's not a nice guy, your father?"

"No, he's not, but that's not important. He's dead."

James Quinlan knew her file inside out. All he needed was to have her flip out on him. He'd found her, he had her now, but she was obviously close to the edge. He didn't want a fruitcake on his hands. He needed her to be sane. He said very gently, his voice, his body movements all calm, unhurried, "That's impossible, you know."

"Yes, I know, but it was still his voice." She was rubbing her hands over her arms. She was staring at that phone, waiting. Waiting for her dead father to call again? She looked terrified, but more than that she looked just plain confused.

"What did he say? This man who sounded like your dead father?"

"It was my father. I'd know that voice anywhere." She was rubbing harder. "He said that he was coming, that he'd be here with me soon and then he'd take care of things."

"What things?"

"Me," she said. "He'll come here to take care of me."

"Do you have any brandy?"

Her head jerked up. "Brandy?" She grinned, then laughed, a small, rusty sound, but it was a laugh. "That's what my aunt's been sneaking into my tea since I got here yesterday. Sure, I've got brandy, but I promise you, even without the brandy I won't get my broomstick out of the closet and fly out of here."

He thrust out his hand. "That's good enough for me. My name's James Quinlan."

She looked at that hand, a strong hand, one with fine black hairs on the back of it, long fingers, well-cared-for nails, buffed and neat. Not an artist's hands, not like Amabel's, but capable hands. Not like Scott's hands either. Still, she didn't want to shake James Quinlan's hand, she didn't want him to see hers and know what a mess she was. But there was no choice.

She shook his hand and immediately withdrew hers. "My name's Sally St. John. I'm in The Cove to visit my aunt, Amabel Perdy."

St. John. She'd only gone back to her maiden name. "Yes, I met her in the World's Greatest Ice Cream Shop. I would have thought she lived in a caravan and sat by a campfire at night reading fortunes and dancing with veils."

She made a stab at a laugh again. "That's what I thought too when I first got here. I hadn't seen her since I was seven years old. I expected her to whip out some tarot cards, but I was very glad she didn't."

"Why? Maybe she's good at tarot cards. Uncertainty's a bitch."

But she was shaking her head. "I'd rather have uncertainty than certainty. I don't want to know what's going to happen. It can't be good."

No, he wasn't going to tell her who he was, he wasn't going to tell her that she was perfectly right, that what would happen to her would suck. He wondered if she'd killed her father, if she hadn't run to this town that was on the backside of the Earth to protect her mother. Others in the Bureau believed it was a deal gone sour, that Amory St. John had finally screwed over the wrong people. But he didn't believe that for a minute, never had, which was why he was here and no other agents were. "You know, I'd sure like some brandy."

"Who are you?"

He said easily, "I'm a private investigator from Los Angeles. A man hired me to find his parents, who disappeared from around here some three years ago."

She was weighing his words, and he knew she was trying to determine if he was lying to her. His cover was excellent because it was true, but even that didn't matter. He was a good liar. He could tell his voice was working on her.

She was so thin, her face still had that bloodless look, the color leached out by the terror of that phone call. Her father? He was coming to take care of her? This was nuts. He could handle sane people. He didn't know what he'd do if she flipped out.

"All right," she said finally. "Come this way, into the kitchen."

He followed her to a kitchen that was straight out of the 1940s—the brownish linoleum floor with stains older than he was. It was clean but peeling up badly near the sink area. All the appliances were as old as the floor, and just as clean. He sat down at the table as she said, "Don't lean on it. One of the legs is uneven. See, Aunt Amabel has magazines under it to make it steady."

He wondered how long the table had been like that. What an easy thing to fix. He watched Susan St. John Brainerd pour him some brandy in a water glass. He watched her pause and frown. He realized she didn't know how much to pour.

"That's just right," he said easily. "Thank you." He waited until she'd poured herself a bit, then gave her a salute. "I need this. You scared the bejesus out of me. Nice to meet you, Susan St. John."

"And you, Mr. Quinlan. Please call me Sally."

"All right—Sally. After all our screams and shouts, why not call me James?"

"I don't know you, even if I did scream at you."

"The way you gouged me in the ribs, I'd give up before I'd let you attack me like that again. Where'd you learn to do that?"

"A girl at boarding school taught me. She said her brother was the meanest guy in junior high and he didn't want a wuss for a sister so he taught her all sorts of self-defense tricks."

He found himself looking down at her hands. They were as thin and pale as the rest of her. She said, "I never tried it before—seriously, I mean. Well, I did, several times, but I didn't have a chance. There were too many of them."

What the hell was she talking about? He said, "It worked. I wanted to die. In fact, I'll be hobbled over for the next couple of days. I'm glad you missed my groin."

He sipped his brandy, watching her. What to do? It had seemed so simple, so straightforward before, but now, sitting here, facing her, seeing her in the flesh as a person and not just as his key to the murder of Amory St. John, things weren't so clear anymore. He hated it when things weren't clear. "Tell me about your father."

She didn't say anything, just shook her head.

"Listen to me, Sally. He's dead. Your damned father is dead. That couldn't have been him on the phone. That means that it must have been either a recording of his voice or a person who could mimic him very well."

"Yes," she said, still staring into the brandy.

"Obviously someone knows you're here. Someone wants to frighten you."

She looked up at him then, and remarkably, she smiled. It was a lovely smile, free of fear, free of stress. He found himself smiling back at her. "That someone succeeded admirably," she said. "I'm scared out of my mind. I'm sorry I attacked you."

"I would have attacked me too if I had burst through the front door like that."

"I don't know if the call was long distance. If it was long distance, then I've got some time to decide what to do." She paused, then stiffened. She didn't move, but he got the feeling that she'd just backed a good fifteen feet away from him. "You know who I am, don't you? I didn't realize it before, but you know."

"Yes, I know."

"How?"

"I saw your photo on TV, also some footage of you with your father and your mother."

"Amabel assures me that no one in The Cove will realize who I am. She says no one besides her has a TV except for Thelma Nettro, who's older than dust."

"You don't have to worry that I'll shout it around. In fact, I promise to keep it to myself. I was in the World's Greatest Ice Cream Shop when I met your aunt. A Sherry Vorhees mentioned that you were visiting. Your aunt didn't say a word about who you were." Lying was an art, he thought, watching her assess his words. The trick was always to lean as much as possible toward the exact truth. It was a trick some of the town's citizens could benefit from.

She was frowning, her hands clasped around the glass. Her foot was tapping on the linoleum.

"Who is after you?"

Again she gave him a smile, but this one was mocking and underlaid with so much fear he fancied he could smell it. She fiddled with the napkin holder, saying while she straightened the napkins that had dumped onto the table, "You name someone and he'd probably be just one in a long line."

She was sitting across from one of those someones. Damnation, he hated this. He'd thought it would be so easy. When would he learn that people were never what they seemed? That smile of hers was wonderful. He wanted to feed her.

She said suddenly, "The strangest thing happened the first night I was here, just two nights ago. I woke up in the middle of the night at the sound of a person's cry. It was a person, I know it was. I went into the hall upstairs to make sure something wasn't happening to Amabel, but when the cry came again I knew it was from outside. Amabel said I'd imagined it. It's true that I'd had a horrible nightmare, a vivid memory in the form of a dream, actually, but the screams pulled me out of the dream. I know that. I'm sure of it. Anyway, I went back to bed, but I know I heard Amabel leave the house after that. You're a private detective. What do you make of that?"

"You want to be my client? It'll cost you big bucks."

"My father was rich, not me. I don't have a cent."

"What about your husband? He's a big tycoon lawyer, isn't he?"

She stood up like a shot. "I think you should leave now, Mr. Quinlan. Perhaps it's just because you're a private detective and it's your job to ask questions, but you've crossed the line. I'm none of your business. Forget what you saw on TV. Very little of it was true. Please go."

"All right," he said. "I'll be in The Cove for another week. You might ask your aunt if she remembers two old folk named Harve and Marge Jensen. They were in a new red Winnebago, and they probably drove into town to buy some of the World's Greatest Ice Cream. Like I told you, the reason I'm here is because their son hired me to find them. It's been over three years since they disappeared." Although he'd already asked Amabel himself, he wanted Sally to ask her as well. He'd be interested to see if she thought her aunt was lying.

"I'll ask her. Good-bye, Mr. Quinlan."

She dogged him to the front door, which, thankfully, was still attached to its ancient hinges.

"I'll see you again, Sally," he said, gave her a small salute, and walked up the well-maintained sidewalk.

The temperature had dropped. A storm was blowing in. He had a lot to do before it hit. He quickened his step. So her husband was off-limits. Was she scared of him? She wasn't wearing a wedding band, but the evidence of one had been in that thick white line on her finger.

He'd really blundered—that wasn't like him. Usually he was very cautious, very careful, particularly with someone like her, someone fragile, someone who was teetering right on the brink.

Nothing seemed straightforward now that he'd met Susan St. John, that thin young woman who was terrified of a dead man who had called her on the phone.

He wondered how long it would be before Susan St. John discovered he'd lied through his teeth. It was possible she would never find out. Just about everything he knew was in the file the FBI had assembled on her. If she found out he knew more than had ever been dished out to the public, would she take off? He hoped not. He was curious now about those human cries she'd heard in the middle of the night. Maybe her aunt had been right and she had dreamed it—being in a new place, she had every reason to be jumpy. And she had admitted to having a nightmare. Who the hell knew?

He looked around at the beautiful small houses on either side of the street. There were flowers and low shrubs planted just about everywhere, all protected from the ocean winds with high-sided wooden slats on the western side. He imagined that storms off the ocean could devastate just about any plant alive. The people were trying.

He still didn't like the town, but it didn't seem so much like a Hollywood set anymore. Actually it didn't look at all like Teresa's hometown in Ohio. There was an air of complacency about it that didn't put him off. He had a sense that everyone who lived here knew their town was neat and lovely and quaint. The townspeople had thought about what they wanted to do and they'd done it. The town had genuine charm and vitality, he'd admit that, even though he hadn't seen a single child or young person since he'd driven in some three hours before.

IT WAS LATE AT NIGHT when the storm blew in. The wind howled, rattling the windows. Sally shivered beneath the mound of blankets, listening to the rain slam nearly straight down, pounding the shingled roof. She prayed there were no holes in the roof, even though Amabel had said earlier, "Oh, no, baby. It's a new roof. Had it put on just last year."

How long could she remain here with Amabel? Now that she was safe, now that she was hidden, she was free to think about the future, at least a future of more than one day's duration. She thought about next week, about next month.

What was she going to do? That phone call—it had yanked her right back to the present, and to the past. It had been her father's voice, no question about that. A tape, just like James Quinlan had said, a tape of a mimic.

Suddenly there was a scream, long and drawn out, starting low and ending on a crescendo. It was coming from outside the house.

She ran toward her aunt's bedroom, not feeling the cold wooden floor beneath her bare feet, no, just running until she forced herself to draw up and tap lightly on the door.

Amabel opened the door as if she'd been standing right there, waiting for her to knock. But that wasn't possible, surely.

She grabbed her aunt's arms and shook her. "Did you hear the scream, Amabel? Please, you heard it, didn't you?"

"Oh, baby, that was the wind. I heard it and knew you'd be frightened. I was coming to you. Did you have another nightmare?"

"It wasn't the wind, Amabel. It was a woman."

"No, no, come along now and let me help you back to bed. Look at your bare feet. You'll catch your death of something. Come on now, baby, back to bed with you.,"

There was another scream, this one short and high-pitched, then suddenly muffled. It was a woman's scream, like the first one.

Amabel dropped her arm.

"Now do you believe me, Amabel?"

"I suppose I'll just have to call one of the men to come and check it out. The problem is, they're all so old that if they go out in this weather, they'll probably catch pneumonia. Maybe it was the wind. What woman would be screaming outside? Yes, it's this bloody wind. It's impossible, Sally. Let's just forget it."

"No, I can't. It's a woman, Amabel, and someone is hurting her. I can't just go back to bed and forget it."

"Why not?"

Sally just stared at her.

"You mean when your papa hit your mama you tried to protect her?"

"Yes."

Amabel sighed. "I'm sorry, baby. You did hear the wind this time, not your mama being punched by your papa."

"Can I borrow your raincoat, Amabel?"

Amabel sighed, hugged Sally close, and said, "All right. I'll call Reverend Vorhees. He's not as rickety as the others, and he's strong. He'll check it out."

When Reverend Hal Vorhees arrived at Amabel's house, he had three other men with him. "This is Gus Eisner, Susan, a fellow who can fix anything with wheels and a motor."

"Mr. Eisner," Sally said. "I heard a woman scream, twice. It was an awful scream. Someone was hurting her."

Gus Eisner looked as if he would have spat if there'd been a cuspidor in the corner. "The wind, ma'am," he said, nodding, "it was just the wind. I've heard it all my life, all seventy-four years, and it makes noises that sometimes have made my teeth ache. Just the wind."

"But we'll look around anyway," Hal Vorhees said. "This here is Purn Davies, who owns the general store, and Hunker Dawson, who's a World War Two vet and our flower expert." Sally nodded, and the reverend patted her shoulder, nodded to Amabel, and followed the other men out the front door. "You ladies stay safe inside now. Don't let anyone in unless it's us."

"The little females," Sally said. "I feel like I should be barefoot and pregnant, making coffee in the kitchen."

"They're old, baby, they're just old. That generation gave their wives an allowance. Gus's wife, Velma, wouldn't know a bank statement if it bit her ankle. But things balance out, you know. Old Gus is night-blind. Without Velma, he'd be helpless after dark. Don't mind their words. They care, and that's a good feeling, isn't it?"

Just as she opened her mouth to reply, there was a third scream, this one fast and loud, and then it ended, cut off abruptly. It was distant, hidden, and now it was over.

Sally knew deep down that there wouldn't be another scream. Ever again. She also knew it wasn't the damned wind.

She looked at her aunt, who was straightening a modern painting over the sofa, a small picture painted in patternless swirls of ochre, orange, and purple. It was an unsettling painting, dark and violent.

"The wind," Sally said slowly. "Yes, no more than the wind." She wanted to ask Amabel if Gus were night-blind, what good would he be out searching for a victim in the dark?

THE NEXT MORNING DAWNED cool and clear, the sky as blue in March as it would be in August. Sally walked to Thelma's Bed and Breakfast. Mr. Quinlan, Martha told her, was having his breakfast.

He was seated in isolated splendor amid the heavy Victorian furnishings in Miss Thelma's front room. On the linen-covered table was a breakfast more suited to three kings than just one man.

She walked straight to him, waited until he looked up from his newspaper, and said, "Who are you?"

IT HAD NEVER occurred to him that she would confront him, not after he'd seen her huddled on the floor when he burst into her aunt's living room. But she had tried to knee him and she'd also punched him just below the ribs. She had fought back. And here she was today, looking ready to spit on him. For some obscure reason, that pleased him. Perhaps it was because he didn't want his prey to be stupid or cowardly. He wanted a chase that would challenge him.

How could she have found out so quickly? It didn't make sense.

"I'm James Quinlan," he said. "Most people call me Quinlan. You can call me whatever you want to. Won't you sit down, Sally? I assure you there's enough food, though when I finish one plate Martha just brings in another one. Does she do the cooking?"

"I don't know. Who are you?"

"Sit down and we'll talk. Or would you like a section of the newspaper? It's the *Oregonian,* a very good paper. There's a long article in here about your father."

She sat down.

"Who are you, Mr. Quinlan?"

"That didn't last long. It was James yesterday."

"I have a feeling that nothing lasts very long with you."

She was right about that, he thought, as he had a fleeting image of Teresa laughing when he'd whispered to her as he'd come inside her that if she ever had another man she would find out what it meant to be half empty.

"What other feelings do you have, Sally?"

"That you love problems, that you get a problem in your hands and shape and mold and twist and do whatever you have to do to solve that problem. Then you lose interest. You look for another problem."

He stared at her and said aloud, though he didn't realize he was doing so, "How the hell do you know that?"

"Mr. Quinlan, how did you know my husband is a lawyer? That wasn't on TV. There was no reason for it to be. Or if he had been shown, they certainly would have had no reason to discuss his profession or anything else about him."

"Ah, you remembered that, did you?"

"Delaying tactics don't become you. What if I told you I have a Colt forty-five revolver in my purse and I'll shoot you if you don't tell me the truth right now?"

"I'd probably believe you. Keep your gun in your purse. It was on TV—your good old husband escorting your mother to your dad's funeral. You just didn't see it." Thank God he'd heard Thelma and Martha discussing it yesterday. Thank God they hadn't really been interested. Washington, D.C., was lightyears from their world. "If you think there's anything private about you now, forget it. You're an open book."

She had seen it, she'd forgotten, just plain forgotten. She'd made a mistake, and she couldn't afford to make any more. She remembered eating that wonderful ham sandwich the first day she'd arrived, sitting with Amabel, watching her black-and-white set, listening and watching and knowing that Scott was with her mother. She hadn't watched TV before or since. She prayed she wasn't an open book. She prayed no one in The Cove would ever realize who she was.

"I forgot," she said and picked up a slice of unbuttered toast. She bit into it, chewed slowly, then swallowed. "I shouldn't have, but I did."

"Tell me about him."

She took another bite of toast. "I can't afford you, remember, James?"

"I sometimes do *pro bono*."

"I don't think so. Have you discovered anything about the old couple?"

"Yes, I have. Everyone I've spoken to is lying through their collective dentures. Marge and Harve were here, probably at the World's Greatest Ice Cream Shop. Why doesn't anyone want to admit it? What's to hide? So they had ice cream—who cares?"

He pulled up short, staring at the pale young woman sitting across from him. She took another bite of the dry toast. He lifted the dish of homemade strawberry jam and handed it to her. She shook her head. He'd never in his life told anyone about his business. Of course, old

Marge and Harve weren't really his business, not really, but then again, why the hell had everyone lied to him?

More to the point, why had he said anything about that case to her? She was a damned criminal, or at least she knew who had offed her father. If there was one thing he was sure of, it was that.

Whatever else she was—well, he'd find out. She had come to him. Confronted him. It saved him the trouble of seeking her out again.

"You're right. That doesn't make any sense. You're sure folk lied to you?"

"Positive. It's interesting, don't you think?"

She nodded, took another bite of toast, and chewed slowly. "Why don't I ask Amabel why no one admits to remembering them?"

"No, I don't think so. I'm the private investigator here. I'll do the asking. It's not your job."

She just shrugged.

"It's too early for the World's Greatest Ice Cream," he said. "Maybe you'd like to go for a walk on the cliffs? You look pale. A walk would put some color in your cheeks."

She gave it a lot of thought. He said nothing more, just watched her eat the rest of that dry toast that had to be cold as a stone. She stood, brushed the crumbs from the legs of her brown corduroy slacks, and said, "I need to put on my sneakers. I'll meet you in front of Amabel's house in ten minutes."

"Excellent," he said, and meant it. Now he was getting somewhere. He'd open her up soon enough, just like a clam. Soon she would tell him all about her husband, her mother, her dead father, who hadn't called her on the phone. No, that was impossible.

She also seemed perfectly normal, and that bothered him as well. When he'd found her hysterical and frightened yesterday, it had been what he'd expected. But this calm, this open smile that, to his critical eye, held no malice or guile, made him feel he'd missed the last train to Saginaw.

When he met her in front of her aunt's house, she smiled at him. Where the hell was her guile?

Fifteen minutes later she was talking as if there wasn't a single black cloud in her world. ". . . Amabel told me that The Cove was nothing until a developer from Portland bought up all the land and built vacation cottages. Everything went smoothly until the sixties, then everyone just forgot about the town."

"Someone sure remembered, someone with lots of money. The place is a picture postcard." He remembered old Thelma Nettro had told him the same thing.

"Yes," she said, kicking a small pebble out of her path. "It's odd, isn't it? If the town died, then how was it resurrected? There's no local factory to employ everyone, no manufacturing of any kind. Amabel said the high school closed back in 1974."

"Maybe one of them has discovered how to tap into the Social Security computer system."

"That would only work in the short term. The fund only has money for, what is it? Fifteen months? It's scary. No one would want to count on that."

They stood on the edge of a narrow promontory and looked down at the fierce white spume, fanning upward when the waves hit the black rocks.

"It's beautiful," she said as she drew in a deep breath of the salt air.

"Yes, it is, but it makes me nervous. All that unleashed power. It has no conscience. It can kill you so easily."

"What a romantic thing to say, Mr. Quinlan."

"Not at all. But I'm right. It doesn't know the good guys from the bad guys. And it's James. You want to climb down? There's a path just over there by that lone cypress tree that doesn't look too dangerous."

"I don't want you fainting on me, if you get too close to all that unleashed power."

"Threaten to knee me and I'll forget about fainting for the rest of my life."

She laughed and walked ahead of him. She quickly disappeared around a turn in the trail. It was a narrow path, strewn with good-sized rocks, snaggled low brush, and it was too steep. She slipped, gasped aloud, and grabbed at a root.

"Be careful!"

"Yes, I will be. No, don't say it. I don't want to go back. We'll both be very careful. Just another fifty feet."

The trail just stopped. From the settled look of all the brush and rocks, there'd been an avalanche some years before. They could probably climb over the rocks, but Quinlan didn't want to take the chance. "This is far enough," he said, grabbing her hand when she took another step. "Nope, Sally, this is it. Let's sit here and commune with all that unleashed power."

There was no beach below, just pile upon pile of rocks, forming strange shapes as richly imagined as the cloud formations overhead. One even made a bridge from one pile to another, with water flowing beneath. It was breathtaking, and James was right, it was a bit frightening.

Seagulls whirled and dove overhead, squawking and calling to each other.

"It isn't particularly cold today."

"No," she said. "Not like last night."

"I'm in the west tower room at Thelma's Bed and Breakfast. The windows shuddered the whole night."

Suddenly she stood up, her eyes fixed on something just off to the right. She shook her head, whispering, "No, no, it can't be."

He was on his feet in an instant, his hand on her shoulder. "What is it?"

She pointed.

"Oh, my God," he said. "Stay here, Sally. Just stay here and I'll check it out."

"No, I won't stay put."

But he just shook his head at her. He set her aside and made his way carefully through the rocks until he was standing just five feet above the body of a woman, the waves washing her against the rocks, then tugging her back, back and forth. There was no blood in the water. "Oh, no," he said aloud.

She was at his side, staring down at the woman. "I knew it," she said. "I was right, but nobody would listen to me."

"We've got to get her out before there's nothing left of her," he said. He sat down, took off his running shoes and socks, and rolled up his jeans. "Stay here, Sally. I mean it. I don't want to have to worry about you falling into the water and washing out to sea."

Quinlan finally managed to haul her in. He wrapped the woman, what was left of her, in his jacket. His stomach was churning. He waved to Sally to start climbing back up the path. He didn't allow himself to think that what he was carrying had once been a living, laughing person. God, it made him sick. "We'll take her to Doc Spiver," Sally called over her shoulder. "He'll take care of her."

"Yeah," he said to himself, "I just bet he will." An old man in this one-horse town would probably say that she'd been killed accidentally by a hunter shooting curlews.

Doc Spiver's living room smelled musty. James wanted to open the windows and air the place out, but he figured the old man must want it this way. He sat down and called Sam North, a homicide detective with the Portland police department. Sam wasn't in, so James left Doc Spiver's number. "Tell him it's urgent," he said to Sam's partner, Martin Amick. "It's really urgent."

He hung up and watched Sally St. John Brainerd pace back and forth over a rich wine-red Bokhara carpet. It was fairly new, that beautiful carpet. "What did you mean when you said you knew it?"

"What? Oh, I heard her scream last night. There were three screams, and at the last one I knew someone had killed her. It was just cut off so quickly, like someone just hit her hard and that was it.

"Amabel thought it was the wind because it was howling—no doubt about that, but I knew it was a woman's scream, just like the one the first night I was here. I told you about that. Do you think it was the same woman?"

"I don't know."

"Amabel called Reverend Vorhees and he came with three other men and they went on a search. When they came back they said they hadn't found anything. It was the wind, they said. Reverend Vorhees patted me again, like I was a child, an idiot."

"Or worse, a hysterical woman."

"Exactly. Someone killed her, James. It couldn't have been an accident. I heard her scream the night I arrived—three nights ago—and then last night. Last night, they killed her."

"What do you mean, 'they'?"

She shrugged, looking a bit confused. "I don't know. It just seems right."

The phone rang and James answered it. It was Sam North calling him back. Sally listened to his end of the conversation.

"Yes, a woman anywhere from young to middle-aged, I guess. The tide washed her in, and she'd been battered against the rocks for a good number of hours. I don't know how long. What do you want to do, Sam?"

He listened, then said, "A little town called The Cove about an hour or so southwest of you. You know it? Good. The local doctor is looking her over now, but they have no law enforcement, nothing like that. Yes? All right. Done. His name is Doc Spiver, on the end of Main Street. You've got the number. Right. Thanks, Sam."

He said as he hung up the phone, "Sam's calling the county sheriff. He says they'll send someone over to handle things."

"Soon, I hope," Doc Spiver said, walking into the small living room, wiping his hands—an obscene thing to be doing, Sally thought, staring at those old liver-spotted hands, knowing what those hands had been touching. There was a knock on the front door and Doc Spiver called out, "Come along in!"

It was Reverend Hal Vorhees. On his heels were the four old men who spent most of their time sitting around the barrel playing cards.

"What the hell's going on, Doc? Excuse me, ma'am, but we heard you'd found a body at the bottom of the cliffs."

"It's true, Gus," Doc Spiver said. "Do all of you know Mr. Quinlan and Sally, Amabel's niece?"

"Yes, we do, Doc," Purn Davies, the man who'd wanted to marry Amabel, said. "Now what's happening? Be quick telling us. I don't want the ladies to hear about it and be distressed."

"Sally and Mr. Quinlan found a woman's body."

"Who is she? Do you recognize her?" This from Hal Vorhees.

"No. She's not from around here, I don't think. I couldn't find anything on her clothes either. You find anything, Mr. Quinlan?"

"No. The county sheriff is sending someone over soon. A medical examiner as well."

"Good," Doc Spiver said. "Look, she could have been killed by anything. Me, I'd say it was an accident, but who knows? I can't run tests, and I haven't the tools or equipment to do an autopsy. As I said, I vote for accident."

"No," Sally said. "No accident. Someone killed her. I heard her screaming."

"Now, Sally," Doc Spiver said, holding out his hand to her, that hand he'd been wiping, "you're not thinking that the wind you heard was this poor woman screaming."

"Yes, I am."

"We never found anything," Reverend Vorhees said. "We all looked a good two hours."

"You just didn't look in the right place," Sally said.

"Would you like something to calm you?"

She stared at the old man who had been a doctor for many more years than her mother had been alive. She'd met him the previous day. He'd been kind, if a little vague. She knew he didn't want her here, that she didn't belong here, but as long as she was with Amabel, he would continue being kind. Come to think of it, all the folk she'd met had been kind, but she still felt they didn't want her here. It was because she was a murdered man's daughter—that had to be it. She wondered if they would turn her in now that she and James had found the woman's body, the woman Sally had heard screaming.

"Something to calm me," she repeated slowly, "something to calm me." She laughed, a low, very ugly laugh that brought Quinlan's head up.

"I'd better get you something," Doc Spiver said, turned quickly, and ran into an end table. The beautiful Tiffany lamp crashed to the floor. It didn't break.

He didn't see it, James realized. The damned old man is going blind. He said easily, "No, Doc. Sally and I will be on our way now. The detective from the Portland police will tell the sheriff to come here. If you'd let them know we'll be at Amabel's house?"

"Yes, certainly," Doc Spiver said, not looking at them. He was on his knees, touching the precious Tiffany lamp, feeling all the lead seams to make certain it wasn't cracked.

They left him still on the floor. All the other men were silent as death in the small living room with its rich wine-red Bokhara carpet.

"Amabel told me he was blinder than a bat," Sally said as they stepped out into the bright afternoon sunlight. She stopped cold.

"What's wrong?"

"I forgot. I can't have the police knowing I'm here. They'll call the police in Washington, they'll send someone to get me, they'll force me to go back to that place or they'll kill me or they'll—"

"No, they won't. I already thought of that. Don't worry. Your name is Susan Brandon. They'll have no reason to question that. Just tell them your story and they'll leave you be."

"I have a black wig I wore here. I'll put it on."

"Couldn't hurt."

"How can you know they'll just want to hear my story? You don't know what's going on here any more than I do. Oh, I see. You don't think they'll believe I heard a woman screaming those two nights."

He said patiently, "Even if they don't believe you, it doesn't make a whole lot of sense that they'd then have a murdered woman on their hands, does it? You heard a woman's screams. Now she's dead. I don't think there's a whole lot of other possible conclusions. Get a grip, Sally, and don't fall apart on me now. You're going to be Susan Brandon. All right?"

She nodded slowly, but he didn't think he had ever seen such fear on a face in all his years.

He was glad she had a wig. No one could forget her face, and the good Lord knew it had been flashed on TV enough times recently.

DAVID MOUNTEBANK HAD hated his name ever since he'd looked it up in the dictionary and read it meant boastful and unscrupulous. Whenever he met a big man, a big man who looked smart, and he had to introduce himself, he held himself stiff and wary, waiting to see if the guy would make a crack. He braced himself accordingly as he introduced himself to the man before him now.

"I'm Sheriff David Mountebank."

The man stuck out his hand. "I'm James Quinlan, Sheriff Mountebank. This is Susan Brandon. We were together when we found the woman's body two hours ago."

"Ms. Brandon."

"Won't you be seated, Sheriff?"

He nodded, took his hat off, and relaxed into the soft sofa cushions. "The Cove's changed," he said, looking around Amabel's living room as if he'd found himself in a shop filled with modern prints that gave him indigestion. "It seems every time I come here, it just keeps looking better and better. How about that?"

"I wouldn't know," Quinlan said. "I'm from L.A."

"You live here, Ms. Brandon? If you do, you've got to be the youngest sprout within the town limits, although there's something of a subdivision growing over near the highway. Don't know why folks would want to live near the highway. They don't come into The Cove except for ice cream, leastwises that's what I hear."

"No, Sheriff. I'm visiting my aunt. Just a short vacation. I'm from Missouri."

Sheriff Mountebank wrote that down in his book, then sat back, scratched his knees, and said, "The medical examiner's over at Doc Spiver's house checking out the dead woman. She'd been in the water a good while, at least eight hours, I'd say."

"I know when she died," Sally said.

The sheriff merely smiled at her and waited. It was a habit of his, just waiting, and sure enough, everything he ever wanted to hear would pop out of a person's mouth just to fill in the silence.

He didn't have to wait long this time because Susan Brandon couldn't wait to tell him about the screams, about how her aunt had convinced her it was just the wind that first night, but last night she'd known—just known—it was a woman screaming, a woman in pain, and then that last scream, well, someone had killed her.

"What time was that? Do you remember, Ms. Brandon?"

"It was around two-oh-five in the morning, Sheriff. That's when my aunt went along with me and called Reverend Vorhees."

"She called Hal Vorhees?"

"Yes. She said he was just about the youngest man and the most physically able. He brought over three elderly men with him. They searched but couldn't find anything."

"That was probably the same group that's over at Doc Spiver's. They were all just sitting around looking at each other. This kind of thing hits a small town like The Cove real hard."

David Mountebank took down their names. He said without pre-amble, without softening, "Why are you wearing a black wig, Ms. Brandon?"

Without a pause she said, "I'm having chemotherapy, Sheriff. I'm nearly bald."

"I'm sorry."

"That's all right."

At that moment, Quinlan knew he would never again underesti-mate Sally Brainerd. He wasn't particularly surprised that the sheriff could tell it was a wig. She was frankly ludicrous in that black-as-sin wig that made her look like Elvira, Mistress of the Dark. No, she was even paler than Elvira. He was impressed that the sheriff had asked her about the wig. Just maybe there'd be a prayer of finding out who the woman was and who had killed her. He could see that David Mounte-bank wasn't stupid.

"Doc Spiver thinks this is all a tragic accident," the sheriff said, writing with his pencil on his pad even as he spoke.

James said, "The good doctor is nearly blind. He could have just as easily been examining the table leg and not the dead woman."

"Well, it appears the doctor admitted that readily enough. He said he just couldn't imagine who could have killed her, not unless it was someone from the outside. That means beyond Highway 101A. The four other fellows there didn't know a blessed thing. I guess they were there for moral support. Now, Mr. Quinlan, you're here on business?"

Quinlan told him about the old couple he was looking for. He didn't say anything about the townspeople lying to him.

"Over three years ago," the sheriff said, looking at one of Amabel's paintings over Sally's head, this one all pale yellows and creams and nearly blueless blues, no shape or reason to any of it, but it was nice.

"Yeah, probably too long a time to turn anything up, but the son wanted to try again. I'm using The Cove as my headquarters, checking here first, then fanning out."

"Tell you what, Mr. Quinlan, when I get back to my office I'll do some checking. I've been sheriff only two years. I'll see what the former sheriff had to say about it."

"I'd appreciate that."

There was a knock at the front door. Then it opened and a small, slender man came into the living room. He was wearing wire-rim glasses and a fedora. He took off his hat, nodded to the sheriff, and bowed to Sally. "Sheriff, ma'am." He then looked at Quinlan, just looked at him, like a little dog ready to go after the mastodon if his master gave the command.

Quinlan stuck out his hand. "Quinlan."

"I'm the medical examiner. We're removing the body now, Sheriff. I just wanted to give you a preliminary report." He paused, a dramatic pause, Quinlan knew, and grinned. He'd seen it many times before. Medical examiners hardly ever had the limelight. It was their only chance to shine, and this man was trying his best to light up the room.

"Yes, Ponser? Get on with it."

That wasn't as good a name as Mountebank, but it was close. Quinlan looked over at Sally, but she was staring at her shoes. She was listening, though; he could see the tension in her body, practically see the air quiver around her.

"Someone strangled her," Ponser said cheerfully. "It's pretty obvious, but I can't say for sure until I've done the autopsy. Perhaps the killer believed it wouldn't be evident after she'd been in the water, but he was wrong. On the other hand, if the tide hadn't washed her in, then her body would never have been found and it would have been academic."

"That's what they wanted," Sally said. "They didn't want her found. Even with the tide washing her up, how many people ever go down there? They're all old. It's dangerous. James and I finding her, that was just plain bad luck for them."

"Yes, it certainly was," the sheriff said. He rose. "Ms. Brandon, could you try to pinpoint the direction and the distance of those screams you heard? Were they from the same direction and distance both nights?"

"That's an awfully good question," Sally said slowly. "It would help, yes, it would. Both nights the screams were close, that or she really screamed loudly. I think they came both times from across the way. It was close, so very close—at least I think it was."

"Ah, there's a nice long row of neat little cottages lining the street across from this house. Surely someone must have heard something. If you remember anything else, here's my card. Call me anytime."

He shook Quinlan's hand. "You know, what I can't figure out is why someone was holding the woman prisoner."

"Prisoner?" Sally said, just staring at the sheriff.

"Naturally, ma'am. If she wasn't being held against her will, then why would you have heard the screams two different nights? The killer was holding her for some reason, a reason so powerful he only killed her that second night when she got loose and screamed again. But I've gotta ask myself, why keep someone prisoner if you're not planning on doing away with her anyway? Or maybe he was thinking of ransom and that's why he kept her alive. Maybe he was planning on killing her all along. Maybe he's a real psycho. I don't know, but I'll find out. I haven't heard a thing about anyone missing.

"Questions, I'm filled with them. As soon as we can get a photograph of the woman, then my deputies will be crawling all over the subdivision like army ants. I hope she's local, I really do."

"It would make your job a whole lot easier," Quinlan said. "Give me a relative or a husband any day and I'll find you a dozen motives."

"Yes, Mr. Quinlan, that's surely the truth."

"Nothing like a good mystery to stir a man's blood."

"I prefer mine to yours, Mr. Quinlan. Finding two missing people after three years isn't likely. Well, I'll be on my way now. A pleasure to meet you, Ms. Brandon."

He said to Quinlan as they walked to the door, "Now, this murdered woman, I'll find out who was holding her and then we'll see what kind of motive we've got for a brutal murder. I wonder why they threw her body over the cliff?"

"Instead of burying her?"

"Yeah. You know what I think now? I think someone was furious that she got loose and made a racket. I think someone was so furious he killed her and just threw her away like so much trash. I want to catch him badly."

"I would too, Sheriff. I think you might just be right."

"You in town long, Mr. Quinlan?"

"Another week or so."

"And Ms. Brandon?"

"I don't know, Sheriff."

"A shame about the cancer."

"Yes, a real shame."

"She gonna be all right?"

"That's what her doctors believe."

Sheriff David Mountebank shook Quinlan's hand, nodded back at Sally—who'd heard everything they said, even though they'd been speaking low—and took his leave.

Sally wondered why her aunt had left before the sheriff came. Amabel had said only, "Why would a sheriff want to talk to me? I don't know anything."

"But you heard the screams, Amabel."

"No, baby, you did. I never did think they were screams. You don't want me calling you a liar in front of the law, do you?" And with that, she took off.

Sally said now to Quinlan, "The sheriff isn't dumb."

"No, he isn't. But you got him, Sally, with that chemo business. Where is your aunt?"

"I don't know. She left."

"But she knew the sheriff would be here."

"Yes, but she said she didn't know anything. She said she didn't hear any screams and didn't want to make me look bad if she had to tell him that."

"You mean like a hysterical girl or a liar?"

"That's about it. When she does talk to him, she'll probably lie. She loves me. She wouldn't want to hurt me."

But she hadn't loved her enough to lie for her this time, Quinlan thought. Strange family.

"Any more phone calls?"

Sally shook her head, her eyes going automatically to the telephone, sitting next to a lamp on an end table.

"But someone knows you're here."

"Yes, someone."

He dropped it. He didn't want to push anymore, at least not right now. She'd been through quite enough for one day. But she hadn't lost it. She'd hung in there. "I'm proud of you," he said, without thinking.

She blinked as she looked up at him. He was still standing by the front door, leaning against the wall, his arms crossed over his chest. "You're proud of me? Why?"

He shrugged and walked over to her. "You're a civilian, but you didn't fall apart."

If only he knew, she thought, as she rubbed where that ring had been, so tight on her finger, paralyzing her.

"Sally, what's wrong?"

She jumped to her feet. "Nothing, James, nothing at all. It's lunchtime. You hungry?"

He wasn't, but she had to be, if that single piece of dry toast was all she'd eaten so far today. "Let's go back to Thelma's and see what's cooking," he said, and she agreed. She didn't want to be alone. She didn't want to be in this house alone.

The old lady was sitting in the dining room slurping minestrone soup, her diary open and facedown in her lap, the old-fashioned fountain pen beside her plate. What the hell did she write in that diary? What could be so bloody interesting? When she saw them, she yelled, "Martha, bring me my teeth. I can't be a proper hostess without my teeth."

She shut her mouth, not saying another word until poor Martha hurried into the dining room and slipped the old lady her teeth. Thelma turned, then turned back, giving them a big porcelain smile.

"Now, what's all this I hear about you two finding a dead body?"

James said, "We're hungry. Any chance for some of your soup?"

Thelma yelled, "Martha, bring two more bowls of your minestrone!"

She waved them to two seats across from her. She stared at Sally, who was no longer wearing her wig. "So you're Amabel's niece, are you?"

Sally nodded. "Yes, ma'am. It's a pleasure to meet you."

The old lady snorted. "You just wonder why I'm not dead yet. But I'm not, and I make sure I see Doc Spiver every day to tell him so. He pronounced me dead three years ago, did you know that?"

Quinlan did. He imagined everybody did, many times over. He just smiled and shook his head. He reached beneath the table and squeezed Sally's hand. She went rigid, then slowly he felt her relax. Good, he thought, she was beginning to trust him. Then he felt like a shit.

Martha set two places in front of them, then served two bowls of soup.

"Martha always had men hanging around her, but they were rotters, all of them. They just wanted her cooking. What did you do with young Ed, Martha? Did you cook for him or demand that he go to bed with you first?"

Martha just shook her head. "Now, Thelma, you're embarrassing poor little Miss Sally here."

"And me, too," Quinlan said and spooned some of the soup into his mouth. "Martha," he said, "I'm not a rotter and I'd surely marry you. I'd do anything for you."

"Go along, Mr. Quinlan."

"A big man like you embarrassed, James Quinlan?" Thelma Nettro laughed. Sally was thankful she was wearing her teeth. "I think you've been around several blocks, boy. I bet I could take off my clothes and it wouldn't faze you."

"I wouldn't bet on it, ma'am," Quinlan said.

"I'll bring in the chicken parmigiana," Martha said. "With garlic toast," she said over her shoulder.

"She keeps me alive," Thelma said. "She should have been my daughter but wasn't. It's a pity. She's a good girl."

This was interesting, Quinlan thought, but not as interesting as the soup. They all gave single-minded concentration to the minestrone until Martha reappeared with a huge tray covered with dishes. The smells nearly put Quinlan under the table. He wondered how long he'd have a hard stomach if Martha cooked all his meals.

Thelma took a big bite of chicken parmigiana, chewed like it was her last bite on earth, sighed, then said, "Did I tell you that my husband, Bobby, invented a new, improved gyropilot and sold it to a huge conglomerate in San Diego? They were hot for it, it being the war and all. Yep, that's what happened. I know it made airplanes fly even more evenly at the same height on a set course than before. With that money, Bobby and I moved here to The Cove. Our kids were grown and gone by then." She shook her head, smiled, and said, "I'll bet that body was a real mess when you found it."

"Yes," Sally managed to say, reeling just a bit. "The poor woman had been thrown over the cliff. Evidently she was caught in the tide."

"So who is she?"

"No one knows yet," Quinlan said. "Sheriff Mountebank will find out. Did you hear a woman screaming, Ms. Nettro?"

"You can call me Thelma, boy. My sweet Bobby died in the winter of 1956, just after Eisenhower was elected—he called me Hell's Bells, but he always smiled when he said it, so I didn't ever get mad at him. A woman screaming? Not likely. I like my TV loud."

"It was in the middle of the night," Sally said. "You would have been in bed."

"My hair curlers are so tight, I can't hear a thing. Ask Martha. If she's not trying to find herself a man, she's lying in bed thinking about it. Maybe she heard something."

"All right," Quinlan said. He took a bite of garlic toast, shivered in ecstasy at the rich garlic and butter taste, and said, "The woman was screaming close by, perhaps just across the way from Amabel's house. She was someone's prisoner. Then that someone killed her. What do you think?"

Thelma chewed another bite of chicken, a string of mozzarella cheese hanging off her chin. "I think, boy, that you and Sally here should go driving someplace and neck. I've never before seen a girl in such a twitter as poor Sally here. She's a mess. Amabel won't say anything except that you've had a rough time and you're trying to get over a bad marriage. She said none of us were to say a word to anybody, that you needed peace and quiet. You don't have to worry, Sally, no one from The Cove will call and tell on you."

"Thank you, ma'am."

"Call me Thelma, Sally. Now, how much does either of you know about that big-time murdered lawyer back in Washington?"

James thought Sally would faint and fall into her chicken parmigiana. She looked whiter than death. He said easily, "No more than anybody else, I suspect. What do you know, Thelma?"

"Since I'm the only one with a real working TV, I know a world more than anybody else in this town. Did you know the missing daughter's husband was on TV, pleading for her to come home? He said he was worried she wasn't well and didn't know what she was doing. He said she wasn't responsible, that she was sick. He said he was real concerned about her, that he wanted her back so he could take care of her. Did you know that? Isn't that something?"

She wouldn't faint into the parmigiana now. Quinlan felt her turn into stone. "Where did you hear that, Thelma?" he asked mildly, even as he doubted he ever wanted another bite of chicken parmigiana in his life.

"It was on FOX. You can find out everything on FOX."

"Do you remember anything else he said?"

That was about it. He pleads real well. Looked very sincere. A handsome man, but there's something too slick about him. From what I could tell he's got a weak chin. What do you two think about that?"

"Not a thing," Sally said, and James was pleased that her voice didn't sound scared, though he knew she had to be.

Thelma didn't seem to realize that her audience had stopped eating. She cackled, saying, "I like James. He's not all soft and smooth like that poor girl's husband. No, James doesn't put all that mousse in his hair. I bet that poor girl's husband wouldn't use that nice big gun James has under his coat. No, he'd have one of those prissy little derringers. No, he's too slick for my tastes.

"Now that James is here, Sally, I recommend that you use him. That's what my husband always said to me. 'Thelma,' he'd say, 'men love to be used. Use me.' I still miss Bobby. He caught pneumonia, you know, back in 1956. Killed him in four days. A pity." She sighed and took another bite of chicken parmigiana.

"I feel like I just swallowed five cloves of garlic," Quinlan said after they managed to escape, Sally pleading a stomachache.

"Yes, but it was delicious until Thelma mentioned Scott."

"He wants to take care of you."

"Oh, I'm sure he does."

He wished she'd tell him about her husband and what he'd done to her. The fear in her voice wasn't as strong as the bitterness. When she'd gotten that phone call from someone pretending to be her father—now, that was fear. She turned to face him. She looked paler, if that were possible, and pinched, as if the life were being drained out of her. "You've been kind to me and I appreciate it, but I've got to be leaving now. I can't stay here any longer. Now that he's gotten on TV about me, someone will have seen it. Someone will call. I've got to leave. And you know what else? Thelma knows. She was just playing with me."

"No one will call because no one saw him. If he'd offered a reward, then I'd bet on Thelma calling up in a flash, cackling all the while. Yes, Thelma knows, but she'll stop at enjoying the hell out of taunting you. Look, Sally, no one else knows who you are. All you are is Amabel's niece. I'd even wager that if anyone did find out they wouldn't say a word. Loyalty—you know what I mean?"

"Actually," she said, "I don't."

Dear God, he thought as he stepped along with her, what the hell had her life been like? He didn't remember a TV in his tower bedroom. He hoped there was one. He wanted to see Scott Brainerd pleading to his wife to return to him.

"Don't go," he said to her when they reached Amabel's cottage. "You know, it isn't all that hard to be loyal if it doesn't cost you anything. There's no need to. Let things spin out, just stay out of it. Besides, you don't have any money, do you?"

"I have credit cards, but I'm afraid to use them."

"They're very easy to trace. I'm glad you didn't use them. Look, Sally, I've got some friends back in Washington. Let me put in a couple of calls and see what's really happening, okay?"

"What friends?"

He smiled down at her. "I can't put a thing over on you, can I?"

"Not when it hits me in the nose," she said, and smiled back at him. "It doesn't matter, James. If you want to talk to some people, go ahead. Just remember, though, I don't have any money to pay you."

"*Pro bono,*" he said. "I hear even government agencies do some work for free."

"Yeah, just like they use our taxes to pay for midnight volleyball."

"Basketball. That was a while back."

"Your friends work for the feds?"

"Yep, and they're good people. I'll let you know what's cooking—if they know anything, of course."

"Thank you, James. But you know, there's still the person who called me pretending to be my father. That person knows where I am."

"Whoever comes, if he comes, has my big gun to contend with. Don't worry."

She nodded, wished he could touch her hand, squeeze it, pat her cheek, anything, to make her feel less threatened, less hunted. But he couldn't, she knew that, just as she knew she didn't know him at all.

So he was her protector now, Quinlan realized, shaking his head at himself. He would protect her from any guy who came here wanting to drag her back or hurt her.

That was a good joke on him, he thought, as he walked back to Thelma's Bed and Breakfast.

He was her main hunter.

WHEN THE PHONE RANG, Sally was in the kitchen slicing a turkey breast Amabel had brought home from Safeway. Her aunt called out, "It's for you, Sally."

James, she thought, smiling, as she wiped her hands. She walked into the living room to see Martha with her aunt, the two of them smiling at her, saying nothing now, which was only polite since they'd probably been talking about her before she'd come into the room.

"Hello?"

"How's my little girl?"

She froze. Her heart pounded fast and painfully hard. It was him. She remembered his voice too well to believe now that it was someone pretending to be Amory St. John.

"You don't want to talk to me? You don't want to know when I'm going to come get you, Sally?"

She said clearly, "You're dead. Long dead. I don't know who killed you, but I wish I had. Go back to hell where you belong."

"Soon, Sally. I can't wait, can you? Very soon now I'll have you with me again."

"No, you won't," she screamed and slammed down the receiver.

"Sally, what is going on? Who was that?"

"It was my father," she said and laughed. She was still laughing as she walked up the stairs.

Amabel called after her, "But Sally, that couldn't have been someone trying to make you believe it was your father. That was a woman on the line. Martha said she sounded all fuzzy, but it was a woman. She even thought it sounded a bit like Thelma Nettro, but that couldn't be. I didn't know of any woman who knew you were here."

Sally stopped on the second step from the top. The steps were narrow, and too steep. She turned slowly and looked back downstairs. She couldn't see her aunt or Martha. She didn't want to see them. A woman? Maybe Thelma Nettro? No way.

She ran back down the stairs into the living room. Placid Martha was looking distressed, her hands clasping and unclasping her pearls, her glasses sliding down her nose.

"My dear," she began, only to stop at the ferocious look of anger on the girl's face. "Whatever is wrong? Amabel's right. It was a woman on the phone."

"When I answered it wasn't a woman on the phone. It was a man pretending to be my father." It had been her father. She knew it, knew it deep down. She was so scared she wondered if a person could die of just being scared, nothing else, just being scared.

"Baby," Amabel said, rising, "this is all very confusing. I think you and I should talk about this later."

Sally turned without another word and walked slowly upstairs. She was leaving now. She didn't care if she had to walk and hitchhike. She knew all the stories about the dangers of a woman alone, but they didn't come close to the danger she felt bearing down on her now. How many people knew she was here? The man pretending to be her father, and now a woman? She thought of that nurse. She'd hated that nurse so much. Sally couldn't even remember her name now. She didn't want to. Could it have been that nurse?

She stuffed her clothes in her duffel bag and then realized she had to wait. She didn't want to fight with Amabel. She heard Amabel lock up the cottage. She heard her walk up the stairs, her step brisk and solid. Sally got quickly into bed and pulled the covers up to her chin.

"Sally?"

"Yes, Amabel. Oh, goodness, I was nearly asleep. Good night."

"Yes, good night, baby. Sleep well."

"All right."

"Sally, about that phone call—"

She waited, not saying a word.

"Martha could have been mistaken. It's quite possible. Her hearing isn't all that good anymore. She's getting old. It could even have been a man disguising his voice like a woman's just in case you didn't answer the phone. I can't imagine that it could have been Thelma. Baby, nobody knows who you are, nobody."

Amabel paused. Sally could see her silhouetted in the doorway from the dim light in the corridor. "You know, baby, you've been through a lot, too much. You're frightened. I would be too. Your mind can do funny things to you when you're frightened. You know that, don't you?"

"Yes, I understand that, Amabel." She wasn't about to tell Amabel that Thelma knew who she was.

"Good. You try to sleep, baby." She didn't come in to kiss her good night, for which Sally was grateful. She lay there, waiting, waiting.

Finally, she slipped out of bed, pulled on her sneakers, picked up her duffel bag, and tiptoed to the window. It slid up easily. She poked her head out and scanned the ground as she'd done earlier. This was the way out. It wasn't far to the ground, and she knew there was no way she could get down those stairs without Amabel hearing her.

No, she'd be just fine. She climbed out the window and sat on the narrow ledge. She dropped the duffel bag and watched it bounce off the squat, thick bushes below. She drew a deep breath and jumped.

She landed on James Quinlan.

They both went down, James rolling, holding her tight against him.

When they came to a stop, Sally reared up on her hands and stared down at him. There was a half-moon, more than enough light to see his face clearly.

"What are you doing here?"

"I knew you'd run after that telephone call."

She rolled off him and rose, only to collapse again. She'd sprained her damned ankle. She cursed.

He laughed. "That's not good enough for a girl who didn't go to finishing school in Switzerland. Don't you know some down and dirty street curses?"

"Go to hell. I sprained my damned ankle and it's all your fault. Why couldn't you just mind your own damned business?"

"I didn't want you out on the road hitchhiking with some lowlife who could rape you and cut your throat."

"I thought of that. I'd rather take that risk than stay here. He knows I'm here, James, you know that. I can't just stay here and wait for him to come and take me. That's what he said. He said soon he'd be here for me."

"I was reading a newspaper when Martha came in all worried and told Thelma about a woman calling you, a woman you said wasn't a woman but your father. She said you were really distressed. She didn't understand why you'd be so upset to hear from your father. I knew you'd probably try to run, that's why I'm here, having you crush me into the ground."

She sat there on the ground next to him, rubbing her ankle, just shaking her head. "I'm not crazy."

"I know that," he said patiently. "There's an explanation. That's why you're not going to run away. Now *that's* crazy."

She came up on her knees, leaning toward him, her hands grasping his jacket lapels. "Listen to me, James. It was my father. No fake, no imitation. *It was my father.* Amabel said it could have been a man disguising his voice as a woman's if I wasn't the one to answer the phone. Then she turned around and told me how much strain I've been under. In other words, I'm crazy."

He took her hands in his, just held them, saying nothing. Then he spoke. "As I said, there's always an explanation. It probably was a man. We'll find out. If it wasn't, if it truly was a woman who asked for you, then we'll deal with that too. Trust me, Sally."

She sat back. Her ankle had stopped throbbing. Maybe it wasn't sprained after all.

"Tell me something."

"Yes?"

"Do you think someone could be trying to gaslight you?"

What did he know? She searched his face for the lie, for knowledge, but saw none of it.

"Is it possible? Could someone be trying to make you crazy? Make you doubt your sanity?"

She looked down at her clasped hands, at her fingernails. She realized that she hadn't chewed her nails since she'd been in The Cove. Not since she'd met him. They didn't look so ragged. She said finally, not looking at him, because it was awful, what she was, what she had been, perhaps what she still was today, right now, "Why?"

"I'd have to say that someone's afraid of you, afraid of what you might possibly know. This someone wants to eliminate you from the game, so to speak." He paused, looking toward the ocean, fancying he could hear the crashing waves, but he couldn't, Amabel's cottage was just a bit too far for that. "The question is why this someone would go this route. You're about the sanest person I know, Sally. Who could possibly think he could make you believe you were nuts?"

She loved him for that. Loved him without reservation, without any question. She gave him a big grin. It came from the deepest part of her, a place that had been empty for so long she'd forgotten that it was possible to feel this good, this confident in herself, and in someone else.

"I was nuts," she said, still grinning, feeling the incredible relief of telling someone the truth, of telling him. "At least that's what they wanted everyone to believe. They kept me drugged up for six months until I finally got it together enough to hide the medication under my tongue and not swallow it. The nurse always forced my mouth open and ran her fingers all inside to make sure I'd taken the pills. I don't know how I managed to keep the pill hidden, but I did. I did it for two days, until I was together enough. Then I escaped. And then I got the ring off my finger and threw it in a ditch."

He knew she'd been in a sanitarium, a very expensive posh little resort sanitarium in Maryland. All very private. But this? She'd been a prisoner? Drugged to her gills?

He looked at her for a long time. Her smile faltered. He just shook his head at her, cupped her face in his hand, and said, "How would you like to come back to Thelma's place and share my tower room with me? I'll take the sofa and you can have the bed. I won't make any moves on you, I swear. We can't just sit here for the rest of the night. It's damp and I don't want either of us to get sick."

"And then what?"

"We'll think more about that tomorrow. If it was a woman who put the call through, then we need to figure out who it could have been. And I want to know why you were in that place for six months."

She was shaking her head even as he spoke. He knew she regretted spilling it to him now. After all, she didn't know him, didn't have a clue if she could trust him or not. She said, "You know, I have another question. Why did Martha answer Amabel's phone and not Amabel?"

"That's a good one, but the answer's probably just as simple as that Martha happened to be standing next to the phone when it rang. Don't get paranoid, Sally."

He carried her duffel bag, his other hand under her arm. She was limping, but it wasn't bad, not a sprain, as she'd feared. He didn't want to haul her over to Doc Spiver's. Only the good Lord knew what that old man might do. Probably want to give her artificial respiration.

He had a key to the front door of Thelma's Bed and Breakfast. All the lights were out. They walked to his tower room without waking Thelma or Martha. James knew there was only one other guest, who had come in just today, an older woman who'd been nice and smiling and had said that she was here to visit her daughter in the subdivision, but she'd always wanted to stay here, in one of the tower rooms. Thank God, she'd said, that there were two. Which meant she was on the other side of the huge house.

He switched the bedside lamp on low only after he had closed the venetian blinds. "There. It's charming, isn't it? There's no TV."

She wasn't looking at him or the window. She was moving as fast as a shot toward the door. She knew she didn't remotely love him anymore. She was afraid. She was in this man's room, a man she didn't know, a man who was sympathetic. She hadn't known sympathy in so long that she'd fallen for it without thought, without question. James Quinlan was quite wrong. She was as nuts as they came.

"Sally, what's wrong?"

She was tugging on the doorknob, trying to turn it, but the door didn't open. She realized the key was still in the lock. She felt like a fool.

He didn't make any movement of any kind. He didn't even stretch out his hand to her. He just said in his calm, deep voice, "It's all right. I know you're scared. Come now and sit over here. We'll talk. I won't hurt you. I'm on your side."

A lie, he thought, another damned lie. The chance of his ever being anywhere near her side was just about nil.

She walked slowly away from the door, stumbled against a small end table, and sat down heavily on the sofa. It was chintz with pale blue and cream flowers.

She was rubbing her hands together, just like Lady Macbeth, she thought. She raised her face. "I'm sorry."

"Don't be dumb. Now, would you like to try to sleep or talk awhile?"

She'd already told him too much. He was probably reconsidering his comment that she was the sanest person he knew. And he wanted to know why she'd been in that place? No, she couldn't bear that. Thinking about it was too much. She couldn't imagine talking about it. If she did, he'd know she was paranoid, delusional.

"I'm not crazy," she said, staring at him, knowing he was in the shadows and so was she, and neither of them could read the other's expression.

"Well, I just might be. I still haven't found out what happened to Harve and Marge Jensen, and you know what? I'm not all that interested anymore. Now, I called a friend at the FBI. No, don't look like you're going to dive for the door again. He's a very good friend, and I just got some information from him." Lies mixed with truth. It was his business, his lies having to be better than the bad guy's lies.

"What's his name?"

"Dillon Savich. He told me that the FBI is looking high and low for you, but no sign as yet. He said they're convinced you saw something the night of your father's murder, that you probably saw the person who killed him, that it was probably your mother, and you ran to protect her. If it wasn't your mother, then it was someone else, or you.

"Your dad wasn't a nice man, Sally. Turns out he was being investigated by the FBI for selling weapons to terrorist countries on our No Way List, like Iraq, Iran, and Syria. In any case, they're convinced you know something." He didn't ask her if it was true. He just sat there on the other end of that chintz sofa with its feminine pale blue and cream flowers and waited.

"How do you know this Dillon Savich?"

He realized then that she might be scared half out of her mind, but she wasn't stupid. He'd managed to say everything that needed to be said without blowing his cover. But she hadn't responded. She still didn't trust him, and he admired her for that.

"We went to Princeton together in the nineties. He always wanted to be an agent, always. We've kept in touch. He's good at his job. I trust him."

"It's difficult to believe he just spilled all this out to you."

Quinlan shrugged. "He's frustrated. They all are. They want you, and you're gone without a trace. He was probably praying that I knew something and would tell him if he whetted my appetite."

"I didn't know about my father being a traitor. But on the other hand, I'm not surprised. I guess I've known for a very long time that he was capable of just about anything."

She was sitting very quietly, looking toward the door every couple of seconds but not saying anything. She looked exhausted, her hair was ratty, there was a smudge of dirt on her cheek from her jump and a huge grass stain on the leg of her blue jeans. He wished she'd tell him what she was thinking. He wished she'd just come clean and tell him everything.

Then, he thought, it might be a good idea to take her to dinner.

He laughed. He was the crazy one. He liked her. He hadn't wanted to. He'd only wanted to see her as the main piece to his puzzle, the linchpin that would bring it all together.

"Did you tell this Dillon Savich anything?"

"I told him I wouldn't go out with his sister-in-law again. She's always popping bubble gum in her mouth."

She blinked at him, then smiled—a small, tight smile, but it was a smile.

He rose and offered her his hand. "You're exhausted. Go to bed. We can deal with this in the morning. The bathroom's through there. It's a treat, all marble and a water-saver toilet in pale pink. Take a nice long shower, it'll help bring down the swelling in your ankle. Thelma even provides those fluffy white bathrobes."

He had let her off the hook, even though he guessed he could have gotten more out of her if he'd tried even a little bit. But she was near the edge, and not just with that damned phone call.

Who the hell was the dead woman they'd found being pulled in and out by the tide at the base of the cliff?

THEY WERE EATING breakfast the next morning, alone in the large dining room. The woman who'd checked in the day before wasn't down
yet, nor was Thelma Nettro.

Martha had said as she took their order, "Thelma sometimes likes
to watch the early talk shows in bed. She also writes in that diary of
hers. Goodness, she's kept a diary for as long as I can remember."

"What does she write in it?" Sally asked.

Martha shrugged. "I guess just the little things that happen every
day. What else would she write?"

"Eat," Quinlan told Sally when Martha placed a plate stacked with
blueberry pancakes in front of her. He watched her butter them, then
pour Martha's homemade syrup over the top. She took one bite, chewed
it slowly, then carefully laid her fork on the edge of the plate.

Her fork was still there when Sheriff David Mountebank walked in,
Martha at his heels offering him food and coffee. He took one look at
Sally's pancakes and Quinlan's English muffin with strawberry jam and
said yes to everything.

They made room for him. He looked at them closely, not saying
anything, just looking from one to the other. Finally he said, "You're a
fast worker, Mr. Quinlan."

"I beg your pardon?"

"You and Ms. Brandon are already involved? Sleeping together?"

"It's a long story, Sheriff," Quinlan said, then laughed, hoping it
would make Sally realize how silly it was.

"I think you're a damned pig, Sheriff," Sally said pleasantly. "I hope
the pancakes give you stomach cramps."

"All right, so I'm a jerk. But what the hell are you doing here? Amabel Perdy called my office real early and told me you'd disappeared. She was frantic. Incidentally, your hair sure grew back fast."

No black wig. Face him down, she thought, just face him down. She said, "I was going to call her after breakfast. It's only seven in the morning. I didn't want to wake her. Actually, I'm surprised Martha didn't call her to tell her I was here."

"Martha must have assumed that Amabel already knew where you were. Now what's going on here?"

"What did her aunt tell you, Sheriff?"

David Mountebank recognized technique when he saw it. He didn't like to have it used on him, but for the moment, he knew he should play along. For a simple PI this man was very good.

"She just said you'd gotten an obscene phone call last night and panicked. She thought you must have run away. She was worried because you don't have a car or any money."

"That's right, Sheriff. I'm sorry she worried you all for nothing."

Quinlan said, "I rescued the damsel, Sheriff, and slept on the sofa. She liked the tower room. She ignored me. Have you found out anything about the murdered woman?"

"Yes, her name was Laura Strather. She lived in the subdivision with her husband and three kids. They thought she was visiting her sister up in Portland. That's why no missing person report was filed on her. The question is, why was she being held a prisoner over here in The Cove and who the hell killed her?"

"Have your people checked all the houses across from Amabel Perdy's cottage?"

The sheriff nodded. "Depressing, Quinlan, depressing. No one knows a thing. No one heard a thing—not a TV, not a telephone, not a car backfiring, not a woman screaming. Not on either night. Not a bloody thing." He looked over at Sally, but couldn't speak until Martha delivered his pancakes.

She looked at each of them, then smiled and said, "I'll never forget my mama showing me an article in the *Oregonian* written by this man called Qumquat Jagger way back in the early fifties. 'The Cove sunsets are a dramatic sight as long as one has a martini in the right hand.' I've long agreed with him on that." She added easily, "It's too early for a martini or a sunset—how about a bloody mary? All of you look on edge."

"I'd love one," Sheriff Mountebank said, "but I can't." Quinlan and Sally shook their heads. "Thank you, though, Martha," Quinlan said.

She checked to see that they had everything they could possibly want, then left the dining room.

After David Mountebank had eaten half the pancakes, he looked at Sally again and said, "If you had called me about hearing that woman screaming, I'm not certain I would have believed you. I would have searched, naturally, but I'd probably have thought you'd had a nightmare. But then you and Quinlan found a woman's body. Was she the woman you heard screaming? Probably so. You were telling the truth then, and all the old folk in this town are deaf. Either of you have any ideas?"

"I didn't even think about calling a sheriff," Sally said. "But I probably wouldn't have. My aunt wouldn't have wanted that."

"No, probably not. The folk in The Cove like to keep things to themselves." The sheriff grinned at her then. "I don't know if you're my best witness in any case, Ms. Brandon, since I find you've slept in Quinlan's tower room. And you lied to me about your hair."

"I have several wigs, Sheriff. I like wigs. I thought you were impertinent to ask me, so I said I had cancer to guilt you."

David Mountebank sighed. Why did everybody have to lie? It was exhausting. He looked at her again. This time he frowned. "You look familiar," he said slowly.

"James tells me I look like his former sister-in-law. Amabel thinks I look like Mary Lou Retton, although I'm nearly a foot taller. My mom said I was the image of her Venezuelan nanny. Don't tell me, Sheriff, that I remind you of your Pekingese."

"No, Ms. Brandon, be thankful you don't look like my dog. His name is Hugo and he's a rottweiler."

Sally waited, trying not to clench her hands, trying to look amused, trying to look like she was all together and not ready to fall apart if he poked his finger at her and said he was taking her in. She watched his frown smooth away as he turned to James.

"I checked the files from the previous sheriff. Her name was Dorothy Willis, and she was very good. Her notes on those missing old folks were very thorough. I made copies and brought them to you." He reached in his pocket and pulled out a thick envelope.

"Thank you, Sheriff," Quinlan said, not knowing for several moments who the hell David Mountebank was talking about. Then he remembered Harve and Marge Jensen.

"I read over them last night. Everybody believed there was foul play, what with their Winnebago being found in a used car lot in Spokane. It's just that nobody knew anything. She wrote that she spoke to nearly everybody in The Cove but came up with nothing. Nobody knew a thing. Nobody remembered the Jensens. She even sent off the particulars to the FBI just in case something like this had happened elsewhere in the country. That's it, Quinlan. Sorry, but there's no more. No leads of any kind." He ate another helping of pancakes, drank his black coffee down, then shoved back his chair. "Well, you're all right, Ms. Brandon, so at least I don't have to worry about you. It's strange, you know? Nobody else heard that woman scream. Real strange."

He shook his head and walked out of the dining room, saying over his shoulder, "You look best with your own hair, Ms. Brandon. Lose the wigs. Trust me. My wife says I've got real good taste."

"Sheriff, what happened to Dorothy Willis?"

David Mountebank stopped then. "A bad thing, a very bad thing. She was shot by a teenage boy who was robbing a local 7-Eleven. She died."

When Thelma Nettro made her appearance some ten minutes later, looking for all the world like a relic from Victorian days, her teeth in her mouth, white lace at her parchment throat, the first words out of her mouth were, "Well, girl, is James here a decent lover?"

"I don't know, ma'am. He wouldn't even kiss me. He said he was too tired. He even hinted at a headache. What could I do?"

Old Thelma threw her head back, and that scrawny neck of hers worked ferociously to bring out fat, full laughs. "Here I thought you were a wimp, Sally. That's good. Now, what's this Martha tells me about how a woman who was really your dead daddy called you at Amabel's last night?"

"There was no woman when I got on the line."

"This is very strange, Sally. Why would anyone do this? Now, if it had been James on the phone, well, that would have been another matter. But if he gets all that tired, well, then maybe you'd just best forget him."

"How many husbands did you have, Thelma?" Quinlan asked, knowing that Sally was reeling, giving her time to get herself together.

"Just Bobby, James. Did I tell you Bobby invented a new improved gyropilot? Yes, well, that's why I've got more money than any of the other poor sods in this place. All because of Bobby's invention."

"It looks to me like everyone has money," Sally said. "The town is charming. Everything looks new, planned, like everyone put money in a pot and decided together what they wanted to do with it."

"It was something like that," Thelma said. "It's all barren by the cliffs now. I remember back in the fifties there were still some pines and firs, even a few poplars close to the cliffs, all bowed down, of course, from the violent storms. They're all gone now, like there'd never been anything there at all. At least we've managed to save a few here in town."

She then turned in her chair and yelled, "Martha, where's my peppermint tea? You back there with young Ed? Leave him alone and bring me my breakfast!"

James waited two beats, then said easily, "I sure wish you'd tell me about Harve and Marge Jensen, Thelma. It was only three years ago, and you've got the sharpest mind in town. Hey, maybe there was something interesting about them and you wrote about it in your diary. Do you think so?"

"That's true enough, boy. I'm sure smarter than poor Martha, who doesn't know her elbow from the teakettle. And she just never leaves those pearls of hers alone. I've replaced them at least three times now. I even let her think for a while that I was the one who called Sally, I like to tease her, it makes life a bit more lively when she's twisting around like a sheet in a stiff wind. I'm sorry, but I don't remember any Harve or Marge."

"You know," Sally said, "that phone call could have been local. The voice was so clear."

"You think maybe I called you, girl, then pretended to be your daddy? I like it, but there's no way I could have gotten a tape of your daddy's voice. Who cares, anyway?"

"So you admit you know who I am?"

"Sure I do. It took you long enough to catch on. No need to worry, Sally, I won't tell a soul. No telling what some of these young nitwits around town would do if they found out you were that murdered big-shot lawyer's daughter. No, I won't tell anybody, not even Martha."

Martha brought in the peppermint tea and a plate filled with fat browned sausages, at least half a dozen of them. They were rolling on the plate in puddles of grease. Sally and Quinlan both stared at that plate.

Thelma cackled. "I want the highest cholesterol in history when I croak. I made Doc Spiver promise that when I finally shuck off this mortal snakeskin, he'll check. I want to be in the book of records."

"You must be well on your way," Quinlan said.

"I don't think so," Martha said, hovering by Thelma's left hand. "She's been eating this for years now. Sherry Vorhees says she'll outlive us all. She says her husband, Reverend Hal, doesn't have a chance against Thelma. He's already wheezing around and he's only sixty-eight, and he isn't fat. Strange, isn't it? Thelma wonders who's going to do her service if Reverend Hal isn't around."

"What does Sherry know?" Thelma demanded, talking while she chewed on one of those fat sausages. "I think she'd be happier if

Reverend Hal would pass on to his just reward, although I don't know how just he'd find it. He might find himself plunked down in hell and wonder how it could happen to him since he's so holy. He's reasonable most of the time, is Hal. It's just when he's near a woman alone that he goes off the deep end and starts mumbling about sin and hell and temptations of the flesh. It appears he believes sex is a sin and rarely touches his wife. No wonder they don't have any kids. Not a one, ever. Fancy that. It's hard to believe, since he is a man, after all. But still, all poor Sherry does is drink her iced tea, fiddle with her chignon, and sell ice cream."

"What's wrong with that?" Sally asked, thinking that the Mad Hatter's tea party couldn't have been weirder than Thelma Nettro at breakfast. "If she were unhappy, wouldn't she just leave?" *Yeah, like you did, but just not in time.* Some of the grease around the sausages was beginning to congeal.

"Her iced tea is that cheap white wine. I don't know how her liver is still holding up after all these years."

Sally swallowed, looking away from those sausages. "Amabel told me that when you first opened the World's Greatest Ice Cream Shop, you stored the ice cream in Ralph Keaton's caskets."

"That's right. It was Helen's idea. She's Ralph's wife and the one who had the recipe. It was her idea that we start the ice cream shop. She used to be a shy little thing, looked scared whenever she had to say anything. If Ralph said boo she'd fade behind a piece of furniture. She's changed now, speaks right up, tells Ralph to put a sock in it whenever she doesn't like something he does. All because of that recipe. She's really blossomed with her ice cream success.

"Poor old Ralph. He needs business, but none of us will die for him. I think he's hoping the husband of that dead woman will ask him to lay her out."

Sally couldn't stand it anymore. She rose, tried to smile, and said, "Thank you for breakfast, Thelma. I've got to go home now. Amabel must be worried about me."

"Martha called her and told her you were here with James. She didn't have a word to say to that."

"I'll thank Martha," Sally said politely. She waited for James to join her. It was raining outside, a dark, miserably gray day.

"Well, damn," James said. He walked back into the foyer and fetched an umbrella from the stand. He said as they walked down the street, "I'll bet you the old men are playing cards in Purn Davies's store. I can't imagine them missing the ritual."

"Sheriff Mountebank will realize who I am, James. It's just a matter of time."

"I don't think so. He probably saw your picture on TV, but that would have been last week at the latest. He won't make the connection."

"I'm sure the authorities would have sent photos out to everyone."

"This is a backwater, Sally. It costs too much to fax photos to every police and sheriff office in the country. Don't worry about it. The sheriff doesn't have a clue. The way you answered him polished it off."

His eyes were as gray as the rain that was pouring down. He wasn't looking at her, but straight ahead, his hand cupping her elbow. "Watch the puddle."

She took a quick step sideways. "The town doesn't look quite so charming in this rain, does it? Main Street looks like an old abandoned Hollywood set, all gray and forlorn, like no one's lived here forever."

"Don't worry, Sally."

"Maybe you're right. Are you married, James?"

"No. Watch your step here."

"Okay. Have you ever been married?"

"Once. It didn't work out."

"I wonder if any marriages ever work out."

"You an expert?"

She was surprised at the sarcasm but nodded, saying, "A bit. My parents didn't do well. Actually . . . no, never mind that. I didn't do well, either. That's just about one hundred percent of my world, and it's all bad."

They were walking past Purn Davies's general store. Quinlan

grinned and took her hand. "Let's go see what the old guys are up to. I'd like to ask them firsthand if it's true that nobody heard anything the night that poor woman was murdered."

Purn Davies, Hunker Dawson, Gus Eisner, and Ralph Keaton were seated around the barrel, a game of gin rummy under way. There was a fire in a wood-burning stove that looked to be more for show than for utility, a handsome antique piece. A bell over the door rang when Quinlan and Sally came through.

"Wet out there," Quinlan said, shaking the umbrella. "How you all doing?"

There were two grunts, one okay, and Purn Davies actually folded his cards facedown and got up to greet them. "What can I do for you folks?"

"You meet Amabel Perdy's niece, Sally St. John?"

"Yep, but it weren't much of a meeting. How you doin', Miz Sally? Amabel all right?"

She nodded. She just hoped she could keep her fake names straight. Brandon for Sheriff Mountebank and St. John for everyone else.

There was more than polite interest in his question about Amabel, and it made Sally smile. "Amabel's just fine, Mr. Davies. We didn't have any leaks during the storm. The new roof's holding up really well."

Hunker Dawson, who was sitting there pulling on his suspenders, said, "You had us all out looking for that poor woman who went and fell off that cliff. It was cold and windy that night. None of us liked going out. There weren't nothing to find anyway."

SALLY'S CHIN WENT UP. "Yes, sir. I heard her scream and of course I would alert you. I'm just sorry you didn't find her before she was murdered."

"Murdered?" The front legs of Ralph Keaton's chair hit hard against the pine floor. "What the dickens do you mean, murdered? Doc said she must have fallen, said it was a tragic accident."

Quinlan said mildly, "The medical examiner said she'd been strangled. Evidently whoever killed her didn't count on her body washing back up to land. More than that, whoever killed her didn't even consider that if she did wash up there would be anyone around down there to find her. The walk down that path is rather perilous."

"You saying that we're too rickety to walk down that path, Mr. Quinlan?"

"Well, it's a possibility, isn't it? You're certain none of you heard her scream during the night? Cry out? Call for help? Anything that wasn't just a regular night sound?"

"It was around two o'clock in the morning," Sally said.

"Look, Miz Sally," Ralph Keaton said, rising now, "we all know you're all upset about leaving your husband, but that don't matter. We all know you came here to rest, to get your bearings again. But you know, that kind of thing can have some pretty big effects on a young lady like yourself, like screwing up how you see things, how you hear things."

"I didn't imagine it, Mr. Keaton. I would think that I had if Mr. Quinlan and I hadn't found the woman's body the very next day."

"There is that," Purn Davies said. "Could be a coincidence. You havin' a dream because of you leaving your husband—that's what

Amabel told us—or hearing the wind howling, and the woman jumping off that cliff. Yeah, all a coincidence."

Quinlan knew there was nothing more to be gained. They'd all dug in their heels. Both he and Sally were outsiders. They weren't welcome, just tolerated, barely. He thought it was interesting that Amabel Perdy seemed to have enough control over the townspeople so none of them had revealed to the cops that Sally was here, no matter how much she was obviously upsetting them. He prayed that Amabel's hold on them would last. Maybe he should tone things down, just to be on the safe side. "Mr. Davies is right, Sally," Quinlan said easily. "Who knows? We sure don't. But, you know, I just wish you'd remember something about Harve and Marge Jensen."

Hunker Dawson turned so fast he fell off his chair. There was pandemonium for a minute. Quinlan was beside him in an instant, making sure that he hadn't hurt himself. "I'm a clumsy old geek," Hunker said, as Quinlan carefully helped him to his feet.

"What the hell happened to you?" Ralph Keaton shouted at him, all red in the face.

"I'm a clumsy old geek," Hunker said again. "I wish Arlene were still alive. She'd massage me and make me some chicken soup. My shoulder hurts."

Quinlan patted his arm. "Sally and I will drop by Doc Spiver's house and tell him to come over here, all right? Take two aspirin. He shouldn't be long."

"Naw, don't do that," Ralph Keaton said. "No problem. Hunker here is just whining."

"It's no problem," Sally said. "We were going to walk by his house anyway."

"Well, all right, then," Hunker said and let his friends lower him back into his chair. He was rubbing his shoulder.

"Yes, we'll get Doc Spiver," Quinlan said. He shook open the umbrella and escorted Sally out of the general store. He paused when he heard the old men talking quietly. He heard Purn Davies say, "Why the hell shouldn't they go to Doc's house? You got a problem with that, Ralph? Hunker doesn't, and he's right. Listen to me, it don't matter."

"Yeah," Gus Eisner said. "I don't think Hunker could make it over there, now could he?"

"Probably wouldn't be smart," Purn Davies said slowly. "No, let Quinlan and Sally go. Yeah, that's best."

The rain had become a miserable drizzle, chilling them to the bone. He said, "None of them is a very good liar. I wonder what all that talk of theirs meant."

All that he was implying blossomed in her mind, and she felt more than the chill, damp air engulfing her. "I can't believe what you're suggesting, James."

He shrugged. "I guess I shouldn't have said anything. Just forget it, Sally."

She couldn't, of course. "They're old. If they do remember the Jensens, it's just that they're afraid to admit it. As for the other, it was harmless."

"Could be," James said.

They walked in silence to Doc Spiver's house, and Quinlan knocked on the freshly painted white door. Even in the dull morning light, the house looked well cared for. Just like all the other houses in this bloody little town.

No answer.

Quinlan knocked again, calling out, "Doc Spiver? It's Quinlan. It's about Hunker Dawson. He fell and hurt his shoulder."

No answer.

Sally felt something hard and dark creep over her. "He must be out with someone else," she said, but she was shivering.

Quinlan turned the doorknob. To his surprise it wasn't locked. "Let's see," he said and pushed the door open. The house was warm, the furnace going full blast.

There were no lights on, and there should have been, what with all the dull gray outside. It was just as gray inside the house, the corners just as shadowy, as it was outdoors.

"Doc Spiver?"

Suddenly James turned, took her by the shoulders, and said, "I want you to stay here in the hallway, Sally. Don't budge."

She just smiled up at him. "I'll look in the living room and dining room. Why don't you check upstairs? He's just not here, James."

"Probably not." He turned and headed up the stairs, Sally felt the impact of the heat. It was hotter now, almost burning, making her mouth dry. She quickly switched on the hallway light. Odd, but it didn't help. It was still too dark in here. Everything was so still, so motionless. There didn't seem to be any air. She tried to draw in a deep breath but couldn't. She looked at the arch that led into the living room.

Suddenly she didn't want to go in there. But she forced herself to take one step at a time. She wished James were right beside her, talking to her, dispelling the horrible stillness. For God's sake, the old man just wasn't here, that was all.

She tried to take another deep breath. She took another step. She stood in the open archway. The living room was just as dim and gray as the hallway. She quickly switched on the overhead lights. She saw the rich Bokhara carpet, the Tiffany lamp that Doc Spiver had knocked over because he hadn't seen it. It wasn't broken or cracked, as far as she could tell. She took a step into the living room.

"Doc Spiver? Are you here?"

There was no answer.

She looked around, not wanting to go farther, to take one more step into that room. She saw a blur, something moving quickly. She heard a loud thump on the hardwood floor, then the raucous sound of a rocking chair. There was a loud, indignant meow, and a huge gray cat leaped off the back of the sofa to land at her feet. Sally shrieked. Then she laughed, a horrible laugh that made her sound crazy. "Good kitty," she said, her voice so thin she was surprised she could breathe. The cat skittered away.

She heard the rocking chair moving, back and forth, back and forth, creaking softly now. She stifled the scream in her throat. The cat had hit the rocking chair and made it move, nothing more. She drew a deep breath and walked quickly to the far side of the living room. The rocker was moving slowly, as if someone were putting pressure on it, somehow making it move. She walked around to the front of the chair.

The air was as still and dead as the old man slumped low in the old bentwood rocker, one arm hanging to the floor, his head bowed to his chest. His fingernails scraped gently against the hardwood floor. The sound was like a gun blast. She stifled a scream behind the fist pressed against her mouth. Then she took several fast breaths. She stared in fascination at the drops of blood that dripped slowly, inexorably, off the end of his middle finger. She turned on her heel and ran back into the hallway.

She yelled, her voice hoarse with terror and the urge to vomit. "James! Doc Spiver is here! James!"

"ONE WONDERS—if you weren't here, Ms. Brandon, would there have been two deaths?"

Sally sat on the edge of Amabel's sofa, her hands clasped in her lap, rocking gently back and forth, just like old Doc Spiver had in that rocking chair. James was sitting on the arm of the sofa, as still as a man waiting in the shadows for his prey to pass by. Now where, David Mountebank wondered, had that thought come from? James Quinlan was a professional, he knew that for sure now, knew it from the way Quinlan had handled the scene at Doc Spiver's house more professionally than David would have, the way he had kept calm, detached. All of it screamed training that had been extensive, had been received by someone who already had all the necessary skills—and that easy, calm temperament.

Quinlan was worried about Sally Brandon, David could see that, but there was something else, something more that was hidden, and David hated that, hated the not knowing.

"Don't you agree, Ms. Brandon?" he asked again, pressing now, gently, because he didn't want her to collapse. She was too pale, too drawn, but he had to find out what the devil was going on here.

She said finally, with great simplicity, "Yes."

"All right." He turned to Quinlan and gave him a slow smile. "Actually, you and Sally arrived at nearly the same time. That's rather an odd coincidence, isn't it?"

He was too close, James thought, but he knew David Mountebank couldn't possibly know anything. All he could do was guess.

"Yes," he said. "It's also one that I would have willingly forgone. Amabel should be back soon. Sally, would you like some tea?"

"His fingernails scraped against the hardwood floor. It scared me silly."

"It would scare me silly, too," David said. "So, both of you were there just because Hunker Dawson fell off his chair and hurt his shoulder."

"Yes," James said. "That's it. Nothing sinister, just being good neighbors. Nothing more except what a couple of the old men said when we were leaving. Something about it didn't matter. That Hunker shouldn't go. To let us go, that it was time."

"You aren't saying that they knew he was dead and wanted you and Sally to be the ones to find him?"

"I have no idea. It doesn't make any sense, really. I just thought I'd pour out everything."

"Do you think he killed himself?"

Quinlan said, "If you look at the angle of the shot, at how the gun fell, at how his body crumpled in, I think it could go either way. Your medical examiner will find out, don't you think?"

"Ponser is good, but he isn't that good. He didn't have the greatest training. I'll let him have a go at it, and if it turns out equivocal, then I'll call Portland."

Sally looked up then. "You really think he could have killed himself, James?"

He nodded. He wanted to say more, but he knew he couldn't, even if the sheriff weren't here. He had to rein in all the words that wanted to speak themselves to her. It was too much.

"Why would he do that?"

Quinlan shrugged. "Perhaps he had a terminal illness, Sally. Perhaps he was in great pain."

"Or maybe he knew something and couldn't stand it. He killed himself to protect someone."

"Where did that come from, Ms. Brandon?"

"I don't know, Sheriff. It's all just hideous. Amabel told me after we found that poor woman that nothing ever happened here, at least nothing more than Doc Spiver's cat, Forceps, getting stuck in that old elm tree in his backyard. What will happen to the cat?"

"I'll make sure Forceps has a new home. I'll just bet one of my kids will beg me to bring the damned cat home."

"David," Quinlan said, "why don't you just break down and call her Sally?"

"All right, if you don't mind. Sally." When she nodded, he was struck again at how familiar she looked to him. But he couldn't nail it down. More likely, she just looked like someone he'd known years ago, perhaps.

"Maybe James and I should leave so nothing else will happen."

"Well, actually, ma'am, you can't leave The Cove. You found the second body. There are so many questions and just not enough answers. Quinlan, why don't you and I make Sally some tea?"

Sally watched them walk out of the small living room. The sheriff stopped by one of Amabel's paintings, this one of oranges rotting in a bowl. Amabel had used globs of paint on those parts of the oranges that were rotting. It was a disturbing painting. She shivered. What did the sheriff want to talk to James about?

DAVID MOUNTEBANK WATCHED Quinlan pour water into the old kettle and turn on the heat beneath it. "Who are you?" he asked.

James stilled. Then he took down three cups and saucers from the cabinet. "You like sugar or milk, Sheriff?"

"No."

"How about brandy? That's what I'm putting in Sally's tea."

"No, thank you. Answer me, Quinlan. There's no way you're a PI, no way in hell. You're too good. You've had the best training. You're experienced. You know how to do things that normal folk just wouldn't know."

"Well, shit," James said. He pulled out his wallet and flipped it open. "Special Agent James Quinlan, Sheriff. FBI. A pleasure to meet you."

"Hot damn," David said. "You're here undercover. What the hell is going on?"

JAMES POURED A finger of brandy into the cup of tea. He grinned when the sheriff held out his hand. "No, hold on a second, I want to give this to Sally. I want to make sure she's hanging in there. She's a civilian. This has been incredibly tough on her. Surely you can understand that."

"Yes. I'll wait for you here, Quinlan."

James returned after just a moment to see the sheriff staring out the kitchen window over the sink, his hands on the counter. He was a tall man, a runner, rangy and lean. He was probably only a few years older than James. He had a quality of utter concentration about him, something that made people want to talk to him. James admired that, but he wasn't about to talk. He was beginning to like David Mountebank, but he wasn't about to let that sway him, either.

Quinlan said quietly, not wanting to startle him, "She's asleep. I covered her with one of Amabel's afghans. But let's keep it down, all right, Sheriff?"

He turned slowly and gave Quinlan a glimpse of a smile. "Call me David. What the hell's going on? Why are you here?"

Quinlan said calmly, "I'm not really here to find out about Marge and Harve Jensen. They're just my cover. But their disappearance remains a mystery. And it's not just them. You were right. The former sheriff sent everything off to the FBI, including reports on two more missing persons—a biker and his girlfriend. Other towns up and down the coast have done the same thing. There's a nice fat file now on folks who have simply disappeared around here. The Jensens were the first, evidently, so I'm just sticking to them. I've told everyone I'm a PI because I don't want to scare these old folks. They'd freak if they knew an FBI agent was in their midst doing God knows what."

"It's a good cover, since it's real. I don't suppose you'll tell me what's really going on?"

"I can't, at least not right now. Can you be satisfied with that?"

"I guess I'll just have to be. You discover anything yet about the Jensens?"

"Yeah—all these respectable old folk are lying to me. Can you beat that? Your parents or grandparents lying through their teeth over something as innocuous as a pair of old people in a Winnebago probably coming into town just to buy the World's Greatest Ice Cream?"

"Okay, then. They do remember Harve and Marge, but they're afraid to talk, afraid to get involved. Why didn't you come talk to me right away? Tell me who you were and that you were undercover?"

"I wanted to keep things under wraps for as long as possible. It makes it easier." Quinlan shrugged. "Hey, then if I didn't find anything, well, no harm done and who knows? I just might discover something about all these old folks who have disappeared."

"You would have succeeded in keeping your cover from me if two people weren't dead. You're just too good, too well trained." David Mountebank sighed, took a deep drink of the brandied tea James handed him, shuddered a bit, then grinned as he patted his belly. "That'll put optimism back in your pecker."

"Yeah," Quinlan said.

"What are you doing with Sally Brandon?"

"I just sort of hooked up with her the first day I was here. I like her. She doesn't deserve all this misery."

"More than misery. Seeing that poor woman's body banging up against the rocks at the base of those cliffs was enough to give a person nightmares for the rest of her life. But finding Doc Spiver with half his head blown off was even worse."

David took another drink of his tea. "I sure won't forget this remedy. You think that by any wild chance these two deaths are related in any way to the FBI missing persons files, to this Harve and Marge Jensen and all the others?"

"That's far-fetched for even my devious brain, but it makes you wonder, doesn't it?"

He was doing it to him again, David thought, without rancor. He was smooth, he was polite, he wasn't about to spill anything he didn't want to spill. It would be impossible to rattle him. He wondered why the devil he was really here. Well, Quinlan would tell him when he was good and ready.

David said slowly, "I know you won't tell me why you're really here, but I've got enough on my plate right now, so I don't plan to stew about it. You keep doing what you're doing, and if you can help me at all, or I can help you, I'll be here."

"Thanks, David. I appreciate it. The Cove is an interesting little town, don't you think?"

"It is now. You should have seen it three or four years ago. It was as ramshackle as you could imagine, everything run-down, only old folks here. All the young ones hightailed it out of town as soon as they could get. Then prosperity. Whatever they did, they did it well and with admirable planning.

"Maybe some relative of one of them died and left a pile of money, and that person gave it to the town. Whatever, the place is a treat now. Yep, it shows that folk can pull themselves out of a ditch if they put their minds to it. You've got to respect them."

David set his empty cup in the sink. "Well, I'm back to Doc Spiver's houses. I've got exactly nothing, Quinlan."

"If I uncover something, I'll call."

"I won't hold the lines open. I just realized that these two deaths have got to be real hard on the townsfolk. Here I am, just about accusing one of them of holding the woman prisoner before killing her. Hey, I was even thinking those four old men already knew that Doc Spiver was dead when you volunteered to go fetch him for Hunker Dawson, that maybe they'd had something to do with it. That's just crazy. They're good people. I want to get this cleared up as soon as possible."

"As I said, I'll tell you if I find something."

David didn't know if that was the truth, but Quinlan sounded sincere enough. Well, he should. He'd been trained by the best of the best. David had a cousin, Tom Neibber, who had washed out of Quantico back in the late eighties, only gotten through the fourth week out of sixteen. He'd thought his cousin had what it took, but he hadn't made it.

David turned in the kitchen doorway. "It's funny, but inescapable. Sally wasn't expected here. Whoever killed Laura Strather was already holding her prisoner. If Sally hadn't heard the woman scream that first night she was here, you can bet no one else would have—but that's exactly what happened. If you and Sally hadn't been out there on the cliffs, that woman's body would never have been found. There would never have been a crime. Nothing, just another missing persons report put out by the husband.

"Now, Doc Spiver, that's different. The killer didn't care if Doc was found, just didn't care."

"Don't forget, it could be suicide."

"I know, but it doesn't smell right, you know?"

"No, I don't know, but you keep smelling, David. I do wonder that nobody heard a blessed thing. Hardly seems possible, does it? People are just too contrary to all agree with each other. Now, that must smell big time to you."

"Yeah, it does, but I still think the old folk are just afraid. I'll be around, Quinlan. Take care of Sally. There's something about her that makes you want to put her under your coat and see that nothing happens to her."

"Maybe right now, but I imagine that usually if you tried that she'd punch your lights out."

"I get the same feeling—probably she would have some time ago, but not now. No, there's something wrong there, but I fancy you're not going to tell me what."

"I'll be talking to you, David. Good luck with that autopsy."

"Oh, yeah, I got to call my wife. I think she can forget me being home for dinner."

"You married?"

"You saw my wedding ring first thing, Quinlan. Don't be cute. I even mentioned one of my kids. I've got three little ones, all girls. When I come through the front door, two of them climb up my legs and the third one drags a chair over to jump into my arms. It's a race to see who gets her arms around my neck first."

David gave him a lopsided grin, a small salute, and left.

NO ONE COULD TALK about anything else. Just Doc Spiver and how two outsiders had found him lying in his rocking chair, blood dropping off his fingertips, half his head blown off.

He'd killed himself—everyone agreed to that—but why?

Terminal cancer, Thelma Nettro said. Her own grandpa had had cancer, and he would have killed himself if he hadn't died first.

He was nearly blind, Ralph Keaton said. Everybody knew he was pleased because when they got the body back, Ralph would lay him out. Yeah, Ralph said, Doc couldn't stand it that he wasn't really an honest-to-goodness doctor anymore.

He was hurt because some woman rejected him, Purn Davies said. Everyone knew that Amabel had turned Purn down some years before and he was still burning with resentment.

He just got tired of life, Helen Keaton said, as she scooped out a triple-dip chocolate pecan cone for Sherry Vorhees. Lots of old people just got tired of living. He just did something about it and didn't sit around whining for ten years until the devil finally took him.

Just maybe, Hunker Dawson said, just maybe Doc Spiver had something to do with that poor woman's death. It made sense he'd kill himself then, wouldn't it? The guilt would drive a fine man like Doc Spiver to shoot himself.

There were no lawyers in town, but the sheriff found Doc Spiver's will soon enough. He had some $22,000 in a bank in South Bend. He left it all to what he called the Town Fund, headed by Reverend Hal Vorhees.

Sheriff David Mountebank was surprised when he was told about the Town Fund. He'd never heard about such a thing. What effect would this Town Fund have had on people's motives? Of course, he didn't know yet if someone had put the .38-caliber pistol in Doc's mouth and pulled the trigger, then pressed the butt into Doc's hand.

Premeditated murder, that was. Or Doc Spiver had put the gun in his own mouth. Ponser called David at eight o'clock that evening. He'd finished the autopsy and now he was equivocating, damn him. David pushed him, and he ended up saying it was suicide. No, Doc Spiver didn't have any terminal illness—at least Ponser hadn't seen anything.

Amabel said to Sally that same evening, "I'm thinking you and I should go to Mexico and lie on a beach."

Sally smiled. She was still wearing Amabel's bathrobe because she just couldn't seem to get warm. James hadn't wanted to leave her, but then it seemed he remembered something that had made him go back to Thelma's. She'd wanted to ask him what it was, but she hadn't. "I can't go to Mexico, Amabel. I don't have my passport."

"Alaska, then. We could lie around on the snowbanks. I could paint and you could do—what, Sally? What did you do before your daddy got killed?"

Sally got colder. She pulled the bathrobe tighter around her and moved closer to the heat register. "I was Senator Bainbridge's senior aide."

"Didn't he retire?"

"Yes, last year. I didn't do anything after that."

"Why not?"

Vivid, frenzied pictures went careening through her mind, shrieking as loudly as the wind outside. She clutched the edge of the kitchen table.

"It's all right, baby, you don't have to tell me. It really doesn't matter. Goodness, what a day it's been. I'm going to miss Doc. He's been here forever. Everyone will miss him."

"No, Amabel, not everyone."

"So you don't think it was suicide, Sally?"

"No," Sally said, drawing a deep breath. "I think there's a madness in this town."

"What a thing to say! I've lived here for nearly thirty years. I'm not mad. None of my friends is mad. They're all down-to-earth folk who are friendly and care about each other and this town. Besides, if you were right, then the madness didn't begin until after you arrived. How do you explain that, Sally?"

"That's what the sheriff said. Amabel, do you really believe that Laura Strather, the woman James and I found, was brought into town by a stranger and held somewhere before he murdered her?"

"What I think, Sally, is that your brain is squirreling around, and it's just not healthy for you, not with everything else upside down in your life. Just don't think about it. Everything will be back to normal soon. It's got to be."

That night, at exactly three o'clock in the morning, a blustery night with high winds but no rain, something brought Sally awake. She lay there a moment. Then she heard a soft tap on the window. At least it wasn't a woman screaming.

A branch from a tree, she thought, turning over and pulling the blanket up to her nose. Just a tree branch.

Tap.

She gave up and slid out of bed.

Tap.

She didn't remember that there wasn't a tree high enough until she'd pulled back the curtain and stared into her father's ghastly white, grinning face.

Amabel found her on her knees in the middle of the floor, her arms wrapped around herself, the window open, the curtains billowing outward, pulled by the wind, screaming and screaming until her throat closed and no sound came from her mouth.

QUINLAN MADE A DECISION then and there. "I'm taking her back to Thelma's. She'll stay with me. If something else happens, I'll be there to deal with it."

She'd called him thirty minutes before, gasping out her words, begging him to come and make her father leave her alone. He'd heard Amabel in the background telling her she was in no shape to be on the phone to anybody, much less to that man she didn't even know, to put down the phone, she was just excited, there hadn't been anyone there, it had just been her imagination. Just look at all she'd been through.

And she was still saying it, ignoring Quinlan. "Baby, just think. You were sound asleep when you heard the wind making strange noises against the window. You were dreaming, just like those other times. I'll bet you weren't even awake when you pulled the curtains back."

"I wasn't asleep," Sally said. "The wind had awakened me. I was lying there. And then came the tapping."

"Baby—"

"It doesn't matter," Quinlan said, impatient now, knowing that Sally would soon think that she was crazy, that she'd imagined it all. He prayed to God that she hadn't. But she had been in that sanitarium, for six months. She'd been paranoid, that's what was in the file. She'd also been depressed and suicidal. They'd been worried that she would harm herself. Her doctor hadn't wanted her released. Her husband had agreed. They wanted her back. Her husband was first in line. He wondered about the legalities of getting a person committed if that person didn't volunteer.

Why hadn't Sally's parents done anything about it? Had they believed her to be nuts too? But she was a person with legal rights. He had to check on how they'd gotten around it.

He said now, "Amabel, could you please pack Sally's things? I'd like all of us to get some sleep before morning."

Amabel pursed her lips. "She's a married woman. She shouldn't be going off with you."

Sally started laughing, a low, hoarse, very ugly laugh.

Amabel was so startled that she didn't say anything more. She went upstairs to pack the duffel bag.

Thirty minutes later, after four o'clock in the morning, Quinlan let Sally into his tower room.

"Thank you, James," she said. "I'm so tired. Thank you for coming for me."

He'd come for her, all right. He'd been off like a shot to get her. Damnation, why couldn't anything turn out the way it was supposed to, the way he'd planned? He was in the middle of a puzzle, and all he had was scattered pieces that didn't look like they would ever fit together. He put her to bed, tucked the covers around her, and without thinking about it, kissed her lightly on the mouth.

She didn't respond, just looked up at him.

"Go to sleep," he said, gently pushing her hair back from her face. He pulled the string on the bedside lamp. "We'll work it all out. Just don't worry anymore."

That was a promise and a half. It scared the hell out of him.

"That's what he said on the phone, that he was coming for me. Soon, he said, very soon. He didn't lie, did he? He's here, James."

"Someone's here. We'll deal with it tomorrow. Go to sleep. I'm sure as hell here, and I won't leave you alone, not anymore."

SHE WAS USUALLY ALONE. At the beginning some of the patients had tried to talk to her, in their way, but she'd turned away from them. It didn't matter really, because most of the time her brain was fuzzy, so completely disconnected from anything she could identify either outside herself or inside that she was as good as lost in a deep cave. Or she was floating up in the ether. There was no reality here, no getting up at six in the morning to run up Exeter Street over to Concord Avenue, covering a good two miles, then run home, jump in the shower, and think about all she had to do that day while she washed her hair.

Senator Bainbridge went to the White House at least twice a week. Many times she was with him, keeping together all his notes for the topics to be discussed. It was easy for her to do that, since she'd written most of the notes and knew more than he did about his stands on his committee projects. She'd done so much, been involved in so many things—press releases, huddling with staff and the senator when a hot story broke and they tried to determine the best position for the senator to take.

There were always fund-raisers, press parties, embassy parties, political parties. So much, and she'd loved it, even when she would fall exhausted into bed.

At first Scott had told her how proud he was of her. He'd seemed excited to be invited to all the parties, to meet all the important players. At first.

Now she did nothing. Someone washed her hair twice a week. She scarcely noticed unless they let water run down her neck. She didn't have any muscles anymore, even though someone took her for long walks every day, just like a dog. She'd wanted to run once, just run and feel the wind against her face, feel her face chapping, but they didn't let her. After that they gave her more drugs so she wouldn't want to run again.

And he came, at least twice a week, sometimes more. The nurses adored him, saying behind their hands how devoted he was. He would sit with her in the common room a few minutes, then take her hand and lead her back to her room. It was a stark white room with nothing in it to use in attempting suicide—nothing sharp, no belts.

He had furnished it for her, she'd heard once, with the advice of Dr. Beadermeyer. It was a metal bed covered with fake wood, fake so that it wouldn't splinter so she could stick a fragment through her own heart. Not that such a thing would ever occur to her, but he talked about it and laughed, saying as he cupped her face in his hand that he would take care of her for a very long time.

Then he'd strip off her clothes and make her lie on her back on the bed. He would walk around the bed, looking at her, talking to her about his day, his work, about the woman he was currently sleeping with. Then he'd unzip his trousers and show her himself, tell her how lucky she was to get to see him, that he would let her touch him but he didn't quite trust her yet.

He'd touch her all over. He'd rub himself. Just before he came, he'd hit her at least once, usually in the ribs.

Once when his head was thrown back in his orgasm, she saw through the fog in her eyes that there were two people at the window opening in the door, staring at them, talking even as they looked. She'd tried to push him away, but it hadn't worked. She had so little strength. He'd finished, then leaned down, seen the hatred in her eyes, and struck her face. It was the only time he had ever hit her in the face.

She remembered once how he'd turned her onto her belly, pulling her back toward him and how he'd said that maybe one day he'd let her have him, let her feel him going into her, deep, and it would hurt because he was big, didn't she agree? But no, she didn't deserve him yet. And who cared? They had years ahead of them, years to do all sorts of things. And he'd told her about when he finally allowed his mistresses to have him and what they did to please him.

She hadn't said anything. He'd struck her for that, with his belt, on her buttocks. He hadn't stopped for a very long time. She remembered screaming, begging, screaming some more, trying to wriggle away from him, but he'd held her down. He hadn't stopped.

IT WAS FIVE A.M. when Quinlan was jerked out of a deep sleep by her scream, loud, piercing, so filled with pain and helplessness that he couldn't bear it. He was at her side in an instant, pulling her against him, trying to soothe her, saying anything that came to mind, just talking and talking to bring her out of the dreadful nightmare.

"God, it hurt so much, but he didn't care, he just kept hitting and hitting, holding me down so I couldn't move, couldn't escape. I screamed and screamed, but nobody cared, nobody came, but I know those faces were looking in the window and they loved it. Oh, God, no, make it stop. STOP IT!"

So it was a nightmare about her time in that sanitarium—at least that's what it sounded like. It sounded sadistic and sexual. What was going on here?

His hand was busy in her hair, stroking up and down her back, talking to her, talking, talking.

Her horrible gasping breaths slowed. She hiccuped. She leaned back, wiping her hand across her nose. She closed her eyes a moment, then began to tremble.

"No, Sally, just stop it. I'm here, it's all right. Just relax against me, that's it. Just breathe real slow. Good, that's just fine." He stroked her back, felt the shivering slowly ease. God, what had she dreamed? A memory distorted by the unconscious could be hideous.

"What did he do to you?" He spoke slowly, softly against her temple. "You can tell me. It'll make it go away faster if you talk about it."

She whispered against his neck, "He came, at least twice a week, and every time he took off my clothes and looked at me and touched me and told me things he'd done that day, the women he'd taken.

"People watched through that window in the door, the same people, as if they had season tickets or something. It was horrible, but most of the time I just lay there because my brain wasn't working. But that one time, it hurt so badly, I remember having my thoughts and feelings come together enough to feel the humiliation, so I tried to get away from him, to fight him, but he just kept hitting me and hitting me, first with his hand, then with his belt. It pleased him that he'd made me bleed. He told me maybe sometime in the future, when I'd earned the honor, he'd come into me. I wouldn't have to worry because he wasn't HIV-positive, not that I would anyway because I was fucking crazy. That's what he said, 'You won't remember a thing, will you, Sally, because you're fucking crazy?'"

Even though Quinlan was so tense he imagined that if someone hit him he would just shatter into myriad pieces, Sally was now leaning limp against him, her breathing low, calmer. He'd been right. Talking about it out loud had eased her, but not him, good Lord, not him.

Could she have imagined it all? For the longest time he couldn't speak. Finally he said, "Was it your husband who did this to you, Sally?"

She was asleep, her breath even and slow against his chest. He realized then that he was wearing only shorts. Who the hell cared? He pushed her back and tried to pull away from her. To his pleasure and consternation, she clutched her arms around his back. "No, please, no," she said. She sounded asleep.

He eased down beside her, lying on his back, pressing her face against his shoulder. He hadn't planned on this, he thought, staring up at the dark ceiling. She was breathing deeply, her leg across his belly now, her palm flat on his chest. Any lower with that hand or any lower with her thigh and he would be in big trouble.

He was already in big trouble. He kissed her forehead, squeezed her more closely against him, and closed his eyes. At least the bastard hadn't raped her. But he'd beat her.

Surprisingly, he fell asleep.

"YEAH, RIGHT," Quinlan said to himself as he got to his feet. There were two nice male footprints below Sally's bedroom window at Amabel's house and, more important, deep impressions where the feet of the ladder had dug into the earth.

There were small torn branches on the ground, ripped away by someone who had moved quickly, dragging that damned long ladder with him. He dropped to his haunches again and measured the footprints with his right hand. Size eleven shoe, just about his own size. He took off his loafer and set it gently into the indentation. Nearly a perfect fit. All right, then, an eleven and a half.

The heels were pretty deep, which meant he wasn't a small man, perhaps about six feet and one hundred eighty pounds or so. Close enough. He looked more carefully, measuring the depth of the indentations with his fingers. One went deeper than the other, which was odd. A limp? He didn't know. Maybe it was just an aberration.

"What have you got, Quinlan?" It was David Mountebank. He was in his uniform, looking pressed and well shaved, and surprisingly well rested. It was only six-thirty in the morning. "You thinking about eloping with Sally Brandon?"

Well, hell, Quinlan thought, rising slowly, as he said in an easy voice, "Actually someone tried to get into the house last night and really scared Sally. And yes, if you're interested, she should still be sleeping in Thelma's tower room, my room."

"Someone tried to break in?"

"Yeah, that's about it. Sally woke up and saw the man's face in the window. It scared the bejesus out of her. When she screamed, it must have scared the bejesus out of the guy as well, because he was out of here."

David Mountebank leaned against the side of Amabel's cottage. It looked like it had been freshly painted not six months ago. The dark green trim around the windows was very crisp. "What the hell's really going on, Quinlan?"

He sighed. "I can't tell you. Call it national security, David."

"I'd like to call that bullshit."

"I can't tell you," Quinlan repeated. He met David's eye. He never flinched. David could have drawn a gun on him and he wouldn't have flinched.

"All right," David said finally. "Have it your way, at least for now. You promise me it doesn't have anything to do with the two murders?"

"It doesn't. The more I mull it over, the more I think the woman's murder is somehow connected to Harve and Marge Jensen's disappearance three years ago, even though just yesterday I told you I couldn't imagine it. I don't know how or why, but you've got things that don't smell right. Well, I have things that just twist and turn in my gut. That's my intuition. I've learned over the years never to ignore it. Things are somehow connected. I just have no idea how or why or if I'm just plain not thinking straight.

"As for Sally, just let it go, David. I'd consider that I owed you good if you'd just let it go."

"It was *two* murders, Quinlan."

"Doc Spiver?"

"Yeah. I just got a call from the M.E. in Portland, a woman who was trained down in San Francisco and really knows her stuff. Would that there were M.E.s everywhere who knew what they were doing. I got his body to her late last night, and she agreed to do the autopsy immediately, bless her. She determined there was no way in hell he would have sat himself down in the rocking chair, put the gun in his mouth, and pulled the trigger."

"That takes care of the theory that Doc Spiver murdered the woman and then felt so guilty that he killed himself."

"Blows it straight to hell."

"You know what it sounds like to me? Just maybe the person really believed everyone would think Doc Spiver killed himself. Maybe an older person who doesn't know all about things a good M.E. can determine. Your man Ponser didn't know, after all. You could say you just lucked out because of how good the M.E. is in Portland."

"That sounds right to me." He sighed. "What we've got is a killer loose, Quinlan, and I'm so stuck I don't know what to do.

"My men and I have been questioning every damned person in this beautiful little town, and just like with Laura Strather, no one knows a damned thing. I still can't buy it that one of the local folk is involved in this."

"One of them is, David, no way around it."

"You want me to take plaster casts of those footprints?"

"No, don't bother. But take a look, one impression goes deeper than the other. You ever see anything like that?"

David was down on his hands and knees, studying the footprints. He measured the depth with his pinkie finger, just as Quinlan had done. "Strange," he said. "I don't have a clue."

"I was thinking the guy had a limp, but it wouldn't look like that if he did. There'd be more of a rolling to one side, but there's not."

"You got me, Quinlan." David stood up and looked toward the ocean. "It's going to be a beautiful day. I used to bring my kids here at least twice a week for the World's Greatest Ice Cream. I haven't wanted them to get near The Cove since that first murder."

And, Quinlan knew, besides that killer, there was another man here who was out to make Sally believe she was crazy. It had to be her husband, Scott Brainerd.

He dusted his hands off on his dark brown corduroy pants. "Oh, David, which one got to you first?"

"What?"

"Which of your daughters got her arms around your neck first?"

David laughed. "The littlest one. She climbed right up my leg like a monkey. Her name's Deirdre."

James left David Mountebank and returned to Thelma's Bed and Breakfast.

When he opened the door to his tower room, Sally was standing in the doorway of the bathroom. Her hair was wet and plastered to her head, strands falling to her shoulders. She had a towel in her left hand. She stared at him.

She was stark naked.

She was so damned thin and so damned perfect, and he realized it in just the split second before she pulled the towel in front of herself.

"Where did you go?" she asked, still not moving, just standing there, wet and thin and perfect, and covered with a white towel.

"He wears an eleven-and-a-half shoe."

She tightened the towel, rolling it over above her breasts. She just stared at him.

"The man pretending to be your father," he said, watching her closely. "You found him?"

"Not yet, but I found his footprints beneath your bedroom window and the indentations of the ladder feet. Yeah, our man was there. What size shoe does your husband wear, Sally?"

She was very pale. Now she was so colorless that he imagined even her hair was fading as he looked at her. "I don't know what size. I never asked, I never bought him shoes. My father wears an eleven and a half."

"Sally, your father is dead. He was murdered more than two weeks ago. He was buried. The cops saw the body. It was your father. The man last night, it wasn't your father. If you can't think of any other man who's trying to drive you nuts, then it has to be your husband. Did you see him the night your father was murdered?"

"No," she whispered, backing away from him, retreating into the bathroom, shaking her head, wet strands of hair slapping her cheeks. "No, no."

She didn't slam the door, just quietly pushed it closed. He heard the lock click on the other side.

He knew he would never look at her in quite the same way again. She could be wearing a bear coat and he knew he would still see her standing naked in the bathroom doorway, so pale and beautiful that he'd wanted to pick her up and very gently lay her on his bed. But that would never happen. He had to get a grip.

"Hi," he said when she came out a while later, wrapped in one of the white robes, her hair dry, her eyes not meeting his.

She just nodded, her eyes still on her bare feet, and began to collect her clothing.

"Sally, we're both adults."

"What's that supposed to mean?"

At least she was looking at him now, and there wasn't an ounce of fear in her voice or in her eyes. He was pleased. She trusted him not to hurt her.

"I didn't mean as in consenting adults. I just meant that you're no more a kid than I am. There's no reason for you to be embarrassed."

"I suppose you'd be the one to be embarrassed since I'm so skinny and ugly."

"Yeah, right."

"What does that mean?"

"It means I think you're very—no, never mind that. Now, smile."

She gave him a ghastly smile, but again, there was no fear in it. She did trust him not to rape her. He heard himself say, completely unplanned, "Was it your husband who humiliated you and beat you in that sanitarium?"

She didn't move, didn't change expressions, but she withdrew from him. She just shut down.

"Answer me, Sally. Was it your damned husband?"

She looked at him straight on and said, "I don't know you. You could be the man calling me, mimicking my father, you could be the man last night at my window. He could have sent you. I want to leave now, James, and never come back here. I want to disappear. Will you help me do that?"

Jesus, he wanted to help her. He wanted to disappear with her. He wanted . . . He shook his head. "That's no answer to anything. You can't run forever, Sally."

"I wouldn't bet on it." She turned, clutching her clothes to her chest, and went back into the bathroom.

He started to shout through the bathroom door that he liked the small black mole on the right side of her belly. But he didn't. He sat down on the chintz sofa and tried to figure things out.

"THELMA," he said after he'd swallowed a spoonful of the lightest, most beautifully seasoned scrambled eggs he'd ever tasted in his life, "if you were a stranger and you wanted to hide here in The Cove, where would you go?"

Thelma ate one of her fat sausages, wiped the grease off her chin, and said, "Well, let me see. There's that dilapidated little shack just up on that hillock behind Doc Spiver's house. But I tell you, boy, I'd have to be real desperate to hole up in that place. All filled with dirt and spiders and probably rats. Nasty place that probably leaks real bad when it rains." She ate another sausage, just forked the whole thing up and stuffed it into her mouth.

Martha came up beside her and handed her a fresh napkin. Thelma gave her a nasty look. "You think I'm one of those old ladies who will dribble on themselves if a handmaiden isn't right on the spot to keep her clean?"

"Now, Thelma, you've been twisting the other napkin around until it's a crumpled ball. Here, take this one. Oh, look, you got some sausage grease on your diary. You've got to be more careful."

"I need more ink. Go buy me some, Martha. Hey, you got young Ed back there in the kitchen? You're feeding him, aren't you, Martha? You're buying my food with my money and you're feeding him just so he'll go to bed with you."

Martha rolled her eyes and looked at Sally's plate. "You don't like the toast? It's a little on the pale side. You want it better toasted?"

"No, no, it's fine, truly. I'm just not hungry this morning."

"No man wants a skinny post, Sally," Thelma said, taking a noisy bite of toast. "A man's got to have something he can hang on to. Just look at Martha, bosom so big young Ed can't even walk past without seeing her poking out at him."

"Young Ed has prostate trouble," Martha said, raising a thick black eyebrow, and she left the dining room, saying over her shoulder, "I'll buy you some black ink, Thelma."

"I'M COMING WITH YOU."

"But—"

Sally just shook her head and walked across the street toward the World's Greatest Ice Cream Shop. She was limping only slightly today. A bell tinkled when she opened the door.

Amabel, dressed like a gypsy with a cute white apron, stood behind the counter, scooping up a peach double-dip cone for a young woman who was talking a mile a minute.

". . . I heard that two people have been murdered here in the last several days. That's incredible! My mama said The Cove was the quietest little place she knew about, she said nothing ever happened here, that it had to be one of those gangs from down south come up here to stir up misery."

"Hello, Sally, James. How are you this morning, baby?"

As she spoke, she handed the cone to the young woman, who immediately began licking and moaning in ecstasy.

"I'm fine," Sally said.

"That will be two dollars and sixty cents," Amabel said.

"Oh, it's wonderful," the young woman said. She alternately dug in her wallet and ate the ice cream.

Quinlan smiled at her. "It is excellent ice cream. Why don't you just keep eating and I'll treat you?"

"Taking ice cream from a stranger is okay," Sally said. "Besides, I know him. He's harmless."

Quinlan paid Amabel. Nothing else was said until the young woman left the shop.

"There hasn't been another call," Amabel said. "Either from Thelma or from your father."

"He knows that I've left your house," Sally said thoughtfully. "That's good. I don't want you in any danger."

"Don't be ridiculous, Sally. There's no danger for me."

"There was for Laura Strather and Doc Spiver," Quinlan said. "You be careful, Amabel. Sally and I are going exploring. Thelma told us about this shack up the hill behind Doc Spiver's house. We're going to check it out."

"Watch out for snakes," Amabel called after them.

Which kind? Quinlan wondered.

Once they were rounding the corner to Doc Spiver's house, Sally said, "Why did you tell Amabel where we were going?"

"Seeding," he said. "Watch your step, Sally. You're not all that steady on your ankle just yet." He held back the stiff, gnarly branch of a yew tree. There was a barren hill behind the house, and tucked into a shallow recess was a small shack.

"What do you mean, seeding?"

"I don't like the fact that your dear auntie has treated you like you're so high-strung no one should trust what you say. I told her that just to see if perhaps something might happen. Then if it does—"

"Amabel would never hurt me, never."

He looked down at her and then at the shack. "Is that what you believed about your husband when you married him?"

He didn't wait for her to answer him, just pushed open the door. It was surprisingly solid. "Watch your head," he said over his shoulder as he stooped down and walked into the dim single room.

"Yuck," Sally said. "This is pretty bad, James."

"Yeah, I'd say so." He didn't say anything else, just began to look around as he imagined the sheriff had done only days before. He found nothing. The small space was empty. There were no windows. It would be pitch black when the door was closed. Just plain nothing. A modicum of hope, that was all he'd had, but still, he was more than a modicum disappointed. "I'd say that if Laura Strather was kept prisoner here, the guy holding her was very thorough cleaning up. There's nothing, Sally, not a trace of anything. Well, hell."

"He's not hiding in here, either," she said. "And that's what we're really doing here, isn't it?"

"Both, really. I have a feeling that your *father* wouldn't lower himself to stay in this place. There aren't even any free bathrobes."

THAT AFTERNOON they ate lunch at the Hinterlands. This week Zeke was serving Spam burgers and variations on meat loaf.

They both ordered Zeke's original-recipe meat loaf.

"The smells make me salivate," Quinlan said, inhaling. "Zeke puts garlic in his mashed potatoes. Breathe deeply enough and no vampire will come near you."

Sally was toying with the curved slice of carrot in her salad. "I like garlic."

"Tell me about that night, Sally."

She'd picked up the carrot and was chewing on it. She dropped it. Then she picked it up again and slowly began eating it. "All right," she said finally. She smiled at him. "I might as well trust you. If you're going to betray me, then I might as well hang it up. The cops are right. I was there that night. But they're wrong about everything else. I don't remember a thing, James, not a blessed thing."

Well, hell, he thought, but he knew she was telling him the truth. "Do you think someone struck you?"

"No, I don't think so. I've thought and thought about it and all I can figure out is that I just don't want to remember, can't bear to, I guess, so my brain just closed it down."

"I've heard about hysterical amnesia and even seen it a couple of times. What usually happens is that you will remember, if not tomorrow, then next week. Your father wasn't killed in a horrific way. He was shot neatly through the heart, no muss, no fuss. So, it would seem to me that the people involved in his death shook you so much that's the reason you've blocked it all out."

"Yes," she said slowly, then turned around and saw the waitress bringing their plates. The smell of garlic, butter, roasted squash, and the rich aroma of the meat loaf filled the air around them.

"I couldn't live here and stay trim," James said. "It smells delicious, Nelda."

"Catsup for the meat loaf?"

"Does a shark have a fin?"

Nelda, the waitress, laughed and set a Heinz bottle between them. "Enjoy," she said.

"Nelda, how often do young Ed and Martha eat here?"

"Oh, maybe twice a week," she said, looking a bit startled. "Martha says she gets tired of her own cooking. Young Ed is my older brother. Poor man. Every time he wants to see Martha, he has to endure Thelma's jokes. Can you believe that old woman is still alive, writing in that diary of hers every day and eating that sausage?"

"That's interesting," James said when Nelda left them. "Eat, Sally. That's right. You're perfect, but I'd be worried for you in a strong wind."

"I used to run every day," she said. "I used to be strong."

"You will be again. Just stick with me."

"I can't imagine running in Los Angeles. All I ever see is pictures of horrible fog and cars stacked up on the freeways."

"I live in a canyon. It's got healthy air and I run there as well."

"Somehow I can't imagine you living in Southern California. You just don't seem the type. Does your ex-wife still live there?"

"No, Teresa is back east. She married a crook, interestingly enough. I hope she doesn't have kids with the guy. Their genetic potential is hair-raising."

She laughed, actually laughed. It felt as wonderful to her as if felt to James hearing it.

"You have any idea how beautiful you are, Sally?"

Her fork stilled over the meat loaf. "You're into crazy freaks?"

"If you ever say anything like that again, you'll piss me off. When I get pissed off I do strange things, like take off all my clothes and chase ducks in the park." The tension fell away from her. He had no idea why he'd told her she was beautiful; it had just slipped out. Actually, she was more than beautiful—she was warm and caring, even while she was living this nightmare. He wished he knew what to do.

"You said you don't remember about that night your father was killed. Do you have other gaps in your memory?"

"Yes. Sometimes when I think about that place, very sharp memories will come to me, but I couldn't swear if they are truly memories or just weird images stewed up by my brain. I remember everything very clearly until about six months ago."

"What happened six months ago?"

"That's when everything went dim."

"What happened six months ago?"

"Senator Bainbridge retired suddenly, and I was out of a job. I remember that I was going to interview with Senator Irwin, but I never got to his office."

"Why not?"

"I don't know. I remember it was a sunny day. I was singing. The top was down on my Mustang. The air was sharp and warm." She paused, frowning, then shrugged. "I always sang when the top was down. I don't remember anything else, but I know I never saw Senator Irwin."

She said nothing more. She was eating her meat loaf. She probably didn't realize she was eating, but he wanted her to keep at it. He guessed he wanted her to eat more than he wanted her to talk. At least for now. What the hell had happened?

James paid their bill and walked outside while Sally went to the women's room. He wondered how he was going to keep his hands off her when they got back to his tower bedroom.

HE HEARD A whisper of sound that didn't belong in that small narrow space beside the Hinterlands. He turned around, wondering if Sally had come out of the cafe without his seeing her. That was when he heard it again. There it was, just a whisper of sound. He pivoted quickly on his heel, his hand inside his jacket on the butt of his SIG-Sauer, a 9mm semiautomatic pistol that fit his hand and his personality perfectly. He was at one with that pistol, as he'd never been with any other before in his professional life. He was pulling it out, smooth and quick, but still, he was too late. The blow struck him just over his left ear. He went down without a sound.

"James?" Sally stuck her head out the door of the cafe. There was no one around. She waved to Nelda, then turned back. Where was James? She frowned and stepped down. She heard a scraping sound, then she knew she heard a whisper—a man's whisper? James? She wheeled about to look in that sliver of space beside the building.

What she saw was James lying on his side on the ground, a trickle of blood trailing down his cheek toward his chin. She yelled his name and skidded onto her knees beside him, shaking him, then drawing back. She sucked in her breath. Gently she laid her fingers on the pulse in his throat. It was strong and slow. Thank God, he was all right. What was going on here? But then she knew.

It was her father, he'd finally come to get her, just as he'd promised he would. He'd hurt James, probably because he'd been protecting her.

She looked up for help, praying to see anyone, it didn't matter how old he was, just anyone. There was no one around, not a single soul.

Oh, God, what should she do? She was leaning down to look at the wound when the blow crashed directly down on the back of her head and she crumpled over James.

SHE HEARD THE SOUND. It came at short intervals. It was water, one drop after another, hitting metal.

Plop.

She opened her eyes but couldn't seem to focus. Her brain felt loose, as if it were floating inside her head. She couldn't seem to think, she could only hear that plop. She knew something wasn't right. She tried to remember but couldn't quite make her brain fasten onto something that would trigger a thought, any thought, anything that had happened to her before she was here, wherever here was.

"You're awake. Good."

A voice, a man's voice, *his* voice. She managed to follow the sound of his voice. It was Dr. Beadermeyer, the man who had tormented her for six long months.

Yes, she remembered that, not all of it, but enough to have it burn through her sleep and terrify her over and over in nightmares that still brought vivid pain.

Suddenly she remembered. She'd been with James. Yes, James Quinlan. He'd been struck on the head. He was lying unconscious on the ground in that small slice of land next to the Hinterlands.

"Nothing to say, Sally? I cut back on the dosage so you could talk to me." She felt a sharp slap on her cheek.

"Look at me, Sally. Don't pretend you're off in outer space. I know this time you can't be." He slapped her again.

He grabbed her shoulders and shook her hard.

"Is James all right?"

He stopped shaking her. "James?" He sounded surprised. "Oh, that man you were with in The Cove. Yes, he's fine. No one wanted to take the risk of killing him. Was he your lover, Sally? You had him less than a week. That's moving fast. He must have been desperate.

"Just look at you, all skinny and pathetic, your hair in strings, your clothes bagging around you. Come on, Sally, tell me about James. Tell me what you told him."

"I told him about you," she said. "I had a nightmare and he helped me through it. I told him what a piece of slime you are."

He slapped her again, not too hard, but hard enough to make her shrink away from him.

"You're rude, Sally. And you're lying. You've never lied well and I can always tell. You might have dreamed, but you didn't tell him about me. You want to know why? It's because you're crazy and I'm so deep a part of you that if you were to tell anyone about me, why, you'd just collapse in on yourself and die. You can't exist without me, Sally.

"You were away from me for just two weeks, and look what happened. You're a mess. You tried to pretend you were normal. You lost all your manners. Your mother would be appalled. Your husband would back away from you in disgust. As for your father, well—well, I suppose it's not worth speculating now that he's shuffled off his mortal coil."

"Where am I?"

"Ah, that's supposed to be the first thing out of your mouth, if books and TV stories are to be believed. You're back where you belong, Sally. Just look around you. You're back in your room, the very same one decorated especially for you by your dear father. I've kept you under for nearly a day and a half. I let up on the dosage about four hours ago. You took your time coming to the surface."

"What do you want?"

"I have what I want; at least I have the first installment of what I want. And that's you, my dear."

"I'm thirsty."

"I'll bet you are. Holland, where are you? Bring some water to our patient."

She remembered Holland, a skinny, furtive little man who'd been one of the two men to stare through the small square window while he was hitting her and caressing her, humiliating her. Holland had thinning brown hair and the deadest eyes she'd ever seen. He rarely said anything, at least to her.

She said nothing more until he appeared at her side, a glass of water in his hand.

"Here you are, Doctor," he said in that low, hoarse voice of his that lay like a covering of loose gravel in all those nightmares, making her want to be drugged so she wouldn't realize he was around her.

He was standing behind Beadermeyer, looking down at her, his eyes dead and hungry. She wanted to vomit.

Dr. Beadermeyer raised her and let her drink her fill.

"Soon you'll want to go to the bathroom. Holland will help you with that, won't you, Holland?"

Holland nodded, and she wanted to die. She fell back against the pillow, a hard, institutional pillow, and closed her eyes. She knew deep down she couldn't keep herself intact in this place again. She also realized that she would never escape again. This time it was over for her.

She kept her eyes closed, didn't turn toward him, just said, "I'm not crazy. I was never crazy. Why are you doing this? He's dead. What does it matter?"

"You still don't know, do you? You still have no memory of any of it. I realized that almost immediately. Well, it isn't my place to tell you, my dear." She felt him pat her cheek. She flinched.

"Now, now, Sally, I'm not the one who tormented you, though I must admit that I enjoyed the one tape I saw. Except you weren't even there, you were just flopping back, your eyes closed, letting him do whatever he wanted.

"You didn't have any fight in you. Why, you were so out of it, you barely flinched when he hit you. But even then you weren't afraid. I could tell. The contrast, at least, made for fascinating viewing."

She felt gooseflesh rise on her arms as remnants of memories flooded her—the movement of his hands over her, the pushing and slapping, the caressing that turned to pain.

She heard the bed ease up and knew that Dr. Beadermeyer was standing beside her, looking down at her. She heard him say softly, "Holland, if she gets away again, I'll have to hurt you badly. Do you understand?"

"Yes, Dr. Beadermeyer."

"It won't be like last time, Holland. I made a mistake on your punishment last time. You rather liked that little shock therapy, didn't you?"

"It won't happen again, Dr. Beadermeyer." Was there disappointment in that frightening little man's voice?

"Good. You know what happened to Nurse Krider when she let her hide those pills under her tongue. Yes, of course you do. Be mindful, Holland.

"I must go now, Sally, but I'll be with you again this evening. We'll have to get you away from the sanitarium, probably tomorrow morning. The decision about what to do with you hasn't been made just yet. But you can't stay here. The FBI, this Quinlan fellow, he's got to know all about this place. I'm sure you did tell him some things about your past. And they'll come. But that isn't your problem.

"Now, let me give you a little shot of something that will make you drift and really feel quite good about things. Yes, Holland, hold her arm for me."

Sally felt the chill of the needle, felt the brief sting. Within moments, she felt herself begin to drift out of her brain, to float in nothingness. She felt the part of her that was real, the part of her that wanted life—such a small flicker, really—struggling briefly before it succumbed. She sighed deeply and was gone from herself.

She felt hands on her, taking off her clothes. She knew it was Holland. Probably Dr. Beadermeyer was watching.

She didn't struggle. There was nothing more to care about.

QUINLAN WOKE UP with a roaring headache that beat any hangover he'd ever had in college. He cursed, held his head in his hands, and cursed some more.

"You've got the mother of all headaches, right?"

"David," he said, and even that one word hurt. "What the devil happened?"

"Someone hit you good just above your left ear. Our doctor put three stitches in your head. Hold still and I'll get you a pill."

Quinlan focused on that pill. It had to help. If it didn't, his brain would break out of his skull.

"Here, Quinlan. It's strong stuff; you're supposed to have just one every four hours."

Quinlan took it and downed the entire glass of water. He lay back, his eyes closed, and waited.

"Dr. Grafft said it would kick in quickly."

"I sure hope so. Talk to me, David. Where's Sally?"

"I'll tell you everything. Just lie still. I found you unconscious in that narrow little strip of alley beside the Hinterlands. Thelma Nettro had reported you and Sally missing, so I started looking.

"You scared the shit out of me. When I found you lying there, I thought you were dead. I slung you over my shoulder and brought you to my house. Dr. Grafft met me here and stitched you up. I don't know about Sally. She's just gone, Quinlan. No trace, nothing. It's like she was never even here."

If he didn't hurt so badly, Quinlan would have yelled. Instead, he just lay there, trying to figure things out, trying to think. For the moment, it was beyond him.

Sally was gone. That was all that was real to him. Gone, not found dead. Gone. But where?

He heard children's voices. Surely that couldn't be right. He heard David say, "Deirdre, come here and sit on my lap. You've got to keep very quiet, okay? Mr. Quinlan isn't feeling well, and we don't want to make him feel worse."

He heard a little girl whisper, but he couldn't make it out. He remembered that Deirdre meant sorrow. He slept.

He awoke to see a young woman with a pale complexion and very dark red hair looking at him. She had the sweetest face he'd ever seen. "Who are you?"

"I'm Jane, David's wife. You just lie still, Mr. Quinlan." He felt her cool palm on his forehead. "I've got some nice hot chicken soup for you. Dr. Grafft said to keep it light until tomorrow. You just open your mouth and I'll feed you. That's right."

He ate the entire bowl and began to feel human. "Thank you," he said, and slowly, her hand under his elbow, he sat up.

"Your head ache?"

"It's just a dull thud now. What time is it? Rather, what day is it?"

"You were hurt early this afternoon. It's eight o'clock in the evening now. I hope the girls didn't disturb you."

"No, not at all. Thank you for taking me in."

"Let me get David. He's tucking the girls into bed. He should be just about through with the bedtime story."

Quinlan sat there, his head back against the cushions of the sofa, a nice comfortable sofa. The headache was gone now. He could get out of here soon. He could find Sally. He realized he was scared to his socks. What had happened to her?

Her father had come for her just as he'd promised he would. No, that was ridiculous. Amory St. John was long dead.

"You want some brandy in hot tea?"

"Nah, my pecker doesn't need optimism." Quinlan opened his eyes and smiled at David Mountebank. "Your wife fed me. Great soup. I appreciate you taking me in, David."

"I couldn't leave you with Thelma Nettro, now, could I? I wouldn't leave my worst enemy there. That old lady gives me the willies. It's the weirdest thing. She always has that diary of hers with her and that fountain pen in her hand. The tip of her tongue is practically tattooed from the pen tip."

"Tell me about Sally."

"Every man I could round up is talking to everybody in The Cove and looking for her. I've got an APB out on her—"

"No APB," James said, sitting up straight now, his face paling. "No, David, cancel it now. It's critical."

"I won't buy any more of this national security shit, Quinlan. Tell me why or I won't do it."

"You're not being cooperative, David."

"Tell me and let me help you."

"She's Sally St. John Brainerd."

David just stared at him. "She's Amory St. John's daughter? The daughter who's nuts and who ran away from that sanitarium? The woman whose husband is frantic about her safety? I knew she looked familiar. Damn, I'm slipping fast. I should have made the connection. Ah, that's the reason for the black wig. Then she just forgot to put it on, didn't she?"

"Yeah, that and I told her to relax, that you would never connect her to Susan Brainerd, at least I prayed you wouldn't."

"I wish I could say I would have, but I probably never would have unless I saw her in person and then saw her again on TV. What were you doing with her, Quinlan?"

Quinlan sighed. "She doesn't know I'm FBI. She bought that story about me being a PI and looking for those old folks who disappeared around here three years ago. I came here because I had this feeling she would run here, to her aunt. I was just going to take her back."

"But why is the FBI involved in a homicide?"

"It's not just a homicide at all. That's only part of it. We're in it for other reasons."

"I know. You're not going to tell me the rest of it."

"I'd prefer not to just yet. As I was saying, I was going to take her back, but then—"

"Then what?"

"Her father phoned her twice. Then she saw his face at her window in the middle of the night."

"And you found her father's footprints on the ground the next morning. Her father's dead, murdered. Quinlan, what's going on here?"

"I don't know. But I've got to find her. Someone was trying to scare the hell out of her—make her believe she was crazy—and that aunt of hers didn't help a bit, kept telling her in an understanding, tender voice that she'd be hearing things and seeing things too if she'd been through all that Sally had, and she had been in that sanitarium for so long, and that would make her think differently, wouldn't it?

"Then the two murders. I've got to find her. Everything else is nuts, but not Sally."

"When you feel well enough, you and I will go see her aunt. I already spoke to her, but she just said that she hadn't seen Sally, that she was staying with you at Thelma's Bed and Breakfast. We searched your tower bedroom. Her duffel bag was gone and all her clothes, her blow dryer, everything. It's like she was never there. Look, Quinlan, maybe when she saw you unconscious, she got really scared and ran."

"No," James said, looking David straight in the eye. "I know she wouldn't leave me, not if I were lying there unconscious. She just wouldn't."

"It's like that, is it?"

"God only knows, but she has a thick streak of honor and she cares about me. She wouldn't have left."

"Then we've got to find her. Another thing—I'm an officer of the law. Now that I know who she is, it's my duty to report her."

"I'd appreciate it if you'd wait, David. There's more at stake here than just Amory St. John's murder, lots more. Trust me on this."

David looked at him for a long time. Finally, he said, "All right. Tell me what I can do to help."

"Let's go see Aunt Amabel Perdy."

DR. ALFRED BEADERMEYER was enjoying himself. Sally didn't know the small new mirror in her room was two-way. No one knew, at least he didn't think so. He watched her sit up slowly, obviously trying to coordinate her arms and legs. Since her brain was fuzzy, it was difficult for her, but she just kept trying. He admired that in her, and at the same time he wanted to destroy it. It seemed to take her several moments to realize she was naked.

Then, very slowly, as if she were an old woman, she rose and walked to the small closet. She pulled out a nightgown she'd left there before she escaped. She didn't know it, but he had bought it for her. She slipped it over her head, teetering a bit but managing finally. Then she walked back to sit on the edge of the bed. She held her head in her hands.

He was getting bored. Wouldn't she do anything? Wouldn't she start yelling? Something? He had nearly turned to go when at last she raised her head and he saw tears streaming down her cheeks.

This was better. Soon she would be ready to listen to him. Soon now. He would hold off on another shot for an hour or so. He turned away and unlocked the door of the tiny room.

Sally knew she was crying. She could feel the wet on her face, taste the salt when it trickled into her mouth. Why was she crying? James. She remembered James, how he lay there, blood streaming from the wound over his left ear. He'd been so still, so very still. Beadermeyer had promised he wasn't dead. How could she believe that devil?

He had to be all right. She looked at the soft silk gown that slithered against her skin. It was a lovely peach color with wide silk straps over her shoulders. Unfortunately it bagged on her now. She looked at the needle marks in her arm. There were five pinpricks. He'd drugged her five times. She felt her head begin to clear, slowly, so very slowly. More things, memories, began to filter through, take shape and substance.

She had to get out of here before he either killed her or took her someplace else, someplace where nobody could find her. She thought of James. He could find her if anyone could.

She forced herself to her feet. She took one step, then another. Soon she was walking slowly, carefully, but naturally. She stood in front of the narrow window and stared out onto the sanitarium grounds.

The mowed lawn stretched a good hundred yards before it butted against a heavily wooded area. Surely she could walk that far; she had before. She just had to get to those woods. She could get lost in those woods, just as she had before. Eventually she'd found her way out. She would again.

She walked back to the closet. There was a bathrobe and two more nightgowns, a pair of slippers. Nothing else. No pants, no dresses, no underwear.

She didn't care. She would walk in her bathrobe, to the ends of the earth if necessary. Then another veil lifted in her brain, and she remembered that she'd stolen one of the nurse's pantsuits that first time, and her shoes. Would it be possible to do that again?

Who had done this to her? She knew it wasn't her father. He was long dead. It had to be the man pretending to be her father, the man who'd called her, who'd appeared at her bedroom window. It could have been Scott, it could have been Dr. Beadermeyer, it could have been some man either of them had hired.

But not her father, thank God. That miserable bastard was finally dead. She prayed there really was a hell. If there was, she knew he was there, in the deepest pit.

She had to get to her mother. Noelle would help her. Noelle would protect her, once she knew the truth. But why hadn't Noelle ever come to see her during the six months here? Why hadn't she demanded to know why her daughter was here? As far as Sally knew, Noelle hadn't done anything to help her. Did she believe her daughter was crazy? Had she believed her husband? Had she believed Sally's husband?

How to get out of here?

AMABEL SAID, "Would either of you gentlemen care for a cup of coffee?"

"No," Quinlan said curtly. "Tell us where Sally is."

Amabel sighed and motioned the two men to sit down. "Listen, James, I already told the sheriff here that Sally must have gotten scared when she saw you were hurt, and she ran. That's the only explanation. Sally's not a strong girl. She's been through a lot. She was even in an asylum. You don't look shocked. I'm a bit surprised that she told you about it. Something like that shouldn't be talked about.

"But listen, she was very ill. She still is. It makes sense that she would run again, just like she ran away from what happened in Washington. If you doubt me, just go to Thelma's. Martha told me that all of Sally's things were gone from your room. Isn't that odd? She left not even a memory of herself in that room.

"It was like she wanted to erase her very self." She paused a moment, then added in a faraway gypsy's voice, "It's almost as if she was never really there at all, as if we all just imagined she was here."

Quinlan jumped to his feet and stood over her. He looked as menacing as hell but David didn't say a word, just waited. Quinlan stuck his face very near hers and said slowly and very distinctly, "That's bullshit, Amabel. Sally wasn't an apparition, nor was she nuts, as you implied to her, like you're implying to us now. She didn't imagine hearing a woman scream those two nights. She didn't imagine seeing her father's face at her bedroom window in the middle of the night. You tried to make her doubt herself, didn't you, Amabel? You tried to make her think she was crazy."

"That is ridiculous."

Quinlan moved even closer, leaning over her now, forcing her to press her back against the chair. "Why did you do that, Amabel? You just said you knew she was in a sanitarium. You knew, didn't you, that someone put her there and kept her for six months drugged to her eyebrows? You didn't try to assure her that she was as sane as anyone—no, you kept on with the innuendos.

"Don't deny it, I heard you do it. You tried to make Sally doubt herself, her reason. Why?"

But Amabel just smiled sadly at him. She said to David, "Sheriff, I've been very patient. This man only knew Sally for a matter of days. I'm her aunt. I love her. There's no reason I would ever want to hurt her. I would always seek to protect her. I'm sorry, James, but she ran away. It's as simple as that. I pray the sheriff will find her. She's not strong. She needs to be taken care of."

Quinlan was so angry he was afraid he'd pull her out of the chair and shake her like a rat. He backed off and began pacing around the small living room. David watched him for a moment, then said, "Mrs. Perdy, if Sally ran, can you guess where she would go?"

"To Alaska. She said she wanted to go to Alaska. She said she preferred Mexico, but she didn't have her passport. That's all I can tell you, Sheriff. Of course, if I hear from her, I'll call you right away." Amabel rose. "I'm sorry, James. You know who Sally is. It's likely you've told Sheriff Mountebank her real name. There's a lot for her to face, and she'll have to face it eventually. As to her mental status, who's to say? All we can do is pray."

James wanted to wrap his fingers around her gypsy neck and squeeze. She was lying, damn her, but she was doing it very well. Sally wouldn't have run away, not with him lying unconscious at her feet. She wouldn't.

That meant that someone had her.

And that someone was the person who had pretended to be her father. James would bet on it. Now he knew what to do. He even had a good idea where she was, and it curdled his blood to think about it.

IT WAS A BLACK MIDNIGHT, not even a sliver of moon or a single star to cast a dim light through that cauldron sky. Roiling black clouds moved and shifted, but never revealed anything except more blackness.

Sally stared out the window, drawing one deep breath after another. They would be here soon to give her another shot. No more pills, she'd heard Beadermeyer say, she just might be able to hide them again in her mouth. He announced that he didn't want her hurt again, the bastard.

There was a new nurse—her name tag said Rosalee—and she was as blank-faced as Holland. She didn't speak to Sally except to tell her tersely what to do and when and how to do it. She watched Sally go to the bathroom, which, Sally supposed, was better than having Holland standing there.

Dr. Beadermeyer didn't want her hurt? That could only be because he himself wanted to be the one to hurt her. She'd seen no one except Beadermeyer and Holland and Nurse Rosalee. They'd forced her to keep to her room. She had nothing to read, no TV to watch. She didn't know anything about her mother or about Scott. Most of the time she was so drugged she didn't care, didn't even know who she was, but now she knew, now she could reason, and she was getting stronger by the minute.

If only Beadermeyer would wait just a few more minutes, maybe fifteen minutes, then she'd be ready.

But he didn't give her even two more minutes. She jumped when she heard him unlock the door. No time to get into position. She stood stiffly by the window in her peach silk nightgown.

"Good evening, my dear Sally. You're looking chipper and really quite lovely in that nightgown. Would you like to take it off for me now?"

"No."

"Ah, so you've got your wits together, have you? Just as well. I'd like to have a conversation with you before I send you back into the ether. Do sit down, Sally."

"No, I want to stay as far away from you as possible."

"As you wish." He was wearing a dark blue crew sweater and black slacks. His black hair was slicked back as if he'd just had a shower. His teeth were white, the front two top teeth overlapping.

"Your teeth are ugly," she said now. "Why didn't you wear braces as a kid?"

She'd spoken without thinking, another indication that her mind wasn't completely clear yet.

He looked as if he wanted to kill her. Without conscious thought, he raised his fingers to touch his teeth, then dropped his arm. There was only a thin veil of shadow separating them now, but she recognized the anger in him, knew he wanted to hurt her.

He got control of himself. "Well, you're a little bitch tonight, aren't you?"

"No," she said, still watching him, her body tensed, knowing he wanted to attack her, hurt her badly. She didn't know she could hate a person as much as she hated him. Other than her father. Other than her husband.

Finally, he sat down in the single chair and crossed his legs. He removed his glasses and put them on the small circular table beside the chair. There was a carafe of water and a single glass on the table, nothing more.

"What do you want?" The carafe was plastic—even if she struck him squarely on the head, it wouldn't hurt him. But the table was sturdy. If only she were fast enough, she could grab it and smash him with it. But she knew she would have to be free of the drugs for at least another hour to be fast enough, strong enough, to bring him down. Could she keep him talking that long? She doubted it, but it was worth a try.

"What do you want?" she said again. She couldn't bring herself to take a step closer to him.

"I'm bored," he said. "I'm making so much money, but I'm never free to leave this place. I want to enjoy my money. What do you suggest?"

"Let me go, and I'll see that you get even more money."

"That would defeat the purpose, wouldn't it?"

"Do you mean that you have other people in here who are perfectly sane? Other people you're holding prisoner? Other people you're being paid to keep here?"

"This is a very small, very private place, Sally. Not many people know about it. I gain all my patients through referrals, carefully screened referrals.

"Just listen to me. This is the first time I've ever talked to you as an adult. Six months I had you with me, six whole months, and you were always as interesting as a jointless doll, except for that time you jumped through the window in my office. If anything proved to your dear mother that you were nuts, that story did. That made me sit up and take notice of you, but not for long. This is much better. If only I could trust you not to try to escape me again, I would keep you just as you are now."

"How do you imagine that I can escape?"

"Unfortunately Holland is quite stupid, and he's the one who tends you most often. I do believe Nurse Rosalee is a bit afraid of you. Isn't that odd? As for Holland, he begged me to let him take care of you, the pathetic creature. Yes, I can imagine you waiting behind that door for him to come in.

"What would you do, Sally? Hit him on the head with this table?

125

That would stun him. Then you could strip off his clothes, though I doubt you'd enjoy stripping him as much as he enjoys stripping you. No, you see, I'm in a bind. And please don't move. Remember, I'm not Holland. Stay where you are or you get a nice big shot right now."

"I haven't moved an inch. Why am I here? How did you find me? Amabel had to call to tell you where I was. But why? And who wanted me back here? My husband? Were you the one who pretended to be my father or was it Scott?"

"You speak of your poor husband as if he's a stranger to you. It's that James Quinlan, isn't it? You slept with him, you enjoyed him, and now you want to dump poor Scott. I would never have taken you for such a fickle woman, Sally. Wait until I tell Scott what you've done."

"When you speak to Scott Brainerd, tell him I fully intend to kill him when I'm free of this place. And I will be free soon, Dr. Beader-meyer."

"Ah, Sally, I'm sure that Scott wants me to make you more mal-leable. He doesn't like women who are aggressive, all tied up in their careers. Trust me to see to it, Sally."

"Either you or Scott called me up in The Cove pretending to be my father. Either you or Scott came to The Cove and climbed that silly lad-der to scare the hell out of me, to make me think I was crazy. There's no one else. My father is dead."

"Yes, Amory is dead. I think personally that you killed him, Sally. Did you?"

"I don't know if you really want the truth. I have no memory of that night. It will come back, though. It has to."

"Don't count on it. One of the drugs I'm giving you is excellent at suppressing memory. No one really knows yet what the long-term side effects will be. And you will be taking it forever, Sally."

He rose and walked to her. "Now," he said. He was smiling. She couldn't help herself. When he reached for her, she cracked a fist as hard as she could against his jaw. His head flew back. She hit him again, kicked him in the groin with all her strength, and ran to grab that table.

But she stumbled, her head spinning, nausea flooding through her. Her legs collapsed beneath her. She fell to the floor.

She heard him panting behind her. She had to get to that table. She struggled to her feet, forced one foot in front of the other. He was close behind her now, panting, panting, he was in pain, she'd hurt him. If she didn't knock him out, he would take great pleasure in hurting her. Please, God, please, please.

She clutched the table, lifted it, turned to face him. He was so close, his arms stretched out toward her, his fingers curved, coming toward her throat.

"Holland!"

"No," she said and swung the table at him. But it was a puny effort, and he blocked it with his shoulder.

"Holland!"

The door flew open and Holland ran into the room.

"Hold the little bitch, hold her!"

"No, no." She backed away from the men, but there was no room, just the narrow bed and the table she held as a shield in front of her.

Dr. Beadermeyer was holding his crotch, his face still drawn in pain. Good, she'd hurt him. Anything he did to her would be worth it. She'd hurt him.

"That's enough, Sally." Holland's voice, soft and hoarse, terrifying.

"I'll kill you, Holland. Stay away from me." But it was an empty threat. Her arms were trembling, her stomach roiling now. She tasted bile. She dropped the table, fell to her knees, and vomited on Dr. Beadermeyer's Italian loafers.

"YOU EITHER HELP ME or you don't, Savich, but you don't tell a soul about this."

"Damnation, Quinlan, do you know what you're asking?" Dillon Savich leaned back in his chair, nearly tipping it over, but not quite because he knew exactly how far to go. His computer screen was bright with the photo of a man's face, a youngish man who looked like a yuppie broker, well dressed, easy smile, well-groomed hair and clothes.

"Yes. You're going with me to that sanitarium and we're going to rescue Sally. Then we're going to clean up this mess. We'll be heroes. You won't be gone from your computer for more than a couple of hours. Maybe three hours if you want to be a hero. Take your laptop and the modem. You can still hook in to any system you want."

"Marvin will cut our balls off. You know he hates it when you try to go off on your own without talking to him."

James said, "We'll give Marvin all the credit. The FBI will shine. Marvin will be grinning from ear to ear. He'll give the credit to his boss, Mr. Maitland, so he won't cut Marvin's balls off. Mr. Maitland will be happy as a loon."

"And on and on it goes. Sally will be safe and we'll get this damned murder solved."

Savich said, "You still ignore the fact that she might have killed her father herself. It's a possibility. What's wrong with you? How can you ignore it?"

"Yes, I do ignore it. I have to. But we'll find out, won't we?"

"You're involved with her, aren't you? It was only one bloody week you were with her. What is she, some sort of siren?"

"No, she's a skinny little blonde who's got more grit than you can begin to imagine."

"I don't believe this. No, shut up, Quinlan, I've got to think." Savich leaned forward and stared fixedly at the man's photo on the computer screen. He said absently, "This creep is probably the one who's killing the homeless people in Minneapolis."

"Leave the creep for the moment. Think, brood, whatever. You're going to try to figure all the odds. You're going to weigh every possible outcome with that computer brain of yours. Have you developed a program for that yet?"

"Not yet, but I'm close. Come on, Quinlan, my brain is why you love me. I've saved your butt at least three times. You wouldn't trade me for any other agent. Shut up. I've got to make an important decision here."

"You've got ten minutes. Not a second more. I've got to get to her. God knows what they're doing to her, what they're giving her. Jesus, she could be dead. Or they could have already moved her. If the guy who hit me bothered to check my ID, then they know I'm FBI. We haven't got much time even if they didn't check. I know they'll move her, it only makes sense."

"Why are you so sure she's at the sanitarium?"

"They wouldn't take the chance of taking her anywhere else."

"'They' who? No, you don't know. Ten minutes, then. No, shut up, Quinlan."

"Thank God, you've already been to the gym this morning or I'd have to wait for you to lift your bloody weights. I'm getting some coffee."

Quinlan walked down to the small lounge at the end of the hall. It wasn't that the fifth floor was ugly and inhospitable. It couldn't be, since they let tourists get within a floor of them. It didn't look all that institutional, just tired. The linoleum was still pale brown with years of grit walked deep into it.

He poured a cup of coffee, sniffed it first, then took a cautious sip. Yep, it still made his Adam's apple shudder, but it kept the nerves finely tuned. Without it an agent would probably just fold up and die.

He needed Savich. He knew that Savich would set up an appropriate backup in case it turned out they couldn't handle the job. He'd been tempted to go directly from Dulles to Maryland to that sanitarium, but he'd given the matter a good deal of thought. He was in this up to his neck, and he wanted to save Sally's neck as well.

He had no idea about the security at Beadermeyer's sanitarium, but

Savich would find out and then they'd get over there. He couldn't take the chance of alerting his boss, Brammer. He couldn't take the chance that Sally could be plowed under in this damned mess.

He drank more coffee, felt the caffeine jolt hit his brain and stomach at about the same time.

He wandered back into Savich's office. "It's been ten minutes."

"I've been waiting for you, Quinlan. Let's go."

"Just like that? No more arguments? No more telling me there's a thirteen percent chance that one of us will end up in a ditch with a knife in his throat?"

"Nope," Savich said cheerfully. He pulled several sheets out of his printer and rose.

"Here's the layout for the sanitarium. I think I've found exactly where it's safest for us to go in."

"You made up your mind before you even kicked me out."

"Sure. I wanted to get a look at the plans, didn't really know if I could get my paws on them, but I did. Come here and let me show you the best way into this place. Tell me what you think."

"DID YOU MAKE HER brush her teeth and wash her mouth out?"

"Yes, Dr. Beadermeyer. She spit the mouthwash on me, but she did get a bit of it in her mouth."

"I hate the smell of vomit," Beadermeyer said as he looked down at his shoes. He'd cleaned them as best he could. Just thinking about what she'd done made him want to hit her again, but it wouldn't gain him any pleasure. She was unconscious.

"She'll be out of it for a good four hours. Then I'll lighten the dose to keep her pleasantly sedated."

"I hope the dose isn't too high."

"Don't be a fool. I have no intention of killing her, at least not yet. I just don't know yet what will happen. I'm taking her out of here tomorrow morning."

"Yes, before he comes to get her."

"Why do you say that, Holland? How the hell do you know anything?"

"I was sitting beside her after you gave her the shot, and she was whispering that she knew he'd come here, she knew it."

"She's fucking crazy. You know that, Holland."

"Yes, Doctor."

Damnation. Quinlan could find out everything he wanted to know about the sanitarium within computer minutes. He felt the wet of his own sweat in his armpits. Damn, this shouldn't have happened. He wondered if he should get her out of there tonight, right now.

They should have killed that damned agent while they'd had him, and because they'd been afraid to, now he would have to deal with it.

If he was smart, if he wanted to make sure he was safe, he'd get Sally out of there now.

Where to take her? Jesus, he was tired. He rubbed the back of his neck as he walked back to his office.

Mrs. Willard hadn't left any coffee for him, damn her. He sat down behind the mahogany desk that kept patients a good three and a half feet from him and leaned back in his chair.

When would Quinlan and his FBI buddies show up? He would show up, Beadermeyer knew it. He'd followed her to The Cove. He would come here for sure. But how soon? How much time did he have? He picked up the telephone and dialed. They would have to make a decision now. There was no more time for playing games.

THE NIGHT WAS BLACK as pitch. Quinlan and Savich left the Oldsmobile sedan about twenty yards down the road from the wide gates of the Beadermeyer sanitarium. The words were scrolled in fancy script letters on top of the black iron gates.

"Pretentious bastard."

"Yeah," Savich said. "Let me think if there's anything more to tell you about our doctor. First of all, I don't think many people have this information.

"He's brilliant and unscrupulous. Word has it that if you're rich enough and discreet enough and you want someone under wraps badly enough, then Beadermeyer will take that person off your hands. It's just rumors, of course, but who knows? Who did Sally piss off enough to get her sent here? Look, Quinlan, maybe she's really sick."

"She isn't sick. Who sent her here? I don't know. She never would tell me. She never even mentioned Beadermeyer by name. But it has to be him. Keep that flashlight down, Savich. Yeah, better. Who knows what kind of security he has?"

"That I couldn't find out, but hey, the fence isn't electrified."

They were both wearing black, including heavily lined black gloves. The twelve-foot-high fence was no problem. They dropped lightly to the spongy grass on the other side.

"So far, so good," Quinlan said, keeping the flashlight low and moving it in a wide arc.

"Let's stay close to the tree line."

The two men moved quickly, hunkered down, the flashlight sending out a low beam just in front of them.

"Not good," Savich said.

"What? Oh, yeah." Two German shepherds came galloping toward them.

"I don't want to kill them."

"You won't have to. Just stand still, Savich."

"What are you going—"

Savich watched Quinlan pull a plastic-wrapped package from inside his black jacket. He peeled it open to show three huge pieces of raw steak.

The dogs were within twelve feet of them. Still Quinlan held perfectly still, waiting, waiting.

"Just another second," he said, then threw one piece of raw steak in one direction and a second piece in the other direction. The dogs were on the meat in an instant.

"Let's get moving. I'm going to save this last piece as getaway meat."

"Not a bad security system," Savich said.

They were running now, keeping low, the flashlight off because there were a few lights on in the long, sprawling building in front of them, enough to light their way.

"You said the patient rooms are all in the left wing."

"Right. Beadermeyer's office is in the far end of the right wing. If the bastard's still here, he's a good distance away."

"There should just be a small night shift complement."

"I hope. I didn't take the time to access their personnel and administration files. I don't know how many employees work the night shift."

"Damned useless machine."

Savich laughed. "Don't accuse me of being married to my computer when you're at your club most weekends wailing away on your sax. Whoa, Quinlan, stop."

They froze in an instant, pressed against the brick building, just behind two tall bushes. Someone was coming, walking briskly, a flashlight in his hand.

He was whistling the theme from *Gone With the Wind*.

"A romantic security guard," Quinlan whispered.

The man waved the flashlight to both sides and back again to the front. He never stopped whistling. The light flowed right over their bent heads, showing the guard only black shadows.

"I just hope she's here," Quinlan said. "Beadermeyer has to know I'll come here. If he's the one who hit me, then he would have checked my ID. What if they've already taken her away?"

"She's here. Stop worrying. If she isn't, well, then, we'll find her soon enough. Did I tell you I had a date tonight? I had a date and look what I'm doing. Playing Rescue Squad with you. Stop worrying. You're smarter than Beadermeyer. She's still here, I'll bet you on it. I get the feeling there's more arrogance in this Beadermeyer than in most folk. I think he believes he's invincible."

They were moving again, bent nearly double, no flashlight, just two black shadows skimming over the well-manicured lawn.

"We've got to get inside."

"Soon," Savich said. "Just ahead. Then it's going to be tricky. Imagine seeing the two of us dressed like cat burglars roaming down the halls."

"We'll find a nurse soon enough. She'll tell us."

"We're nearly to the back emergency entrance. Yeah, here we are. Help me pull up the doors, Quinlan."

Well oiled, thank God, Quinlan thought when they gently eased the doors back down. He turned on the flashlight. They were in an enclosed space that could hold at least six cars. There were four cars there. They made their way around them, then Quinlan turned and trained his flashlight on the license plates.

"Look, Savich. Good guess, huh? The bastard would have a luxury plate—BEADRMYR. So he's still here. I wouldn't mind running into him."

"Marvin would not be a happy camper."

Quinlan laughed.

Savich used one of his lock picks to get into the door. It only took a moment.

"You're getting good at this."

"I practiced for at least six hours at Quantico. They have about three dozen kinds of locks. They use a stopwatch on you. I came in sixth."

"How many agents were entered?"

"Seven. Me and six women."

"I want to hear more about this later."

They were in a long hallway, low lights giving off a dim, mellow glow. There were no names on the doors, just numbers.

"We've got to get us a nurse," Savich said.

They turned a corner to see a nurses' station just ahead. There was only one woman there, reading a novel. She looked up every once in a while at the TV screen in front of her. They were nearly upon her when she saw them. She gasped, her novel dropping to the linoleum floor as she tried to scoot off her chair and run.

Quinlan grabbed her arm and gently pressed his hand over her mouth. "We won't hurt you. Just hold still. You got her chart, Savich?"

"Yep, here it is. Room two twenty-two."

"Sorry," Quinlan said quietly as he struck her in the jaw. She collapsed against him and he lowered her to the floor, pushing her under the desk.

"We passed two twenty-two. Quick, Savich, I've got a feeling that our charmed existence is about to be shot down in flames."

They ran swiftly down the hallway, back the way they had come. "Here it is. No light. Good."

Quinlan slowly pushed at the door. The damned thing was locked, just as he'd known it would be. He motioned Savich forward. Savich examined the lock, then pulled out a pick. He didn't say a word, just changed to another pick. After a good three minutes, the lock slid open.

Quinlan pushed the door open. The soft light from the hallway beamed into the room, right on the face of a man who was seated on a narrow bed, leaning over a woman.

He whipped around on the bed, half rising, his mouth open to yell.

"I DIDN'T KNOW you could move that fast," Savich said in admiration after Quinlan had leaped across to the bed and slammed his fist into the man's mouth before he could let out a single sound. He dumped him off the bed to the floor.

"Is this Sally Brainerd?"

Quinlan looked briefly at the small man whose nose was flooding blood, then up at the woman on the bed. "It's Sally," he said, such rage in his voice that Savich stared at him for a moment. "Let me get that door closed and then we'll use our flashlights. Take the little guy and tie him up with something."

Quinlan shone the flashlight in her face. He was shocked at her pallor and the slackness of her flesh. "Sally," he said, gently slapping her face.

She didn't respond.

"Sally," he said, shaking her this time. The covers slid down and he saw that she was naked. He looked over at the slight man who was now tied up as well as unconscious. Had he been planning to rape her?

She was deeply unconscious. He shone the light on her bare arms. There were six needle marks.

The damned bastards. "Look, Savich. Just look what they've done to her."

Savich ran his fingers lightly over the needle marks. "It looks like they gave her a real heavy dose this time," he said as he leaned down and pulled up her eyelids. "Real heavy dose."

"They'll pay. See what kind of clothes are in the closet."

Quinlan noticed that her hair was neatly brushed and smoothed back from her forehead. That little man who'd been leaning over her, he'd done that. Quinlan knew it. He felt himself shiver. Jesus, what went on in this place?

"Here's a nightgown and a robe and a pair of slippers. Nothing more."

Quinlan got her into the gown and robe within minutes. It was difficult dressing an unconscious person, even a small one. Finally, he lifted her over his shoulder. "Let's get the hell out of here."

They were through the back emergency door and nearly out of the garage when the sirens went off.

"The nurse," Quinlan said. "We should have tied her up, dammit."

"We've got time. We'll make it."

When Quinlan tired, Savich took Sally. They were almost to the fence when the German shepherds, barking louder than the hounds of Baskerville, came racing smoothly toward them.

Quinlan tossed out the other piece of meat. They didn't stop to see what the dogs did with it.

When they got to the fence, Quinlan climbed it faster than he'd ever climbed anything in his life. At the top, he straddled the fence on his belly and leaned back toward Savich as far as he could. "Hand her up to me."

"She's like a boneless Foster Farms chicken," Savich said, trying to get a firm grip on her. On the third try, Quinlan got hold of her wrists. He slowly pulled her up. He held her around the waist until Savich was on top of the fence beside him. His arms were cramping by the time Savich swiveled around and leaped to the ground. He brought her around and began to lower her. "Hurry, Quinlan, hurry. Okay, just another couple of inches. There, I've got her. Get down here!"

The dogs were barking louder. The meat had stopped them for all of forty-five seconds.

They heard several men yelling.

Guns fired, one bullet sparked off the iron fence, so close to Quinlan's head that he felt the searing heat from it.

A woman's sharp yell sounded behind the men.

"Let's get the hell out of here," Quinlan said as he hefted Sally over his shoulder and ran as fast as he could toward the Oldsmobile.

The guns didn't stop until they'd raced around the bend and were out of sight.

"If they let the dogs out on us, we're in trouble," Savich said.

Quinlan hoped they didn't. He didn't want to shoot those beautiful dogs.

He was relieved when they slammed the car doors some two minutes later. "Thank God for good-sized favors."

"You've got that right. Hey, that was fun. Now, your apartment, Quinlan?"

"Oh, no, we're going to Maryland, just another hour up the road, Savich. I'll give you directions. What surprises me is that they took her back to this place at all. They must have figured I'd come here first thing. I'll just bet you she would have been gone tomorrow morning. So, I'm not going to be as stupid. No way we're going back to my place."

"You're right. When someone hit you over the head in The Cove, he would have searched your pockets. They know you're FBI. That's why they didn't kill you, I'd bet my StairMaster on it. It would have been too big a risk for them."

"Yeah. We're going to my parents' lake cottage. It's safe. No one knows about it except you. You haven't told anyone, have you?"

Savich shook his head. "What are you going to do with her, Quinlan? This is highly irregular."

Quinlan was holding her in his lap, her head cradled on his arm. He'd covered her with his black jacket. It was warm in the car. "We're going to wait until she comes out from under this drug, then see what she knows. Then we're going to clean everything up. How's that sound to you?"

"Like we'll be a couple of damned heroes." Savich sighed. "Marvin won't like it. He'll probably try to transfer us to Alaska for not being team players. But, hey, don't sell a hero short."

SHE WOKE UP to see a strange man looking down at her, his nose not more than six inches from hers. It took her a moment to realize that he was indeed flesh and blood and not some specter dredged up from a drugged vision. Her lips felt cracked. It was hard to make herself talk, but she did.

"If Dr. Beadermeyer sent you, it won't matter." She spit on him.

Savich jerked back, wiped the back of his hand across his nose and cheek. "I'm a hero, not a bad guy. Beadermeyer didn't send me."

Sally tried to sift through his words, make some sense of them. Her brain still felt like it wanted to sleep, like parts of it were numb, like an arm or leg that had been in a single position for too long. "You're a hero?"

"Yeah, a real live hero."

"Then James must be here."

"You mean Quinlan?"

"Yes. He's a hero too. He was the first hero I ever met. I'm sorry I spit on you, but I thought you were another one of those horrible men."

"It's okay. You just lie still and I'll get Quinlan."

What did he think she would do? Jump up and race out of here, wherever here was?

"Good morning, Sally. Don't spit on me, okay?"

She stared up at him, so thirsty she could barely squeak out another word. Her brain was at last knitting itself back together, and all she could do was throw up her arms and pull him down to her. She said against his throat. "I knew you'd come. I just knew it. I'm so thirsty, James. Can I have some water?"

"You all right? Really? Let me up just a little, okay?'

"Yes. I'm so glad you're not dead. Someone hit you and I was bending over you." She pulled back from him, her fingers lightly tracing over the stitched wound over his left ear.

"I'm okay—don't worry about it."

"I didn't know who'd done it to you. Then someone hit me over the head. I woke up with Beadermeyer leaning over me. I was back in that place."

"I know, but you're with me now and no one can possibly find you." He said over his shoulder, "Savich, how about some water for the lady?"

"It's the drugs he gives me. They make my throat feel like a desert."

She felt the tightening in him at her words.

"Here, I'll hold the glass for you."

She drank her fill, then lay back and sighed. "I'll be back to normal in about ten more minutes—at least that's my best guess. James, who is that man I spit on?"

"He's a good friend of mine, name of Dillon Savich. He and I got you out of the sanitarium last night. Savich, come and say hello to Sally."

"Ma'am."

"He said he was a hero, just like you, James."

"It's possible. You can trust him, Sally."

She nodded, such a slight movement really, and he watched her eyes close again. "You're not ready to eat something?"

"No, not yet. You won't leave, will you?"

"Not ever."

He would have sworn that the corners of her mouth turned up just a bit into a very slight smile. Without thinking, he leaned down and kissed her closed mouth. "I'm glad I've got you again. When I woke up in David Mountebank's house, my head pounding like a watermelon with a stake in it, he told me you were gone. I've never been so scared in my life. You're not going to be out of my sight again, Sally."

"That sounds good to me," she said. In the next moment, she was asleep. Not unconscious but asleep, real sleep.

Quinlan rose and looked down at her. He straightened the light blanket over her chest. He smoothed her hair back on the pillow. He thought of that little man they'd found in her room and knew that if he ever saw him again, he'd kill him.

And Beadermeyer. He couldn't wait to get his hands on Dr. Beadermeyer.

"How does it feel to be the most important person in the whole universe, Quinlan?"

Quinlan kept smoothing down the blanket, his movements slow and calm. Finally he said, "It scares the shit out of me. You want to know something else? It doesn't feel bad at all. How much credit am I going to have to give you?"

THAT EVENING, the three of them were sitting on the front veranda of Quinlan's cottage, looking out over Louise Lynn Lake. For an evening in March, it was balmy. The cottage faced west. The sun was low on the horizon, making the water ripple with golds and startling pinks.

Quinlan said to Sally, "It's narrow, not all that much fun for boaters unless you're a teenager and like to play chicken. And you can see at least four different curves from here. Well, the sucker has so many curves that—"

"So many curves that what?" Savich asked, looking up from the smooth block of maple he was carving.

"We are not a comedy routine," Quinlan said, grinning to Sally. "Come on now, the lake has so many curves that it very nearly winds back onto itself."

Savich said, as he watched a curling sliver of maple drift to the wooden floor, "You sometimes don't know if you're coming or going."

"You're very good friends," Sally said. "You know each other quite well, don't you?"

"Yeah, but we're not going to get married. Quinlan snores like a pig."

She smiled. It was a good smile, Dillon thought, not a forced smile. Now, that showed she knew she was safe here.

"You want some more iced tea, Sally?"

"No, I like sucking on the ice. There's plenty."

Quinlan lifted his legs and put his feet on the wooden railing that circled the front veranda. He was wearing short, scuffed black boots, old faded blue jeans that looked quite lovely on him—it was surely a shock that she could even think of something like that—and a white shirt with the sleeves rolled up to the elbows.

He was also wearing a shoulder holster, and there was a gun in it. She hadn't realized that all private investigators wore guns all the time. He was comfortable with it, like it was just another item of clothing. It looked part of him. He was long and solid and looked hard as nails. She remembered how she'd hauled his face down to hers when she'd come out of the drugged sleep. How he'd let her. How he'd kissed her when he thought she was asleep again. She'd never met a man like him before in her life— a man to trust, a man to believe, a man who cared what happened to her.

"Has your head cleared?" Savich asked. She turned to see him gently rubbing his thumbs over the maple, over and over and over.

"Why are you doing that?"

"What? Oh, it warms the wood and makes it shine."

"What are you carving?"

"You, if you don't mind."

She blinked at him, swallowed a piece of ice she was sucking, and promptly fell to coughing. James leaned over and lightly slapped her between the shoulder blades.

When she got her breath, she said, "Why ever would you want to immortalize me in any way? I'm nothing at all, nothing—"

"Dammit, shut up, Sally."

"Why, James? Someone wants me out of the way, but that doesn't make me important. It just makes what I appear to know of interest to someone."

"I guess maybe it's time we got to that," Savich said. He set down the piece of maple and turned to face Sally.

"If we're to help you, you must tell us everything."

She looked from Dillon Savich to James. She frowned down at her hands. She carefully set the glass down on the rattan table beside her.

She looked at James again, nodding at his shoulder holster. "I was just thinking that I never realized that private investigators wore guns all the time. But you do, don't you? Another thing—it looks natural on you, like you were born wearing it. You're not a private investigator, are you, James?"

"No."

"Who are you?"

He was very still, then he looked at her straight in the face and said, "My name is James Quinlan, just as I told you. What I didn't tell you was that I'm Special Agent James Quinlan, FBI. Savich and I have worked together for five years. We're not really partners, since the FBI doesn't operate that way, but we're on a lot of cases together.

"I came to The Cove to find you."

"You're with the FBI?" Just saying the words made gooseflesh ripple over her arms, made her feel numb and cold.

"Yes. I didn't tell you immediately because I knew it would spook you. I wanted to get your confidence and then bring you back to Washington and clear up all the mess."

"You certainly succeeded in gaining my confidence, Mr. Quinlan."

He winced at her use of his surname. He saw that Savich wanted to say something, and held up his hand. "No, let me finish it. Look, Sally, I was doing my job. Things got complicated when I got to know you. And then there were the two murders in The Cove, your dear father calling you on the phone and then appearing at your bedroom window.

"I decided not to tell you because I didn't know what you'd do. I knew you were in possible danger and I didn't want you running away. I knew I could protect you—"

"You failed at that, didn't you?"

"Yes." Damn, but she was angry, it was sharp and clear in her voice. He wished he could change things, but he couldn't. He just had to try to make her understand. If he didn't get her to come around, then what would happen?

She rose slowly to her feet. She was wearing blue jeans that looked like a second skin. Savich had misjudged and bought her a pair of girl's jeans at the Kmart in the closest town, Glenberg. Even the blouse was tight, the buttons pulling apart.

The look on her face was remote, distant, as if she really weren't standing on the old veranda any longer, between the two of them. She said nothing for a very long time, just stared at the lake. Finally she said, "Thank you for getting me out of that place last night. He wouldn't leave my head clear enough so I could figure out how to escape again. I don't think I would ever have gotten free. I owe you both a lot for that. But now I'm leaving. I have a good number of things to resolve. Goodbye, James."

"YOU'RE NOT LEAVING, Sally. I can't let you leave."

She gave him a look that was so immensely damning of what he was and what he'd done, he couldn't stand it.

"Listen, Sally, please. I'm sorry. I did what I believed was right. I couldn't tell you, please understand that. You were coming to trust me. I couldn't take a chance that you'd react the way you're reacting now."

She laughed. Just laughed. She said nothing at all.

Savich rose, saying, "I'm going for a walk. I'll be back to make dinner in an hour."

Sally watched him stride down the narrow trail toward the water. She supposed he was a fine-looking man, not as fine-looking as James, of course. She didn't like all his big muscles, but she supposed some people did.

"Sally."

She didn't want to turn back to him. She didn't want to speak to him anymore, give him any of her attention, listen to his damning words that made so much sense to him and had utterly destroyed her.

No, she'd rather watch Dillon Savich, or the two boats that were rocking lazily in the smooth evening waters. It would be sunset soon. The water was beginning to turn the color of cherries.

"Sally, I can't let you leave. Besides, where would you go? I don't know where you'd be safe. You thought you'd have a refuge in The Cove. You didn't. Your dear auntie Amabel was in on it."

"No, that's impossible."

"Believe it. I have no reason to lie to you. David and I both visited her after I got on my feet again. She claimed you'd seen me unconscious and decided to run away. She said that you had probably run to Alaska, that you couldn't go to Mexico because you didn't have a passport. She said that you'd been ill—in an institution, as a matter of fact—and that you were still unstable, still very weak in the head. My gut tells me that your auntie is in this mess up to her eyeballs."

"She welcomed me. She was sincere. You're wrong, James, or you're just plain lying."

"Maybe she was sincere at first. But then someone got to her. What about the two murders in The Cove, Sally? The woman's screams you heard that Amabel claimed were a result of the wind, that or the result of you being so bloody nuts."

"So you used those old people—Marge and Harve, who drove to The Cove in their Winnebago and then disappeared—as your, what do you call it? Oh, yes, your cover. The sheriff believed you completely, didn't he?"

"Yes, he did. And what's more, the investigation will open again, since a whole bunch of other folk have disappeared in that area as well. Being a PI hired by their son from L.A. was my cover. It worked. After the murders happened, I didn't know what to think. I knew it couldn't have anything to do with you directly."

He stopped, plowing his fingers through his hair. "Damn, we're getting off the subject, Sally. Forget about The Cove. Just forget Amabel. She and her town are three thousand miles away. I want you to try to understand why I did what I did. I want you to understand why I had to keep silent about who I really am and why I was at The Cove."

"You want me to agree that it was fine for you to lie to me, to manipulate me?"

"Yes. You lied to me as well, if you'll recall. All you had to do was scream your head off when your so-called father called you, and I was manipulated up to my ears. A beautiful woman appealing to my macho side. Yeah, I was hooked from that moment."

She was staring at him as if he'd lost his mind.

"Jesus, Sally, I came flying into the room like a madman to see you on the floor, staring at that damned phone like it was a snake ready to bite you, and I was a goner."

She waved away his words. "Someone was after me, James. Nobody was after you."

"It didn't matter."

She began to laugh. "Actually there were two someones after me, and you were the second, only I was too stupid, too pathetically grateful to you, to realize it. I'm leaving, James. I don't want to see you again. I can't believe I thought you were a hero. God, when will I stop being such a credulous fool?"

"Where will you go?"

"That's none of your business, Mr. Quinlan. None of what I do is any of your business anymore."

"The hell it isn't. Listen, Sally. Tell me the truth about something. When Savich and I got into your room at the sanitarium, there was this pathetic little guy who looked crazy as a loon sitting on the bed beside you, looking down at you. Did he ever hurt you? Beat you? Rape you?"

"Holland was there in my room?"

"Yeah, you were naked and he was leaning down over you. I think he'd combed and straightened your hair. Did he rape you?"

"No," she said in a remote voice. "No one raped me. As for Holland, he did other things, that Beadermeyer told him to do. He never hurt me, just—well, that's not important."

"Then who the hell did hurt you? That bloody Beadermeyer? Your husband? Who was that man you told me about in your nightmare?"

She gave him a long look, and again that look was filled with quiet rage. "You are nothing more to me. None of this is any of your business. Go to hell, James."

She turned away from him and walked down the wooden steps. It was chilly now. She wasn't wearing anything but that too-small shirt and jeans.

"Come back, Sally. I can't let you go. I won't let you go. I won't see you hurt again."

She didn't even slow down, just kept walking, in sneakers that were probably too small for her as well. He didn't want her to get blisters. He'd planned to go shopping for her tomorrow, to buy her some clothes that fit her, to—damn, he was losing it.

He saw Savich standing near the water line, unaware that she was walking away.

"Sally, you don't know where you are. You don't have any money."

Then she did stop. She was smiling as she turned to face him. "You're right, but it shouldn't be a problem for long. I really don't think I'm afraid of any man anymore. Don't worry. I'll get enough money to get back to Washington."

It sent him right over the edge. He slammed his hand down on the railing and vaulted over it to land lightly only three feet away from her. "No one will ever hurt you again. You will not take the chance of some asshole raping you. You will stay with me until this is over. Then I'll let you go if you don't want to stay."

She began to laugh. Her body shook with her laughter. She sank slowly to her knees, hugging herself, laughing and laughing.

"Sally!"

She stared up at him, her palms on her thighs. She laughed, then said, "Let me go? You'd keep me if I didn't want to leave? Like some sort of pathetic stray? That's good, James. I haven't known a single person for a very long time who cared one whit about anyone, including me, not that it mattered. Please, no more lies.

"I'm a case for you, nothing more. If you solve it, just think of your reputation. The FBI will probably make you director. They'll kiss your feet. The president will give you a medal."

She gasped, out of breath now, hiccuping through the laughter that welled up from her throat. "You should have believed my file, James. Yes, I'm sure the FBI has a very thick file on me, particularly my stint in the loony bin. I'm crazy, James. No one should believe I'm a credible witness, despite the fact that you want very badly to have someone to lock up, anyone.

"I won't tell you anything. I don't trust you, but I do owe you for rescuing me from that place. Now let me go before something horrible happens."

He came down on his knees in front of her. Very slowly, he pulled her arms to her sides. He brought her forward until her face was resting against his shoulder. He rubbed his hands up and down her back. "It's going to be all right, I swear it to you. I swear I won't fuck up again."

She didn't move, didn't settle against him, didn't release the terrible rage that had been deep inside her for so long she didn't know if she could ever confront it, or speak about it, because it could very well destroy her, and the sheer magnitude of it would destroy others as well.

It bubbled deep, that rage, and now with it was a shattering sense of betrayal. She'd trusted him and he'd betrayed her. She felt stupid for having believed him so quickly, so completely.

Sally marveled that she felt such passion, such a hideous need to hurt as she'd been hurt. She'd thought he'd drained such savage feelings out of her long ago. It felt incredible to feel rage again, to feel sweat rise on her flesh, to want to do something, to want vengeance. Yes, she wanted vengeance.

She just lay against him, thinking, wondering, calming herself, and in the end of it all, she still didn't know what to do.

"You've got to help me now, Sally."

"If I don't, then you'll take me to the FBI dungeon and they'll give me more drugs to make me tell the truth?"

"No, but the FBI will get all the truth sooner or later. We usually do. Your father's murder is a very big deal, not just his murder but lots of other things that are connected to it. Lots of folk want to be in on catching his murderer. It's important for a lot of reasons. No more crap about you not being credible. If you'll just help me now, you'll be free of all this evil."

"Funny that you call it evil."

"I don't know why I did. That sounds a bit melodramatic, but somehow it just came out. Is it evil, Sally?"

She said nothing, just stared ahead, her thoughts far away from him, and he hated it. He wanted to know what was going through her mind. He imagined it wasn't pleasant.

"If you help me, I'll get your passport and take you to Mexico."

That brought her back for a moment. She said with a quirky smile that she probably hadn't worn on her face in a very long time, "I don't want to go to Mexico. I've been there three times and got vilely sick all three times."

"There's this drug you can take before going. It's supposed to keep your innards safe from the foreign bugs. I used it once when I went down to La Paz on a fishing trip with my buddies and I never got sick and we were on the water most of the time."

"I can't imagine you ever getting sick from anything. No bug would want to take up residence inside you. Too little to show for it."

"You're talking to me."

"Oh, yes. Talking calms me. It makes all that bile settle down a bit. And just listen to you, talking to the little victim, trying to soothe and calm her, gain her trust. You're really very good, the way you use your voice, your tone, your choice of words.

"Forget it, James. I've got even more to say. In fact, I think I've got it all together now.

"If you'll notice, Mr. Quinlan, I've got your gun pointed at your belly. Try to squeeze me or hurt me or jerk it away from me with one of your fancy moves, and I'll pull the trigger."

He felt then the nose of his SIG-Sauer pressing against his gut. He hadn't felt it even a second before. How the hell had she gotten it out of his shoulder holster? The fact that she'd gotten it without his realizing it scared him more than knowing the pistol had a hair trigger and her finger was on it.

He said against her hair, "I guess this means you're still pissed at me, huh?"

"Yes."

"I guess this means you don't want to talk about Mexico anymore? You don't like deep-sea fishing?"

"I've never done it. But no, the time for talking is over."

He said very quietly and slowly, "That gun is perfectly balanced and will respond practically to your thoughts. Please be careful. Sally, don't think any violent thoughts, okay?"

"I'll try not to, but don't push me. Now, James, just fall over onto your back and don't even think about kicking out with your feet. No, don't stiffen up like that or I'll shoot you. I've got nothing to lose, don't ever forget that."

"It's not a good idea, Sally. Let's talk some more."

"FALL ON YOUR BACK!"

"Well, hell." He dropped his arms to his sides as he keeled over backward. He could have tried kicking up, but he couldn't be sure that he wouldn't hurt her badly. He lay on his back watching her rise to stand over him, the pistol in her hand. She looked very proficient with that damned gun. She never looked away from him, not even for an instant.

"Have you ever fired a gun before?"

"Oh, yes. You needn't worry that I'll shoot myself in the foot. Now, James, don't even twitch." She backed away from him, up the steps to the veranda. She got his jacket, felt inside the breast pocket and found his wallet. "I hope you've got enough money," she said.

"I went to the cash machine just before coming to rescue you, dammit."

"That was nice of you. Don't worry, James." She gave him a small salute with his gun, then threw his jacket over her arm. "Your good buddy will be back soon to make your dinner. I think I heard him talking about some halibut. The lake doesn't look polluted, so maybe it won't poison you. Did I ever tell you that my father headed up this citizens' committee that was always haranguing against pollution?

"But who cares, when it comes right down to it? No, don't say it. I'm talking. It feels rather good actually. So you see, no matter what else the bastard did, he did accomplish some good.

"Oh, yeah, Mr. Quinlan, you wanted to know all the juicy details about who did what to me in the sanitarium. You're dying to know who did it, who put me there. Well, it wasn't Dr. Beadermeyer or my husband. It was my father."

And how, she wondered, could she ever get vengeance on a dead man? She was off in a flash, running faster than he'd thought she could, dust kicking up behind her sneakers.

She was at the car when he jumped to his feet. He didn't think, just sprinted as fast as he could toward the Oldsmobile. He saw her stop by the driver's door and aim quickly, then he felt the dirt spray his jeans leg as a bullet kicked up not a foot from his right boot. Then she was inside. The car engine revved. She was fast.

He watched her throw the car in reverse, watched her back it out of the narrow driveway onto the small country road. She did it well, coming close to that elm tree but not touching the paint job on the car, which was nice of her because the government was never pleased when it had to repaint bureau cars.

He was running after her again, knowing he had to do something, but not knowing what, just accepting that he was a fool and an incompetent ass and running, running.

Her father had beat her and fondled her and humiliated her in the sanitarium? He'd been the one to put her there in the first place?

Why?

It was nuts, the whole thing. And that's why she hadn't told him. Her father was dead, couldn't be grilled, and the whole thing did sound crazy.

"Rein in, Quinlan," Savich shouted from behind him. "Come on back. She's well and truly gone."

He turned to see Savich run up behind him. "Last time I checked your speed on the track you couldn't beat an accelerating Olds."

"Yeah, yeah. Damn, it's all my fault. You don't have to say it."

"There's hardly any need to say it. How did she get your gun?"

Quinlan turned to his longtime friend, shoved his hands in the pockets of his jeans, and said in the most bewildered voice Savich had ever heard from him, "I was holding her against me, trying to make her understand that I did what I had to do and I wasn't betraying her, really I wasn't, and I thought perhaps she was coming around.

"Looks like I really screwed up on this one. I never felt a thing. Nothing. Then she told me she was pointing the gun in my gut. She was."

"I don't think I like having a partner who's so besotted that he can't even keep his own gun in his holster."

"Is that some sort of weird sexual innuendo?"

"Not at all. My cell phone's inside. I hope she didn't take it."

"She never went inside the cottage."

"Thank God for small favors. It's about time we got one."

Quinlan said, "Are your connections good enough to get us another one?"

"If not, I'll call my aunt Paulie. Between her Uncle Abe, they've got more connections than the pope."

SHE KNEW JAMES would come here, maybe not immediately, but soon enough. She also knew she had time. Too bad she hadn't thought to take their cell phones. That would have really slowed him up. But she had enough of a head start.

She pulled the Oldsmobile into an empty parking spot just off

Cooperton Street. She locked the door and walked slowly, wearing James's jacket, which should make her look very hip, toward number 337, the gracious Georgian red-brick home on Lark Street. Lights were on downstairs. She prayed Noelle was there and not the police or the FBI.

She huddled low and ran along the tap line of shrubbery toward the downstairs library. Her father's office. The room where she'd first seen her father strike her mother. That had been ten years ago. Ten years. What had happened to those years? College, with nightly phone calls and more visits than she cared to make, even unexpected visits during the week to make sure her father wasn't beating her mother.

She'd sensed the festering anger in her father at her interference, but his position, more highly visible by the year, his absolute horror of anyone finding out that he was a wife beater, kept him in line, at least most of the time. As it turned out, she found out that if he was pissed off, he would beat her mother as soon as Sally left to go back to college. Not that her mother would ever have told her.

On one visit she'd forgotten a sweater and had gone quickly back home to get it. She'd opened the front door with her key and walked into the library, in on a screaming match with her mother cowering on the floor and her father kicking her.

"I'm calling the police," she said calmly from the doorway. "I don't care what happens. This will stop and it will stop now."

Her father froze, his leg in mid-kick, and stared at her in the doorway. "You damned little bitch. What the hell are you doing here?"

"I'm calling the police now. It's over." She walked back into the foyer to the phone that sat on the small Louis XVI table, beneath a beautiful gilt mirror.

She'd dialed 9-1- when her hand was grabbed. It was her mother. It was Noelle, and she was crying, begging her not to call the police, begging, on her knees, begging and begging, tears streaming down her face.

Sally stared down at the woman who was clutching at her knees, tears of pain grooving down her cheeks. Then she looked at her father, who was standing in the doorway to the library, his arms crossed over his chest, his ankles crossed, tall and slender, beautifully dressed in cashmere and wool, his hair thick and dark, with brilliant gray threading through it, looking like a romantic lead in the movies. He was watching her.

"Go ahead, do it," he said. "Do it and just see what your mother will do when the cops get here. She'll say you're a liar, Sally, that you're a jealous little bitch, that you don't want her to have my affection, that you've always resented her, resented your own mother.

"Isn't that why you're coming home all the time from college? Go ahead, Sally. Do it. You'll see." He never moved, just spoke in that intoxicating, mesmerizing voice of his, one that had swayed his colleagues and clients for the past thirty years. He kept a hint of a Southern drawl, knowing it added just the right touch when he deftly slurred the word he wanted to emphasize.

"Please, Sally, don't. Don't. I'm begging you. You can't. It would ruin everything. I can't allow you to. It's dangerous. It's all right, Sally. Just don't call, please, don't call."

She gave her mother and her father one last look and left. She did not return until after her graduation seven months later.

Maybe her father was beating her mother less simply because Sally wasn't coming home anymore.

Funny that she hadn't been able to remember that episode until now. Not until . . . not until she'd gone to The Cove and met James and her life had begun to seem like a life again, despite the murders, despite her father's phone calls, despite everything.

She must really be nuts. The damned man had betrayed her. There was no way around that. He'd saved her too, but that didn't count, it was just more of the job. She still marveled at her own simplicity. He was FBI. He'd tracked her down and lied to her.

She huddled down even more as she neared the library windows. She looked inside. Her mother was reading a book. She was sitting in her husband's favorite wing chair, reading a book. She looked exquisite.

Well, she should. The bastard had been dead for a good three weeks. No more bruises. No more chance of bruises.

Still, Sally waited. No one else was in the house.

"YOU'RE SURE SHE'S GOING HOME, Quinlan?"

"Not home. She's going to her mother's house. Not her husband's house. You know my intuition, my gut. But to be honest about it, I know her. She feels something for her mother. That's the first place she'll go. I'll bet you both her father and her husband put her in that sanitarium in the first place. Why? I haven't the foggiest idea. I do know, though, that her father was a very evil man."

"I assume you'll tell me what you mean by that later?"

"Drive faster, Savich. The house is number three thirty-seven on Lark. Yeah, I'll tell you, but not now. Let's get going."

"HELLO, NOELLE."

Noelle St. John slowly lowered her novel to her lap. Just as slowly, she looked up at the doorway to see her daughter standing there, wearing a man's jacket that came nearly to her knees.

Her mother didn't move, just stared at her. When she was younger, her mother was always holding her, hugging her, kissing her. She wasn't moving now. Well, if she believed Sally was crazy, then it made sense. Did Noelle think her daughter was here to shoot her? She said in a soft, frightened voice, "Is it really you, Sally?"

"Yes. I got away from the sanitarium again. I got away from Dr. Beadermeyer."

"But why, darling? He takes such good care of you. Doesn't he? Why are you looking at me like that, Sally? What's wrong?"

Then nothing mattered, because her mother was smiling at her. Her mother jumped to her feet and ran to her, enfolding her in her arms. Years were instantly stripped away. She was small again. She was safe. Her mother was holding her. Sally felt immense gratitude. Her mother was here for her, as she'd prayed she would be.

"Mama, you've got to help me. Everyone is after me."

Noelle stood back, smoothing Sally's hair, running her hands over her pale face. She hugged her again, whispering against her cheek. "It's all right, sweetheart. I'll take care of everything. It's all right." Noelle was shorter than her daughter, but she was the mother and Sally was the child, and to Sally she felt like a goddess.

She let herself be held, breathed in her mother's fragrance, a scent she'd worn from Sally's earliest memories. "I'm sorry, Noelle. Are you all right?"

Her mother released her, stepping back. "It's been difficult, what with the police and not knowing where you were and worrying incessantly. You should have called me, Sally. I worried so much about you."

"I couldn't. I imagined that the police had your phone bugged. They could have traced me."

"I don't think there's anything wrong with the phones. Surely they wouldn't dare plant devices like that in your father's home?"

"He's dead, Noelle. They'd do anything. Now, listen. I need you to tell me the truth. I do know that I was here the night that he was murdered. But I don't remember anything about it. Just violent images, but no faces. Just loud voices, but no person to go with the voices."

"It's all right, love. I didn't murder your father. I know that's why you ran away. You ran away to protect me, just as you tried to protect me for all those years.

"Do you believe me? Why would you think I'd know anything about it? I wasn't here myself. I was with Scott, your husband. He's so worried about you. All he can talk about is you and how he prays you'll come home. Please tell me you believe me. I wouldn't kill your father."

"Yes, Noelle, I believe you—although if you had shot him I would have applauded you. But no, I never really believed that you did. But I can't remember. I just can't remember, and the police and the FBI, they all believe I know everything that happened that night. Won't you tell me what happened, Noelle?"

"Are you well again, Sally?"

She stared at her mother. She sounded vaguely frightened. Of her? Of her own daughter? Did she think she would murder her because she was insane? Sally shook her head. Noelle might look a bit frightened, but she also looked exquisite in vivid emerald lounging pajamas. Her light hair was pinned up with a gold clip. She wore three thin gold chains. She looked young and beautiful and vital. Perhaps there was some justice after all.

"Listen to me, Noelle," Sally said, willing her mother to believe her. "I wasn't ever sick. Father put me in that place. It was all a plot. He wanted me out of the way. Why? I don't know. Maybe just plain revenge for the way I'd thwarted him for the past ten years. Surely you must have guessed something. Doubted him when he told you. You never came to see me, Mama, never."

"Your father told me, and you're right, I was suspicious, but then Scott broke down—he was in tears—and he told me about all the things you'd done, how you simply weren't yourself anymore and there hadn't been any choice but to put you in the sanitarium. I met Dr. Beadermeyer. He assured me you would be well cared for.

"Oh, Sally, Dr. Beadermeyer told me it would be better if I didn't see you just yet, that you were blaming me for so many things, that you hated me, that you didn't want to see me, that seeing me would just make you worse and he feared you'd try to commit suicide again."

But Sally wasn't listening to her. She felt something prickle on her skin, and she knew, she *knew* he was close. She also knew that her mother wasn't telling her the truth about the night her father was murdered. Why? What had really happened that night? There just wasn't time now.

Yes, James was close. There was no unnatural sound, no real warning, yet she knew.

"Do you have any money, Noelle?"

"Just a few dollars, Sally, but why? Why? Let me call Dr. Beader-meyer. He's already called several times. I've got to protect you, Sally."

"Good-bye, Noelle. If you love me—if you've ever loved me—please keep the FBI agent talking as long as you can. His name is James Quinlan. Please, don't tell him I was here."

"How do you know the name of an FBI agent?"

"It's not important. Please don't tell him anything, Noelle."

"MRS. ST. JOHN, we saw the car parked on Cooperton. Sally was here. Is she still here? Are you hiding her?"

Noelle St. John stared at his ID, then at Savich's. Finally, after an eternity, she looked up and said, "I haven't seen my daughter for nearly seven months, Agent Quinlan. What car are you talking about?"

"A car we know she was driving, Mrs. St. John," Savich said.

"Why are you calling my daughter by her first name? Indeed, Sally is her nickname. Her real name is Susan. Where did you get her nickname?"

"It doesn't matter," Quinlan said. "Please, Mrs. St. John, you must help us. Would you mind if we looked through your house? Her car is parked just down the street. She's probably hiding here in the house waiting for us to leave before she comes out."

"That's ridiculous, gentlemen, but look to your hearts' content. None of the help sleep here, so the house is empty. Don't worry about frightening anyone." She smiled at them and walked with her elegant stride back into the library.

"Upstairs first," Quinlan said.

They went methodically from room to room, Savich waiting in the corridor as Quinlan searched, to ensure that Sally couldn't slip between adjoining rooms and elude them. When Quinlan opened the door to a bedroom at the far end of the hall, he knew immediately that it had been hers. He switched on the light. It wasn't a frilly room with a pink or white canopied bed and posters of rock stars plastering the walls. No, three of the walls were filled with bookshelves, all of them stuffed with books. On the fourth wall were framed awards, writing awards beginning with ones for papers she'd written in junior high school on the U.S. dependence on foreign oil and the gasoline crisis, on the hostages in Iran, on the countries that became communist during Carter's administration and why. There was a paper that had won the Idleberg Award and appeared in the *New York Times* on the U.S. hockey win against the Russians at Lake Placid at the 1980 Olympics. The high school awards were for papers that ran more toward literary themes.

Then they stopped, somewhere around the end of high school—no more awards, no more recognition for excellent short stories or essays, at least no more here in this bedroom. She'd gone to Georgetown University, majored in English. Again, no more sign that she'd ever written another word or won another prize.

"Quinlan, for God's sake, what are you doing? Is she in there or not?"

He was shaking his head when he rejoined Savich. He said, "Sally isn't here. Sure, she was here, but she's long gone. Somehow she knew we were close. How, I don't know, but she knew. Let's go, Savich."

"You don't think her mother would have any idea, do you?"

"Get real." But they asked Mrs. St. John anyway. She gave them a blank smile and sent them on their way.

"What now, Quinlan?"

"Let me think." Quinlan hunched over the steering wheel, wishing he had a cup of coffee, not good coffee, but the rotgut stuff at the bureau. He drove to FBI headquarters at Tenth and Pennsylvania, the ugliest building ever constructed in the nation's capital.

Ten minutes later, he was sipping on the stuff that could be used to plug a hole in a dike. He took Savich a cup and set it near the mouse pad at his right hand.

"Okay, she's got the Oldsmobile."

"No APB, Savich."

Savich swiveled around in his chair, the computer screen glowing behind his head. "You can't just keep this a two-man hunt, Quinlan. We lost her. You and I, my friend, lost a rank amateur. Don't you think it's time to spread the net?"

"Not yet. She's also got my wallet. See what you can do with that."

"If she keeps purchases below fifty dollars, chances are no one will check. Still, if someone does check, we'll have her almost instantly. Hold on a minute and let me set that up."

Savich had big hands, long, blunt fingers. Quinlan watched those unlikely fingers race over the computer keys. Savich hit a final key and nodded in satisfaction. "There's just something about computers," he said over his shoulder to Quinlan. "They never give you trouble, they never contradict you. You tell 'em what to do in simple language and they do it."

"They don't love you, either."

"In their way they do. They're so clean, Quinlan. Now, if she uses one of your credit cards and there's no check, then I've got her within eighteen hours. It's not the best, but it'll have to do."

"She might have to use a credit card, but she'll keep it below fifty dollars. She's not stupid. Did you know she won a statewide contest for a paper she wrote about how much credit card crooks cost the American public? You'd better believe she knows she's bought eighteen hours, and she might figure that's just enough, thank you."

"How do you know that? Surely you had other things to talk about with her? You had two murders in that little picturesque town, and the two of you found both bodies. Surely that's enough fodder for conversation for at least three hours."

"When I was in her bedroom I saw that the walls are loaded with awards for papers, short stories, essays, all sorts of stuff that she wrote. That credit card essay was one of them. She must have been all of sixteen when she wrote it."

"So she's a good writer, even a talented writer. She's still a rank amateur. She's scared. She doesn't know what to do. Everyone is after her, and we're probably the best-meaning of the lot, but it didn't matter to her. She still poked your own gun in your belly."

"Don't whine. She has around three hundred dollars in cash. That's not going to take her far. On the other hand, she got all the way across the country on next to no money at all riding a Greyhound bus."

"You don't keep your PIN number in your wallet, do you?"

"No."

"Good. Then she can't get out any more cash in your name."

Quinlan sat down in a swivel chair beside Savich's. He steepled his fingers and tapped the fingertips together rhythmically. "There's something she said, Savich, something that nearly tore my guts apart, something about no one she'd been around cared about anybody but himself. I think she trusted me so quickly because something inside her desperately needs to be reaffirmed."

"You're sounding like a shrink."

"No, listen. She's scared just like you said, but she needs someone to believe her and care about what happens to her, someone to accept that she isn't crazy, someone simply to believe her, without reservation, without hesitation.

"She thought I did, and she was right, only, you know the answer to that. She was locked up in that place for six months. Everyone told her she was nuts. She needs trust, complete unquestioning trust."

"So who would give her unconditional trust? Her mother? I can't believe that, even though Sally went to see her first. There's something weird going on with Mrs. St. John. Sure as hell not her husband, Scott Brainerd, although I'd like to meet the guy, maybe rearrange his face a bit."

Quinlan got out her file. "Let's see about friends."

He read quietly for a very long time while Savich put all systems in place to kick in whenever Sally used one of the credit cards.

"Interesting," Quinlan said, leaning back and rubbing his eyes. "She had several very good women friends, most of them associated with

Congress. Then after she married Scott Brainerd, the friends seemed to fade away over the period before Daddy committed her to Beadermeyer's charming resort."

"That cuts things down, but it doesn't help us. You don't think she'd go to her husband, do you? I can't imagine it, but—"

"No way in hell."

There was a flash and a beep on the computer screen. "Well, I'll be swiggered," Savich said, rubbing his hands together. He punched in several numbers and added two more commands.

"She used a credit card for gas. The amount is just twenty-two fifty, but it's their policy to check all credit cards, regardless of the amount. She's in Delaware, Quinlan, just outside of Wilmington. Hot damn."

"Wilmington isn't that far from Philadelphia."

"It isn't that far from anywhere, except maybe Cleveland."

"No, that's not what I meant. Her grandparents live on the Main Line just outside of Philadelphia. Real ritzy section. Street name's Fisher Road."

"Fisher Road? Doesn't sound ritzy."

"Don't let the name fool you. I have a feeling Fisher Road will wind up being one of those streets with big stone mansions set back a good hundred feet from the road. Gates too, I'll bet."

"We'll see soon enough. It's her mother's parents who live there. Their name is Harrison. Mr. and Mrs. Franklin Ogilvee Harrison."

"I don't suppose Mrs. Harrison has a name?"

"Nah, if the guy is rich and old, that's the way they do it. I've wondered if sometimes they just make up that highbrow middle name for effect."

17

"I MEANT TO tell you why Sally used a credit card and not some of your three hundred bucks."

Savich was driving, handling his Porsche with the same ease and skill he used with computers.

Quinlan was reading everything he had on the grandparents with a small penlight. He had to look up every few minutes so he wouldn't throw up. "I hate reading in a car. My sister used to read novels all the time—in the back seat—never bothered her for an instant. I'd look at a picture and want to throw up. What did you say, Savich? Oh, yeah, why Sally used the credit card. While you were getting your coat, I checked the rest of the information they gave on the credit card check. The license plate number was different. She bought a clunker, probably used about every cent of that three hundred bucks."

Savich grunted. "Hand me the coffee. Another hour and we'll be there."

"It took time for her to sell the Olds and buy the clunker. It cut down on her lead. Let's say she's got two hours on us. That's not too bad."

"Let's hope she doesn't realize you're anywhere in the vicinity, like you seem to believe she did last time at her mother's."

"She did know. Listen to this. Mr. Franklin Ogilvee Harrison is the president and CEO of the First Philadelphia Union Bank. He owns three clothing stores called the Gentleman's Purveyor. His father owned the two largest steel mills in Pennsylvania, got out before the bottom fell out, and left his family millions. As for Mrs. Harrison, she comes from the Boston Thurmonds, who are all in public office, lots of old money from shipping. Two daughters, Amabel and Noelle, and a son,

Geoffrey, who's got Down's syndrome and is kept at a very nice private place near Boston."

"You want to stop at that gas station in Wilmington? We'll be there in half an hour."

"Let's do it. Someone will remember the kind of car she was driving."

"If she got something for three hundred bucks, it would really stand out."

But the guy who'd sold her the gas had gone home. They drove straight on to Philadelphia.

SALLY LOOKED from her grandfather Franklin to her grandmother Olivia. She'd seen them two or three times a year every year of her life, except this past year.

Their downstairs maid, Cecilia, had let her in, not blinked an eye at her huge men's coat over the too tight blouse and jeans, and calmly led her to the informal study at the back of the house. Her grandparents were watching *Friends* on TV.

Cecilia didn't announce her, just left her there and quietly closed the door. Sally didn't say anything for a long time. She just stood there, listening to her grandfather give an occasional chuckle. Her grandmother had a book on her lap, but she wasn't reading, she was watching TV as well. They were both seventy-six, in excellent health, and enjoyed the Jumby Bay private resort island off Antigua twice a year.

Sally waited for a commercial, then said, "Hello, Grandfather, Grandmother."

Her grandmother's head jerked around, and she cried out, "Susan!"

Her grandfather said, "Is that really you, Susan? By all that's holy, my poor child, whatever are you doing here?"

Neither of them moved from the sofa. They seemed nailed to their seats. Her grandmother's book slid from her lap to the beautiful Tabriz carpet.

Sally took a step toward them. "I hoped you could give me some money. There are a lot of people looking for me, and I need to hide someplace. I only have about seventeen dollars."

Franklin Harrison rose slowly. He was wearing a smoking jacket and an ascot—she hadn't known those things were still even made. She suddenly had an image of him wearing the same thing when she'd been a very young girl. She remembered how he'd held her and let her stroke the soft silk of the ascot. His white hair was thick and wavy, his eyes a dark blue, his cheekbones high, but his mouth was small and tight. It seemed smaller and tighter now.

Olivia Harrison rose as well, straightening the silk dress she was wearing. She held out her hand. "Susan, dear, why aren't you with that lovely Dr. Beadermeyer? You didn't escape again, did you? That's not a good thing for you, dear, not good for you at all, particularly with all the scandal that your father's death has produced."

"He didn't just die, Grandmother, he was murdered."

"Yes, we know. All of us have suffered. But now we're concerned about you, Susan. Your mother has told us how much Dr. Beadermeyer has done for you, how much better you've gotten. We met him once and were very impressed with him. Wasn't that nice of him to come to Philadelphia to meet us? You are better, aren't you, Susan? You aren't still seeing things that aren't there, are you? You're not still blaming people for things they didn't do?"

"No, Grandmother. I never did any of those things." Strange how neither of them wanted to come close to her.

"You know, dear," her grandmother continued in that gentle voice of hers that masked pure iron, "your grandfather and I have discussed this, and we hate to say it, but it's possible that you're like your uncle Geoffrey. Your illness is probably hereditary, and so it isn't really your fault. Let me call Dr. Beadermeyer, dear."

Sally could only stare at her grandmother. "Uncle Geoffrey was born with Down's syndrome. It has nothing to do with mental illness."

"Yes, but it perhaps shows that instability can be somewhat genetic, passed down from a mother or a father to the daughter. But that's not important. What's important is getting you back to that nice sanitarium so Dr. Beadermeyer can treat you. Before your father died, he called us every week to tell us how much better you were getting. Well, there were weeks with setbacks, but he said that in the main, you were improving with the new drug therapies."

What could she say to that? Tell them all the truth as she remembered it and watch their faces go from disbelief to fury on her account? Not likely.

She saw the years upon years of inflexibility, the utter rigidity, in her grandmother. She remembered what Aunt Amabel had told her about when Noelle had come home, beaten by her husband, when Sally was just a baby. How they hadn't believed Noelle.

It had always been there, of course, this rigidity, but since Sally had seen her grandmother so infrequently, she'd never had it turned on her. More clearly than ever, Sally could see now how her grandmother had treated her daughter Noelle when she'd come here begging for help. She shuddered.

"Well," her grandfather said, all hale and hearty, so good-natured, so weak, "it's good to see you, dear. I know you don't have time to stay, do you? Why not let us send you back to Washington? Like you grandmother said, this Beadermeyer fellow seemed to be doing you a great deal of good."

She looked from one to the other. Her grandfather, as tall as James, or at least he used to be, a man who had lived his life by a set of rules of his wife's making—or perhaps his father's—a man who didn't mind if someone strayed from the proper course but who wouldn't defend that person if his wife was anywhere near.

She'd always believed him so dear, so kind, but he wasn't coming anywhere near her, either—she wondered what he really thought of her. She wondered why he had that tight, mean mouth. She said, "I was in The Cove. I stayed for a while with Aunt Amabel."

"We don't speak of her," her grandmother said, taller now because her back had gotten stiffer. "She made her bed and now she must—"

"She's very happy."

"She can't be. She disgraced herself and her family, marrying that absurd man who painted for a living, *painted pictures!*"

"Aunt Amabel is an excellent artist."

"Your aunt dabbled at many things, nothing more. If she were a good painter, then why haven't we heard of her? You see, no one has. She lives in this backwater town and exists on a shoestring. Forget about Amabel. Your grandfather and I are sorry you saw her. We can't give you money, Susan. I'm sure your grandfather would agree. Surely you understand why."

She looked her grandmother right in the eye. "No, I don't understand. Tell me why you won't give me money."

"Susan, dear," her grandmother said, her voice all low and soothing, "you're not well. We're sorry for it and a bit stunned, since this sort of thing has never before been in the family except, of course, for your uncle Geoffrey.

"We can't give you money because you could use it to hurt yourself even more. If you would just sit down here, even stay the night, we will call Dr. Beadermeyer and he can come and get you. Trust us, dear."

"Yes, Susan, trust us. We've always loved you, always wanted the best for you."

"You mean the way you sent your daughter, my mother, back to a man who beat her?"

"Susan!"

"It's true, and both of you know it. He beat the living shit out of her whenever he felt like it."

"Don't use that kind of word in front of your grandmother, Susan," her grandfather said, and she saw that mouth of his go stern and tight.

She just looked at him, wondering why she'd even come here, but still, she had to try. She had to have money.

"I tried to protect Noelle for years, but I couldn't save her because she let him do it—do you hear me?—Noelle let him beat her. She was just like all those pathetic women you hear about."

"Don't be stupid, Susan," her grandmother said in a voice that could have crushed gravel. "Your grandfather and I have discussed this, and we know that battered wives are weak and stupid women. They're dependent. They have no motivation. They have no desire to better themselves. They aren't able to leave their situations because they've bred like rabbits and the men they're married to drink and don't have any money."

"Your grandmother is perfectly correct, Susan. They aren't our kind at all. They are to be pitied, certainly, but don't ever put your dear mother in that class."

"Amabel told me how Noelle came here once—it was early on in her marriage—and told you both what my father was doing. You didn't want to hear about it. You insisted she go back. You turned her away. You were horrified. Did you even think she was making it up?"

Sally thought for a wild moment that this was surely the wrong way to go about getting money from them. She hadn't realized all this resentment toward them was bottled up inside her.

"We will not speak of your mother to you, Susan," her grandmother said. She nodded slightly to her husband, but Susan saw it. He took a step toward her. She wondered if he would try to hold her down and tie her up and call Dr. Beadermeyer. In that moment, she truly wanted him to try. She wouldn't mind hitting that tight, mean mouth of his that masked weakness and preached platitudes.

She took a step back, her hands in front of her. "Listen, I need some money. Please, if you have any feeling for me at all, give me some money."

"What are you wearing, Susan? That's a man's jacket. What have you done? You haven't harmed some innocent person, have you? Please, what have you done?"

She'd been a fool to come here. What had she expected? They were so set in their ways that a bulldozer couldn't budge them. They saw things one way, only one—her grandmother's way.

"You're not well, are you, Susan? If you were, you wouldn't be wearing those clothes that are so distasteful. Would you like to lie down for a while and we can call Dr. Beadermeyer?"

Her grandfather was moving toward her again, and she knew then that he would try to hold her here.

She had a trump card, and she played it. She even smiled at the two old people who perhaps had loved her once, in their way. "The FBI is after me. They'll be here soon. You don't want the FBI to get me, do you, Grandfather?"

He stopped cold and looked at his wife, whose face had paled.

She said, "How could they possibly know you were coming here?"

"I know one of the agents. He's smarter than anyone has a right to be. He also has this gut instinct about things. I've seen him in action. Count on it. He'll be here soon now with his partner. If they find me here, they'll take me back. Then everything will come out. I'll tell the world how my father—that larger-than-life, very rich lawyer—beat my mother and how you didn't care, how you ignored it, how you pretended everything was fine, happy to bask in the additional glory that such a successful son-in-law brought you."

"You're not a very nice girl, Susan," her grandmother said, two spots of bright red appearing on her very white cheeks. Anger, probably. "It's because you're ill, you know. You didn't used to be this way."

"Give me money and I'll be out of here in a flash. Keep talking, and the FBI will be here and haul me off."

Her grandfather didn't look at his wife this time. He pulled out his wallet. He didn't count the money, just took out all the bills, folded them, and thrust them toward her. He didn't want to touch her. She wondered about that again. Was he afraid he'd go nuts if he did?

"You should immediately drive back to Dr. Beadermeyer," he said to her, speaking slowly, as if she were an idiot. "He'll protect you. He'll keep you safe from the police and the FBI."

She stuffed the bills into her jeans pocket. It was a tight fit. "Good-bye, and thank you for the money." She paused a moment, her hand on the doorknob. "What does either of you know about Dr. Beadermeyer?"

"He came highly recommended, dear. Go back to him. Do as your grandfather says. Go back."

"He's a horrible man. He held me prisoner there. He did terrible things to me. But then again, so did my father. Of course, you wouldn't believe that, would you? He's so wonderful—rather, he was so wonderful. Doesn't it bother you that your son-in-law was murdered? That's rather low on the social ladder, isn't it?"

They just stared at her.

"Good-bye." But before she could leave the room, her grandmother called out. "Why are you saying things like this, Susan? I can't believe that you're doing this. Not just to us but to your poor mother as well. And what about your dear husband? You're not telling lies about him, are you?"

"Not a one," Sally said and slipped out of the room, closing the door behind her. She grinned briefly.

Cecilia was standing in the hall. She said, "I didn't call the cops. No one else is here. You don't have to worry. But hurry, Miss Susan, hurry."

"Do I know you?"

"No, but my mama always took care of you when your parents brought you here every year. She said you were the brightest little bean and so sweet. She told me how you could write the greatest poems for birthday cards. I still have several cards she made me that have your poems on them. Good luck, Miss Susan."

"Thank you, Cecilia."

"I'M AGENT QUINLAN and this is Agent Savich. Are Mr. and Mrs. Harrison here?"

"Yes, sir. Come with me, please." Cecilia led them to the study, just as she'd led Sally Brainerd there thirty minutes before. She closed the door after they'd gone in. She thought the Harrisons were now watching the Home Shopping Network. Mr. Harrison liked to see how the clothes hawked there compared with his.

She smiled. She wasn't about to tell them that Sally Brainerd now had money, although she didn't know how much she'd gotten from that niggardly old man. Only as much as Mrs. Harrison allowed him to give her. She wished Sally good luck.

SALLY STOPPED at an all-night convenience store and bought herself a ham sandwich and a Coke. She ate outside, well under the lights in front of the store. She waited until the last car had pulled out, then counted her money.

She laughed and laughed.

She had exactly three hundred dollars.

She was so tired she was weaving around like a drunk. The laughter was still bubbling out. She was getting hysterical.

A motel, that was what she needed, a nice, cheap motel. She needed to sleep a good eight hours, then she could go on.

She found one outside Philadelphia—the Last Stop Motel. She paid cash and endured the look of the old man who really didn't want to let her stay but couldn't bring himself to turn away the money she was holding in her hand.

Tomorrow, she thought, she would have to buy some clothes. She'd do it on a credit card and only spend $49.99. Fifty dollars was the cutoff, wasn't it?

She wondered, as she finally fell asleep on a bed that was wonderfully firm, where James was.

"WHERE TO NOW, Quinlan?"

"Let me stop thinking violent thoughts. Damn them. Sally was there. Why wouldn't they help us?"

"They love her and want to protect her?"

"Bullshit. I got cold when I got within three feet of them."

"It was interesting what Mrs. Harrison said," Savich said as he turned on the ignition in the Porsche. "About Sally being ill and she hoped soon she would be back with that nice Dr. Beadermeyer."

"I'll bet you a week's salary that they called the good doctor the minute Sally was out of there. Wasn't it strange the way Mrs. Harrison tried to make Mr. Harrison look like the strong, firm one? I'd hate to go toe-to-toe with that old battle-ax. She's the scary one in that family. I wonder if they gave her any money."

"I hope so," James said. "It makes my belly knot up to think of her driving a clunker around without a dime to her name."

"She's got your credit cards. If they didn't give her any money, she'll have to use them."

"I'll bet you Sally is dead on her rear. Let's find a motel, and then we can take turns calling all the motels in the area."

They stayed at a Quality Inn, an approved lodging for FBI agents. Thirty minutes later, Quinlan was staring at the phone, just staring, so surprised he couldn't move.

"You found her? This fast?"

"She's not five miles from here, at a motel called the Last Stop. She didn't use her real name, but the old man thought she looked strange, what with that man's coat she was wearing and those tight clothes he said made her look like a hooker except he knew she wasn't, and that's why he let her stay. He said she looked scared and lost."

"Glory be," Savich said. "I'm not all that tired anymore, Quinlan."

"Let's go."

SALLY TOOK OFF her clothes—peeled the jeans off, truth be told, because they were so tight—and lay on the bed in the full-cut girls' cotton panties that Dillon Savich had bought for her. She didn't have a bra, which was why she had to keep James's coat on. The bra Savich had bought—a training bra—she could have used when she was eleven years old.

The bed was wonderful, firm—well, all right, hard as a rock, but that was better than falling into a trough. She closed her eyes.

She opened her eyes and stared at the ceiling. Through the cheap drapes she could see an all-night flashing neon sign: HOT HARVEY'S TOP-LESS GIRLS.

Great part of town she'd chosen.

She closed her eyes again, turned on her side, and wondered where James was. In Washington? She wondered what Noelle had said to him. Why hadn't Noelle told her the truth about that night? Maybe she would have if there'd been more time. Maybe. Had Noelle told her the truth, that both her father and her husband had conspired to put her in Beadermeyer's sanitarium? Both of them? And Noelle had bought it?

She wondered if her grandparents had called Dr. Beadermeyer, and if the Nazi was on his way to Philadelphia. No, he'd wait. He wouldn't want to chase shadows, and that's exactly what she was and planned to be. No one could catch her now. The three hundred dollars would get her to Maine. She'd go to Bar Harbor, get a job, and survive. The tourists would flow in in only three months, then she would have more cover than she'd ever need. No one would find her there. She knew she was seeing Bar Harbor through a seven-year-old's eyes, but it had been so magical; surely it couldn't be all that different now.

Where was James? He was close, she just knew it. She hadn't exactly felt him close, but as she'd told her grandparents, he was smarter than he had a right to be.

She devoutly hoped he was at home in Washington, in bed fast asleep, the way she should be right now but wasn't. How close was he?

"Damnation," she said aloud. She thought about it a few more minutes, then got out of bed. She would just get to Bar Harbor sooner than expected. Still, she'd spent $27.52 on this room. To waste that money was appalling, but she couldn't sleep.

She was out of the room within five minutes. She revved up her motorcycle and swung back onto the road, the garish lights from Hot Harvey's Topless Girls haloing around her helmeted head. It was odd, she thought, as she passed a Chevrolet—she could have sworn that James was nearby. But that wasn't possible.

JAMES WAS THE NAVIGATOR and on the lookout for the Last Stop Motel. When she pulled out not fifty feet ahead of them, at first he couldn't believe it. He shouted, "Good God. Wait, Savich, wait. Stop."

"Why, what's wrong?"

"My God, it's Sally."

"What Sally? Where?"

"On the motorcycle. I'd recognize my coat anywhere. She didn't buy a clunker, she bought a motorcycle. Let's go. What if we'd been thirty seconds later?"

"You're sure? That's Sally on that motorcycle? Yeah, you're right, that is your coat. It looks moth-eaten even from here. How do you want me to curb her in? It could be dangerous, what with her on that damned bike."

"Hang back for a while and let's think about this."

Savich kept the Porsche a good fifty feet behind Sally.

"That was a smart thing she did," Savich said. "Buying a motorcycle."

"They're dangerous as hell. She could break her neck riding that thing."

"Stop sounding like you're her husband, Quinlan."

"You want me to break your upper lip? Hey, what's going on here?"

Four motorcycles passed the Porsche and accelerated toward the single motorcycle ahead.

"This is all we need. A gang, you think?"

"Why not? Our luck has sucked so far. How many rounds of ammunition do you have?"

"Enough," Savich said briefly, his hands still loose and relaxed on the steering wheel, his eyes never leaving the road ahead. Traffic was very light going out of Philadelphia at this time of night.

"You feeling like the Lone Ranger again?"

"Why not?"

THE FOUR MOTORCYCLES formed a phalanx around Sally.

Just don't panic, Sally, Quinlan said over and over to himself. Just don't panic.

She'd never been so scared in her life. She had to laugh at that. Well, to tell the truth, at least she hadn't been this scared in the last five hours. Four of them, all guys, all riding gigantic Harleys, all of them in dark leather jackets. None of them was wearing a helmet. She should tell them they were stupid not to wear helmets. Maybe they didn't realize she was female. She felt her hair slapping against her shoulders. So much for that prayer.

What to do? More to the point, what would James do?

He'd say she was outnumbered and to get the hell out of there. She twisted the accelerator grip hard, but the four of them did the same, seemingly content for the moment just to keep their positions, hemming her in and scaring the hell out of her.

She thought of her precious two hundred and seventy-something dollars, all the money she had in the world. No, she wouldn't let them take that money. It was all she had.

She shouted to the guy next to her, "What do you want? Go away!"

The guy just laughed and called out, "Come with us. We've got a place up ahead you'll like."

She yelled, "No, go away!" Was the idiot serious? He wasn't a fat, revolting biker, like the stereotype was usually painted. He was lean, his hair was cut short, and he was wearing glasses.

He swerved his bike in closer, not a foot from her now. He called out, "Don't be afraid. Come with us. We're turning off at the next right. Al—the guy on your right—he's got a nice cozy little place not five miles from here. You could spend some time with us, maybe sack out. We figure you must have rolled some guy for that coat, whatever, it doesn't matter. Hey, we're good solid citizens. We promise."

"Yeah, right," she shouted, "just like the pope. You want me to come with you so you can rob me and rape me and probably kill me. Go to hell, buster!"

She sped up. The bike shot forward. She could have sworn she heard laughter behind her. She felt the gun in James's coat pocket. She leaned down close to the handlebars and prayed.

"LET'S GO, Savich."

Savich accelerated the Porsche and honked at the bikers, who swerved to the side of the highway. They heard curses and shouts behind them. Quinlan just grinned.

"Let's just keep us between her and the bikers," Quinlan said. "What do you think? Are we going to have to follow her until she runs out of gas?"

"I can get ahead of her, brake hard, and swing the car across the road in front of her."

"Not with the bikers still back there, we can't. Just stay close."

"In exactly one more minute she's going to look back," Savich said. "She's never seen the Porsche."

"Great. So she'll think not only some insane bikers are after her but also a guy in a sexy red Porsche."

"If I were her, I'd opt for you."

WHY DIDN'T the car pass her?

She pulled even farther over toward the shoulder. Still the car didn't pull around. There were two bloody lanes. There were no other cars around. Did the idiot want three lanes?

Then something slammed into her belly. The guy in that Porsche was after her. Who was he? He had to be connected with Quinlan— she'd bet her last dime on it.

Why hadn't she stayed in her motel room, quiet on that nice hard bed, and counted sheep? That's probably what James would have done, but no, she had to come out on a motorcycle after midnight.

Then she saw a small, gaping hole in the guardrail that separated the eastbound lanes from the westbound. She didn't think, just swerved over in a tight arc and flew through that opening. There was a honk behind her from a motorist who barely missed her. He cursed at her out his window as he flew by.

There was lots of traffic going back into Philadelphia. She was safer now.

"Jesus, I can't believe she did that," Quinlan said, his heart pounding so loud in his chest that it hurt. "Did you see that opening? It couldn't have been more than a foot. I'm going to have to yell at her when we catch her."

"Well, she made it. Looked like a pro. You told me she had grit. I'd say more likely she's got nerves of steel or the luck of the Irish. And yeah, you're sounding like you're her husband again. Stop it, Quinlan. It scares me."

"Nothing short of a howitzer firing would scare you. Pay attention now and stop analyzing everything I say. We'll get her, Savich. There's a cut-through just ahead."

It took them some time to get her back in view. She was weaving in and out of the thicker traffic going back into the city.

"Hellfire," Quinlan said over and over, knowing that at any instant someone would cut her off, someone else wouldn't see her and would change lanes and crush her between two cars.

"At least she thinks she's lost us," Savich said. "I wonder who she thought we were."

"I wouldn't be surprised if she guess it was me."

"Nah, how could that be possible?"

"It's my gut talking to me again. Yeah, she probably knows, and that's why she's driving like a bat out of hell. Jesus, look out, Savich! Oh, my God! Hey, watch out, bubba!" Quinlan rolled down the window and yelled at the man again. He turned back to Savich. "Damned Pennsylvania drivers. Now, how are we going to get her?"

"Let's just tail her until we get an opportunity."

"I don't like it. Oh, shit, the bikers are back, all four of them."

The four bikers fanned through the traffic, coming back together when there was a break, then fanning out again.

Sally was feeling good. She was feeling smart. She'd gotten them, that jerk driving that Porsche and the four bikers. She'd gone through that opening without hesitation, and she'd done it without any problem. It was a good thing she hadn't had time to think about it, otherwise she would have wet her pants. She was grinning, the wind hitting hard against her teeth, making them tingle. However, she was going in the wrong direction.

She looked at the upcoming road sign. There was a turn onto Rancor Road half a mile ahead. She didn't know where Rancor Road went, but from what she could see, it wove back underneath the highway. That meant a way back east.

She guided her bike over to the far right lane. A car honked, and she could have sworn she felt the heat of it as it roared past her. Never again, she thought, never again would she get on a motorcycle.

Although why not? She was a pro.

She'd driven a Honda 350, just like this one, for two years, beginning when she was sixteen. When she told her father she was moving back home, he refused to buy her the car he'd promised. The motorcycle was for the interim. She saved her money and got the red Honda, a wonderful bike. She remembered how infuriated her father had been. He'd even forbidden her to get near a motorcycle.

She'd ignored him.

He'd grounded her.

She hadn't cared. She didn't want to leave her mother in any case. Then he'd just shut up about it. She had the sneaking suspicion that he wouldn't have cared if she'd killed herself on the thing.

Not that it mattered. He'd gotten his revenge.

She didn't want to think about that.

She took the turn onto Rancor Road. Soon now, she'd be going back in the other direction, and no one would be after her this time. The road was dark, no lights at all. It was windy. There were thick, tall bushes on both sides. There was no one on the road. What had she done? She smelled the fear on herself. Why the hell had she turned off? James wouldn't have turned off.

She was a fool, an idiot, and she'd pay for it.

It happened so fast she didn't even have time to yell or feel scared. She saw the lead biker on her left, waving to her, calling to her, but she couldn't understand his words. She jerked her bike to the right, hit a gravel patch, slid into a skid, and lost control. She went flying over the top of the bike and landed on the side of the two-lane road, not on the road but in the bushes that lined the road.

She felt like a meteor had hit her—a circle of blinding lights and a whoosh of pain—then darkness blacker than her father's soul.

Quinlan didn't want to believe what he'd just seen. "Savich, she's hurt. Hurry, dammit, hurry."

The Porsche screeched to a halt not six feet from where the four bikers were standing over Sally. One of them, tall, lanky, short hair, was bending over her.

"Okay, guys," Quinlan said, "back off now."

Three of them twisted around to see two guns pointed at them. "We're FBI and we want you out of here in three seconds."

"Not yet." It was the lead biker, who was now on his knees beside her.

"What are you doing to her?"

"I'm a doctor—well, not fully trained, but I am an intern. Simpson's the name. I'm just trying to see how badly hurt she is."

"Since you're the one that knocked her off the road, that sounds weird."

"We didn't force her off the road. She went into a skid. Actually, we followed because we saw you go back after her. Hey, man, we just want to help her."

"As I said, we're FBI," Quinlan repeated, looking at the man. "Listen, she's a criminal. A big-time counterfeiter. Is she going to be all right? Can you tell if she broke anything? Savich, keep an eye on these bozos."

Quinlan dropped to his knees. "Can I take off her helmet?"

"No, let me. I guess maybe we should wear helmets. If she hadn't had one on, she might have scrambled her brains, and not necessarily left them inside her head. You're really FBI? She's really a criminal?"

"Of course she is. What are you doing? Okay, you're seeing if her arms are broken. She'd better be all right or I'll have to flatten you. You scared the shit out of her. Yeah, she's your typical criminal type. Why isn't she conscious yet?"

At that moment Sally moaned and opened her eyes. It was dark. She heard men's voices, lots of them. Then she heard James.

"No," she said. "No, it's not possible you caught me. I didn't think it could be you. I was wrong again."

He leaned down over her and said one inch from her nose, "I

caught you, all right. And this is the last time I'm going to do it. Now just be quiet and lie still."

"I wouldn't have guessed she was a criminal," Simpson said. "She looks as innocent and sweet as my kid sister."

"Yeah, well, you never know. It's taken us a long time to catch up with her. We didn't know she'd gotten ahold of a bike. She was in a car six hours ago."

"All right, Sally, are you all right? Anything hurt? Nothing's broken, right? Can't you take off her helmet now?"

"Okay, but let's do it real carefully."

Once the helmet was off, she breathed a sigh of relief. "My head hurts," she said. "Nothing else does except my shoulder. Is it broken?"

The biker felt it very gently. "No, not even dislocated. You probably landed on it. It'll be sore for a while. I think you should go to the hospital and make sure there are no internal injuries."

"No," she said. "I want to get on my bike and get out of here. I've got to get away from this man. He betrayed me."

"What do you mean, he betrayed you?"

"He drew me in and made me trust him. I even slept with him one night, but that was in Oregon. Then he had the gall to tell me he'd lied to me, he was an FBI agent. He told me that here, not in Oregon."

"You're sure her brains aren't scrambled?" Savich asked, pressing a bit closer.

"She made perfectly good sense," Quinlan said. "If you can't add anything sensible, Savich, just keep quiet."

Quinlan touched the biker's arm. "Thanks for your help. The four of you can go now."

"Can I see identification?"

Quinlan smiled through his teeth. "Sure thing. Savich, show the man our ID again. He didn't get a good enough look the first time."

The biker studied it closely, then nodded. He looked back down at Sally, who'd propped herself up on her elbows. "I still can't believe she's a crook."

"You should see her grandmother. A glacier, that old lady. She's the head of the counterfeiting ring. Leads her husband around by the ear. She's a terror, and this one is going to be just like her."

Once the bikers had roared off, Quinlan said to Sally, "We're going to take you to the hospital now."

"No."

"Don't be an idiot. You could have hurt your innards."

"If you force me to a hospital, I'll announce to the world who I am and who you are."

"No, you won't."

"Try me."

He realized he was being blackmailed, but not for anything he had done. She would be the only one to be hurt if she did as she promised. He believed her.

"How are you, Sally?"

"Agent Savich? You were the jerk driving the Porsche? And James was sitting right beside you telling you what to do. I should have known. Well, I did know, deep down."

"Yeah," Savich said, wondering why it didn't occur to her to give him any of the credit. "Let me help you up. You don't look half bad in Quinlan's coat. A little long, but other than that, it's a perfect fit. Anyone who can ride a motorcycle like you do has to have the broadest shoulders in the land."

"How did you find me? Oh, dear, my head." She shook her head, then blinked her eyes. "It's just a bit of a headache. My shoulder hurts a little, but that's all. No hospital."

Quinlan couldn't stand to see her weaving around, his coat torn at the left shoulder, two buttons popped on her blouse. "You're not wearing a bra."

Sally looked down at the gaping blouse. There was no way she could pull it together. She just buttoned James's coat. "This blind man here got me a training bra when he went out, and bought all these charming duds that are three sizes too small. I couldn't even get the thing fastened."

"Well, I didn't know what size. Sorry it didn't get the job done."

She kicked him in the shin.

"I didn't mean it like that, dammit," Savich said, rubbing his leg. "I'll think of something and tell you later."

"You'd better not."

Quinlan took her arm and gently pulled her toward him. "It's all right now, Sally. It's all right."

He pulled her against him. "Are you sure you don't want to have a doctor check you out?"

"No doctor. I hate doctors."

That made sense to him. He didn't point out that a doctor wasn't the same as a shrink. He wondered in that moment if Beadermeyer even was a doctor. He said to Savich, "When you get a minute, do some checking on Beadermeyer. I'm beginning to wonder if he's just a ruthless crook." To Sally he said, "All right. But you need to rest. Let's find a place to stay the night."

"How did you find me?"

"We just missed you at your grandparents' house, just as we did at your mother's. We figured you had to be as tired as we were, so we called all the motels in this area. It was easy. You've got a lot to learn about running, Sally."

She realized then that she'd lost, she'd really lost. And it had been so easy for them. If they hadn't tracked her down on the highway, then James would have just come into her motel room. Easy, too easy. She was a turkey. She looked down at her dead Honda 350, at its twisted frame and blown back tire.

"My bike is ruined. I just bought it. I was just getting it broken in."

"It's all right. It doesn't matter."

"That bike cost me nearly all my money."

"Since it was my three hundred dollars, I'm willing to write it off."

Everything had turned upside down. Nothing was as it should be. She eased her hand into the coat and pulled out his gun. She pressed it against his lower ribs.

"NOT AGAIN, SALLY," he said, but still he was careful not to move.

"She's got your gun on you again, Quinlan?"

"Yes, but it's okay. I think she's learned a bit more since the last time she did it.

"Sally, it's over now. Come on, sweetheart, pull that sucker back. Whatever you do, don't forget that hair trigger. Damn, I think I'll have it modified a bit next time I'm at Quantico. Actually, if you could slip it back into my shoulder holster once we're in the car, I'd appreciate it. My shoulder holster's been empty since you stole my gun. I feel half-dressed."

"I don't want to shoot you, James, but I do want to get away from you. You did betray me. You know I can't trust you. Let me go, please."

"Nope, not ever again. You know you can trust me. It pisses me off that you're even questioning that. Listen up, Sally. You're with me now until all this is over. Would you rather trust your mother or your grand-parents? Oh, yeah, your sweet little granny is a piece of work."

"No, I don't trust any of them. Well, I do trust Noelle, but she's all confused and doesn't know what to believe—whether I'm a lunatic or not. I'd bet that all of them have called Beadermeyer, even Noelle. If she called him it wasn't to turn me in, it was to get some answers. Oh, God, do you think Beadermeyer would hurt her?"

Quinlan didn't think he would hurt her unless her own skin was in really deep trouble, which it would be shortly, but not just yet. But he said, "I don't know. Beadermeyer could do anything if he felt threatened, which he probably does, since we busted you out of his sanitarium. Hey, did you know I even threw meat to those dogs to save you?"

She looked up at him in the darkness. "What dogs?"

Savich said, "There were guard dogs at the sanitarium, Sally. James tossed meat to them so they wouldn't tear our throats out. One of the dogs was leaping up trying to get James's ankle when he was carrying you up that fence."

She could see the shadows and blurred lines of his face. "Well," she said at last, aware that she couldn't hold that gun up for much longer because her shoulder hurt like the very devil, "shit."

"That's what we've been thinking for the past six hours," Savich said. "Come on, Sally, give it up. Quinlan's determined to help you. He's determined to protect you. Let him be possessive. I've never before seen him like this. It's a real treat."

"Now, come on, you guys. Let's get out of here before some motorists come by and stop or worse, someone calls the local cops."

Quinlan didn't even think about it, he just scooped her up in his arms and carried her to the Porsche.

"You're no he-man," she said in the bitterest voice he'd ever heard. "It was just a six-foot walk. A nerd could have carried me that far."

"It's my gun," he said, leaning down and lightly kissing her ear. "It's heavy." When he settled her on his lap in the passenger side of the Porsche, he held out his hand for the gun.

She looked at him for a very long time. "You're really feeling possessive about me?"

"You stole my money, my credit cards, my car, and the photos of my nieces and nephews. I had to catch you so I could get that stuff back."

"Bastard." She gave him the gun.

"Yeah, that's me," he said. "Thanks, Sally. No more trying to run away from me?" he asked as he tossed the gun into the back seat.

"I don't know."

"Tell you what, I won't strain your options. I'll handcuff you to me, how's that?"

She didn't answer, her head pressed against his shoulder. She hurt, he realized, and here he'd been teasing her. "Just rest," he said. He looked at Savich. "How about finding us a nice motel?"

"Contradiction in terms. Are you paying or is the FBI?"

"Hell, I'm rich now that I've got my credit cards back. It's on me, all except your room."

"TOMORROW WE'LL BUY you some clothes that fit."

She was standing there, staring at the large motel room. There was a sitting area and a TV and a king-size bed.

She turned to look at him. "It's payback time?"

He cocked his head to one side. "What do you mean?"

She nodded toward the bed. "I gather I'm to sleep with you in that bed."

"I was going to ask that you take the sofa. It's too short for me."

She gave him a baffled look, then walked to the bathroom, saying over her shoulder, "I don't understand you. Why aren't you furious with me? Why aren't you yelling? I'm not used to reasonable people, particularly reasonable men. Just look at you, the very image of long-suffering Job."

A bruise was coming up along her jaw. He wondered just how badly her shoulder was hurt. "I would be pissed at you if I hadn't seen you go flying off that motorcycle. You gave me a gray hair with that stunt."

"I hit gravel. There was nothing I could do."

"Take a nice long shower. It should help your aches and bruises."

Five minutes later there was a knock on the adjoining door.

Quinlan opened it up. "She's in the shower. Come on in."

Savich was carrying a big bag from Burger King and a container holding three big soft drinks. He set them down on the table and sat down on the sofa.

"What a mess. At least it seems like she's not going to try to run again. I didn't know you had such charm."

"Hang around and maybe you'll get a few pointers."

"What are we going to do, Quinlan? We've got to call Brammer. We don't even know what's going on with the rest of the investigation."

"It just occurred to me that it's the weekend. This is Friday night—well, actually Saturday morning. We're sort of off duty. We've got until Monday before we have to be the good guys again, right?"

Savich was leaning back against the sofa, his eyes closed. "Brammer will have our balls for breakfast."

"Nah. He would have had our balls if we'd lost Sally. But we didn't. Everything will be fine now."

"I can't believe your wild-eyed optimism," Savich said, opening his eyes and sitting up when he heard the shower turn off. "They have all sorts of those little shampoos and conditioners and stuff in the bathrooms."

"Your point?"

The blow dryer went on.

"No point, really. Let's eat," Savich said. He took the beef patty out of his hamburger bun, took a big bite, and said, with his mouth full, "I'm stressed. I need to work out. Thank God tomorrow's Saturday. But damn, the gym will be crowded."

IT WAS NEARLY THREE o'clock in the morning. It was quiet and dark in the room. He knew she was still awake. It was driving him nuts.

"Sally?" he said finally. "What's wrong?"

"What's wrong?" She started to laugh. "You have the feelings of a rhino. You ask me *what's wrong?*"

"Okay, you have a point, but you need to sleep and so do I. I can't go to sleep until you do."

"That's nonsense. I haven't made a sound."

"I know, that's what's so crazy about it. I know you're scared to death, but if you'll remember, I promised you I'd protect you. I promised that we'd get this mess all cleared up. You know I can't do it without you."

"I told you, James, I don't remember that night. Not a single thing. There are just images and sounds, but nothing solid. I don't know who killed my father. He may not even have been killed when I was there. On the other hand, I could have shot him. I hated him more than you can begin to imagine. Noelle swore to me she didn't kill him. There was more, but she didn't have time to tell me—if, that is, she would have told me in any case."

"You know you were there when he was shot. You know very well you didn't shoot him. But we'll get back to that later."

"I think my mother didn't tell me the truth because she knows I did shoot him. She's trying to protect me, not the other way around."

"No, you didn't shoot him. Maybe it was because she didn't have time since we showed up. Or maybe it was because she's protecting somebody else. We'll find out everything. Trust me. She told the cops and us that she'd been out all evening, alone, at a movie."

"Well, she told me she'd been with Scott. Which means she had a witness to prove she didn't kill my father."

"Scott? Your husband?"

"Don't be cute. You know he's my husband, but for only a very short time longer."

"All right. We'll take care of things. Now, it's late. We've got to get some sleep.

"I just wanted to tell you that you ran a good race, Sally, real good. When I just happened to spot you leaving the motel on that motorcycle, I nearly dropped my teeth. That was real smart of you to ditch the car and buy a bike. It took us totally by surprise."

"Yes, but it didn't matter when it came right down to it, did it?"

"No, thank God. Savich and I are good. That and lucky as dogs on the loose in an Alpo factory. Where were you going?"

"To Bar Harbor. My grandfather gave me three hundred dollars. It was all he had in his wallet. When I counted it, I became aware of a certain irony."

"You're kidding. Three hundred exactly?"

"Right on the button."

"I didn't particularly care for your grandparents. The maid showed us into this back study. They were watching some Home Shopping show. I've got to say that was a surprise. Mr. Franklin Ogilvee Harrison and wife watching that plebian show."

"That would have surprised me too."

"Sally, would you like to come here to the big bed? No, don't freeze up on me. I can see you freezing from here. I'll bet your shoulder aches too, doesn't it?"

"Just a little bit. More sore than aches. I was very lucky."

"You're right about that. Come on now, I promise not to attack you. Remember how well we both slept in The Cove in my tower bedroom? It can't have bothered you all that much, since you were willing to tell the bikers about it quick enough."

The silence lasted for a full minute. She said, "Yes, I remember. I don't know why I opened my mouth and blabbed it to total strangers. I had that horrible nightmare."

"No, you remembered what had happened to you. It was a nightmare, but it was real. It was your father. At least you finally told me that.

"Come here, Sally. I'm exhausted and even you—super female—have got to be teetering on the edge just a bit."

To his relief and pleased surprise, she was standing beside the bed in the next moment, looking down at him. She was wearing one of his white undershirts. He pulled the cover back.

She slipped in and lay on her back.

He lay on his back four inches away from her.

"Give me your hand."

She did. He squeezed her fingers. "Let's get some sleep."

Surprisingly, they did.

When Quinlan awoke early the following morning, she was sprawled on top of him, her arms wrapped around his neck, her legs parted, lying directly on top of his. The undershirt had ridden up to her waist.

Oh, damn, he thought, trying not to move, trying to tell himself that this was just something else a professionally trained FBI agent had to learn how to deal with. So it hadn't been covered in the sixteen-week training course at Quantico. No big deal. He had experience. He wasn't sixteen. He breathed through his teeth.

Yes, he would handle this situation with poise and composure. He felt the heat of her through his boxer shorts. He was just a smidgen of material away from her, that was all, and he knew that composure was a big thing at this point.

"Sally?"

"Hmmmm?"

He was harder than his uncle Alex's divining rod. No way he was going to scare her. As gently as he could, he pushed her off him onto her back. The only thing was that she didn't let go of him. He had no choice but to come down over her. Now Uncle Alex's divining rod was between her legs, just where it belonged.

What the hell was poise anyway? It didn't seem too important right at that moment.

"Sally, I'm in a bad way. Let me go, okay?"

Her arms eased around his neck but she kept her fingers laced.

He could have easily pulled away from her, but he couldn't bring himself to do it. She was slight and warm and he thought where he was and where she was a very nice thing. He loved the feel of her arms tight about his neck. He liked her warm breath against his neck.

He thought having her here beneath him until he croaked would be a very nice thing.

He was staring down at her. He opened his mouth and said, "Sally, would you marry me?"

Her eyes came open in a flash. "What did you say?"

"I asked you to marry me."

"I don't know, James. I'm already married."

"I forgot that. Sally, please don't move. Do you want to take your arms off my neck?"

"No, not really. You're warm, James, and I like your weight on me. I feel safe and like everything just might be all right. Somebody would have to go through you to get to me. They'd never make it, you're too solid, too strong. Please don't roll off me."

Solid and strong was he? He turned even harder. "You're sure you're not afraid? After what happened to you at the sanitarium, I don't want to scare you."

She frowned even as she tightened her arms around his neck. "It's odd, but you never scared me except when you came roaring through Amabel's door like a bull that day, that day when my father called me for the first time. But after that, not at all, not even when you walked in on me and I'd just come out of the shower."

"You were so beautiful, I thought I'd lose it for sure."

"Me? Beautiful?" She snorted, and he was charmed. "I'm a stick, but you're nice to say it."

"But it's true. I looked at you and thought, She's perfect. I really like that little black mole on the side of your belly, just beside your left pelvic bone."

"Oh, dear, you saw that much of me?"

"Oh, yes. A man's eyes can move real fast when the motivation is there. Why don't you dump Scott Brainerd and then you can marry me?"

"I don't think he'll mind at all," she said after a moment. "Actually he's already dumped me, despite those pleas he made on TV." She was rubbing her hands over his shoulders and upper back. His skin was warm and smooth. "Shortly after we were married, I knew it had been a mistake. I was as busy as he was, always on the go, always going out to meetings and parties and functions in the evenings, always talking to people on the phone, always having people over. I loved it, and he seemed to at first.

"Then he told me he'd thought I would give all that up when we got married. Evidently he expected me to sit around until he got home and then feed him and probably rub his back and listen to him talk about his day, and then strip if he wanted sex. At least that's what he'd expected. Where he got that idea I'll never know.

"I tried to talk to him about it, but he would just shake his head and tell me over and over that I was a crummy wife, that I was unreasonable. He said I'd lied to him. That wasn't true. It came as a total shock to me after we were married when he started pitching fits over my schedule. While we were dating it had been just the same and he never said a word. Once he even told me how proud he was of me.

"When I finally told him that I knew he was having an affair and that I wanted out, he said I was imagining things. He said I was being silly, at least at first he said that. Then just days later he said I was losing it, that I was paranoid but that he wouldn't divorce me because I was going crazy. It wouldn't be right. No, he wouldn't do that to me. I didn't understand what he was talking about until about four days later.

"He was sleeping with another woman, James, I would bet my life on it. After I was locked away in Beadermeyer's sanitarium, I don't know what he did. I was kind of hoping that I'd never have to see him again. And I didn't. Just my father came out. But Scott had to be in on it with my father. He was and is my husband, after all. And he had told me I was nuts."

Interesting, he thought. "Yes," he said. "He was in on it, up to his little shyster's ears. Who was he having an affair with?"

"I don't know. Probably someone at work, at TransCon. Scott's big into power."

"I'm sorry," he said, and dipped down and kissed her ear, "but you're going to have to see him again, at least one more time. Good thing is, I'm your hero and I'm even official, so you don't have to worry.

"Sally, maybe Scott killed your father. Maybe your mother is protecting him."

"No, Scott's a worm. He's a stingy, cowardly little worm. He wouldn't have the guts to kill my father."

"All right." So much pain, he thought, too much. It would all work out, it just had to.

He leaned down and kissed her mouth this time. Her lips parted, and he wanted more than anything to go deep into her mouth, just as he wanted to go deeply inside her body, but he realized her world was spinning out of control right now. He didn't want to add any more confusion to her life. Good Lord, he'd asked her to marry him.

"Perhaps that would be good," she said and pulled him down so she could kiss him.

"What would be good?" he said in her mouth.

"To get married. To you. You're so normal, so big and normal. You didn't have a screwed-up childhood, did you?"

"No. I've got two older sisters and an older brother. I was the baby of the family. Everyone spoiled me rotten. My family wasn't particularly dysfunctional. No one hit anyone. We kids beat the crap out of each other, but that's normal enough. I was big into sports, any and every sport, but my passion was and still is football. Sundays were created for football. I always go into withdrawal after the Super Bowl. Do you like football?"

"Yes. I had a woman gym teacher at my school who was from San Francisco. She was nuts about football and taught us the game. We got very good. The only problem was that there wasn't another girls' team around for us to play. I don't like basketball or baseball."

"I can live with that. I'll even play touch football with you."

She kissed his neck. He shuddered as he felt her opening even more beneath him. He said quickly, "My big screw-up was marrying Teresa Raglan when I was twenty-six. She was from Ohio, seemed just perfect for me.

"She's a lawyer, just like your husband and dear old dad. It turned out she fell in love with a guy in the Navy who was selling secrets to whoever was interested. I was the one who caught him. She defended him. She got him off, then left me and married him."

"That's pretty amazing, James. What happened to her?"

"They live in Annandale, Virginia. The guy's some sort of lobbyist, gets paid really well, and they seem to be doing just great. I see them every once in a while. No, don't romanticize it and pretend that I was a brokenhearted wreck. I wasn't. I was shocked and furious for a while, before Savich pointed out the absurdity of it all.

"The good guy catches the bad guy. The good guy's wife defends the bad guy and gets him off and then marries him. Pretty deep stuff to walk in. He was right. The whole thing was like a bad melodrama or a TV soap."

"James, you're wonderful. Even in all this mess, you can laugh and make me laugh, and you weren't angry that I poked a gun in your stomach and stole your car. I had to just ditch the car, James. Then I bought the motorcycle. I had to get away. I think if you could forget who you are and come to Bar Harbor with me, everything would be better than what it's going to be soon. I used to love life, James, before—well, that's not important right now."

"It is important. You want to know something else? Something else that will prove how great I am?"

"What's that?"

"I didn't even get pissed when you pulled my gun on me the second time."

"Well, that settles it then, doesn't it?" She moved beneath him, and he thought he'd lose it for sure. He was hard against her, and his heart was pounding deep and fast against her chest.

He hadn't intended to let things get this out of hand, at least he hadn't before she shifted beneath him, her legs wide now, his legs between hers.

He kissed her, then said into her mouth. "You're beautiful, and you can feel how much I want you. But we can't let this happen. I don't have any condoms. The last thing you need is to get pregnant."

He heard Savich moving about in the adjoining room. "Besides, Savich is awake and up. It's nearly seven o'clock. We need to get back home."

She turned her face away from him. Her eyes were closed. He thought she must be in pain, from either her head or her shoulder. Without thinking, he reared back and pulled his undershirt over her head. She blinked up at him and made a move to cover herself.

No, he thought, she wasn't ready for this. "It's all right. I want to see how badly your shoulder is hurt. Hold still."

He was on his knees between her legs, bending over her, his hands gentle as they lightly touched her left shoulder. She winced. "There. Okay, hold still, let me feel around just a bit more." She looked like the Italian flag, the bruises raw and bright, slashing downward to her breasts and over her shoulder cap to her upper arm. Some of the colors were smearing into each other, green the predominant one.

He leaned down and kissed her shoulder.

He felt her hands clenching his arms. "I'm sorry you got hurt." He kissed her again, on her left breast this time. He laid his cheek against her breast and listened to her heartbeat, so clear and strong, and now it was speeding up. Why not? he thought. He raised his head and smiled at her.

"A woman who's lived with as much stress as you must have release. It's the best medicine." He kissed her again, and eased off her onto his side. He slid his palm down her body, lightly caressing her belly, then his fingers found her. He caressed her even as he kissed her, knowing that she was scared, nervous, but he didn't stop. His fingers went deeper, changing rhythm, even as his breath speeded up as he felt her relax, as he felt the excitement of what he was doing to her break through her embarrassment.

He lifted his head and smiled at her dazed face. "It's all right, sweetheart. You need this. God knows I do, too."

He began kissing her again, talking into her mouth, sex words that were crude and raw and exciting. When she came, he took her cries in his mouth, held her tightly against him, and wished like mad that he could come inside her. He hurt, he was pressing hard as a board against her thigh.

But he couldn't.

Savich knocked lightly on the adjoining door.

"Quinlan, Sally, you guys awake?"

He looked down at the bluest eyes he'd ever seen. She was just staring at him as if she couldn't believe what had happened.

"You okay?"

She just stared at him, mute.

"Hey, Quinlan, you up? Come on, you guys, we've got miles to go."

"That's the guy who owns the Porsche," Quinlan said. "We've got to hang on to him." He kissed the tip of her nose and forced himself to leave her.

"I LIKE YOUR apartment."

He grinned at the back of her head. "Easy for you to say since it's got more character than that motel room—"

She turned to face him, no longer dressed in the too-tight jeans, his coat that had hung halfway down her legs, and the blouse that had gaped open over her breasts.

They'd stopped at the Macy's in Montgomery Plaza on the way back to Washington. Savich had bowed out, heading for the computer software store in the mall. James and Sally had enjoyed themselves immensely, arguing over everything from the color of her nightgown to the style of her shoes. She left wearing dark brown corduroy slacks that fit her very nicely, a cream pullover wool sweater over a brown turtleneck, and neat brown leather half boots.

He was carrying his own coat—the one she'd taken—over his arm. He doubted the dry cleaners would be able to get out the grease stains from her motorcycle accident.

"I've heard that men living alone usually live in a dump—you know, empty pizza cartons all over everywhere, including the bathroom, dead plants, and horrible furniture they got from their mother's attic."

"I like to live well," he said, and realized it was true. He didn't like mess or secondhand furniture, and he loved plants and impressionist paintings. He was lucky to have Mrs. Mulgravy live next to him. She saw to everything when he was gone, particularly his precious African violets.

"You do very well with plants."

"I think the secret is that I play my sax to them. Most of them prefer blues."

"I don't think I like the blues," she said, still looking at him intently.

"Have you ever listened to Dexter Gordon? John Coltrane? Gordon's album *Blue Notes* wrings your withers."

"I've heard of Gato Barbieri."

"He's great too. I learned a lot from him and Phil Woods. There's hope for you yet, Sally. You'll get an earful tonight. You've got to give the wailing and the rhythm a chance."

"That's your hobby, James?"

He looked just a bit embarrassed. "Yeah, I play the saxophone at the Bonhomie Club on Friday and Saturday nights. Except when I'm not in town, like last night."

"Are you playing tonight?"

"Yes, but no, not now. You're here."

"I'd love to hear you. Why can't we go?"

He gave her a slow smile. "You'd really like to go?"

"I'd really like to go."

"Okay. The chances are nobody would even begin to recognize you, but let's get you a wig anyway, and big dark glasses." He knew that tomorrow he, Sally, and Savich would leap into this mess feetfirst. He couldn't wait to meet Scott Brainerd. He couldn't wait to meet Dr. Bea-dermeyer. He hadn't told Sally yet. He wanted to give her today with no hassles from him, from anybody. He wanted to see her smile.

"James, do you think I could call a couple of my friends?"

"Who are they?"

"Women who work on the Hill. I haven't spoken to them since more than six months ago. Well, I did call one of them just before I left Washington to go to The Cove. Her name is Jill Hughes. I asked her for a loan. She agreed, very quickly, and wanted to meet me. There was something about how she acted—I didn't go. I'd like to call Monica Freeman. She was my very best friend. She was out of town before. I want to see how she acts, what she has to say to me. Perhaps I'm paranoid, but I just want to know who's there for me."

She didn't sound the least bit sorry for herself. Still, he felt a knife twist in his gut.

"Yeah," he said easily, "let's give Monica a call and see if someone's gotten to her as well."

She called Monica Freeman, a powerhouse administrator in HUD. She was embarrassed because she had to call Information for the number. She'd known it as well as her own before Scott.

The phone rang twice, three times, then, "Hello."

"Monica? It's Sally."

James was bent over, writing something.

There was a long pause. "Sally? Sally Brainerd?"

"Yes. How are you, Monica?"

"Sally, where are you? What's going on?"

James slid a sheet of paper under her hand. Sally read it, nodded slowly, then said, "I'm in trouble, Monica. Can you help me? Can you loan me some money?"

There was another long pause. "Sally, listen. Tell me where you are."

"No, Monica, I can't do that."

"Let me call Scott. He can come and get you. Where are you, Sally?"

"You never called him Scott before, Monica. You didn't like him, remember? You used to call him a jerk when you knew I was listening. You wanted to protect me from him. You used to tell me he was into power and that he was trying to separate me from all my friends. Don't you remember how you'd call after Scott and I were first married and ask me first thing if Scott was gone so we could really talk? You didn't like him, Monica. Once you told me I should kick him in the balls."

There was utter silence, then, "I was wrong about him. He's been very concerned about you, Sally. He came to me hoping you would call and that I would help him.

"Scott's a good man, Sally. Let me call him for you. He and I can meet you someplace, we—"

Sally very gently punched the off button on the portable phone.

To her surprise James was grinning. "Hey, just maybe we've got your husband's lover. Am I jumping too fast here? Yeah, probably, but what do you think? Maybe he's a real stud, may he's got both Jill and Monica? Could he do it, do you think?"

She'd been thinking that hell couldn't feel worse than she felt right now, but he'd put a ridiculous twist on it, like the best of the spin doctors. "I don't know. She's certainly changed her tune, just like Jill. Two? I doubt it, James. He was always so busy. I think his deals were more exhilarating to him than mere sex."

"What kind of deals?"

"He was in my dad's law firm, something I didn't know until after we were married. That sounds weird but it's true. He didn't want me to know, obviously, until after we were married. He was in international finance, working primarily with the oil cartel. He would come home rubbing his hands together, telling me how this deal or that deal would impress everybody, how he'd gotten the better of such and such a sheikh and had just brought in a cool half million. Deals like that."

"How long were you married to him?"

"Eight months." She blinked and fiddled with the leaves of a healthy philodendron. "Isn't it odd? I don't count the six months in the sanitarium."

"That's not a very long time for a marriage, Sally. Even mine—a semi-unmitigated disaster—lasted two years."

"I realized right after we were married that my father was as much a part of the marriage as we were. I'm willing to bet he offered me up to Scott as part of a deal between the two of them."

She drew a deep breath. "I think my father put me in the sanitarium as revenge for all those years I protected Noelle. I'm willing to bet that another part of the revenge was to get Scott to marry me. He got to Scott, and Scott did what he was told. All revenge.

"When I told Scott I wanted a divorce, he told me I was crazy. I told him that he could marry my father if he wanted a St. John so badly. Maybe two days after that, I was in that sanitarium—at least I think it was two days. The time still gets all scrambled up."

"But he had a lover. Perhaps Monica, perhaps Jill. Perhaps someone we don't know at all. How quickly were you sure about this affair?"

"About three months after we were married. I'd decided to try to make a go of it, but when I found a couple of love notes, unsigned, and two motel receipts, I didn't care enough to try. Between that and my father, always in the background, I just wanted to get out."

"But your father didn't let you get out."

"No."

"Obviously your father knew everything about your marriage. Scott must have told him immediately when you asked for a divorce for your father to have taken action so quickly. Who knows? Maybe it was Scott's idea. Do you want to call anyone else?"

"No, that leaves just Rita. I don't think I could take it if Rita started on me about calling Scott. This was enough—much too much, as a matter of fact."

"Okay, no more work today, all right?"

"That was work?"

"Certainly. We just filled in another piece of the puzzle."

"James, who knocked both of us out in The Cove and brought me back to Dr. Beadermeyer's?"

"Beadermeyer or a henchman. Probably not Scott. It was probably the guy who played the role of your father that night in your bedroom window. But now that you've got me, you don't have to be depressed at the number of bad people in the world."

"They all seem to have congregated around me. Except Noelle."

He wanted to ask her to go over everything with him, from the day she met Scott Brainerd to now, but he didn't. Give her the day off, make her smile. Maybe they could make love in front of the fireplace. He wanted to make love to her very much. His fingers itched remembering the feel of her, the way she moved against his fingers, the softness of her flesh. He tried to focus on his African violets.

THAT EVENING she pulled her hair back tight, securing it with a clip at the nape of her neck. She put on a big pair of dark sunglasses. "No one would recognize you," Quinlan said, coming up behind her and putting his hands lightly on her shoulders.

"But let's get you a wig anyway. You know something? Your father was killed, what, three weeks ago or so? It was splashed all over TV, all over every tabloid, every newspaper. You, the missing daughter, got the same treatment. Why take the chance on someone recognizing you? I have to tell you, I like you in those sunglasses. You look mysterious. Are you really the same woman who's agreed to marry me? The same woman who woke me up this morning lying on top of me?"

"I'm the same woman. James, really, the other—I thought that was just a glitch on your part. You really mean it?"

"Nah, I just wanted to get you in bed and make you come."

She hit him in the stomach.

"Yeah, Sally, I really meant it."

THE BONHOMIE CLUB on Houtton Street was in an old brick building set in the middle of what they called a "border" neighborhood. It was accepted wisdom to take a cab to and from the club or else take a huge risk of losing your entire car, not just the hubcaps.

James had never really thought about the possible dangers in this area until he handed Sally out of the cab. He looked around at the streetlights, many of them shot out.

There was litter on the sidewalks, none in front of the club because Ms. Lilly didn't like trash—real trash, white trash, any kind of trash.

"Like I told you, boy," she'd said when she hired him some four years before, "I like the look of you. No earrings, no tattoos, no bad teeth, and no paunch.

"You'll have to watch the gals, now, they're a horny bunch and one look at you and they're gonna have visions of sugar cocks dancing in their heads." And she howled at her own humor while James, an experienced agent, a man who'd heard just about every possible combination of crude words, just stood there, embarrassed to his toes. She tweaked his earlobe between two fingers with inch-long bright pink fingernails and laughed some more. "You're gonna do just fine, boy, just fine."

And he had. At first the customers, a loyal bunch, the large majority of them black, had looked at him like he was something escaped from the zoo, but Lilly had introduced him, made three off-color jokes about his sax playing, his sex playing, and his red sox playing.

She was one of his best friends. She'd even given him a raise in January.

"You'll like Ms. Lilly," Quinlan said to Sally as he shoved open the heavy oak door of the club. "I'm her token white." Marvin the Bouncer was just inside, a heavy scowl on his ugly face until he saw it was Quinlan.

"Hullo, Quinlan," he said. "Who's the chicky?"

"The chicky is Sally. You can call her Sally, Marvin."

"Hello, Marvin."

But Marvin wasn't up for names. He just nodded. "Ms. Lilly is back in her office playing poker with the mayor and some of his lame-assed cronies. No, James, there ain't no drugs. You know Ms. Lilly, she'd shoot anybody before she'd let 'em take a snort.

"She'll be out before it's time for you to play. As for you, Chicky, you just stay in my eyesight once James is up there wailing his heart out on the stage, all right?"

"She's a cute little chicky, Quinlan. I'll take care of her."

"I appreciate it, Marvin. She is cute, and a lot of bad people are chasing her. If you could keep an eye on her, I can wail on my sax without worry."

"Ms. Lilly is going to try to feed her, Quinlan. She doesn't look like she's had a good meal in a month. You hungry, Chicky?"

"Not yet, but thank you, Marvin."

"A chicky with real good manners. It warms a man's heart, Quinlan."

"Amazing," Sally said and nothing more. But she was smiling. She gave Marvin a small wave.

"He'll watch over you, not to worry."

"Actually I hadn't even thought about it. I can't believe you just spit out the truth to him."

"Ah, Marvin didn't believe me. He thought I was worried some guy would try to pick you up, that's all."

Sally looked around the dark, smoky interior of the Bonhomie Club. "It's got lots of character, James."

"It gains more by the year. I think it's because of the aging wood. That bar is over a hundred years old. It's Lilly's pride. She won it in a poker game from a guy up in Boston. She always calls him Mr. Cheers."

"Lots of character."

He grinned down at her. "Tonight's just for fun, all right? You look gorgeous, you know that? I like that sexy little top."

"You're into jet beads, are you?" But she was pleased. He'd insisted on buying it for her at Macy's. She actually smiled. She felt good, light and easy. Tonight, she thought, tonight was for fun. It had been so long. Fun. She'd simply forgotten.

Nightmares could wait for tomorrow. Maybe when James took her home he'd want to kiss her some more, maybe even make love to her. She could still feel the warmth of his fingers on her.

"You want a drink?"

"I'd love a white wine. It's been so long."

He raised an eyebrow. "I don't know if Fuzz the Bartender has ever heard of such a thing. You sit down and let the atmosphere soak into your bones. I'll go see what Fuzz has got back there."

Fuzz the Bartender, she thought. This was a world she'd never imagined. She'd cheated herself.

She looked up to see James gesturing back at her and an immense black man with a bald head shiny as a cue ball grinning at her, waving a dusty wine bottle. She waved back and gave a thumbs-up.

Where did the name Fuzz come from?

There were only about half a dozen whites in the club, four men and two women. But no one seemed to care what color anyone was.

An Asian woman with long, board-straight black hair to her waist was playing the flute on the small wooden stage. The song was haunting and soft.

The conversation was a steady hum, never seeming to rise or fall. James put a glass of white wine in front of her.

"Fuzz said he got the wine a couple of years ago from this guy who wanted whiskey but was broke. Fuzz got this bottle of wine in trade."

She sipped it and gulped. It was awful and she wouldn't have traded it for a glass of Balen-Craig. "It's wonderful," she called out to Fuzz the Bartender.

James sat beside her, a beer in his hand. "The wig's not bad, either. A little too red for my taste, a little too curly, but it'll do for tonight."

"It's hot," she said.

"If you can just hold out, I'll try to think of something indecent to do with that thing when we get home."

At nearly nine o'clock, he kissed her mouth, tasted the white wine, and grimaced.

"That's rotgut."

"It's wonderful rotgut. Don't say anything to Mr. Fuzz."

James laughed, swung his saxophone case off the other chair, and wove his way through the tables to the stage.

She couldn't take her eyes off him. He hugged the flautist, then pulled a lower stool forward to the microphone. He took his saxophone out of the case, polished it a bit with a soft cloth, checked the reed. Then he began to warm up.

She didn't know what she'd expected, but the sound coming out of his instrument would make the devil weep. He played scales, bits and pieces of old songs, skipped from high notes to low ones, testing, soft, then loud.

"So you're the little white girl that's hooked my Quinlan, are you?"

"I WON'T BE so little in another six months."

"Why's that?"

"I'm not usually so skinny. I'll fatten up."

"Maybe my Quinlan will even get you pregnant. You just watch out, Sally, all the ladies salivate while he's playing. Poor boy, he tells himself it's because of his beautiful music. And he does look so soulful while he's playing."

She shook her head, her voice mournful. "I don't have the heart to tell him it's his sexy body and gorgeous eyes. Ah, now he's playing Sonny Rollins, my favorite. Well, aren't I forgetful? I'm Lilly," the huge black woman said, grinned wide, and pumped Sally's hand.

"I'm Sally."

"I know. Fuzz told me. Then Marvin told me. They said it looks like my Quinlan has got it real bad. He's never had it even mild before. This should be interesting. Hey, you aren't planning on having your way with him and then kissing him off, are you?"

"Kiss him off? Kiss off James?"

"What I mean is, you aren't married, are you? You're not using my Quinlan just to take care of your needs? I hear he's a treat in bed, so that would make sense, even though I don't like it."

"Actually, no, I'm not going to kiss him off," Sally said. She sipped at Mr. Fuzz's white wine. "I like your dress. It's magnificent."

Ms. Lilly preened and pressed her huge arms against her even more impressive breasts. The resulting cleavage made Sally stare. She'd never seen so much outside of a *Playboy* magazine.

"You like the white satin? So do I. I hear tell that a woman built along statuesque lines like I am isn't supposed to wear white, but hey, I like it. It makes me feel young and virginal. It makes me feel ready to go out and try a man for the first time.

"Now, you just sit here and listen to my Quinlan. That's Stan Getz he's playing now. He makes old Stan sound like a sinful angel. Quinlan's good. You really listen now, and don't just think about having your way with him."

"I'll listen good."

Ms. Lilly patted her on the back, nearly sending her face into the glass of wine, and moved away like a ship under sail to a booth that was very near the stage.

Quinlan began to play a sexy, weeping, slow blues song. It sounded like John Coltrane, but she couldn't be completely sure. It was still so new to her.

She noticed for the first time that no one was talking. There was total quiet in the club. Everyone was focused on James.

She watched at least four women get up and move closer to the stage. God, he played beautifully. His range was excellent, each note full and sweet, enough to break your heart. She felt a lump in her throat and swallowed. The song he was playing cried torrents, the notes sweeping lazily from a high register to low, deep notes that tore at the soul. His eyes were closed. His body was swaying slightly.

She knew she loved him, but she wasn't about to admit it here and now, knowing that it was his damned music that was making her feel as mushy as the grits Noelle had tried to make for her once. Men in uniforms and men playing soul music—a potent combination.

James spoke into the microphone. He said, "This one's for Sally. It's from John Coltrane's *A Love Supreme.*"

If she'd ever doubted what he felt about her, that damned song put an end to it. She gulped down Mr. Fuzz's white wine and her tears.

Two more women moved closer to the stage, and Sally smiled.

When James finished, he waved to her. Then he cleared his throat and called out, "I got a request for Charlie Parker."

She listened, took a last sip of Mr. Fuzz's wine, and realized she had to go to the bathroom.

She slipped out of her chair, looked at Fuzz the Bartender, who was pointing to an open door just beside the bar. She smiled and walked past him, saying, "Can I have another glass when I come out, Mr. Fuzz?"

"You sure can, Sally. I'll have it waiting." When she came out of the women's bathroom, she was smiling. She could hear James getting into his next song, one she recognized, a soft, searching song she hadn't realized was blues.

Suddenly she knew she wasn't alone. She felt someone very close to her, just behind her. She heard breathing, a lot of soft breathing.

The corridor was narrow. There hadn't been any other women in the bathroom. But that was silly. It had to be another woman, she thought on the edge of her brain, her attention on the song James was playing.

But it wasn't a woman.

It was Dr. Beadermeyer. There were two men standing just behind him. One of them was holding a needle in his hand.

He took her arm with a lover's light grasp. It changed quickly enough. She felt her skin pulling and sinking in at the increasing pressure of his fingers.

With his other hand, he grabbed her jaw to hold her still. He leaned over and lightly kissed her.

"Hello, Sally. How lovely you look, my dear. You shouldn't be drinking, you know, it doesn't go well with the kind of drugs your body is used to. I watched you drinking that dreadful stuff. Why are you here? I assume that man up there making a fool of himself in this backwater hole-in-the-wall is James Quinlan, that FBI agent you were with in The Cove? He's not bad looking, Sally. Now I know he's your lover. A man like that wouldn't stay with a woman unless she delivered.

"How desolate poor Scott will be when he finds out. Let's go now, my dear girl. It's time you came back to your little nest. A different nest. This time that bastard won't come to get you." It couldn't be him, but it was. Her father was dead. Why did he still want her so badly?

"I'll hold her. Bring the needle. Let's get out of this godforsaken place."

"I wouldn't go to heaven with you."

"Of course you will, my dear girl."

He was gripping her arm hard now, pulling her back against him, one hand over her mouth. She shoved her right elbow hard into his stomach.

He sucked in his breath, and she jerked free. "James! Marvin!" Then she screamed, just once before a hand smashed down over her mouth.

"Damn it, grab her! Gag her. Give her the shot!"

She grabbed the edge of a small table below the public telephone and gave it a shove, sending it crashing over, knocking against one of the men with Beadermeyer. She screamed once more, just a whisper of sound this time because the man's hand was hard over her mouth, covering her nose as well and she couldn't breathe. She was jerking, kicking back with her heels, feeling flesh, but still the man held her.

She felt fingers fumbling around her arm.

A needle.

He was going to shove a needle into her arm. He was going to make her into a zombie again. She kicked back as hard as she could. For an instant the man's hand loosened over her nose and mouth.

She leaned down and bit the man's hand, the hand that held that needle, and yelled again. "James!"

The hand went back over her mouth. A man was cursing, another man was jerking at her other arm, but she managed to send her left arm back hard, hitting him in the belly. The touch of the needle fell away. She heard a thunk on the wooden floor. He'd dropped the needle.

"I should have known you two goons would fuck it up. Pick up the damned needle, you idiot. Jesus, it's dark in here, but not dark enough. I knew I should have just knocked her out. Or shot the little bitch. Damn, let's just get out of here. Forget the needle, forget her."

It was Dr. Beadermeyer and he was furious.

Then she heard Fuzz the Bartender yelling the ripest obscenities she'd ever heard. The man released her. She staggered, then screamed, "You've lost, you damned bastard. Run and take your two dogs with you or James will kill you!"

He was panting hard, enraged. "I thought it would be easy, just slip a needle into your arm. You've changed, Sally, but this isn't the end of it."

"Oh, yes, it is. I'm going to put you out of business, you Nazi worm. I'm going to put you in jail, and I hope every one of those big inmates takes a fancy to you."

He raised his arm to hit her, but his two men crashed into him as they tried to get down the narrow hallway to the exit.

"Stop it, you fools," he screamed at them. Then they were all racing toward the back emergency exit. The door pounded open, then slammed shut.

She looked up to see Marvin the Bouncer bolting toward her like a runaway train. She heard Fuzz the Bartender crashing through the tables, yelling even riper obscenities.

She realized the whole incident had taken only seconds. It had seemed longer than a winter blizzard.

She took two steps forward. She saw James leaping off the stage. She saw him pull out his gun.

She saw Ms. Lilly pick up a baseball bat and stride toward her like an amazon angel.

It had all happened so quickly. Yet she'd felt the fear of a lifetime. To have a needle shoved into her arm again. No, she couldn't have borne that, not again.

Then she realized that the fear was dimming, releasing her, and she shook her head.

She'd won. She'd beaten him. She wished she could have shot him. Or stuck a knife in his guts.

Marvin the Bouncer took one quick look at her, then slammed open the emergency exit door and ran outside.

Fuzz the Bartender streaked past her and out the door behind Marvin. She heard pounding footsteps. Lots of them. She prayed they'd catch Beadermeyer.

She suddenly felt so weak she couldn't hold herself up. She sank to her knees and leaned against the wall. She wrapped her arms around her bent knees and leaned her face against her legs.

"Sally, hang on, I'll be right back." It was James running after Marvin and Fuzz.

"Well, my girl, Marvin told me that James said you had bad guys after you. I don't mind this—even though it did interrupt one of my favorite songs. What fools those guys were to try to get you here. They must have really been desperate. Either that or stupid. I'll bet stupid."

Ms. Lilly shook her head, the thick black coils of hair never budging. "You ready to get up now, Sally?"

"Is the little chicky all right?"

"Yes, Marvin, she's just catching her breath. I think she did a good job on those guys. I don't suppose you nabbed the jerks?"

"No, Ms. Lilly. We got close, but they pulled away in this big car.

Quinlan put a bullet through the back window, but then he stopped. He said he knew who it was and he was going to get the bastard tomorrow. Then he laughed and rubbed his hands together. It was hard because he was still holding that cannon of his."

Marvin the Bouncer turned. "Ain't that right, Quinlan?"

"It was Beadermeyer, wasn't it, Sally?"

She raised her head. She wasn't hyperventilating anymore. She was feeling just fine, thank you.

Ms. Lilly grabbed her arm and pulled her to her feet. "There you go. Fuzz, get Sally some more of that wonderful white wine you've got stashed."

"Yes, it was Beadermeyer with two goons and a needle. I think the needle's still over there on the floor. I managed to knock it away."

Marvin gave her an approving nod. "I knew you were skinny but not helpless. That was good, Chicky."

"Thank you, Marvin. Thank all of you."

"You're welcome," Ms. Lilly said. She turned and shouted, "Okay, everyone back to their tables. Everything's okay now. This will teach any of you who want to screw around with Marvin that it isn't smart. They beat the shit out of the guys who were trying to mug Sally. It's all over now.

"Quinlan, get your very nice butt back up there on the stage and play me my Dexter Gordon. What do you think I pay you for anyway?"

"My music," James said. "Sally, I want you right next to the stage, all right?" But before he left, he picked up the needle, wrapped it in a napkin, and put it in his shirt pocket.

"I want to know what the bastard was going to give you. We'll take this to the FBI lab tomorrow. Come on, Sally."

"I'll bring the wine," Fuzz said.

HE PACED FROM ONE END of the living room to the other, back and forth. Savich was sitting comfortably in a big overstuffed chair, hunched over the keyboard of his laptop, MAX.

Sally wasn't doing anything except watching James. "I guess I've had enough," she said finally.

Both men looked at her.

She smiled. "I don't want to wait until tomorrow. I want to get it over with tonight. Let's go see my mother. She knows what happened that night my father was murdered. At least she knows a lot more than she's told you or the police or me. I'd like to know the truth."

"Better yet," Savich said, looking back down at his computer screen, "let's get all three of them together—your mother, your husband, and Dr. Beadermeyer. You think the time is right, Quinlan?"

"I don't know," Quinlan said. "Maybe it's too soon." He gave Sally a worried look. "You really sure about this, Sally?"

She looked strong, her thin shoulders back, those soft blue eyes of hers hard and steady. She looked ready to take on a grizzly. "I'm sure."

It was all he needed. Yeah, it was time to find out the truth. He nodded.

"Maybe they'll be tired," Savich said. "Hot damn. Finally I've found it." He gave them a big grin. "I'm good," he said, rubbing his hands together. "Real good."

"What are you talking about?" Quinlan said, striding over to Savich. He leaned down to look at the screen.

"Everything we ever wanted to know about Dr. Alfred Beadermeyer. His real name is Norman Lipsy and he's Canadian. He did go to medical school—McGill, in Montreal.

"My, my, he has a specialty in plastic surgery. And there's lots more. Sorry it took me so long. I just never considered that he'd be Canadian, not with a name like Beadermeyer. I wasn't getting into the right databases." He rubbed his hands together. "I found him on a cosmetic surgeons roster, along with a photo. Said he graduated from McGill."

"This is incredible," Quinlan said. "Excellent, Savich."

"Now, before we're off, let me try just a couple more things on Scott Brainerd. Where'd he get his law degree, Sally?"

"Harvard."

"Yeah, it does show him graduating Harvard in 1992 with honors. Too bad. I was hoping maybe he'd lied about that."

Quinlan said, "You're still sure, Sally? You ready to see Scott? Beadermeyer? After what he tried tonight? You're sure?"

"Yes, I'm sure. No more. It's crazy. It's got to end. If I killed my father, I want to know. If Noelle or someone else did, then let's find out. I won't fall apart, James. I can't stand this fuzziness anymore, this constant mess of blurred images, the voices that are all melting together."

Quinlan said very slowly, in that wonderful soothing voice of his, "Before we leave I want to go over some more things with you. You up to it?"

"Oh, yes," she said. "I'm ready. We already talked about Scott and my father." She stopped, her fingers rubbing the pleats in her corduroy slacks.

"What is it?"

"It's about my father. And my mother." She looked down at her hands. Thin hands, skinny fingers, short fingernails. At least she hadn't bitten them since she'd met James.

"What is it, Sally? Come now, no more secrets."

"He beat my mother, viciously. I caught him doing it when I was just sixteen. That was when I moved back from the girls' school in Virginia. I tried to protect her—"

Savich's head came up. "You're saying your father, the senior legal counsel of TransCon International, was a wife beater?"

"Why am I not surprised?" Quinlan said. He sat beside her and took one of her hands and waited, saying nothing more, just holding her hand. She'd lived through that?

"My mother—Noelle—she wouldn't do anything about it. She just took it. I guess since he was so well known and respected and rich, and she was part of it, she couldn't bear the humiliation or losing all she had.

"I remember I always looked forward to parties, diplomatic gatherings—he was invited to all of them—those lavish lobbyist banquets, intimate little power lunches where wives were trotted out to show off, magazine interviews, things like that, because I knew he wouldn't dare hit Noelle then—there'd be photos taken of the two of them together. He knew that I knew, and that made him hate me even more.

"When I didn't leave the District to go to college, I thought he would kill me. He'd really counted on my leaving. He hadn't dreamed that I'd still be at home, watching him. He actually raised his hand, but then he lowered it, very slowly.

"I'll never forget the hatred in his eyes. He was very handsome, you know, thick, dark hair with white threaded through, dark blue eyes, tall and slender. High cheekbones, sculpted elegantly to make him look like an aristocrat.

"Actually, he's just an older version of Scott. Isn't that strange that I thought I fell in love with a man who looked like my father?"

"Yeah," Savich said. "I'd say that's plain not good. It's a good thing that Quinlan here doesn't look like anybody except himself."

"I came home at random times. He knew I would. Once when I'd been visiting Noelle, after I left to go back to my apartment, I realized I'd forgotten my sweater. I went back into the house and there he was, kicking my mother. I went to the phone to dial nine-one-one. As far as I was concerned, it was the last straw. I just didn't care anymore. He was going to pay. You won't believe it, but my mother crawled to me, grabbed my leg, and begged me not to call the cops. My father stood there in the library doorway and dared me to do it. He dared me, all the while watching my mother sobbing and pleading, on her knees, her nails digging into my jeans. Jesus, it was horrible. I put down the phone and left. I never went back. I just couldn't. Nothing I did mattered, not really. If I was there for a while, he just waited until I left. Then he probably beat her more viciously than if I'd never been there at all. I remember I wondered if he'd broken her ribs that time, but I never asked. What good would it have done?"

"But he didn't take his revenge until six months ago," Savich said. "He waited—what?—some five years before he went after you."

"That's not quite true. He started his revenge with Scott. I'm convinced of that now. Yes, he was behind my marriage to Scott. There weren't any men in my life before that. I worked for Senator Bainbridge right out of college. I was happy. I never saw my parents. I had friends. I'd see my father every once in a while, by accident, and I could tell that he still hated my guts.

"I remember once at a party, I ran into my mother in the women's room. She was combing her hair and her long sleeve had fallen away. There was a horrible purple bruise on her arm. I remember just looking at it and saying, 'What kind of monster in you allows you to let that bastard beat you?'

"She slapped me. I guess I deserved it. I didn't see her again until that night I went to her for money when I was running away from you."

"You do remember actually going to your parents' house the night your father was killed?"

"Yes, but nothing else is clear. How was I sure my father was dead? I don't know. But I did know, and I guess I must have believed that Noelle finally couldn't stand the beatings anymore. Yes, that's what I must have thought, although all that isn't particularly clear."

She began to rub her temples with the palms of her hands. "No, I don't know, James. I think I remember screams, I think I can see a gun, but nothing else, just these images. And maybe blood. I remember blood. But my father? Dead? Was Noelle there? I just can't swear to anything. I'm sorry. I'm no help at all."

But Quinlan wasn't worried. He looked over at Savich whose fingers were tap-dancing on his laptop, nary a furrow of worry on his brow. He knew that Savich was hearing everything they said. He also knew that Savich wasn't worried either.

Quinlan had pulled this off before. They had lots to work with. Sally was ready.

He said slowly, more to himself really, so she would get calm again, "So your father bided his time."

"Yes. It wasn't until after we were married that I found out my father was Scott's boss. He'd never told me what firm he was with. He was vague and I didn't really pay attention. It was all downhill from there, once I found out."

Quinlan paced his living room, not nervous pacing, just rhythmic strides. Savich worked MAX's keyboard. Sally rubbed the dust off the small rubber tree that sat in a beautiful oriental pot next to the sofa.

Quinlan stopped. He smiled at Sally. "I think it's time you made some phone calls, Sally. I think it's time we get the gang together and do some rattling. We'll see what falls out." He handed her the phone.

"Mom, then Scott, then Beadermeyer."

"YOU WANT TO KNOW what's driving me crazy?" Savich said, looking up from the keyboard and stretching his muscles. "I want to know why Beadermeyer is still after you. It was your father who had you put away there. He's dead. Why the hell would Beadermeyer care anymore? Who's following in your old man's footsteps? You said Scott had to be in on it? But why would he care now? Wouldn't he just want that divorce so he could get on with his life? You sure you're up for this, Sally?"

"Yes, I'm up for it. In fact, I can't wait. I want to spit in Beadermeyer's face. As for why they took me again, I've thought and thought, but I can't think of a decent reason. Now let me make those calls."

She took the phone and dialed. There wasn't any wait at all. "Mom? It's me, Sally. I wondered if I could come over. I need to talk to you, Mom. Yes, right now. Is that all right?"

Slowly, she pressed the off button. She started to dial Scott's number. Quinlan lightly touched his hand to hers and shook his head. "No, I think your mom just might get the other players there."

"He's right," Savich said. "If she doesn't, then we'll talk to her alone. We need to anyway. We need to know exactly where she stands in all of this mess."

"James is right," Sally said and swallowed hard. "The others will be there. But know this—she was protecting me. I'd bet my life on it."

He wanted to hug her, but he didn't. He watched her blink back the tears and swallow until she had control again. Sally had guts. She also had him.

He said, "Okay. Let me make some phone calls, then we'll get this show on the road."

Thirty minutes later James tapped the griffin-head knocker of the St. John home.

Noelle St. John answered the door herself. She was wearing a silk dress in a pale blue. Her hair, blonder than Sally's, was twisted up in a neat chignon. She looked elegant, tense, and very pale. She hesitated a moment, then held out her arms to her daughter. Sally didn't move. Noelle St. John looked as if she was ready to burst into tears. She lowered her arms to her sides.

She said quickly, her words running together as if she couldn't get them out fast enough, "Oh, Sally, you've come. I've been so worried. When your grandparents called me I didn't know what to do. Come in, love, come in. We'll get this all straightened out." Then she saw Quinlan in the shadows.

"You."

"Yes, ma'am. May I come in as well?"

"No, you may not. Sally, what's going on here?"

"Sorry—no me, then no Sally."

She looked from Sally to Quinlan, shaking her head. She looked confused.

"Noelle, it's all right. Let us in."

She was shaking her head, back and forth. "But he's FBI, Sally. I don't want him here. He was here before with another man, and they searched the house looking for you. Why would you want him with you? It doesn't make sense. The last person you want around you is a cop. He's lied to you. He's manipulating you. He's just making you more confused."

"No, Noelle, I'm not confused at all about this."

"But Sally, when your grandparents called me, they told me he was right behind you and you claimed you knew he would be. You said he was smart. But they said you wanted to escape and go into hiding. You said the same thing to me. Why are you with him? Why do you want to be with him?"

"He caught me. I'm an amateur and he's not. And trust me, you want him with me, too." Sally took a small step forward and lightly laid her fingertips on her mother's arm.

"That's me, ma'am, real smart. Special Agent James Quinlan. I'm pleased you remember me."

"I wish I didn't remember, sir," Noelle said. She looked back over her shoulder. James smiled, knowing now that there was someone else in the living room. Scott Brainerd? Dr. Beadermeyer? Or both of them? He sure as hell hoped both of them were. "Both of us or neither of us," he said. "It's chilly out here. Make up your mind, ma'am."

"All right, but I don't know why you're with her. You've no right, none at all. Sally's my daughter, she's ill, the FBI can't hold her since she's mentally unstable, nor can the police. She's my responsibility, I'm her guardian, and I say she's going back to the sanitarium. It's the only way she can be protected."

"All that?" James said, looking amazed. Noelle looked at him as if she'd like to smack his face. "She doesn't look unstable to me. I'll bet she could withstand being beaten with rubber hoses, even having her fingernails yanked out. There's not an unstable cell in Sally's brain."

"She's been very ill for the past six months," Noelle said, as she stood back.

They walked past her into the foyer. There were fresh flowers on the beautiful antique table with the large gilded mirror hanging over it. There had always been fresh flowers in that hideous oriental vase, Sally thought, usually white and yellow chrysanthemums.

"Come along into your father's study, Sally. Let's get this over with. Then I'll make certain you're safe again."

"Safe again?" Sally whispered. "Is she nuts?"

Quinlan hugged her quickly against him, and when she looked up at him, he winked at her. "Don't worry."

"Well, well, what a surprise," he said when he saw Dr. Beadermeyer standing by the fireplace. He'd studied the man's photo so many times he felt as if he'd interviewed him, even though they'd never met in the flesh before. Was he the bastard who'd struck him on the head at The Cove? He'd find out soon enough.

He turned to the other man. "And this, I take it, is your husband, Sally? That famous deal-maker Scott Brainerd? Who worked for your father? Who probably married you because your father ordered him to?"

"Her name's Susan," the man said. "Sally is a little girl's name. I never liked it. I call her Susan." He took a step forward, then stopped. "You're looking a bit on edge, Susan, and no wonder. What are you doing with him? Noelle just told me he's an FBI agent—"

"Special agent," Quinlan said, wanting to goad this damned man until he gnashed his teeth. "I've always been a special agent."

"He caught up with her," Noelle said, "and he brought her back. I don't know why he's here, but we must convince him that since Sally isn't well, she wasn't responsible for killing her father. We can protect her. Dr. Beadermeyer can take her back to the sanitarium and keep her safe."

"Since Father's dead," Sally said, staring her mother right in the eye, "that raises a whole lot of questions. For example, since he's no longer with us, then who will come and beat me and fondle me and humiliate me every week?"

Her mother stared at her, her mouth working, but no sound came out. Her face was leached of color. She looked sick now, and uncertain. "Oh, God, no, Sally, that's not possible. Your father and Scott and Dr. Beadermeyer, they all told me every week how well you were doing, what fine care you were getting. No, this can't be true."

"She shouldn't speak of her dead father like that," Dr. Beadermeyer said.

"He's right. This just proves how ill she is," Scott said. "She's making this up. Amory beat his own daughter? Fondled her? That's crazy, she's crazy, she just proved it."

"It's classic," Dr. Beadermeyer said from his staged pose by the fireplace. "Some patients fantasize so strongly that they begin to believe what their minds dredge up. It's usually things that they've always wanted, deep down.

"Your father was a handsome man, Sally. Girls have sexual feelings about their fathers. It's nothing to be ashamed of. The only reason you fantasize that he's come to you is because you wanted it so badly. The beating part, the humiliating part, is just so you can forgive yourself for these feelings by making yourself helpless so that you couldn't prevent it."

"What a bunch of shit," Quinlan said. "You're Dr. Beadermeyer, I take it. Such a pleasure to finally meet you."

"Sorry I can't say the same about you. I'm here to take Sally back with me, and even though you're FBI there's nothing you can do about it."

"Why did you try to kidnap her from the Bonhomie Club three hours ago?"

"Alfred? What's he talking about?"

"A mere misunderstanding, my dear Noelle. I found out where Sally was. I thought I could simply take her with no fuss no bother but it didn't work out."

"It didn't work out?" Sally repeated. "You tried to kidnap me and shove a needle in my arm, and all you can say is it didn't work out?"

He merely smiled at her and shrugged again.

"He brought two goons with him, Noelle," Quinlan said. "All three of them grabbed Sally when she came out of the bathroom and tried to give her a shot." He turned back to Beadermeyer. He wanted very badly to wring the bastard's neck. "We nearly got you, you miserable excuse for a human. At least you have to have your rear window replaced."

"No problem," Beadermeyer said. "It wasn't my car."

"What is going on here?" Scott said. "Noelle told me that Sally escaped. Now she's with an FBI agent. Dr. Beadermeyer told me Sally met this man in this hick town in Oregon and they're lovers. That's not possible. Sally, you're still my wife. What's going on here?"

Quinlan smiled benignly at all of them. "Why don't you just consider me a sort of lawyer for her? I'm here to see that you don't run all over her or that the good doctor here doesn't try to shove another needle into her."

He eyed Scott Brainerd. Tall, slim, beautifully dressed, but that handsome face of his looked haggard. There were dark circles beneath his eyes. He didn't look happy about any of this, and more, he looked scared. He should. Quinlan could tell that he wasn't carrying a gun. He was nervous, part of him always moving, his hands fidgeting. He pulled a pipe out of the pocket of his lovely English jacket. A shoulder holster would ruin the line of that jacket. The bastard.

Quinlan said nothing more, just watched him light his pipe. He imagined that he used the delay to good advantage when he was in negotiations. It also gave his hands something to do when he was nervous or scared shitless.

"You're the man who took Sally away from me, aren't you? You're the one who broke into the sanitarium?"

James smiled at Beadermeyer. "Yeah, right on both counts. How are the German shepherds? They're fine dogs, both with a taste for good raw steak."

"You had no right to break into my facility. I'll sue your butt off."

"Just be quiet, Alfred," Noelle said, "and you too, Mr. Quinlan. Sally, why don't you sit down? Would you like a cup of tea? You look exhausted. You need to rest. You're so thin."

Sally looked at her mother and slowly shook her head. "I'm sorry, Noelle, but I'm afraid you'd let Dr. Beadermeyer drug the tea."

The woman looked as if she'd been hit. She looked frantic. She took a step toward Sally, her hand out. "Sally, no, I'm your mother. I wouldn't hurt you. Please, don't do this. All I want is what's best for you."

Sally was shaking. James took her arm in a firm grip and led her to a small settee. He stayed close to her, knowing it was important for her to feel him beside her, feel the warmth of him, the solidness of him. He put his hands behind his head and eyed them all from beneath his lowered lashes.

He said to Scott Brainerd, who was now puffing furiously on his pipe, "Tell me about how you first met Sally."

"Yes, Scott, do tell him," Sally said.

"If I do, will you tell him to get the hell out of our lives?"

"It's a possibility," Quinlan said. "Tell you what I can promise for sure. I won't throw Sally in the slammer."

"Good," Noelle said. "She needs to be kept safe. Dr. Beadermeyer will see to it. He's promised me he would."

Their litany, Quinlan thought, their damned litany. Was Noelle a part of this? Or could she be this gullible? Couldn't she really see Sally? See that she was perfectly all right?

Scott began to pace, looking at Noelle, who was staring intently at her daughter, as if to read her thoughts, then at Beadermeyer, who was lounging in his large wing chair, trying to copy the damned agent.

"I met her at the Whistler exhibition at the National Gallery of Art. It was an exciting evening. They were displaying sixteen of Whistler's Japanese paintings. Anyway, Sally was there partying with her friends, like she always did. One of the Smithsonian lawyers introduced us. We talked, then had coffee. I took her to dinner.

"That's how it began, nothing more, nothing less. We discovered we had a lot in common. We fell in love. We married."

Beadermeyer rose and stretched. "Vastly romantic, Scott. Now, it's late and Sally needs her rest. It's time for us to leave, Sally."

"I don't think so," Sally said, her voice as calm as could be. James felt the shaking in her arm. "I'm twenty-six years old. I'm perfectly sane. You can't make me go back with you. Incidentally, Scott, you didn't tell James why you neglected to mention that you worked for my father until after we were married."

"You never asked, did you, Sally? You were caught up with your own career, all your fancy parties and wild friends. You didn't really care what I did. You never asked, damn you."

"I asked, but you never came right out with it. You told me it was a law firm and left it at that. I remember asking you, but you wouldn't give much out, ever."

Quinlan felt the ripple beneath the flesh of her hand. He squeezed slightly but kept quiet. She was doing just fine. He was pleased and optimistic. He was fast getting the measure of all three people. Soon, he thought, soon now.

Sally paused just a moment, then said calmly, "I certainly didn't care after I found out you were having an affair."

"That's a lie! I wasn't having an affair. I was faithful to you. I've always been faithful to you, even during these past six months."

Noelle cleared her voice. "This is leading nowhere. Sally, you're saying that you're sane, that indeed your father abused you in the sanitarium—"

"So did Dr. Beadermeyer. He had this creepy little attendant called Holland who liked to bathe me, strip me, fix my hair, and sit on the side of my bed just staring at me."

Noelle turned to Beadermeyer. "Is this true?"

He shrugged. "Just a bit of it. She did have an attendant named Holland. He's gone now. Perhaps once he might have been out of line. These things happen, Noelle, particularly when a patient is as sick as Sally is. As for the rest of it, it's just part of her illness—the delusions, the dark fantasies. Believe me, just as you believed your husband and Scott. Scott lived with her. He saw the disintegration. Isn't that right, Scott?"

Scott nodded. "It was frightening. We're not lying, Noelle."

Noelle St. John did believe them. Quinlan saw it on her face, the look of new resolve, the new certainty, the profound pain she felt.

She said to her daughter, "Listen, Sally, I love you. I've loved you forever. You will get better. I don't care what it costs. You'll have the best care. If you don't like Dr. Beadermeyer, then we'll find you another doctor. But for now, please, go back with him to the sanitarium so you can be protected.

"You were judged mentally incompetent by Judge Harkin. You don't even remember the hearing, do you? Well, no wonder. You were so ill, you just sat through the whole thing, didn't say a thing, just stared straight ahead. I spoke to you, but you just looked through me. You didn't even recognize me. It was horrible.

"I'm your guardian now that your father is dead. Both Scott and I are, as a matter of fact. Please trust me, Sally. I only want what's best for you. I love you."

Scott said, "Mr. Quinlan, you could hold her for a day, maybe, but that's all. The judge has already ruled that she isn't responsible for her actions. You can't do anything to her. No one would consider having her stand trial for the murder of her father."

She kept her head, though Quinlan knew that shook her. This was some group. He still couldn't make up his mind about her mother. She seemed so sincere, so caring, but . . . Now they seemed certain she'd murdered her father? It was almost time for him to intervene, but not just yet.

Sally said, raising her hand to stem her mother's words, "Noelle, did you know that Dr. Beadermeyer kept me drugged all the time? That's why I don't remember the hearing. I told you that my father came and beat me twice a week, but did you know that Dr. Beadermeyer watched? Oh, yes, Doctor, I know about that two-way mirror. I also know you let others look through the door window when my father was fondling himself while I was lying naked on the bed."

She jumped to her feet, and Quinlan was sure she was going to attack Beadermeyer. He lightly touched her arm. Her muscles were frozen. She yelled, "Did you enjoy it, you filthy slug?"

She whirled around to face her mother. "I don't remember the hearing because he kept me drugged up so I wouldn't fight him or any of his keepers. Don't you understand? There was no way in hell they could let up on the drugs. I would have blown them out of the water. Did you also know that sometimes my father would have him lighten the dosage so I'd be more alert when he came to abuse me? That's right, Noelle, believe it. My father, your husband. I'm not lying to you. I'm not making this up to defend my shattered ego. My father was a monster, Noelle. But you know that, don't you?"

Her mother screamed at her, "No more of that, Sally! No more of your crazy lies. I can't stand it, I just can't."

Scott Brainerd shouted, "That's right, Sally. That's more than enough. Apologize to your mother for those horrible things you're saying about her husband."

"But they're all true, and you know they are, Scott. Father couldn't have had me committed without your being in on it. Why did you want me put away, Scott?"

"It nearly killed me to have you committed," Scott said. "Nearly killed me. But we had to. You were going to harm yourself."

To Quinlan's relief, Sally actually managed to laugh. "Oh, that's really good, Scott. You're a wretched liar. Now, Noelle, when my father was beating me, or just holding me down while he stood over me, he'd laugh, tell me how he finally had me right where he wanted me, where I deserved to be.

"Goodness, I remember it all now. He said it was his revenge for all the years I tried to protect you, Noelle. He said being in this nice place would keep my mouth shut about the other, but I don't know what he meant by that."

"I do," Quinlan said. "We'll get to that later."

She smiled at him and nodded, then turned back to her mother. "Did he tell you how much he hated me? But I guess locking me away wasn't enough for him. I guess he wasn't beating you enough, Noelle, since he had to come and beat me as well. Twice a week. Like clockwork. He was a man of disciplined habits. I was so drugged I sometimes didn't even know, but Holland, that pathetic little creep, he would say, 'Yep, every Tuesday and Friday, the old guy's here to knock you around and beat off.'

"Of course, I do remember many of the times, particularly when they lightened the drugs. It pleased him—to know I knew it was him and I was helpless to stop him doing anything he wanted to do."

Noelle St. John turned on Dr. Beadermeyer. "She is sick, isn't she, Alfred? This can't be true, can it? And not just Amory but Scott too. Why, he's sworn to me that she's very ill. Just as you have."

Beadermeyer shrugged. It was the man's favorite response, Quinlan thought. "I think she believes what she's saying is true. She really is very ill. Because she believed he did this to her, she had to murder him to assuage her own guilt. I told you how she managed to hide the sedatives beneath her tongue and escape the sanitarium. She came straight here, like a homing pigeon, took her father's gun from his desk, and when he came in, she shot him. You heard the shot, Noelle. So did you, Scott. By the time I got here she was standing over him, watching the blood leak out of his chest, and all of you were just staring at her. I tried to help her, but she turned that gun on me and escaped again."

Quinlan sat forward on the sofa. Ah, now it would come out. It was time. None of this surprised him. In a few minutes it wouldn't surprise Sally either.

Beadermeyer turned to Sally, and his voice was gentle as a soft rain on the windowpanes. "Come, my dear, I'll protect you from the police. I'll protect you from the FBI, from the press, from everyone. You must leave this man. You don't even know who he is."

"Susan," Scott said, "I'm sorry for all this, but I know you couldn't help yourself. All those delusions, those dreams, those fantasies, Dr. Beadermeyer told us you had. You did shoot Amory, you had the gun in your hand. Noelle and I saw you holding that gun, leaning down over him. We just want to help you, protect you. We didn't tell the police a thing. Dr. Beadermeyer left before they even came. No one accused you. We've been protecting you all along."

"I didn't kill my father."

"But you told me you didn't remember anything," Noelle said. "You told me you were afraid I'd done it and that was why you ran away. To protect you, I made the police suspect me, acted as guilty as I could, even though I hadn't killed him. What saved me was that they couldn't ever find the gun. Neither Scott nor I ever told the police that we were practically witnesses to the shooting. In fact, Scott didn't even tell them he was here. That made me a better suspect. They couldn't find you. The police are certain that you know I did it and that's why you ran. But I didn't, Sally, I didn't. You did."

"And I know she didn't, Susan," Scott Brainerd said, his pipe dangling loose in his right hand, cold now. "I met her in the hallway, and we came into the living room together. You were there, leaning over him, the gun in your hand. You have to go with Dr. Beadermeyer or else you'll wind up behind bars."

"Ah, yes," said Quinlan. "The good Dr. Beadermeyer, or should I call you Norman Lipsy, from the fair nation of Canada to our north?"

"I prefer Dr. Beadermeyer," the man said, with exquisite calm. He lounged more comfortably in his chair, a man without a care, relaxed, at ease.

"What's he talking about?" Scott said.

"Your good doctor here is a fake," Quinlan said. "That little hideaway of his is nothing more than a prison where he keeps folks that family or others want out of the way. I wonder how much money Sally's father paid him to keep her? Maybe you know, Scott? Maybe some of it was your money. I'll just bet it was."

"I am a doctor, sir. You are insulting. I will sue you for libel."

"I have been to the sanitarium," Noelle said. "It's a clean, modern facility. The people there couldn't have been nicer. I didn't get to see Sally simply because she was so ill. What do you mean, people pay for Dr. Beadermeyer to hold their enemies prisoner?"

"It's true, Mrs. St. John, the simple truth. Your husband wanted Sally out of the way. Was it his final revenge against her for trying to protect you? I'll bet that's sure one part of it."

Quinlan turned to Sally. "I think you might have wasted your time protecting your mom, Sally. It seems to me that she would just as soon throw you right back to the hounds."

"That's not true," Noelle said, twisting her hands now. "Don't believe him, Sally."

Quinlan just smiled at her. "In any case, your husband, Mrs. St. John, paid Norman Lipsy here a ton of money every month to keep his daughter drugged to her ears, to let him come visit his little girl and abuse her. Oh, yes, he did abuse her, humiliate her, treat her like a little sex slave. We have a witness."

DR. BEADERMEYER DIDN'T change position or expression.

Scott actually jumped. As for Noelle, she turned as white as the walls.

"No," she whispered. "A witness?"

"Yes, ma'am. FBI agents picked up Holland. Just before we came here, they called. He's singing, Norman. His little lungs are near to bursting with all the songs pouring out of his mouth.

"It's not just Sally who was kept there. There's a senator's daughter. Her name is Patricia. Dr. Beadermeyer gave her a lobotomy—and botched it, by the way."

"That isn't true, none of it."

"Now, Norman, the FBI will be at the sanitarium shortly with a search warrant, and they'll go through that office of yours like ants at a picnic lunch. All your dirty little secrets will be out. I have a friend at the *Washington Post*. All the world will soon know your secrets. All those poor people you've kept at your prison will be free again.

"Now, given all this, Noelle, do you still want to put any stock in this guy's word?"

Noelle looked from Quinlan to Dr. Beadermeyer. "How much did my husband pay you?" It was suddenly a new Noelle—straight shoulders, no longer pale and fragile-looking, but a strong woman whose eyes were narrowed now, whose jaw was locked and hard. He saw rage in those soft blue eyes of hers.

"It was just for her care, Noelle, nothing more. Her case is complex. She's paranoid schizophrenic. She's been mentally ill for some time. We tried a number of drugs to relieve her symptoms. But we were never fully successful. This thing she dreamed up about her father—it gave her enough to focus to escape and come to kill him. It's that simple and that complex. I did nothing wrong.

"This Holland—poor fellow—I took him in. He's very simple in the head. It's true he attended Sally. He was very fond of her in his moronic way. Only a fool would believe anything he said. He'd say whatever anyone wanted him to say. They'll realize quickly enough that he'll say anything, just to please them."

"For someone who's not a shrink, you're not bad, Norman," Quinlan said.

"What do you mean he's not a shrink?" Scott said.

"He's a plastic surgeon. He deals with the outside of the head, not the inside. He's a fake. He's a criminal. And he watched your husband hurt his own daughter. I have no reason to lie to you, Mrs. St. John."

"Bastard," Dr. Beadermeyer said. "All right, Noelle, if you no longer believe me, no longer trust my word, then I won't take Sally back with me. I'll leave. I've got nothing more to say. The only reason I came here was to help Sally."

He took a step forward, but Quinlan was up in an instant. Three steps and he had Dr. Beadermeyer's tie in his fist. He said very softly, right in his face, "Who is paying you to hold Sally now that her father's dead? Scott here? If so, why? Why was she put away? It wasn't just revenge, was it?" Quinlan knew, but he wanted to hear it out of Beadermeyer's mouth.

"Noelle is paying me only for her regular treatment, the same as I've always received."

"Bullshit. Who's paying you? You still want to lie, do you? Well, I'll be able to tell you, Mrs. St. John, exactly the amount your dear husband was paying this little bastard, just as soon as the FBI finishes going through all his crooked little books."

"I'm calling my lawyer. You can't do this. I'll sue you, all of you."

"If Mrs. St. John was paying you just for Sally's care, then why did you come to The Cove, knock both Sally and me on the head, and haul her back to your sanitarium? Did you bill Noelle for the airfare? And your little excursion to the Bonhomie Club with those two goombas— will you send Noelle a bill for their services? How about that rear window I shot out? Don't you bill for overtime, Norman? No comment this time? Don't you even want to insist that you're such a dedicated doctor that you'll do anything to help your poor patients?" Quinlan turned to Noelle, who looked as if she'd love to have a knife. She was looking at Dr. Beadermeyer with very new eyes. "When I got to Sally in the sanitarium she was so drugged it took more than a day to clear her out. That sounds like great treatment, doesn't it, Noelle?"

"Oh, I believe you, Mr. Quinlan. I believe you now."

Dr. Beadermeyer just shrugged and looked down at his fingernails.

"Maybe," Quinlan said, "it's Scott here who wants his wife kept under wraps?"

"That's ridiculous," Scott Brainerd yelled. "I never did anything, just told her father how worried I was about her."

Noelle said very calmly, "No, Scott, that isn't true. You're lying as well. All of you lied to me. If it had been just Amory, I wouldn't have bought it for a minute, but no, all of you were just like this Greek chorus, telling me the same thing over and over until I believed you. Goddamn you, I believed you! I allowed you to put my little girl in that goddamn institution!"

Quinlan quickly stepped out of the way when he saw her coming. She dashed to Beadermeyer and slammed her fist into his jaw before he even had a chance to twitch. He reeled back against the mantelpiece. Noelle stepped back, panting. "You bastard." She whirled around to face Scott. "You vicious little shit, why did you do this to my daughter? How much did my husband pay you?"

Sally rose from the sofa. She walked to her mother. She put her arms around her. "Thank you," she said against her mother's hair. "Thank you. I hope I can hit Beadermeyer myself before this is all over."

Sally wiped her damp hands on her pants legs. She felt such a surge of relief that it made her mouth dry. She actually smiled as she said to Scott, "I'm divorcing you. It shouldn't take long, since I don't even want my poor ivy plant that's probably already dead anyway. My lawyer will serve the papers on you as soon as I can arrange it."

"You're fucking crazy. No lawyer is going to do a thing you say."

"If you take another step toward her, Brainerd, I'll just have to kill you. That or I'll let Noelle at you. Look at poor Norman, his lip is bleeding. You know, I like the thought of Sally as a widow."

Quinlan walked calmly up to Scott Brainerd, pulled back his fist, and rammed it into his stomach. "That's for Sally, Noelle, and me."

Scott yelped, bent over, breathing like he'd been shot, his arms clutching his middle.

"Sally," Quinlan said, rubbing his knuckles, wanting to hit Scott Brainerd again but knowing it wouldn't be smart, "one of my sisters-in-law is a lawyer. She'll handle the paperwork on the divorce. Severing ties with this slug shouldn't be difficult. It takes six months. Maybe I should kill him. You want to try running away, Scott?

"Oh, yes, I forgot to tell you guys, the FBI is also all over the private books in Amory St. John's firm. They've been doing that for a while now. That's the real reason the FBI got involved in the first place. It's all delicate stuff, so that's why we've kept it under wraps, but there's no reason for you not to know.

"Selling arms to places like Algeria, Iraq, and Libya—well, we do tend to frown on stunts like that. And that's got to be the other reason, Sally, that your father and your husband locked you away. They must have believed that you would say something incriminating, something to prove that they were traitors."

"But I never saw a thing, never," Sally said. "Is that it, Scott?"

"No, damn you. I didn't have a thing to do with that."

"And her father manipulated you into coming on to Sally, into marrying her?"

"No, that's not true. All right, so I did agree to have her put away. That's because I believed she was sick."

"Why did you believe I was sick, Scott?"

He didn't say anything, just waved his pipe at her. "You weren't a good wife. Your dad swore to me that your career was just something for you to do until you got married. He said you were just like your mother, a woman who really wanted a husband to take care of and children to look after. I wanted a wife to stay home and take care of me, but you wouldn't do it. I needed you there, to help me, to understand me, but no, you never stayed there for me."

"That doesn't make her sick, Scott," Quinlan said.

"I refuse to say anything more about it," Scott said.

"Why am I not surprised that he was a traitor?" said Noelle. "But I'm not. Then maybe one of his clients murdered him. Maybe it wasn't Sally after all. Such a pity it wasn't Scott who murdered him. That's what you were, isn't it, Scott, you pathetic jerk?"

Good, Quinlan thought, she was trying to explain her husband's murder another way. He was pleased. He said, "That's what he was, Mrs. St. John. Now, you said you walked in here with Scott and found Sally literally standing over him with the smoking gun."

Noelle was frowning, her mouth working. She was thinking real hard. "Well, yes, but she said that she'd heard the shot and come running. She said she had picked the gun up. She said she was here to get money from me and leave."

Quinlan pulled a folded piece of paper out of his breast pocket. He unfolded it and scanned it. "This is your statement to the cops, Noelle. No mention of Sally. Too bad a neighbor reported seeing her running from the house. But you tried, Noelle, you tried.

"Were you really with Scott that night? Did you really run in here with him to see Sally over your husband's body?"

Scott threw his pipe at the fireplace. It fell with a loud crack against the marble hearth. "Damn you! Of course I was with her! I was with her all evening."

Scott was still rubbing his belly, and that made Quinlan feel good. That damned bloody little worm. He turned back to Noelle.

"I'm pleased you tried to protect Sally. But I did wonder if you weren't in it along with these other sterling characters."

"I don't blame you," Noelle said. "I'd think I was a jerk too. But I'm not. I'm just plain stupid."

Sally smiled at her mother. "I'm stupid too. I married Scott, didn't I? Just take a good look at him."

Quinlan said, "Listen, Noelle. Only a real bad person would turn on her daughter after what she tried to do for you since she was sixteen. She was just a girl, and yet she tried to protect you. I want you to tell me this isn't true. Tell me you didn't kill your husband. Tell me you didn't kill that monster who'd been abusing you."

"I didn't kill him, I didn't. Oh, God, you believe me, don't you, Sally? You don't believe I killed your father, do you?"

There was no hesitation. Sally took her mother in her arms. "I believe you."

"But there's so much more, Sally," Quinlan said, his voice soft and smooth, the promise of truth in that voice. "It's time now to get it all out. I want you to think back now. Look at Noelle and think back to that night."

Sally drew back, her eyes on her mother. Then, slowly, she turned to Quinlan. "I now have a clear picture of my father, lying right over there, blood all over his chest. I'm sorry, James, but I don't remember anything else."

"Your mother said you had a gun. You don't remember taking the gun with you, Sally?"

She started to shake her head, then she stared down at her brown boots.

Quinlan said, "It was an antique Roth-Steyr pistol your father probably bought off an old English soldier from World War One. It has a ten-round clip, ugly devil, about nine inches long."

"Yes," Sally said slowly, moving away from him, walking toward the spot on the floor where she'd found her father's body, right in front of his huge mahogany desk. "Yes, I remember that pistol. He was very proud of it. The English ambassador gave it to him back in the 1970s. He'd done him a big favor.

"Yes, now I can see it clearly. I remember picking it up now, holding it. I remember thinking it was heavy, that it weighed my hand down. I remember that it felt hot, like it had just been used."

"It is heavy. The sucker weighs a bit more than three pounds. Are you looking at it, Sally?"

She was standing there, apart from him, apart from all of them, and he knew she was remembering now, fitting those jagged memory pieces together, slowly, but he'd known she could do it.

"It's hot, Sally," he said. "It's burning your hand. What are you going to do with it?"

"I remember that I was glad he was dead. He was wicked. He'd hurt Noelle all those years and he'd never paid for it. He'd always done exactly what he'd wanted to do. He'd gotten me. There'd never been any justice, until then.

"Yes, I can remember that's what I was thinking. 'You're dead, you miserable bastard, and I'm glad. Everyone is free from you now. You're dead.'"

"Do you remember Noelle coming in? Do you remember her screaming?"

She was looking down at her hands, flexing her fingers. "The gun is so hot. I don't know what to do with it. I can see you now, Noelle, and yes, there's Scott behind you. But you have your coats on. You weren't here at the house, you'd been out. Just Father is here, no one else.

"You started screaming, Noelle. Scott, you didn't do a blessed thing. You looked at me like I was some sort of wild dog, like you wanted to put me down."

"We thought you'd killed him," Scott said. "He wasn't even supposed to be at home that night. He was supposed to be in New York, but he came back unexpectedly. You grabbed that gun and you shot him."

But Sally was just shaking her head, looking not frightened but thoughtful, her forehead furrowed. "No, I remember that when I got here I tried the front door. I didn't expect it to be unlocked, but it was. Just as I turned the knob, I heard a shot. I ran into this room and there he was, on the floor, his chest covered with blood.

"I remember—" She paused, frowning ferociously. Then she pressed her knuckles against her forehead. "It's so vague, so fuzzy. Those damned drugs you gave me—God, I could kill you for that."

Quinlan said, "He's in so much trouble now, Sally, that killing him would be letting him off lightly. I want to see him spend all his money on lawyers. Then I want to see him rot in prison for the rest of his miserable life. Don't worry about him. You can do this. It's all vague, but it's there. What do you see?"

She was staring down at where his body had sprawled, arms flung out, his right palm up. So much blood. There had been so much blood. Noelle had laid a new carpet. But there'd been something strange, something she couldn't quite put her finger on, something . . .

"There was someone else there," she said. "Yes, there was someone else in the room."

"How did you get the gun?"

She said without hesitation, "It was on the floor. He was bending down to pick it up when I came into the room. He straightened up real fast and ran to the French doors."

She turned slowly and looked at the floor-to-ceiling windows that gave onto a patio and yard. There were high bushes and a fence between this house and the one next door.

"You're sure it was a man?"

"Yes, I'm sure. I can see his hand opening the handle on the French doors. He's wearing gloves, black leather gloves."

"Did you see his face?"

"No, he—" Her voice froze. She began to shake her back and forth, back and forth. "No," she whispered, looking toward those French doors. "It's not possible, it's just not possible."

"You see him now, Sally?" Quinlan's voice was steady and unhurried.

She looked at James, then at her mother, at Scott, and finally at Dr. Beadermeyer. She said, "Maybe they're right, James. Maybe I am crazy."

"Who was he, Sally?"

"No, no, I'm crazy. I'm delusional."

"Who was he?"

She looked defeated, her shoulders bowed, her head lowered. She whispered, "He was my father."

"Ah," Quinlan said. Everything was falling neatly into place, though not yet for the others.

Noelle whispered, "Your father? Oh, Sally, that's impossible. Your father was lying dead on the floor. I saw him, I went down on my knees beside him. I even shook him. It was your father. I couldn't be wrong about that."

Scott waved his pipe at her, shaking his head, saying, "She's bloody crazy, crazier than we thought. Your father's dead, Sally, just like Noelle said. I saw him dead too. Don't forget there were the two of us."

Dr. Beadermeyer said, "It's all right, Sally. It's another symptom of your illness. Will you come with me now? I'll call your father's lawyer, and he can come and make sure this man doesn't take you to jail."

Quinlan let all their voices float over him for a moment. He stood up and walked to Sally. He took her hands in his. "Well done," he said, leaned down, and kissed her.

"You bastard, that's my wife! I don't want her, but she still is my wife."

He kissed her again. "Everything makes sense now." He turned to Dr. Beadermeyer. "Now it all fits. You're a plastic surgeon, Norman. You must be very good at it. Where did you find the man whose face you reworked into Amory St. John's?"

"You don't know what you're talking about. The murdered man was Amory St. John. No one doubted it. Why should they? There were no questions."

"That's because there was no reason to doubt it. Why would anyone check dental records, for example, if the wife of the deceased identified the body, if the face on the body looked like all the faces on all the photographs on the desk? It does bother me though that the medical examiner didn't see the scars from the surgery. You must be very good, Norman."

"God, did you really do that, Dr. Beadermeyer?" Scott said. "Did you really plan with Armory St. John to kill another man and have him take Amory's place? Was he planning to leave me to take the fall? Dammit, it's the truth, isn't it? I'd be the one blamed because he was supposedly dead. And I didn't do all that much, I swear. There was Sally, but that was necessary because we knew she'd read several short messages that I'd forgotten were in my briefcase. There wasn't any choice. I went along with him because I had to."

Quinlan hit him again, this time in the jaw. He rather hoped he'd broken it.

Beadermeyer looked down at Scott, who was now lying on his side, unconscious. "What a piece of nothing he is, but that's not my problem. Now, Quinlan, all this is nuts. Armory St. John was the one who died. I've had enough of this. I'm sorry, Sally. I've tried to help you, but now I just don't care. I'm leaving."

"When the devil leaves hell, Dr. Beadermeyer," she said. "That's when I'd go with you."

"Best you find another comparison, Sally," Quinlan said. "I know for a fact that the devil roams all over the world. We've got two of his minions right here. So Sally's father is still paying you. That surely answers the rest of my questions."

"I'm leaving," Dr. Beadermeyer said and walked toward the door.

"I don't think you want to leave just yet," Savich said, stepping into the room.

"When that worm wakes up I want to hit him," Noelle St. John said. "Well, maybe I won't wait." She walked over to Scott and kicked him in the ribs. "As for you," she said to Dr. Beadermeyer, "if only Mr. Quinlan will give me a rubber hose, I'll work you over but good. What all of you did to my daughter . . . Jesus, I'd like to kill you."

"I'll make sure you get that rubber hose, Noelle," Quinlan said.

"I'm going to sue all of you. Police brutality, that's it, and libel. Just look at poor Scott."

Sally went over and kicked Scott in the ribs. Then she walked into her mother's arms.

SAVICH NODDED TO Quinlan and smiled at Sally. "That was well done. Quinlan's good at helping people remember."

He turned to Dr. Beadermeyer. "I don't think you want to leave just yet. I've got lots more buddies coming any minute now. And they're all special agents, which means they can shoot off the end of your pinkie finger at fifty yards and make you sing out every secret you've had since you were two years old. They're really very good, so it's best that you just stay put, Dr. Beadermeyer."

Noelle was staring at Dr. Beadermeyer. "I hope you rot in the deepest pit they can find to throw you in. Now, you miserable ass, where is my husband? Who was the poor man both of you murdered?"

"That's an excellent question," Quinlan said. "Tell us, Norman."

It happened quickly. Dr. Beadermeyer pulled a small revolver out of his coat pocket. "I don't have to tell you anything, you son of a bitch. You've ruined my life, Quinlan. I have no home, no money, damn you, nothing. God, I'd love to kill you, but then I'd never know peace, would I?"

They heard several car doors slam.

"It's too late to whine, Norman," Quinlan said. "Now you're going to the slammer. You might consider cutting a deal. Tell us where Amory St.

John is hiding. Tell us the name of that guy whose face you rearranged. Tell us the whole sordid story."

"Go to hell, Quinlan."

"Not for many years yet, I hope," Quinlan said. "So it was Amory St. John who was continuing to pay you to keep Sally a prisoner. Was it indeed her father who followed her to The Cove and peered at her through her bedroom window that night? Were you with him? Did the two of you knock us out and take Sally back to your wonderful sanitarium? Yeah, that sounds right. It was Amory St. John on the phone to his daughter, his own face staring in at her through the bedroom window."

"It's all a lie, all of it. I'm leaving now. Come here, Noelle. I don't think anyone will shoot if you're with me."

Sally said, "My father must have been furious when I saw him run out of this room. He would have thought I'd shout it to the world. That's why he wanted you to keep me in the sanitarium."

"Don't be ridiculous, Sally," Dr. Beadermeyer said. "You're crazy. You escaped from a mental institution. Even if you'd spouted all this out as soon as the cops got here, no one would have believed you, not a single soul."

"But it would have raised questions," Quinlan said. "I would have wondered and chewed on it. I'm a real FBI nerd when it comes to things like that. I wouldn't have let it go. Sally's right. That's why you and her father wanted to keep her locked up. She was out of the way permanently. And her father still believed she knew he was a traitor, or at least suspected that he wasn't a solid citizen."

"Shut up. Come here, Noelle, or I'll shoot your bloody daughter."

"How much money are we talking here, Norman? A couple million? More? It just occurred to me why you wanted Sally so badly. She was your insurance policy, wasn't she? With her, you didn't have to worry that Amory St. John would kill you. Of course, he could have killed Sally too, but that would have raised questions inevitably.

"No, better for him to just keep paying you off until he came up with a bright idea to rid himself of you. Have I gotten anything wrong, Norman? I love real-life wicked plots. Novels can't even come close."

Dr. Beadermeyer waved the gun. "Come here, Noelle."

Scott stirred on the floor, shook his head, and slowly sat up. He moaned and rubbed his ribs. "What's going on here? What are you doing, Dr. Beadermeyer?"

"I'm leaving, Scott. If you want to come along, you can. We've got Noelle. The cops won't take a chance of shooting because they just might hit her. Come here, Noelle." He pointed the revolver at Sally. "Now."

Noelle walked slowly to where he stood. He grabbed her left arm and pulled her tightly against him. "We'll just go out through the French doors. Nice and slow, Noelle, nice and slow. Ah, Scott, why don't you just stay put? I never really liked you, always thought you were a no-account worm. Yes, you just stay here."

"What you're doing isn't smart, Norman," Quinlan said. "Believe me, it isn't smart at all."

"Shut up, you bastard." He kicked open the French doors and pulled Noelle through them. Quinlan didn't move, just shook his head. Savich said, "You did warn him, Quinlan."

There were voices, two shots. Then dead silence. Savich ran outside.

"Noelle!" Sally ran through the open French doors onto the patio, yelling her name over and over.

They turned to see Noelle stumble toward her daughter. The women embraced.

Quinlan said, "Now, Scott, why don't you tell us which woman is your lover—Jill or Monica?"

"Neither, damn you. I'm gay!"

"Jesus, that's a kicker," Quinlan said.

Savich came back in. There was a huge grin on his face. "Poor old Norman Lipsy just got a nick in the arm. He'll be just fine."

"I'm glad about that," Quinlan said.

"Scott is gay, James?" Sally stared at her husband. "You're gay and you married me?"

"I had to," Scott said. "Your father's ruthless. I'd done just a little fiddling with some clients' accounts, but he discovered it. That's when he got me into the arms deals and told me I had to marry you. He also paid me, but believe me, it wasn't enough to bear you for those six months."

Quinlan laughed and pulled Sally against him. "I hope this doesn't depress you too much."

"I think I'll kick up my heels."

They heard Dr. Beadermeyer cursing outside, then moaning, complaining loudly that his arm was bleeding too much, that he'd die from blood loss, that the bastards wanted him to die.

They heard Savich laugh and say loudly, "Justice. I do like to see justice done."

Sally said, "There's no justice yet. James, where is my father?"

He kissed her on the mouth and hugged her. "We'll check first to see if his passport is gone. If it isn't, we'll have him soon enough."

"Another thing," Savich said, "where is that bloody Roth-Steyr pistol?"

"I remember running after my father out the French doors. I threw it in the bushes."

"The cops would have found it. They didn't."

"Then that means her father saw her throw it away and doubled back to get it," Quinlan said. And he smiled. "That pistol IDs him better than fingerprints."

"That poor man Dr. Beadermeyer operated on. I wonder who he was?"

"I don't think we'll ever know, Sally, unless Beadermeyer talks. He was cremated. Damnation, all the clues were there, staring me right in the face. Your father had made out a new will about eight months ago, specifying that he wanted to be cremated immediately. Norman Lipsy was a plastic surgeon. You were certain it was your father on the phone.

I should have believed you, but I truly believed that what you heard was some sort of spliced tape recording of his voice. We'll get him, Sally. I promise."

Quinlan took her home and made her promise to stay there. He had to go to the office and see how the investigation was going.

"But it's after midnight."

"This is a big deal. The FBI building will be lit up from top to bottom, well, at least part of the fifth floor."

"Can I go with you?"

He pictured thirty men and women all talking at the same time, going over reams of paper, one group reviewing what they'd recovered from Amory St. John's office, another group delving into Dr. Beadermeyer's papers.

Then there was Dr. Beadermeyer to interview—ah, he wanted to get Norman in a room alone, just the two of them and a tape recorder and go at it. He nearly rubbed his hands together.

"Yes," he said, "you can come, but agents will latch on to you and question you until you want to curl up in the fetal position and sleep."

"I'm ready to talk," she said and grinned up at him.

"Oh, James, I'm so relieved. Scott is gay and my mother wasn't in on anything. There *is* someone here for me besides you."

MARVIN BRAMMER, assistant director and head of the Criminal Investigative Division, wanted her examined by FBI doctors and shrinks.

Quinlan talked him out of it. Sally didn't get to see him do it, but she just bet he was very good.

She ended up talking at length to Marvin Brammer. He, without realizing it, was positively courtly with her.

By the end of the hour-long interview, he'd gotten even more details of that night from her. Brammer was one of the best interviewers in the FBI, an organization known for its excellent interview skills. Maybe he was even better than Quinlan, but she doubted if James would admit that.

When she came out of Marvin Brammer's office, Brammer behind her with his hand lightly holding her elbow, there was Noelle sitting in the small waiting area, asleep. She looked young and very pretty. She looked, Sally thought, just like she should look. But she was worried about her father. What if he got to Noelle again? What if he got to her? She'd said all that to Mr. Brammer, but he'd reassured her again and again that they would have guards on the two of them. There was no chance Amory St. John would get near either of them. Besides, he couldn't imagine the man being that stupid. No, everything would be all right.

"That's my mother," Sally said. "Isn't she beautiful? She's always loved me." She gave Brammer a smile that would have disarmed a rabid cynic.

Brammer cleared his throat. He ran his fingers lightly through his thick white hair. The word was that his interview skills had increased exponentially when his hair had turned white overnight after a shoot-out five years before in which he'd nearly been killed. You looked at him and you trusted him.

"From what Quinlan told me—he insisted on talking to Scott Brainerd—it seems that Scott did indeed embezzle client funds on a very small scale. But your father caught him, and that was it. He did some of your father's dirty work, so your father really had him. Ah, you were right, he did have a lover, a guy named Allen Falkes, in the British embassy. I'm sorry."

"Actually, all of this comes as quite a relief. I'm not hurt, Mr. Brammer," she said, and it was true. "I'm just surprised by all of it. I've really been used, haven't I?"

"Yes, but a lot of people are used every day. Not as grossly as you've been, but manipulated by those who are more powerful, those who are smarter, those who have more money. But as I said, that won't be a problem anymore, Mrs. Brainerd."

"Call me Sally. After all this, I don't think I ever want to have the Brainerd name attached to me again."

"Sally. A nice name. Warm and funny and cozy. Quinlan likes your name. He said it was a name that made him feel good, made him feel like he'd always get a ready smile, and probably a good deal more, but he didn't add that. Sometimes Quinlan has discretion, at least when he's on the job—or rather, when he's talking to me, his boss."

She said nothing to that.

Brammer really didn't know why he was doing it, but this thin young woman who'd been through more than her fair share for a lifetime, who didn't know the first thing about getting information out of people, had made him spill his guts—and she hadn't said a thing.

Actually, he wanted to take her home with him and feed her and tell her jokes until she was smiling and laughing all the time.

He said, impelled by all the protective instincts she fostered in him, "I've known Quinlan for six years. He's an excellent agent. He's smart and he's intuitive. He's got this sort of extra sense that many times puts him nearly in another person's head—or heart. Sometimes I'm not sure which. Sometimes I have to rein him in, yell at him because he plays a lone hand, which we don't like to have happen. Bureau agents are trained to be team players, except for those in New York City, of course, and Quinlan down here at the Metro office. But I always know when he's doing it, even though he thinks he's fooling me.

"He also has this knack for making people remember things buried deep in their brains. He did that with you tonight, didn't he?"

"Yes. But, on the other hand, Mr. Brammer, you got even more out of me."

"Ah, but that's just because Quinlan opened the spigot, so to speak. Now, in addition to being one of the best agents in this office, he's a very talented man. He plays the saxophone. He's from a huge family sprawled out all over the East Coast. His father retired two years ago, a big-time investment banker. His first wife, Teresa, was a big mistake, but that's over with. He hunkered down for a while, rethought lots of things, and then he came out of hibernation, and he got well. Now he's met you, and all he can do is smile and rub his hands together and talk about the future. Treat him well, Sally."

"As in be gentle with him?"

Marvin Brammer laughed. "Nah, beat on him, give him a run for his money, don't let him pull any of his smart-ass pranks on you."

"Pranks?"

He gave her a surprised grin, then just shook his head. "You haven't known him all that long. You'll see, once you're married, Sally. Maybe even before you're married. I've heard that Quinlan's daddy is just the same. But Quinlan has something his daddy doesn't have."

"What's that?"

"You," Marvin Brammer said. He touched his palm lightly to her cheek. "Don't worry, Sally. We'll get your father, and he'll pay for what he's done. Quinlan was talking a mile a minute to bring me up to date. He told me about your father calling you twice and his face appearing in your bedroom window when you were staying at your aunt's house in this small town called The Cove. Of course, he thought it was someone mimicking your father, that or a spliced tape. He said you knew it was your father. And that scared you. He told me he'd never doubt you about anything again. Now, Sally, let's get honest here. It's not just the murder of that unknown man, it's not just what he did to you, although that turns my stomach—it's the dirty dealings he's been pulling for several years now, the arms sales to very bad people. The feds will chew him up for that, and that, naturally, is why we got involved in the first place after his murder. I'm sorry he had to be your father. We believe that's another reason he locked you away in Beadermeyer's sanitarium. He did believe, according to Scott Brainerd, that you had seen some compromising papers. You don't remember seeing any papers that could have implicated your father in the arms dealing?"

She shook her head. "No, really, Mr. Brammer. But you do believe this was one of the reasons my father had me admitted to Dr. Beadermeyer's sanitarium?"

"It sounds probable. The other thing—the revenge angle—it seems reasonable, but frankly I don't think it's enough of a motive in itself. No, I think it was a bunch of things, but primarily that he knew Scott was losing you, and thus he, Amory St. John, was losing control. And he believed you'd seen some incriminating papers about the arms deals. There's more than enough there, Sally. What was uppermost in your father's mind? I don't know. We'll never know."

"You don't know how much he hated me. I'll bet even my mother believes it's enough of a motive."

"We'll find out when we catch him," Marvin Brammer said. "Then we'll make him pay. I'm sure sorry about all this, Sally. Not much of a decent childhood for you, but there's rottenness in some people, and that's just the way it is."

"What will happen to Dr. Beadermeyer?"

"Ah, Norman Lipsy. If only we'd thought to put Savich on him earlier. That man can make a computer tap-dance. We all laugh that he's not a loner like Quinlan because he's always got his computer tucked under his arm, a modem wrapped around his neck like a stethoscope. He can get into any system on the planet. He's amazing. We kid him that he sleeps with the bloody thing. I think that even if someone gave him a turn-of-the-century telephone, he could invent a modem that would work. Agents in the bureau don't have partners like cops do, but Quinlan and Savich, well, they always do well together.

"Good Lord, why'd I get off on that? You wanted to know about Norman Lipsy. He'll go to jail for a very long time. Don't spend any time worrying about him. He refused to say a thing. Said that Holland was a moron and a liar. But it doesn't matter. We've got the goods on him."

She shivered, her arms wrapped around herself. He wanted to comfort her somehow, but he didn't know what to do.

He said, "Believe me, Lipsy is going down hard. We don't as yet know all the people he's holding there against their will. Our people will interview each one, look at each one's file, speak to all the relatives. It'll shake out soon enough. I think when it's all over, lots of very rich, very famous folk aren't going to be happy.

"Also, Lipsy's an accessory to murder. He's gone for good, Sally. No need for you to worry about him."

Jesus, what had that man done to her? He couldn't imagine. He really didn't want to be able to.

When Quinlan walked up, his eyes alight with pleasure at the sight of Sally, all skinny and pale, her hair mussed, her own eyes bright with the sight of him, Marvin Brammer wandered back into his office thinking that he couldn't remember the last time he'd talked so much.

She would pry every secret out of Quinlan and he wouldn't even know what she was doing. Better yet, she didn't even realize the effect she had on people.

Good thing she wasn't a spy, they'd all be in deep shit. He was also mighty relieved that her mama hadn't been in on the nastiness.

QUINLAN BROUGHT HER home to his apartment, to his bedroom, to his bed, and now he was holding her, lightly stroking his hand up and down her back.

She was so very thin. He could feel her pelvic bones, the thinness of her arms through her nightgown. He had the urge to phone out for Chinese food—lots of sugar in Szechwan beef and pot stickers—but he decided he'd rather be doing what he was doing. Besides, he'd already stuffed her to the gills with spaghetti, lots of Parmesan on top, and hot garlic bread that wasn't nearly as good as Martha's.

"James?"

"You're supposed to be asleep."

"Mr. Brammer was very nice to me. He told me a thing or two about you, too."

Quinlan stared at her. "You're kidding. Brammer is the biggest closed-mouth in the FBI. If they gave awards for it, he'd win hands down."

"Not tonight. Maybe he was tired or excited, like you were. Yep, he told me lots of things."

This was interesting. Quinlan cleared his throat against her hair. "Um, was all he talked about—it was all the case and the players?"

"Most of it, but not all." He felt her fingers playing over his bicep. He instantly flexed the muscle. A man, he thought, he was just a man who wanted his woman to know he was strong. He nearly laughed aloud at himself.

"What was the 'not all'?"

"You. He told me about you and your father and Savich."

"You'll like my old man. He's a kick. He had a heart attack last year but he seems okay now, thank God. He makes you so mad you want to punch his lights out, and then in the next second you're clutching your stomach, you're laughing so hard."

"A lot like you. That's what Mr. Brammer said."

She was caressing his bicep again. He flexed again. A man was a man. He guessed there was just no getting away from it.

"He also said that you liked to play a lone hand but that he always knew what you were doing even if you would swear he didn't know a thing."

"I wouldn't doubt it, that old con man. He's got moles everywhere."

"Maybe now he's got a mole who's living with you."

"That's okay," Quinlan said and kissed her.

She was soft and giving, but she wasn't with him, not yet, and he couldn't blame her at all for that. He said against her warm mouth, "There's only your father left, Sally. We'll get him. He won't get away. There'll be a huge scandal, a big trial. Can you deal with that?"

"Yes," she said, her voice suddenly very cold and hard. "I can't wait, actually. I want to face him down. I want to tell the world how he beat his wife. I want to tell the world what he did to me. James?"

"Yeah?"

"Was there another woman in my father's life? Someone he was going to leave the country with?"

"Not that we know of, but that's a good thought. We'll have to keep an eye on it. It's early, very early. As I said, we have people going through every scrap of paper in your father's house and at his office. Everything will be scrutinized.

"You ain't seen scrutiny until you've seen the FBI do it. As for our Norman Lipsy, the plastic surgeon, he won't be going anywhere even with the best lawyers he can buy. He'll be questioned by agents until at least next Wednesday. It doesn't mean a thing that he hasn't talked yet. He will. Already they've found more than enough evidence to convict him on innumerable counts—kidnapping, collusion, conspiracy, that's just the beginning. Now, Sally, you're still withdrawn from me. What is it? What's going on?"

"James, what if I was wrong? What if I was still drugged up so that I saw things that weren't really there? What if it wasn't my father running out those French doors? What if it was someone else? What if I didn't see anybody? What if I did shoot him and all the rest—well, it's games being played in my mind."

"Nah," he said and kissed her again. "Not in a million years. If there's one thing I know, it's crazy. You aren't crazy. I'll bet you don't even get PMS."

She hit his arm—he flexed the muscle—and she giggled.

"Now that's a wonderful sound. Just forget all that crazy stuff, Sally. You saw your father. There's not one single doubt in my mind or in Brammer's mind or in Savich's or, I'll bet, in Ms. Lilly's, when we tell her.

"Your father must have stopped, seen you throw that prized pistol of his away and gone back to get it. That in itself is convincing, don't you see? If he didn't go back for the gun, then where is it? When we find him I'll bet you a Mexican meal at Taco Charlie's that he's got that Roth-Steyr."

She leaned up and kissed his mouth. "Goodness, I hope so. You were so sure I'd remember."

"I prayed harder than I did when I was seventeen and afraid Melinda Herndon might be pregnant."

"I'm so glad I didn't shoot him, regardless of the fact that I would have liked to. I wonder where he is."

"We'll find him. His passport's still here. The agents had Noelle go through his safe at home and his safety-deposit boxes. He could have had another passport made, but that's tough to do today. They found some bankbooks from the Caymans and Switzerland. We'll get him. It won't take long."

She was quiet, utterly still against him. He liked to feel her push against him, he liked her touching him. He was still on an adrenaline high, but she had to be exhausted. She'd been through quite an experience. He sighed. He settled for a light kiss on her mouth. "You ready to sleep now?"

"I have this feeling, James," she said slowly, her breath warm against his neck. "It's weird and I can't explain it, but I just don't think he's gone anywhere. That is, I don't think he's left the country. He's here, somewhere. I just can't imagine where. We don't have a beach house or a mountain cabin that I know of."

"That's interesting. We'll ask Noelle tomorrow. Now come on, Sally, I'm supposed to be the one with the famous intuition, the hyper gut instinct. You trying to show me up?"

Quinlan shifted his weight. He was still wearing his pants and shirt. He wished he wasn't wearing anything. Sally was in one of her new nightgowns, a cotton thing that came nearly up to her chin and went down to her ankles. He wished she wasn't wearing anything either. He sighed and kissed her right ear.

He wished all the adrenaline in his body would clear out. He was high and horny. To distract himself, he said, "I forgot to tell you. I got a call from David Mountebank—you remember the sheriff, don't you?"

"He's very nice. He took care of you." He felt her fingertips lightly touch where the stitches had been in his head. "Hardly even a ridge now."

"Yes, well, he still hasn't got a clue about the two murders, and yes, Doc Spiver was murdered, no doubt about it. He wants FBI help, officially, and he'll get it since we're talking about interstate shenanigans. He's convinced everybody that the older couple—Harve and Marge Jensen—were killed around there and that all the other missing folks are linked together as well. There'll be agents from the Portland office, and I'll be there from the Washington office. They'll crawl all over that damned town."

She was kissing his neck, her fingers lightly tugging on his chest hair. He said slowly, "I'm going, Sally. And yes, Brammer knows I'm going. He thinks it's a good idea. He wants me to talk to Amabel. We all want to know how she fits into all this. And, believe me, she's got to fit in somewhere. I think you should consider coming with me, Sally."

He had weighed the danger of her being in that small little town on the Oregon coast against the danger of her remaining here, without him, her father still at large. No, he wanted her with him. It was the only way he could protect her. There'd be enough agents hanging around The Cove, no one would have a chance of hurting her.

"How could she be involved, James? She loves me, doesn't she? She took me in. She—"

"Don't turn blind on me now. She's involved. When she told David and me how you would probably run because you were scared, well, then I was as sure as I could be that she was involved. How deeply, we'll find out."

"I've got my mother back now. I'd sure like to have Aunt Amabel, too. I'm praying really hard that she isn't involved."

"Not only do you have your mama back, you've got me, and you'll never lose me, I swear it. And you'll have all my family. They're obnoxious, loving pains in the butt, all in all a great family. Now, if Amabel is somehow involved with all this, we'll deal with it, you and I together."

He felt her palm slide down his chest, felt her fingers slip inside his shirt to caress him. He nearly bowed off the bed. No, she was exhausted, he couldn't let her do this, not now, not tonight.

He'd made up his mind. No way was he going to rush her on this. He shook his head and said, "Sally, are you certain?"

"Oh, yes," she said and kissed his chest. "Let me get this shirt off you, James."

He laughed. He was still laughing when her mouth was on his belly, then lower, closing over him. He moaned and jerked with the power of it. He didn't think he'd ever stop moaning, stop wanting, until he was deep inside her. That was what he wanted more than anything, to be deep inside her and for her to accept him completely, to love him, to shout it to him, and to the world.

And when he was deep inside of her, he knew it was right, better than right. She was his lifeblood, his future. It was about the best thing he'd ever managed in his life.

She whispered against his chest, "I love you, James." He was shaking, heaving over her like a wild man, but she was just as wild, and that made him even wilder.

A man, he thought just before his body shattered into orgasm, a man needed to belong as much as a woman. A man needed to be desired, to be cherished, as much as a woman.

When she bit his neck, then cried out, he knew everything would be just fine. "I love you, too," he said, his breath warm in her open mouth.

Life, he thought, just before he fell into a deep sleep, was weird. He'd gone to The Cove to find a crazy woman who could have murdered her father.

Instead he'd found Sally.

Actually, life was dandy.

THE DAY WAS WARM, the air salty with the ocean spray, the sun high overhead. The Cove had never looked more beautiful, Quinlan thought, as he helped Sally out of their rental car.

"It's a picture postcard," she said, looking around. "There are the four old men playing cards around the barrel. Look, there are at least six cars parked in front of the World's Greatest Ice Cream Shop. There's Martha coming out of the Safeway with two sacks of groceries. There's Reverend Vorhees walking with his head down like he's got to tell some-one that he's sinned badly. How could anything bad happen here? It looks perfect. All calm, nobody running around waving an ax, yelling, no kids ruining buildings with graffiti."

"Yeah," Quinlan said. He was frowning.

"What's wrong?"

He just shook his head. His intuition. She poked him in the ribs. He grabbed her hand and said only, "It's too perfect. Why is that, I wonder? How did it get to be so perfect? Look at all that paint, Sally. It's fresh. Nothing's run-down. Nothing's old. Everything is in tip-top shape.

"But enough of this postcard place. We're meeting David and two FBI agents from the Portland office over at Thelma's at two o'clock. It's just about two now."

"I'll meet them and then go to Amabel's house, all right?"

He looked worried, and she punched him again on his arm. "Do you think she's going to lock me in a root cellar? Don't be silly, James. She's my aunt."

"Okay. I'll be along as soon as I can. Make sure Amabel knows that."

David Mountebank looked tired. He looked harassed. When he

introduced Quinlan to the man and woman agents, he didn't sound like a happy camper. He sounded like he was being bossed around, which occasionally did happen when the feds came in and treated the local law as yokels. It had happened a lot in the past, but not as much now. He sure hoped that wasn't the case here. In the sixteen-week training program at Quantico, agents were told never to usurp local prerogatives.

Maybe he was wrong. Maybe David was just depressed about these killings. He knew he'd be as depressed as hell.

Corey Harper and Thomas Shredder didn't look too happy either. They all shook hands and sat down in Thelma Nettro's parlor. Martha came in and beamed at them. "Sally. Mr. Quinlan. How nice to see you again. Now, would everyone like some coffee? And some of my special New Jersey cheesecake?"

"New Jersey cheesecake, Martha?" Quinlan asked as he kissed her cheek.

"It's better than any cheesecake from New York," she said and gave Sally a brief hug. "You folks just get on with your business. I'll be right back."

"How's Thelma doing, Martha?" Sally asked.

"She's primping right now. Not for you, Sally, but for Mr. Quinlan. She even had me go out and buy her some pumpkin peach lipstick, if you can imagine." Martha tsked and left the large parlor.

"I'd like to get to work here," Thomas Shredder said with just enough impatience in his voice to make Quinlan want to loll back, lock his arms behind his head, and take a snooze, just to aggravate him.

Shredder was about thirty, tall and lanky, and very intense, one of those men Quinlan tried to avoid like the plague. They made him nervous simply because they never laughed, wouldn't know a joke if it bit them, usually saw the forest but never the individual trees.

As for the woman, Special Agent Corey Harper, she hadn't said anything yet. She was tall, with light hair and very pretty blue-gray eyes. She also looked eager, sitting on the edge of the sofa, her notebook on her knee, her ballpoint pen poised above an open page. She looked as if she hadn't been out of Quantico for very long. He'd bet the Portland office was her first assignment.

"Corey told me all the excitement you had back in Washington," David Mountebank said, ignoring Thomas Shredder. "Jesus, that was something. You okay, Sally?"

"Yes, fine now. They still haven't caught my father, but James promises me they will. It's just a matter of time."

Quinlan thought that Thomas Shredder was going to explode. He smiled at the man and said, "I came here looking for Sally. I was a private investigator—that was my cover—hired to locate two old people who disappeared over three years ago in this area. And that was true. These folk did disappear in this area. Funny thing was that when I started asking questions, bad things started happening. Sally, tell them about the woman's screams."

She did, leaving out the fact that Amabel hadn't believed it was really a woman screaming.

"We came across a woman's body the following morning when we were walking down the cliffs," Quinlan said. "She'd been murdered and thrown off the cliffs. Not a very nice thing to do. It's difficult not to believe that this was the same woman Sally heard screaming on two different nights. She must have been held prisoner somewhere close to Sally's aunt's cottage. Why was she being held prisoner? We have no idea. Now, I'm willing to wager the farm that the murders are tied directly to these missing folks."

"Yes, yes, we know all this," Shredder said, and he actually swatted at Quinlan as if he were a fly to be removed from the bread.

"We also know your opinion about this so-called tie-in. However, as yet we don't have any real proof that there is a tie-in. What we've got is two murders, one a longtime local in Doc Spiver and the other a woman from the subdivision, not at all local in the same sense. What we need is a tie-in between the two of them, not between them and the disappearance of these old folk over three years ago."

"Well, then," Quinlan said, "David, why don't you bring me up to date. What have you done since I flew home last week?"

Shredder interrupted, his voice fast and sharp, "Sheriff Mountebank didn't do much of anything. Ms. Harper and I have been here since Monday, not long enough to solve the crimes yet, but we're getting close, very close."

Corey Harper cleared her throat. "Actually, David had collected interviews from just about everyone in town. They're very thorough, but no one could tell him much of anything. Everyone is shocked and very depressed about the deaths, particularly Doc Spiver's."

"We've already started to repeat the interviews," Thomas Shredder said. "Someone must have seen something. We'll get it out of them. Old people have difficulty remembering unless they're prodded just right. It takes special training to learn just how to do it."

"Nah," Quinlan said. "I did it perfectly even before my training. Another thing, David knows all these people. He'd know when they were lying and what about."

"That remains to be seen," Shredder said. Corey Harper looked embarrassed.

Martha appeared in the doorway, a huge tray resting on her arms.

Quinlan got up and took it from her. "He's such a nice boy," she said to Sally.

"Right there, Mr. Quinlan. Yes, that's right. Now, I know you don't want me listening to all this important talk, so I'll just leave you with everything. You'll manage?"

"Yes, thank you, Martha," Quinlan said. "How's Ed?"

"Oh, that poor man. Thelma just won't leave him alone. Now she's accusing him of compromising me on the kitchen table, and she's going to buy a shotgun. He's in the hospital right now having tests for that prostate of his. Poor man."

Thomas Shredder looked at Corey Harper, then at the tray. She bit her lip and began to place cups on saucers. Quinlan grinned at her and began to do the same. Sally poured a cup and said, "Cream, David?"

Thomas Shredder sat there while everyone served each other. Quinlan gave him a big grin and pointed to the last cup on the tray. "Help yourself, Thomas. Ah, best hurry—I bet these New Jersey cheesecakes are going to be inhaled."

"My, this is beyond delicious," Corey Harper said and took the last bite of her slice of cheesecake.

"James and I want to ask Martha to come back to Washington with us," said Sally. "She's the best cook I know. Her pasta makes you weep."

Quinlan knew that Shredder was going to blow up any minute. Well, he'd pushed the ass far enough. He said easily, "Forget the interviews, Thomas. We need to come at this from another angle. I know it sounds weird that the missing persons would have anything to do with the two murders, but the thing is that up until about the time Marge and Harve Jensen disappeared, The Cove was a run-down old shanty of a town. No paint on anything, potholes in the road, fences falling over, even the trees sagging, all the kids gone, just old people left, living on Social Security. My question is, why is The Cove so different now from what it was three years ago? Why did everything here begin to wake up about the same time that Harve and Marge disappeared?"

"My God," Corey said. "I didn't realize the timing."

"I did," David said, "but I never questioned it, Quinlan, for the simple reason that it was common knowledge that Doc Spiver had come into a lot of money right around then. Since he didn't have any heirs, he invested the money and used all the proceeds to improve the town. But you don't think so, Quinlan?"

"I think it's worth checking into, closely. I remember you telling me that in Doc Spiver's will he left his estate to the town and it amounted to about twenty thousand dollars. If he was that low, then the town would start sliding again, really soon, don't you think? Makes you wonder, doesn't it?

"I'll call Savich—he's a computer nerd at the bureau—and get him going on it. Tell me which bank and the account number, David. Sally and I will be staying here. Just give me a call, and I'll get to Savich."

"Is that Dillon Savich?" Corey Harper asked, looking up.

"Yeah, he's a genius with a computer, but don't tell him that because he'll just think you're sucking up."

"I know. I did tell him that when I was in training at Quantico. He gave a couple of great lectures, and yeah, he probably did think I was sucking up."

"I've never heard of this Savich guy, at least not more than three times," Thomas Shredder said. "Who cares about a computer nerd? They're fine in their place, but this is the real world. What we do here is what really counts. Let's get back to why we're here in this godforsaken place."

David said slowly, "Regardless of whether or not the missing persons are somehow involved in these murders, what you're implying in a very subtle way is a tough pill to swallow, Quinlan. I've known these people most all my life. They're a bunch of tough old birds, they've had to be to survive all the economic disasters we've had. Jesus, just realizing that one of them is a murderer curdles my breakfast. More than one of them murderers? No way."

"It's more than a tough pill," Thomas Shredder said with a goodly dose of sarcasm. "You're paranoid, Quinlan. That's nuts."

Quinlan just shrugged. "This town looks like a Hollywood set. I remember that was my first thought when I came here. I want to know why and how that happened."

"All right, we've got a lead," David said, leaning forward. "I'm going to check more closely into Doc Spiver's bank account. Now, I've gotten together all the accounts for all the missing persons reported in this area for the past three years." David drew a deep breath. "There's about sixty."

"Whoa," Corey Harper said.

"James is wrong about this," Sally said. "My aunt has lived here for more than twenty years. She couldn't be part of a murder conspiracy of this magnitude. She couldn't."

"I hope I am wrong, Sally," he said as he took her hand. It was cold.

He poured her some coffee and put the fragile china cup between her hands to warm them. "But there's lots of questions here. I can't think of another way to go on this."

"I can't either," David said.

"Well, I can," said Thomas Shredder, rising to stand in front of the fireplace. He struck a pose, looking like Hercule Poirot ready to deliver his solution. All he needed was a mustache to twirl.

"I hope this is good, Thomas," Quinlan said. "We've paid our admission. Now on with the show."

"Pinning these murders on several of the townspeople just doesn't make sense. As to tying it all to David's missing persons, let's just forget about that."

"But, Thomas," Corey began, but he raised a hand to silence her.

"It's a theory, nothing more. What we've got is solid fact. Let's get specific. I looked into Reverend Hal and Sherry Vorhees. They've lived here for twenty-seven years, true, but before that, they were in Tempe, Arizona. They had two little adopted boys. The two little boys ended up dead within a year after they came to the Vorheeses. One fell out of a tree and broke his neck. The other one got himself burned to death when he turned on the gas stove. Both were accidents, at least that's what was reported and accepted. Everyone felt real bad about it, said the Vorheeses were the nicest people, and he was a reverend, and why would God take both their children?

"But there were questions. It seems a couple of other children had accidents during the time the Vorheeses lived there. Then the Vorheeses left and came here. There weren't any more children. Who the hell knows?"

He waited for applause and he got it.

"That's something," David Mountebank said. "Good going, Thomas. You got any more?"

"There's also some history on Gus Eisner, the old guy who fixes everything on wheels in this town. Turns out his wife, Velma, isn't his first wife. His first wife was murdered. He was accused of the crime, but the DA never had enough evidence to bring him to trial. One month later Gus marries Velma and they move here. From Detroit. Hell, we've got to check on every single soul in this town. Corey's checking on the Keatons."

"Yeah, you're right. We've got to check on all of them," Quinlan said, at which the other man stared at him, utterly surprised, a flicker of pleasure in those dark eyes of his. "I hope it's one or the other. But it still doesn't feel right."

"Look, Quinlan," Thomas Shredder said. "Since the doctor was murdered, we looked all through his background."

"Well, Thomas," Corey Harper said, interrupting him, "actually David ran all the checks on him."

"Yes," David said, sitting forward. "He came here in the late forties with his wife. She died in the mid-sixties of breast cancer. They had two boys, both dead now, one in Vietnam, the other in a motorcycle accident in Europe. There was a rich uncle who died. That's all I could find out, Quinlan."

"We'll see, won't we? If the money didn't come from Doc Spiver, then it had to come from someplace else."

An ancient throat cleared in the doorway, grabbing their attention.

"Well, now, you're back, Sally, and you, Mr. Quinlan. I hear from Amabel that the FBI has nearly everything cleared up back in that capital of ours, that foul den of iniquity." She paused a moment, shaking her head. "Goodness, I'd sure like to visit there."

Thelma Nettro had opened the door and was standing there, leaning on her cane, beaming at all of them, the pumpkin peach lipstick smeared, some of it on her false front teeth.

"Hello, Thelma," Quinlan said and rose to go to her. He leaned down and kissed her cheek. "You're looking like a French model. How's tricks?"

27

"YOU'VE GOT A smart mouth on you, boy," Thelma said in high good humor. She patted Quinlan's cheek. "Help me to my chair and I'll tell you all about my tricks."

Once Quinlan had her settled, she said, "Now, what's this I hear on FOX—that Sally's father killed a man he'd paid some plastic surgeon to make look like him? He locked you up, Sally? Then he skipped out?"

"That's about it, Thelma," Sally said. "My father is still free, more's the pity, but they'll catch him. His face has been all over the TV. Someone will spot him. He didn't leave the country, his passport isn't missing."

"He could have gotten another passport," Thomas Shredder said. "Even today it can be done."

"Damn," Quinlan said. "Excuse me, Thelma. I didn't think of that. You're right, Thomas."

"I've heard worse things than a little damn in my lifetime, Quinlan. So, you got some more FBI agents here. You want to solve those murders, huh?"

"Yes, ma'am," Corey Harper said.

"We all thought Doc had killed himself, but that woman from Portland said it wasn't so."

"The medical examiner," David said. "I was lucky she's so well trained and was available. Otherwise it might have passed as a suicide."

"Poor Doc," Thelma said. "Who'd want to stick a gun in his mouth? It isn't civilized—you know?"

"No, it isn't."

"As for that young woman with the three children, well, that was a pity too, but after all, she wasn't one of us. She was from that wretched subdivision."

"Yeah, Thelma, she lived all of five miles away," Quinlan said, seeing his irony floating gently over Thelma's head. "Fact is, though, she did die right here."

Quinlan sat himself back down beside Sally on the brocade sofa. When he spoke again, Sally immediately recognized that voice of his, low and soothing, intimate. That voice would get information out of a turnip. "Now, did you ever meet that rich uncle of Doc Spiver's, Thelma?"

"Nope, never did. I don't even remember where he lived, if I ever did know. But everyone knew about him and how he was older than God and how if we could just hang on a bit longer then he'd croak and Doc would get the money.

"Of course, I have money, but not as much as that rich uncle had. We were all afraid that the old codger would use it all up on nursing homes, but he just died in his sleep, Doc said, and then Doc got that big fat check. More zeros than anybody in this town had ever seen before, I'll tell you."

"Thelma," David said, "do you know of anyone in town who could have met his uncle?"

"Don't know, but I'll find out. Martha!"

The screech hurt Sally's ears. She winced even as she smiled because Corey had jumped and dropped her pen and notebook.

"Healthy set of lungs," Quinlan said.

Martha appeared in the doorway, wiping her hands on her apron.

"What are you making for dinner, Martha? It's getting on toward four o'clock."

"Your favorite eggplant parmigiana, Thelma, with lots of Parmesan cheese on top and garlic bread so snappy it will make your teeth dance, and a big Greek salad with goat cheese."

"The uncle, Thelma," Quinlan said easily.

"Oh, yes. Martha, did you ever meet Doc Spiver's rich uncle?"

Martha frowned deeply, then slowly shook her head. "No, just heard about him for years. Whenever things were looking real bad, we'd talk about him, discuss how old he was, what kind of ailments he had, try to figure out when he'd pass on. Don't you remember, Thelma? Hal Vorhees was always telling us we were ghouls, that it surely had to be a sin to discuss that poor old man, like we were holding prayer meetings for him to die."

"We were," Thelma said. "I'll bet Hal did a little praying when none of us were around. Well, I wasn't praying for myself because I wasn't poor like the rest of the town, but when Doc got that check, I was shouting along with everyone else."

"You've lived here since the forties, haven't you, Thelma?" David asked.

"Yes. I came here with my husband, Bobby Nettro, back in 1949. We already had grown kids, and we were rattling around in that big old house in Detroit. Came out here and decided this was the place for us." She gave a lusty sigh that sent a whistling sound through her false teeth. "Poor Bobby, he passed on in 1956, right after Eisenhower was reelected. He died of pneumonia, you know.

"But he left me well off, real well off. I got Martha to come live with me in the early seventies, and we did just fine. She was teaching school down in Portland, and she didn't like it, all those gangs and drugs and that young lust. Since I knew her mama before she passed on, I also knew Martha. We all kept in touch. But you know, Quinlan, I did fail her mama. I still can't find Martha a husband, and I promised her I would. Lord knows, I've been looking for more years now than I've got teeth."

"You don't have any teeth, Thelma," Martha said. "Why don't you just chew on that nice pumpkin peach lipstick and think about that eggplant parmigiana?"

"Well, I used to have a healthy set of choppers. I'll tell you, Quinlan, it don't seem to matter how revved up she gets and how much she sticks her bosom out there for the old codgers to ogle. Now, take poor Ed—"

Martha rolled her eyes and left the room.

"Well, actually, could you tell us about your kids, Thelma?" Quinlan asked.

"Two boys, one died in the war—the Big War, not Korea or Vietnam. The other one, well, he lives back in Massachusetts. He's retired now, has grown-up grandkids, and they got kids, and that makes me so old I can't bear to think about it."

Sally smiled as she stood up and walked over to kiss Thelma's soft, wrinkled cheek. "I'm going to see Amabel now, Thelma, but James and I will be staying here in the tower room."

"You still taking advantage of him, huh, Sally? Poor little boy, he doesn't have a chance. The first time I saw the two of you together I knew you'd have his pants off him in no time at all."

"Thelma, have a piece of my New Jersey cheesecake."

Thelma turned to frown at Martha, who had just come back into the room with another tray of her cheesecakes.

"You're such a prude, Martha, such a prude. I'll just bet you're frigid and Ed has to beg you for every little favor."

"I'll see you later," Sally said, grinning back at the two dumbstruck special agents from Portland, James, and David Mountebank.

"I'll be along shortly, Sally," Quinlan said. He was already asking Thelma more questions when Sally went out the front door of Thelma's Bed and Breakfast.

The day was beautiful, warm, just a slight nip in the air, the salty tang swept in from the ocean soft as a bird's wing on her face.

Sally breathed in deeply. Sherry Vorhees was standing in front of the World's Greatest Ice Cream Shop. Sally waved, and Sherry waved back. Helen Keaton, whose grandmother had invented the ice cream recipe, came out of the shop behind her, looked over at Sally, and waved herself. Such nice women. Surely they couldn't know anything about the murders or those missing people.

"Our flavor this week is banana walnut cream," Helen called out. "Do come and try it with your Mr. Quinlan. My granny didn't exactly make it, but I like to try new flavors. Ralph loves the banana walnut, says it's so good it's got to be real bad for you."

Sally remembered that Ralph Keaton was the undertaker. She saw old Hunker Dawson, the World War II veteran, who always wore his two medals across the pocket of his flannel shirts. He hiked up his baggy pants and yelled, "You're famous, Sally Brainerd. We didn't find out until after you'd left that you were crazy. But now you're not even crazy, are you? I think the news media were pissed about you not being crazy. They like crazy and evil better than innocence and victims."

"Yeah," Purn Davies called out, "the media all wanted you to be crazier than a loon and out offing folk. They sure didn't want to report that you weren't crazy. Then, though, they got your daddy."

"I'm glad they finally did," Sally called.

"Don't you worry none about your daddy, Sally," Gus Eisner yelled. "His face has been shown more times than the president's. They'll get him."

"Yeah," Hunker Dawson yelled. "Once the media get their hooks in him all right and proper, they'll forget everything else. They always do. It's always the grossest story of the day for them."

"I sure hope so," she yelled back.

"My wife, Arlene, was wavering on her rocker," Hunker shouted matter-of-factly, tugging on his old suspenders. "Wavering for years before she passed over."

Purn Davies yelled, "Hunker means she was a mite off in her upper works."

"These things happen," she said, but probably not loud enough for them to hear.

The four old men had suspended their card game and were all looking at Sally. Even when she turned away, she knew they were watching her as she walked down that beautiful wooden sidewalk, the railing all fresh white paint, toward Amabel's cottage. She saw Velma Eisner, Gus's wife, and waved to her. Velma didn't see her, just kept walking, her head down, headed for Purn Davies's general store.

Amabel's cottage looked fresh as spring, with newly planted beds of purple iris, white peonies, yellow crocus, and orange poppies, all perfectly arranged and tended. She looked around and saw flower boxes and small gardens filled with fresh flowers. Lots and lots of orange pop-pies and yellow daffodils. What a beautiful town. All the citizens took pride in how their houses looked, how their gardens looked. Every short sidewalk was well swept.

She wondered if The Cove now had a sister Victorian city in England.

She thought about what James had said about all those missing people. She knew the direction of his thoughts, but she wouldn't accept it.

She just couldn't. It was outrageous. She stepped onto Amabel's small porch and knocked on the door.

No answer.

She knocked again and called out.

Her aunt wasn't home. Well, she'd doubtless be back soon.

Sally knew where she wanted to go, had to go.

SHE STOOD IN THE CENTER of the cemetery. It was laid out like a wheel, with the very oldest graves in the very center. It was as well tended as the town. The grass was freshly mowed, giving off that won-derful grass scent. She laid her hand lightly on top of a marble head-stone that read:

ELIJAH BATTERY

BEST BARTENDER IN OREGON

DIED JULY 2, 1897

81 RIPE YEARS

The lettering grooves had been carefully dug out and smoothed again. She looked at other headstones, some incredibly ornate, others that had begun as wooden crosses and had obviously been replaced many times. Those that hadn't weathered well had been replaced.

Was nothing in this town overlooked? Was everything to be perfect, including every headstone?

She walked out from the center of the cemetery. Naturally, the headstones became newer. She finished with the 1920s, the 1930s, the 1940s, all the way into the 1990s. The planners of the cemetery had been very precise indeed, working outward from the middle so that if you wanted to be buried here now, you'd be nearly to the boundaries.

She found Bobby Nettro's grave, on the fourth circle out from the center. It was perfectly tended.

As far as she could tell, they'd kept to this wheel plan since the beginning. There were so many graves now. She imagined that when the first townspeople decided to put the cemetery here they'd considered the plot of ground they were setting aside to be immense. Well, it wasn't. There was little space left, since the west side of the cemetery was bounded by the cliffs, and the east and north were bounded by the church and someone's cottage. The south nearly ran into the single path that led along the cliff.

She walked to the western edge of the cemetery. The graves here were new, as well tended as the others. She leaned down to look at the headstones. There were names, dates of birth and death, but nothing else. Nothing clever, nothing personal, nothing about being a super husband, father, wife, mother. Just the bare information.

Sally pulled a small notebook out of her purse and began to write down the names on the headstones. She walked around the periphery of the cemetery, ending up with a good thirty names. All the people had died in the late nineties to early this year.

It didn't seem right. Thing was, this was a very small town, grown smaller with each decade. Thirty people had died in a period of only five years? Well, it was possible, she supposed. Some kind of flu epidemic that killed off old folk.

Then she noticed something else and felt the hair rise on her arms.

Every one of the headstones bore a man's name. Not a single woman's name. Not one. Not a single child's name. Not one. Just men's names. On one of the graves, it just said BILLY with a date of death.

Nothing more. What was going on here? No women died during this period of time, just men? It made no sense.

She closed her eyes a moment, wondering what the devil she'd discovered. She knew she had to get this list to David Mountebank and to James. She had to be sure that these people had lived here and died here. She had to be sure that these people had nothing to do with all the reported missing folk. The thought that there might be a connection made her want to grab James and run out of the town as fast as she could.

She shook her head even as she stared down at one headstone in particular. The name was strange—Lucien Gray. So it was an odd name; it didn't matter. All these names were legitimate, they had to be. These were all local people who'd just happened to die during this eight-year stretch. Yeah, and only men died. She found herself looking for Harve Jensen's grave. Of course there wasn't one. But there was that one headstone with Lucien Gray scripted on it. It looked very new, very new indeed.

She was beginning to sweat even as her brain raced ahead.

No, no. This town was for real.

This town was filled with good people, not with evil, not with death, more death than she could begin to imagine.

She put her notebook back in her purse. She didn't want to go back to Amabel's cottage.

She was afraid.

Why had that poor woman whose screams she'd heard on two different nights been taken prisoner in the first place?

Had she seen something she shouldn't have seen? Had she heard something she shouldn't have heard?

Why had Doc Spiver been murdered? Had he killed the woman and someone else in town found out about it and shot him so there would be a kind of justice?

She tried to empty her mind. She hated to be afraid. She'd been afraid for too long.

SHE STOPPED AT the World's Greatest Ice Cream Shop. Amabel wasn't there, but Sherry Vorhees was.

"Sally, how good to see you. You here with that cute Mr. Quinlan?"

"Oh, yes. Can I try the banana walnut?"

"It's yummy. We've sold more of this flavor in a week than any other in the history of the store. We have so many repeat customers now—coming in regularly from a fifty-mile radius—that we might have to hire on some of those lazy old codgers out there playing cards around their barrel."

Velma Eisner came in from the back room, which was curtained off from the shop by a lovely blue floral drape. She snorted. "Yeah, Sherry, I can just see those old coots selling ice cream. They'd eat it all and belch at us and try to look pathetic."

She turned to Sally and smiled. "We discussed having the men involved. Of course, they'd grouse and complain and say it was women's work. But we decided to keep them out of it just so we'd be the ones bringing in all the profits."

"You're probably right," Sally said and accepted her ice cream cone. She took a bite and thought her taste buds had gone to heaven. She took another bite and sighed. "This is wonderful. I wonder if Helen would marry me."

The women laughed.

Sherry said, "We've come a long way since we used to store ice cream in Ralph Keaton's caskets, haven't we, Velma?"

Velma just smiled as she took $2.60 from Sally.

Sally took another bite. "I went to Amabel's cottage, but nobody's home."

Helen came in from the back room. "Hi, Sally. Amabel went to Portland."

"For art supplies and shopping," Velma said. "She'll be back in a couple of days, she said. Probably by Friday."

"Oh."

She licked at the ice cream, felt the taste explode in her mouth, and closed her eyes. "This has to be more sinful than eating three eggs a day."

"Well," Helen said, "if you eat just one ice cream cone a week, what does it matter?" She turned to say to Velma, "I saw Sherry eat three cones last Tuesday."

"I did not!"

"I saw you. They were all double dip chocolate."

"I didn't!"

The three women started sniping at each other. It was obvious they'd been doing this for years. They knew each other's red buttons and were pushing them with abandon. Sally just watched, eating her banana walnut ice cream cone. Velma had the last word. Before Sherry or Helen could pipe up, she turned to Sally. "No, we won't let the men get behind the counter. They'd eat everything."

Sally laughed. "I'd be as bad as the men. I'd eat the entire stock in one morning." She finished her cone and patted her stomach. "I don't feel quite so skinny now."

"Stay here, Sally, and you'll look all pillowy and comfortable like us in no time," Sherry Vorhees said.

"I was admiring the town," Sally said. "It's so beautiful, so utterly perfect. And all those flowers, every spring flower that will bloom is out and planted and wonderfully tended. Even the cemetery. The grass is mowed, the headstones are well cared for. I was wondering if you ever forgot anything at all that would make the town look even more perfect?"

"We try to think of everything," Helen said. "We have a town meeting once a week and discuss improvements or things that should be repaired or brought up to date."

"Whatever were you doing in the cemetery?" Velma asked, as she wiped her wet hands on her apron, the same cute blue floral pattern as the drape.

"Oh, just wandering around after I realized that Amabel wasn't at home. I noticed something kind of unusual."

"What was that?" Helen asked.

For a moment, Sally wondered if she shouldn't just keep her mouth shut. But no, these women were sniping at each other about ice cream, for God's sake. They knew who had died and when. They'd tell her. Why not? There was nothing frightening going on here. "Well, there were about thirty graves on the perimeter of the cemetery. All of them were men. There was nothing special on the headstones, just a name and dates of birth and death. The other headstones have personal stuff. There was one in particular, just said BILLY. I just thought it was strange. Maybe everyone got tired of being personal. So many men died, not a single woman. You must have been surprised at that."

Sherry Vorhees sighed deeply and shook her head. "A terrible thing it was," she said. "Hal was so depressed that we lost so many of the flock in those years. And you're right, Sally, it was all men who died. All different reasons for their deaths, but it still hurt all of us."

Helen Keaton said quickly, "Don't forget that quite a few of those deaths came from folk living in the subdivision. Their relatives thought our cemetery was romantic, set near the cliff as it is, with the sea breezes blowing through. We let them bury their dead here."

"Did that poor woman Mr. Quinlan and I found at the base of the cliffs get buried here?"

"No," Velma Eisner said. "Her husband was a rude young man. He was yelling around that we were somehow responsible. I told him to look at our muscles and do some thinking. As if we could have had something to do with his wife's death. He stormed out of here."

"He didn't even buy an ice cream cone," Helen said. "We had vanilla with fresh blueberries that week. He's never been back."

"Well, that wasn't very nice of him," Sally said. "I've got to go now.

Thank you for the ice cream." She turned at the door. "I didn't see Doc Spiver's grave."

"He isn't there," Velma said. "He wanted to be cremated and sent back to Ohio. He said there was no way in hell he was going to let Ralph Keaton lay him out."

Helen Keaton laughed. "Ralph was put out, I can tell you."

"No, Helen," Sherry said. "Ralph was pissed. Put out is something you are when Ralph doesn't throw his shorts in the hamper."

The women laughed, Sally along with them. She walked straight across the street to Thelma's Bed and Breakfast.

SHERRY VORHEES FLIPPED the curtain back down on the windows of the World's Greatest Ice Cream Shop. She said to the two other women, "There are three FBI agents in town and Sheriff David Mountebank."

"Those big shots should keep everyone safe," Velma said.

"Oh, yes," Helen said, slowly licking a swipe of ice cream off her fingers. "Safe as bugs in a miner's winter blanket."

QUINLAN FINALLY HUNG up the phone. "It took a while to read out all those names and dates. Savich is right on it. Finding out the stats on all those guys will be a piece of cake for him. He'll get back to us soon."

Sally said slowly, "I told the women at the World's Greatest Ice Cream Shop that I hadn't seen Doc Spiver's grave. They told me he was cremated and sent back to Ohio."

"Interesting," Quinlan said, and picked up the phone again. "Savich? It's Quinlan again. Find out if a Doc Spiver was cremated and sent back to Ohio, okay? No, it isn't as important as the other names, just of interest to Sally and me. Supposedly Doc had no relatives alive. So why would they cremate him and not bury him here in their own cemetery?

"Now, don't say that. It isn't polite. I bet Sally heard that. Yes, she did, and she's shaking her head at your language."

He was grinning, still listening. "Anything else? No? All right, call us as soon as you've got something. We're staying here for dinner and the evening." When he hung up, he was still grinning. He said to Sally, "I love to hear Savich curse. He doesn't do it well, just keeps repeating the same thing over and over. I tried to teach him more vocabulary—you know, some phrases that connected a good number of really bad words, animal parts, metaphysical parts, whatever—but he just couldn't get the hang of it." He gave her some examples, adopting a different pose for each example. "Here's the one that Brammer does best, but only when he's really pissed at one of the agents."

She rocked back on the bed, she was laughing so hard. Then she sobered. Laughing?

"Stop it, Sally. It's fine to forget. It's great to hear you laugh. Keep doing it. Now that I've taken care of all of your lewd instincts, let's go have Martha's cooking."

It was a feast, better than Thanksgiving, Corey Harper said. Martha brought in a huge platter with a pot roast in the center, carrots, potatoes, and onions placed artistically around it. There was a huge Caesar salad with tart dressing, garlic bread that indeed made your teeth snap, and for dessert, an apple crisp. And there was eggplant parmigiana on the side. Thelma hadn't waited. She'd wanted her eggplant at four-thirty.

Martha appeared at just the right times to refill their wineglasses with the nicest Cabernet Sauvignon anyone had tasted in a long time.

She clucked primarily around the men, encouraging them to eat, until finally Quinlan dropped his fork, sat back in his chair, and groaned. "Martha, any more and God will strike me down for gluttony. Just look at David—his shirt buttons are about to pop off. Even Thomas, who's skinny, would fill out in no time here with you. Since I'm polite, I won't refer to how much the women poked down their gullets."

Sally threw the rest of her garlic bread at him. She turned to a beaming Martha. "You said apple crisp, Martha?"

"Oh, yes, Sally, with lots of Basque vanilla ice cream from the World's Greatest Ice Cream Shop."

They had coffee with Amaretto, a treat from Thelma—who was eating in her room since Quinlan had worn her out earlier with all her talk, or so she claimed according to Martha. Actually, Thelma had to sleep off all that eggplant parmigiana she'd eaten.

After Martha returned to the kitchen, Sally told Thomas Shredder, Corey Harper, and David Mountebank, who had easily been persuaded to return for dinner and another conference, about the cemetery.

Quinlan said, "I called Savich. Knowing how fast he is, I'll probably hear back from him tonight. If it's something weird, I'll wake all of you up."

"I don't know if anyone will be able to wake me up," David said, as he sipped at his coffee. "Forget the coffee as a stimulant. This is the best Amaretto I've ever tasted. I'm already feeling like I want to put on my jammies. I hope my girls don't try to climb up my body when I get home. With luck, Jane will already have them in bed."

Sally didn't say anything. She hated Amaretto, always had. She'd taken one drink, then discreetly poured her coffee into Quinlan's cup while Corey Harper was telling a story about a guy in training school at Quantico who'd arrested some visiting brass by mistake after a bank robbery in Hogan's Alley, the fake USA town set up at Quantico for training. The biggest of the brass had thought it a great exercise until one of the trainees had clapped handcuffs on him and hauled him off.

Quinlan promised he would call if Savich found out anything urgent. But he couldn't imagine waking up even if the phone rang off the wall.

"I think you're tipsy," he told Sally as he held her up with one arm and unlocked the tower room door with the other.

"I'm tipsy?"

"I think Ms. Lilly would get a kick out of seeing you now."

"Next time I see her, I'll have to tell her that even though I was tipsy I had your pants off you in record time."

She was laughing so hard that when she jumped on him, he wrapped his arms around her back and brought her down to the bed, on top of him. He was kissing her, his breath warm with the tart taste of Amaretto.

"For a small favor I won't tell Martha what you did. You know, pouring your Amaretto in my coffee cup. Now, what's this about getting my pants off?"

She tried to give him a sultry look. He nearly doubled over laughing. Then she touched him and he groaned, his laughter choking in his throat. His eyes closed, his neck muscles convulsed.

He began kissing her, his tongue in her mouth, and she loved the feel of him, the taste of him. His hands were on her bottom, strong hands kneading her, pressing her against him. He was hard as the bars on her windows at Beadermeyer's sanitarium. Oh, God, why had she thought that?

She felt a shiver of cold. No, that was just a horrible memory that belonged in the past. It couldn't touch her now. She kissed him again. His mouth was slack. He wasn't so hard now against her belly. He wasn't rubbing his palms over her.

She lifted herself on her elbows and stared down at him, preparing to see him wink at her, preparing to have him toss her over onto her back.

"James?"

He smiled vaguely at her, not moving, not winking, nothing. "I'm tired, Sally," he said, his words soft and slurred. "Aren't you?"

"Just a bit," she said, leaned down, and kissed him again. Suddenly he closed his eyes, and his head fell to the side.

"James? James!"

Something was wrong. He wasn't teasing her. Something was

very wrong. She pressed her fingers to the pulse in his throat. Slow, steady. She flattened her palm over his heart. The beat was solid and slow. She lifted his eyelids and called his name again. She slapped his face.

No response.

He was unconscious. The damned coffee had been drugged. She'd had just a single sip of it, thank God, and that's why she was still conscious. There was no other explanation. She tried to pull herself off Quinlan, and she did manage it, but her arms and legs felt soft and wobbly. Just one drink of that amaretto was doing this to her?

She had to get help. She had to get to Thomas Shredder and Corey Harper. They were staying here, just down the hall. Not far, not far at all. Oh, God, they'd drunk the coffee too. And so had David, and he was driving. She had to see if Thomas and Corey were unconscious. She had to go to their rooms and see. She could make it.

She fell off the bed and rolled. She lay there a moment on her back, staring up at the beautiful molding that ran around the edge of the ceiling. There were even Victorian cherubs at each corner, naked, holding up harps and flowers.

She had to move. She got herself up on her hands and knees. What room was Corey Harper in? She'd told her, but she couldn't remember. Well, it didn't matter, she would find both of them. Their rooms had to be just down the hall. She crawled to the door. Not far at all. She managed to stretch up and turn the knob to open the door.

The hallway stretched forever to her left, the lighting dim and shadowy. What if the person who had drugged the coffee was waiting in those shadows, waiting to see if someone didn't succumb to the drug, waiting to kill that person? She shook her head and managed to heave herself to her feet. She made her feet move, one step at a time, that was all she needed to do, just one foot in front of the other. She'd find Thomas and Corey. Finally, a door appeared on her left—number 114. She knocked.

There was no answer.

She called out, her voice only a miserable whisper, "Thomas? Corey?"

She knocked again. Still no answer. She turned the knob. To her surprise, the door opened. It opened quickly, and she stumbled into the room, her knees buckling under her. She fell on her side.

She called out, "Thomas? Corey?"

She managed to get onto her hands and knees. There was only a single lamp burning, on top of the bedside table. Thomas Shredder was lying on his back, his arms and legs sprawled out away from his body. He was unconscious. Or he was dead. She tried to scream. She wanted to scream, but only a small cry came out of her mouth.

She heard footsteps behind her. She managed to get herself turned around to face the open doorway. James? Was he all right now? But she didn't call out his name. She was afraid it wasn't him. James had drunk a whole cup of that coffee. It couldn't be him. She was afraid of who it might be.

The light was dim. Shadows filled the room, filled her vision. There was a man standing in the doorway, his hands in his pockets.

"Hello, Sally."

"NO," SHE SAID, staring at that shadowy figure, knowing it was him, accepting it, but still she said again, "No, it can't be you."

"Of course it can, dear. You'd know your father anywhere, wouldn't you?"

"No." She was shaking her head back and forth.

"Why can't you get up, Sally?"

"You drugged us. I just drank a little bit, but it must have been very strong."

"Didn't get enough, did you?" He was coming toward her now, quickly, too quickly.

"Dr. Beadermeyer got to try so many new drugs on you. Actually, I was surprised you survived with your brain intact. Well, I'll take care of that."

He leaned down, grabbed the hair at the back of her neck, and yanked her head back. "Here, Sally." He poured liquid down her throat. Then he threw her away from him, and she fell hard onto her back.

She stared up at him, seeing him weave and fade in the dim light. She tried to focus on him, watching him closely, but his features blurred, his mouth moved and grew bigger. His neck stretched out, becoming longer and longer until she could no longer see his head. Surely this was the way Alice in Wonderland must have felt. Off with her head. "Oh, no," she whispered. "Oh, no."

She fell onto her side, the smooth oak boards of the floor cool against her cheek.

HER FATHER WAS HERE. That was her first thought when she woke up. *Her father.*

No doubt about it. Her father. He was here. He had drugged her. He would kill her now. She was helpless again, just as helpless as she'd been for days upon weeks, weeks upon months.

She couldn't move, couldn't even lift a single finger. She realized her hands were tied in front of her, not all that tightly, but tight enough. She shifted her weight a bit. Her ankles were tied, too. But her mind wasn't fettered. Her mind was clear—thank God for that. If she'd been vague and blurry again, she would simply have folded up on herself and willed herself to die. But no, she could think. She could remember. She could also open her eyes. Did she want to?

James, she thought, and forced her eyes open.

She was lying on a bed. The springs squeaked when she shifted from one side to the other. She tried to make out more detail but couldn't. There was only a dim light coming from a hallway. It looked to be a small bedroom, but she couldn't tell anything more about it.

Where was she? Was she still in The Cove? If so, where?

Where was her father? What would he do?

She saw a shadowy figure walk into the bedroom. The light was too dim for her to make out his face. But she knew. Oh, yes, she knew it was him.

"You," she said, surprised that the word had come from her mouth. It sounded rusty and infinitely sad.

"Hello, Sally."

"It is you. I was praying I'd been wrong. Where am I?"

"It's a bit soon to tell you that."

"Are we still in The Cove? Where's James? And the other two agents?"

"It's a bit soon to tell you that as well."

"Damn you, I was praying desperately you'd left the country, that, or you were dead. No, actually I was praying that they would catch you and put you in prison for the rest of your miserable life. Where am I?"

"How poor Noelle suffered for years from that tongue of yours. You were always sniping at her, always moralizing, always telling her what she should do. You wanted her to call the police. You wanted her to leave me. The fact is, she didn't want to, Sally. Maybe at first she did, but not later. But you just wouldn't stop. You depressed her with all that criticism of yours, with your contempt. That's why she never came to see you in the sanitarium. She was afraid you'd preach at her some more, even though you were fucking crazy."

"That's bullshit. Naturally you can say anything you want about anybody now. Noelle isn't here to tell you what she really thinks of you. I'll bet you she'll be the happiest woman in Washington once she truly realizes that she doesn't have to be your punching bag anymore. I'll bet you she's already wearing short-sleeved dresses and shirts again. No more fear of showing bruises. I'll bet she'll even try two-piece bathing suits this summer. How many years couldn't she wear them? You loved to punch her in the ribs, didn't you? You brutalized her. If there's any justice at all, you'll pay. Too bad you didn't die."

"That's more out of you than I've heard in more than six months. You were blessedly silent most of the time during your too brief stay at the sanitarium. Too bad that Dr. Beadermeyer is out of business, thanks to that bastard Quinlan.

"Everything got so complicated, and it was all your fault, Sally. We had a lid on everything until Quinlan got you away from Dr. Beadermeyer again."

"His name's Norman Lipsy. He's a plastic surgeon. He's a criminal. He gave that poor man your face, but you're the one who killed him. You're a filthy murderer, not just a wife beater. And a traitor to your country."

"Why do you denounce me only for my more pedestrian deeds? I did one really good thing, something I'm quite proud of that you haven't mentioned.

"I put my darling daughter away for six months. I do believe that was my favorite project in the last few years.

"Putting you away. Having you under my control. Never having to see the contempt and hatred on your face when you happened to see me. God, how I enjoyed seeing you like a rag doll, your mouth gaping open, looking so stupid and vague that it wasn't even much fun watching that pathetic Holland take off your clothes and bathe you and then dress you again like you were his dolly.

"Toward the end there, I didn't even enjoy slapping you to get your attention. You didn't have any to get, and you got too thin. I told Dr. Beadermeyer to feed you more, but he said all he could do was keep you stabilized. Then you escaped by hiding the pills beneath your tongue.

"To see you in my house, in my study, just after I'd shot Jackie. It was a shock."

He struck a pose she'd seen many times in her life. He propped his elbow up on his other arm and cupped his chin in his hand. It was his intellectual, thoughtful look, she supposed. All he needed was Scott's pipe and perhaps Sherlock Holmes's hat.

"There you were, leaning over poor Jackie—that greedy little bugger—then you turned and saw me, saw me as clear as day. I could see the recognition in your eyes. You picked up my gun. I'd put it down to get some papers from my desk. But then you picked it up, and I had no choice but to run. I hid outside and watched you shake your head, clearly disbelieving you'd seen me. I saw Noelle and Scott come running in. I heard her scream and scream. I saw Scott nearly chew through that damned pipe of his.

"Then you ran, didn't you, Sally? You ran and you threw my prized pistol in the bushes. I couldn't get you then and I'll tell you the truth, I was scared. I had to get my gun first, though, and I did. But I'll tell you, I was worried, and I stayed worried for a long time. So what if you told the world you'd seen me, your father? If you did, even though you were certifiably crazy, they might have insisted on doing a lot more than just an autopsy—fingerprints, dental records compared. But you were so afraid you just ran. You ran here, to The Cove, to Amabel.

"I didn't find out for a good four days that you'd blocked it all out. That you ran because you believed that either you'd killed me or dear Noelle had."

She was trying to take it all in, to realize that she'd never been wrong, to at last understand what this man was. She said slowly, "Quinlan made me remember. That and re-creating the scene, I guess you'd say. I saw everything then, everything."

"I bet you want to know who the man was who looked like me. He was just a guy I discovered in Baltimore one day when I was meeting one of the Iraqi agents. He was broke, looked remarkably like me—same height, nearly the same weight—and then I knew when I saw him, just knew that he'd be the one to save me."

Why, she wondered, was he talking so much? Why was he just

standing there pouring all this out to her? And she realized then that it pleased him to brag about his brilliance to her. To make her realize how truly great he was. After all, she'd been in the dark about everything. Oh, yes, he was enjoying himself.

"Jackie who?"

"You know, I really don't remember his last name. Who cares? He played his role and played it perfectly." Amory St. John laughed. "I promised him a truckload of money if he could impersonate me. I wish you could have heard him practicing my voice tones, my accent. It was pathetic, but both Dr. Beadermeyer and I told him he had a great ear, that he had all my mannerisms, that he could play me to perfection. That's what he believed would happen. He believed he was going to take my place at a big conference. It was his chance to do something, his chance to make a big score. He was a credulous fool."

"Now he's a dead fool."

"Yes."

She began to pull on the ropes ever so slightly as she said, "Dr. Beadermeyer is down, but you already know all that. He'll spend the rest of his miserable life in prison. Holland told the FBI everything. All those people—people like me—will be let out of that prison that you call a sanitarium, like it's a resort where people go to recuperate and rest."

"Yes, but who cares about all those other people? They weren't my problem, just you. I only regret that the sanitarium will be closed down. It was such a perfect place for you. Out of the way for good. It all fell into place once I met Jackie. I already knew Dr. Beadermeyer and all about that little racket of his. Nearly seven months ago, it all came together.

"I got you out of the way—with Scott's help, of course. He was so weak and pathetic, afraid he'd get caught, but I'll tell you, he sure liked the money he got from helping me. And, you see, I knew all about his lover. At least I made sure you didn't get AIDS. I threatened Scott that if he made love to you—if he could force himself to do the deed—then he had to use a condom. Dr. Beadermeyer checked your blood. Thanks to me, you're well. But Scott did play his part. Once he was free of you, he spent his money and dallied openly with his lover. He was a good pawn. Where was I? Oh, yes, then Jackie went under the knife, and I finalized my plans. But you had to butt in, didn't you, Sally? I had you all locked away and still you got out. Still you had to try to ruin my plans. Well, no more."

"Do you hate me so much just because I tried to protect my mother from your fists?"

"Actually not. It was natural that I wouldn't like you very much."

"It's because you believed that I'd learned about your illegal arms sales?"

"Did you?"

"No."

"My dealings with other governments had nothing to do with it. Scott was afraid you'd seen something, but I knew you would have acted in a flash if you had. No, that didn't concern me. Fact of the matter is, you're not my daughter. You're a fucking little bastard. And that, my dear Sally, is why Noelle never left me. She tried once, when you were just a baby. She didn't believe me when I told her she was in this for life. Perhaps she thought she'd test me. She ran back to her rich, snotty parents in Philadelphia, and they acted true to form just as I knew they would. They told her to get back to her husband and stop making up lies about me. After all, I'd saved her bacon. How could she say such things about me, a wonderful man who'd married her when she was pregnant with another man's child?"

He laughed, a long, deep laugh that made her skin crawl. She kept lightly tugging on the ropes. Surely they were a little bit looser now, but she wasn't really thinking about those ropes. She was trying to understand him, to really take in what he was saying. But it was so hard.

He continued, his voice meditative. "When I think about it now, I realize that Noelle really hadn't believed me. She hadn't believed that my price to marry her, other than the five hundred thousand dollars I got from her parents, was that she stay with me forever, or until I didn't

want her anymore. When she came dragging back with you—a screaming little brat—I took you away from her and held you over a big fire in
the fireplace. The fire was blowing really good. It singed off the little
hair you had and your eyebrows. Oh, how she screamed. I told her if
she ever tried anything like that again, I'd kill you.

"I meant it, you know. I bet you wonder who your father was."

She felt as though she'd had a ton of drugs pumped into her body.
She couldn't grasp what he was saying. She understood his words—he
wasn't her father—but she couldn't seem to get it to the core of herself.

"You're not my father," she repeated, staring beyond his left shoulder toward the open door. She wanted to cheer. She didn't have any of
this monster's blood. "You kept Noelle with you by threatening to kill
me, her only child."

"Yes. My dear wife finally believed me. I can't tell you the pleasure
it gave me to beat that rich little bitch. And she had to take it. She had
no choice.

"Then you were sixteen and you saw me hit her. Too bad. It
changed everything, but then I had good reason to get rid of you.
Remember that last time? You came back into the house and I was kicking her and you got on the phone to call for help and she crawled—
actually crawled—over to you and begged you not to call? I enjoyed
that. I enjoyed watching you simply disconnect from her.

"I kicked her a couple more times after you left. She really moaned
delightfully. Then I had sex with her and she cried the whole time.

"After that I was free of you for a long while. Life was really quite
good those four years you were out of my house, out of your mother's
life. But I wanted to pay you back. I got Scott to marry you. That got you
away for a little while, but you didn't want him, did you? You realized he
was a phony almost immediately. Well, it didn't matter.

"I just had to bide my time. When I saw Jackie I knew what to do.
You see, the feds were closing in. I'm not stupid. I knew it was only a
matter of time. I'd gotten very rich, but arms sales to places like Iraq are
always risky. Yes, it was just a matter of time. I wanted to pay you back

for all the trouble you caused me. Those six months you were in Dr. Beadermeyer's sanitarium were wonderful for me. I loved to have you beneath me, watching me fondle you, fondle myself. I adored hitting you, watching you wince in pain. But then you got away and ruined everything." He leaned down and slapped her, her left cheek, then her right cheek. Once, again, and yet again.

She tasted blood. He'd split her lip.

"You fucking coward." She spit at him, but he jerked away from her in time. He slapped her again.

"I never wanted to have sex with you in the sanitarium," he said, close to her face now, "though I could have. I saw you naked enough times, but I never wanted you. Hell, Scott wouldn't even look at you. He only came that one time because I insisted. Now that little bastard will take the fall because I won't be around. Come on, Sally, spit at me again. I'm not the coward, you are."

She spit at him, and this time she didn't miss. She watched him wipe his mouth and his cheek with the back of his hand. Then he smiled down at her. She had a stark memory of him smiling down at her in the sanitarium. "No," she whispered, but it didn't change anything.

He struck her hard and she fell into blackness. Her last thought was that she was grateful he hadn't given her more drugs.

"WE'RE IN DEEP shit," Quinlan said and meant it, but he wasn't thinking about himself and the other agents, he was thinking about Sally. If she was here in this black hole, she was still unconscious. Or dead.

There was a grunt from Thomas Shredder and a "yeah" from Corey

Harper. It was true. They were in very deep shit. It was also true that it was as black as the bottom of a witch's cauldron in this room where they were being kept.

No, it wasn't a room. It was a shed with a dirt floor—the shed behind Doc Spiver's cottage.

"Look," Thomas said, "Quinlan's right. We are in deep shit, but we're trained agents. We can get out of this. If we don't, they'll fire us. We'll lose our careers and our federal pensions. I sure as hell don't want to lose my federal health benefits."

Corey Harper laughed despite the cramps in her ankles. Her hands were okay. They hadn't tied them all that tightly, probably because she was a woman. Still, the knots were secure and weren't about to slip or slide.

"That's the funniest thing I've ever heard you say, Thomas."

Quinlan said, as he tugged at the ropes at his wrists, "One of these clowns must have been in the Navy in World War Two. These ropes are very well tied, not a bit of give to them. Anybody want to try hands or teeth?"

"I would," Corey said, "but I'm tied to the wall over here. Yeah, there's a rope around my waist, and I can feel it's wrapped around one of the wall boards. And yes, it's solid. Even with big teeth and a long reach, I couldn't get to you."

"I'm tied too," Thomas said. "Damn."

"At least everyone's alive," Quinlan said. "I wonder what happened to David?" But he was wondering about Sally. He was just afraid to say her name aloud.

"He probably ran off the road," Thomas said matter-of-factly. "He isn't here. Maybe he's already dead."

"Or maybe somebody rescued him," Corey said.

"What do you mean 'already dead'?" Quinlan said, wishing he could see just an outline of something, anything. He kept working on the ropes, but they wouldn't budge.

"Do you think they're going to keep us here for the next ten years?"

"I hope not," Quinlan said. "They're all so old they'd be dead themselves by then. I'd hate to be forgotten."

"You're not funny, Quinlan."

"Maybe not, but I'm trying."

"Keep trying," Corey said. "I don't want to fall into a funk. We've got to think. First of all, who did this to us?"

"That's pretty damned obvious, isn't it?" Thomas said. "That damned old relic. She probably had Martha bring her the Amaretto and she put something into it. I was out like a light the second I lay down on my bed."

"Where's Sally?" Corey asked suddenly.

"I don't know," Quinlan said. "I don't know."

He'd prayed she was locked up with them, still unconscious from the drug. "Everyone stretch your legs out in front of you. Let's see how big this shed is."

Quinlan could just barely touch Thomas's toe.

"Now lean to one side and then the other."

Quinlan got a pinch of Corey's blouse.

No Sally.

"Sally isn't in here with us," Quinlan said. "Where'd they take her?" Oh, Jesus, why had he asked that question aloud? He didn't want to hear what Thomas had to say.

Thomas said, "Good question. Why would they bother to separate us anyway?"

"Because," Quinlan said slowly, "Sally's aunt Amabel is a part of this. Maybe she has Sally. Maybe she'll protect her."

Thomas sighed. To Quinlan's surprise, he said, "Let's pray you're right. My head feels like a drum in a rock band."

"Mine too," Corey said. "But I can still think. Now, Quinlan, you think the whole town is part of a conspiracy? You think the whole bloody town has killed at least sixty people in the past three to four years? For their money? And then they buried all of them in their cemetery?"

"It shows respect," Quinlan said. "Can't you just see all those old folk, stroking their chins as they look down at an old couple they've just offed, saying, 'Well, Ralph Keaton can lay 'em out, then we'll bury 'em really nice and Reverend Vorhees can say all the right words.' Yeah, Corey, the whole bloody town. What other possibility is there?"

"This is nuts," Thomas said. "An entire town killing people? No one would believe that in a million years, particularly since most of them are senior citizens."

"I believe it," Quinlan said. "Oh, yeah, I believe it. I'll just bet it started with an accident. They got money from that accident. It gave them—or maybe just one of them or a couple of them—an idea of how to save their town. And it grew and grew."

Corey said slowly, "The way they lure victims here is that big advertising sign on the highway."

"Right," Quinlan said. "The World's Greatest Ice Cream Shop. By the way, it is the best ice cream I've ever eaten."

He had to make jokes, he had to or else he'd go nuts. Where was Sally? Could Amabel really be protecting her? He had to doubt it.

"Come in and buy your last ice cream cone," Thomas said. "That's the bottom line."

"What about that woman who was murdered? And Doc Spiver?" Corey said.

Quinlan said, even as he was working furiously on the ropes at his wrists, "The woman must have heard something she shouldn't have heard. They held her prisoner for at least three nights, probably more. She must have gotten her mouth free, because Sally heard her screaming that first night she was here in The Cove. Then, two nights later, she heard her screaming again. The next morning Sally and I found her body. My guess is they had to kill her. They didn't want to, but they did. They knew it was either the woman or them. No choice really. They killed her. They must have been pissed—they just threw her off that cliff, didn't bother laying her out or burying her in their precious cemetery."

"What about Doc Spiver?" Thomas said. "Damn, these ropes are strong. I can't get even a micron of play in them."

"Keep working on them, everybody," Quinlan said. "Now, Doc Spiver. I just don't know. It's possible he was a weak link. That as a physician, all the killing had turned him. Maybe the woman's murder was the last straw. He just couldn't stand it anymore. He cracked. They shot him in the mouth, trying to make it look like a suicide. Again, they saw it as they had no choice."

Corey Harper said, "Do you guys know that most FBI agents never get close to the big trouble we're in now? Some of them never even draw their guns. They spend their whole careers interviewing people. I've been told that quite a few agents, when they retire, become psychologists—they're that good at getting information out of people."

Quinlan laughed. "We'll get out of this, Corey. Believe it."

"You think you're so bloody smart, Quinlan. How the hell are we going to get free? And a swarm of little old people are going to show up any minute. Do you think they'll form a firing squad? Or just beat us to death with their canes?"

Corey said quietly, "Don't, Thomas. Let's get loose. There's got to be a way. I don't want to be helpless when someone comes, and you both know they'll come."

"What, dammit?" Thomas shouted. "What can we do? The ropes are too tight. They even tied us to the wall so we couldn't get to each other. We're in the dark. So what are we going to do?"

"There's got to be something," Corey said.

"Just maybe there is," Quinlan said.

SALLY'S JAW HURT. She opened and closed her mouth, working it until the pain eased to a dull throb. She was lying in the dark, the only light coming through the open doorway from the hall.

She was alone. Her hands were still tied in front of her. She lifted her hands to her mouth and began to tug with her teeth on the knot.

She was concentrating so hard that she nearly screamed when a quiet voice said, "It's really no use, Sally. Just relax, baby. Don't move. Just relax."

"No," Sally whispered. "Oh, no."

"Don't you recognize where you are, Sally? I thought you'd know right away."

"No, it's too dark in here."

"Look toward the window, dear. Just maybe you'll see your dear father's face again."

"I'm in the bedroom just down the hall from yours."

"Yes."

"Why, Amabel? What's going on?"

"Oh, Sally, why'd you have to come back? I'd give anything if you hadn't shown up on my doorstep that day. I had to take you in. I really didn't want you involved, but here you are again, and there's nothing I can do."

"Where are James and the other two agents?"

"I don't know. They're probably in that little tool shed behind Doc Spiver's cottage. That's a sturdy prison. They'll never get out."

"What are you going to do to them?"

"It's really not up to me."

"Who is it up to?"

"The town."

For a long moment, Sally couldn't breathe. It was true. The whole bloody town. "How many people has the town killed, Amabel?"

"The first old couple, Harve and Marge Jensen, the ones Quinlan was supposedly here to look for, they were both accidents. Both of them keeled over with heart attacks. We found cash in their Winnebago. Next there was this biker. He started hitting on poor old Hunker, and Purn cracked him over the head with a chair to protect Hunker. It killed him. Another accident.

"Then the biker's girlfriend realized he was dead. Sherry Vorhees had no choice but to kill her. She slammed her over the head with an industrial blender.

"It got easier after that, you know? Someone would spot a likely old couple or just someone who looked rich. Or maybe one of the women who was working in the World's Greatest Ice Cream Shop saw a whole lot of cash when the person pulled open his wallet. Then we just did it. Yes, it got easier. It got to be nearly a game, but don't misunderstand me, Sally. We always treated them with greatest respect after they were dead.

"You've told me how beautiful the town is now. Well, it was a run-down mess before. But now, our investments are doing well, everyone is quite comfortable, and many tourists come here not just for the World's Greatest Ice Cream but also to see the town and buy souvenirs and eat at the cafe."

"How wonderful for you. More people to choose from. You could discuss it among yourselves. Did that couple look richer than that one over there? You played Russian roulette with people's lives. That's disgusting."

"I wouldn't put it so crassly, but as we've gotten to be more of a tourist attraction we've been able to be more selective. But we've killed only old people, Sally. They had all had a full life."

"That biker's girlfriend didn't."

Amabel shrugged. "It couldn't be helped."

Sally was just shaking her head back and forth on the pillow, believing but still incredulous. "Amabel, you've killed people. Don't you understand that? You've killed innocent people. It doesn't excuse anything that they were old. You robbed them. You buried them in the cemetery—what? Oh, I see. You buried them two to each grave. Only you used just a man's name. Does one of you have a list identifying who's really in each grave?"

"No, but we left identification on the bodies. Don't sound so appalled, Sally. We were dying here. We desperately wanted to survive. We have. We've won."

"No, everything's coming down on your heads now, Amabel. There are three FBI agents here, and Sheriff David Mountebank knows everything they know, maybe more. You kill the agents, and you'll all be in the gas chamber. Don't you understand? The FBI is involved!"

"Oh, Sally, here you are, going on and on about something that really doesn't concern you. What about yourself, baby? What about your father?"

"He's not my father, thank God. At least I found that out."

"Good, there's anger there. I was afraid you were still trying to believe he was a nightmare come back to haunt you."

"You're saying he's here with you, Amabel? You want him here?" She knew the answer. But she didn't want to hear it.

"Of course, Sally."

She stared beyond her aunt to the man illuminated in the doorway. Her father. No, not her father, thank God. It was the bastard who raised her, the bastard who beat the shit out of her mother and locked her away in Dr. Beadermeyer's sanitarium, the bastard who beat her just because it pleased him to do so.

"So how does our little bastard feel, Ammie?"

Ammie? What was this?

"I'm not the bastard. You are."

"Sally, I hesitate to hit you in front of your aunt. It bothers her, even though she knows what a vicious mouth you have, even though she knows I've got to do it to control you."

"Amabel, why do you have him here with you? He's a murderer. He's a traitor to our country."

Amabel sat down beside her. Her fingertips were light and soft as they drifted over Sally's forehead, pushing her hair behind her ears, lightly smoothing her eyebrows.

"Amabel, please. When I was here before, I knew it was him on the phone to me. He admitted that he'd looked in through the bedroom window."

"Yes, dear."

"Why was he here, Amabel?"

"He had to come here, Sally. He had to take you back to the sanitarium. He hoped to make you doubt your sanity with the phone calls and his face at the window."

"But how could he possibly know I was even here?"

"I called him. He was staying at a small inn in Oklahoma City. He took the next plane to Portland, then drove here. But you knew even as you asked that question, didn't you, Sally?

"Ah, but you didn't doubt your sanity at all. That was due in part to Quinlan. That man. His being here made everything more difficult. Isn't it strange? Quinlan made up that story about coming here to try to find a trace of those old folk? All he wanted was you. He didn't care about any missing old people. Just you. He thought you'd either killed your father or were protecting your mother.

"I've always been amused by the ways of fate. Well, I'm not amused now. There are big problems now."

"Now, Ammie, do you think it was fate that brought all those nice old people here to buy the World's Greatest Ice Cream so you could then kill them and steal all their money?"

Amabel turned and frowned at him. "I don't know, and neither do you, Amory. Now, I don't care what happens to Quinlan and the others, but I don't want Sally hurt."

"He doesn't agree with you, Aunt Amabel," Sally said. "He hates me. You know he's not my father. He has no latent tender feelings for me. As for my mother, did you know that he forced Noelle to stay with him?"

"Why, of course, Sally."

Sally gaped at her. She couldn't help it. On the other hand, why was she so surprised? Her world had flipped and turned more times in the past seven months than she could cope with. It seemed she'd never known who she really was or why things were the way they were. And she'd hated her mother for her weakness. She'd felt contempt for her, wanted to shake her herself for letting her husband knock her around.

"Who's my father?"

"Now she wants to know," Amory St. John said, as he strolled into the small bedroom, his hands in his pants pockets.

"Who?"

"Well, dear," Amabel said, "actually your father was my husband. And yes, he was my husband before he met Noelle and the two of them fell in love—"

"In lust, you mean, Ammie."

"That too. Anyway, Noelle was always rather stupid, and Carl wasn't all that much of this earth himself. Knowing both of them as well as I did, I had difficulty figuring out who got whom into bed. But they must have managed it. She got pregnant. Fortunately she was seeing Amory at the time, and things got worked out to everyone's satisfaction."

"Not to my mother's."

"Oh, yes, she was thrilled that she wouldn't have to abort you, Sally. She would have, of course, if it meant no husband as a cover.

"I brought my Carl out here to The Cove so he could paint and spend the rest of his meaningless little life doing landscape oils that sell at airport shows for twenty dollars, and that includes their vulgar gold-painted frames. Carl never roamed again. In fact, he begged my forgiveness, said he'd do anything if only I wouldn't leave him. I let him do quite a bit before he died twenty years ago."

"You didn't kill him, did you?"

"Oh, no. Amory did that, but Carl was already very ill with lung cancer. He never would stop smoking unfiltered Camels. Yes, it was a blessing for Carl that his brakes failed, and he died so quickly. Thank you, Amory."

"You're welcome, Ammie."

"So how long have you been lovers?"

Amabel laughed softly, turning to look at the man who was standing in the doorway. "A very long time," she said.

"So you don't mind him beating you, Amabel?"

"No, Amory, don't!" Amabel walked quickly to him and put her hand on his arm. She said over her shoulder, "Listen to me, Sally. Don't talk like that. There's no reason to make your father angry—"

"He's not my father."

"Nevertheless, mind your tongue. Of course he doesn't hit me. Just Noelle."

"He hit me too, Amabel."

"You deserved it," Amory said.

Sally looked from one to the other. In the dim light she couldn't see either of them clearly. Amory took Amabel's hand, pulled her closer to his side. The shadows seemed to deepen around them, moving into them, drawing them into one. Sally shivered.

"I thought you loved me, Amabel."

"I do, baby, indeed I do. You're my husband's child and my niece. And I agreed with Amory that you were better off in that nice sanitarium. You weren't doing well. He told me how erratic you'd become, how you were cheating on your husband, how you'd gotten in with the wrong people and were taking drugs.

"He said that Dr. Beadermeyer would help you. I met Dr. Beadermeyer. An excellent doctor, who said you were doing nicely but that you needed complete rest and constant supervision by professionals."

"That was all a lie. Even if you don't want to believe he's such a monster, just think about it. You've read the papers, seen the news. Everyone is looking for him. Everyone knows that many of the patients in Dr. Beadermeyer's sanitarium were prisoners, just like I was."

"Oh, baby, don't do this. I don't want to put a gag in your mouth, but I will. I won't let you talk about him like this."

"All right, but didn't you wonder about how crazy I was when he showed up here, knocked me over the head, and drugged me? When he nearly killed James?"

Amory St. John pulled away from Amabel. He walked to the bed and stood there, staring down at Sally. "In this dim light I can't tell if you're going to be bruised or not."

"You really hit her that hard, Amory?"

"Don't fret, Ammie. She deserved it. She spit on me. Over the years I learned exactly how hard I could hit Noelle to get a certain kind and color of bruise. But everyone's skin is different. We'll just have to wait and see, won't we?"

"You're nuts," Sally said. "You're a monster."

"I would have whipped you if you'd ever said that when you lived under my roof."

"It doesn't matter, Amory. She's frightened. She doesn't know what's going to happen to her."

Sally said, "I know exactly what's going to happen to me. He doesn't have Dr. Beadermeyer to hold me prisoner for him anymore. No, he's going to kill me, Amabel. You know that as well, otherwise you wouldn't have admitted everything to me. No, don't deny it. You've already accepted it. But I don't really count. What will bring both of you down is hurting the FBI agents. You try killing James, and all hell will break loose. I know his boss, and you can count on it."

"They're stupid, all of them," Amory said. He shrugged. "I know things will get even more difficult, but we'll deal with it. Actually I've already set things in motion. It's true I just didn't count on that bastard getting you away from Dr. Beadermeyer again. That's what ripped it apart. All my plans, Sally, everything has had to be rearranged. It has put me out. Now I'm no longer dead, thanks to the two of you. Now I'll have to leave the country forever."

"Just try it. They'll catch you. With those arms sales to terrorist countries, you've got the feds ready to tear the world apart looking for you."

"I know. Such a pity. But it will be fine. I got most of my money out of the Caymans and Switzerland nearly a year ago. I left just a bit in all those foreign accounts, just to tantalize the feds, just so they'd realize I knew exactly what I was doing. It will make them crazy, and they won't catch me."

"James will catch you."

"Your James Quinlan isn't going to catch a cold. He won't have time before he's sent six feet under."

She felt such rage she couldn't stop herself. She heaved up, hitting him in the face with her bound fists. Hard. He cursed, shoving her back, his own fist raised.

She heard Amabel yell, "Don't, Amory!"

But that fist just kept coming down, not toward her face but toward her ribs.

"WELL HELL," Quinlan said. "Sorry, guys, but the old codgers were thorough. My army knife is gone. I always taped it to my ankle. Damn."

Thomas said, "Damn is right. Corey, what are you doing? Why are you heaving around like a gutted fish? Why are you making those weird groaning sounds?"

She was breathing hard. "You'll see. I didn't count on Quinlan finding that knife. Just wait a moment, I've nearly made it through."

"Made what through?" Quinlan said, desperately straining to see her in the darkness.

"I was a gymnast. I have the dubious honor of being the most flexible agent to go through the program at Quantico. I'm getting my arms beneath my butt and pushing on through and in just a minute—Jesus, this is tougher than it used to be when I was younger and skinnier—" She stopped, breathing hard, straining. "There."

She was panting, laughing. "I did it!"

"What, Corey? For God's sake, what did you do?"

"My hands are now tied in front of me, Thomas. Thank heaven they left enough leeway between me and the wall. The rope around my waist was higher than the rope tying my wrists together. Now, I'm going to turn around and untie the rope around my waist. When I'm free, I can do my feet and then get to you guys."

"Corey," Quinlan said, "if you get us out of this, both Thomas and I will recommend that you become the special agent in charge of the Portland field office. Right, Thomas?"

"If she gets us out of this, I'll beg her to marry me, and be the SAC."

"Thomas, you're a sexist. I won't ever marry a sexist."

"Corey, how are you doing?" Quinlan said.

"It's coming. The knot at my waist is pretty easy."

"Good. Just hurry."

But how much time did they have left before the old folk came for them? Where was Sally? Quinlan hadn't prayed much in his life, but he was praying now. Did Amabel have her?

"Got it! Now let me get my feet."

"I hear something," Thomas said. "Hurry, Corey, hurry!"

"DON'T HIT HER, Amory!"

Amabel grabbed his arm, jerking it away. It slammed against the bed just an inch from Sally's ribs.

He was panting. He wheeled about, his fist raised. "You shouldn't have done that, Ammie. You shouldn't have done it."

Sally reared up, yelling, "Don't you dare hit her, you cretin!"

But he did, his fist hard against Amabel's jaw, knocking her against the wall. She slid down to the floor.

Sally didn't say a word. She was staring at her aunt, praying she wasn't dead.

"How could you?" She stared up at the man who had to be mad. "You're lovers. She called to tell you I was here so you could come and get me. You hit her just like you hit Noelle."

"Actually," he said, rubbing his knuckles, "it's the first time I've ever had to discipline her. She won't go against me in the future now. I wonder how her skin will bruise."

NO BLINDING LIGHT came through the door as it creaked open—just a tiny bit, then wider until all three of them could see the stars and the half-moon.

"You awake in here?" It was an old man's voice. Which one of them? Quinlan wondered. Was there just one of them come to check on their prisoners, or more? He prayed it was just the one old man.

"It ain't quite morning yet, but you should be awake."

"Yeah," Thomas said, "we're awake. What? You hoped you'd killed us?"

"Nah, there weren't enough of that stuff Doc had on hand to put your lights out. It would have been easier that way, though. Now, well, it ain't going to be any fun."

Quinlan nearly jumped out of his skin when he heard Corey whimper. "Oh, please, I don't feel well. Please take me to a bathroom. Please." She was moaning quietly, very effectively.

"Oh, shit," the old man said. "It's just you, little gal?"

"Yes," Corey managed to choke out. "Please, hurry."

"All right. Damn, I didn't expect any of you to be sick. Nobody was ever sick before."

Corey was slumped over, straight ahead of the old guy, against the back wall. The old man opened the door wider as he came into the shed. Quinlan recognized Purn Davies, the old coot who owned the general store. He saw that Corey had her hands behind her back, as if they were still tied there.

"Please hurry," she whispered. She sounded god-awful, like she would puke at any moment.

Quinlan looked at Thomas and shook his head.

Just as Purn Davies passed Quinlan, he whipped up his feet and kicked the old man on his thighs, knocking him right onto Corey's lap.

"Gotcha!" Corey said. When the old man began to struggle, she raised her fists and knocked him cold.

"Well done, Corey," Thomas said. "You sure you won't marry me? What if I promise to change?"

"Ask me again if we get out of this alive," she said. "Okay, guys, I'm going to untie Quinlan's wrists, then yours, Thomas. Keep an eye on the old man."

It took her only about three minutes to untie Quinlan. In another three minutes all of them were free. They rose and stretched and tried to get the blood moving back into their legs and arms. "I think I'll tie him up real good," Corey said and dropped to her knees. "Look, Quinlan, he's got one of our guns."

"Thank God," Quinlan said. He looked outside the shed. "It's near dawn. I don't see a soul. I guess they just sent him here to make sure we were still alive. Why, I don't know. There's no way they could have afforded to keep us alive, no way at all.

"Ah, look here. The old man brought us some sandwiches. They're out here on a tray. How the hell did he expect us to eat them with our hands tied behind our backs?"

"All done," Corey said, standing behind the two men. "What now, Quinlan?"

"Thomas, bar the shed door, then let's get into Doc Spiver's house and pray the phone's still connected. We can get the cavalry here. Then we'll go find Sally."

"HE'S MAD, Amabel, utterly mad."

Amabel was rubbing her jaw. She looked bewildered. "He's never hit me before, never," she said slowly. "He's always caressed me and loved me. He's never hit me. I always thought it was Noelle who brought that out in him, like she made him hit her, like she was sick and needed it."

"No, she hated it. He demeaned her, Amabel, and she stood for it all because he'd threatened to kill me if she didn't stay with him, if she didn't take his abuse. He hasn't hit you because you're not with him all that much and because if he did, you'd probably shoot him or just leave. Noelle couldn't leave. She had to stay to protect me. Now that he's got you, he'll beat you whenever he feels like it."

"No. I'll tell him that if he ever hits me again, I'll leave him."

"You can try it, but I bet he'll find a way to keep you, just like he did your sister."

"You're wrong. You've got to be wrong. We've been intimate for twelve years, Sally. Twelve years. I know him. He loves me. The only reason he hit me tonight is because he's afraid. He's upset and worried that we won't get away. And you pushed. Yes, you made him furious. It's your fault."

"Wake up, Amabel, he's insane."

"Shush, Sally, here he comes."

"Quick, Amabel, untie me. We can escape."

"Now what's this? My two girls conspiring against me?"

"No, dear," Amabel said, rising to go to him. She hugged him, then kissed him on the mouth. "Oh, no. Poor Sally thinks just because you hit me this one time you'll do it again and again. I know you won't, will you?"

"Of course not. I'm sorry, Ammie, I've been under so much stress, and you were arguing with me. Please, forgive me. I won't ever touch you again."

"He's lying," Sally said. "If you believe him you're stupid, Amabel. Yeah, come on, you lousy human being, come on over here and hit me again. I'm tied, so I can't hurt you much. You're safe. Come on, you pitiful excuse for a man, come and hit me."

He was heaving with rage, the veins in his neck red and thick. "Shut up, Sally."

"Look at him, Amabel. He wants to kill me. He has no control. He's crazy."

Amory turned to Amabel. "I'll take care of her. I know what to do. I swear I won't kill her."

"What are you going to do?"

"Trust me, Ammie. Can't you trust me? You have for the past twelve years. Trust me now."

"You think he won't kill me, Amabel? He's a filthy liar. Do you want to be an accessory to murder?" Her words swallowed themselves. Amabel was already an accessory to murder maybe sixty times over. Maybe she'd even killed some of the people. Sally shut her mouth.

Amory St. John laughed, low and mean. "I see you understand, Sally. Ammie belongs with me. We're two of a kind. Now, Ammie, untie her feet. I'm taking her out of here."

She couldn't stand up because her legs were numb. Amabel dropped to her knees and massaged her ankles and calves. "Is that better, Sally?"

"Why didn't you just kill me before? Why go through this charade with Amabel?"

"Be quiet, you little bitch."

"You swear you won't hurt her, Amory?"

"I told you," he said, so impatient that Sally wondered how Amabel couldn't hear it, couldn't know that he was ready to strike out. "I won't kill her."

When she could stand and walk, Amory took her arm and pulled her out of the small bedroom. "Stay here, Ammie," he called over his shoulder. "I'll be back shortly and then we'll leave."

Sally said, "While you're waiting, Amabel, call Noelle. Tell her how you let him kill me. Yeah, tell her that, Amabel."

He pulled her out of Amabel's sight, then sent his elbow into her ribs. She doubled over, gasping with the pain. He yanked her back up.

"Keep your mouth shut, Sally, or I'll just keep hurting you. Do you want that?"

"What I want," she said when she could finally speak, "is for you to die. Very slowly and very painfully."

"Not in your lifetime, my dear," he said, and laughed.

"They'll get you. There's no way you can escape, not with the FBI after you."

He was still laughing softly, highly amused with her. It made no sense. Then he walked beneath a strong light at the head of the stairs and stopped. He laughed again. "Look, Sally. Look at me."

She did. It wasn't Amory St. John.

THE PHONE SERVICE was still on. Thomas called the Portland office. When he hung up, he said, "They're bringing a helicopter up here. Thirty minutes, tops."

"What about David?" Corey said.

"Here, let me call his wife." David's lovely sweet wife, Jane, who'd taken him in when they cracked him over the head, who'd fed him soup. He prayed David was alive. Please, let him be alive.

Quinlan said, "This is Quinlan. Please tell me David's there. What? Oh, no. I'm sorry. Tell his doctors that he was drugged. That's why he banged himself up. No, no, things are under control here. No, I'm going to call his office and get his three deputies here. Yeah, I'll speak to you soon. Sally? I don't know. We're going to hunt for her now."

He hung up the phone. "David's in a coma. They medivaced him to Portland. His condition's stable so far. Nobody knows anything yet, just that he ran off the road into the only oak tree in his neighborhood. His wife was the first person to get to him. She said the doctors told her that if he hadn't been transported so quickly to the hospital he probably would have died."

"This is a nightmare," Corey said. "The whole town, all of them murderers. I want to get them, Quinlan."

"I sure want them to lose their Social Security," Thomas said. "No means testing."

"That wasn't funny," Corey said, but she laughed.

"It's Shakespearean. You know, comedy mixed with tragedy."

"No," Quinlan said, "it's evil. It didn't start out evil, but they've made it all the way, haven't they? Let's go find my future wife."

IT WAS AMORY ST. JOHN, but it wasn't. She blinked up at him. No, the light here was excellent. "Dr. Beadermeyer changed your face, just like he did the man you murdered."

"Yes. I didn't want to be completely different, just different enough that if an old friend happened to see me he wouldn't wonder. He did his nicks and cuts and sutures just after we got you back from The Cove that first time." He patted his neck. "Gravity was taking a bit of a toll, but no longer. He tucked that all up, too. Would you go out with me, Sally, a young woman your age?"

She didn't say anything. She was afraid if he hit her again she'd lose consciousness. She couldn't let that happen. Her legs were free. The numbness was nearly gone. Surely she could run now. She had to get away from him. She had to find Quinlan and the others. What if they were already dead? No, she wouldn't think like that. They weren't dead. There was still time.

She looked up at him. She hated him more than she believed it possible for one human being to hate another. She wanted to break him. She wanted him to suffer, to realize he'd lost, to realize that he wasn't as smart as he thought he was. "Scott told the FBI everything you'd done. He's cooperating with them, hoping to save his wretched little hide."

"Who cares what the little prick does? Shut up now, and let's get you out of here."

He forced her down the stairs. As if he guessed she would try something, he grabbed her hair and went down behind her.

What to do?

There was a noise at the front door. His hand jerked her hair upward. She didn't even notice. She heard him under his breath. She knew the moment when he drew a gun. "Let's just hope it's one of the old folk."

But it wasn't. The door slowly opened. If only they'd been upstairs no one would have heard anything. She stared at that opening door, mesmerized.

She saw Quinlan's face. She didn't think, just acted. She raised her arms, grabbed his hair, and dropped down. Amory stumbled over her head and rolled over and over down the stairs. He landed on his back, panting hard, but still conscious. Quinlan was on him in an instant, the gun pointed at his temple.

"Who the hell are you?"

"It's Amory St. John," Sally said. "Dr. Beadermeyer changed his face just like he did that other man's."

Quinlan's SIG-Sauer pressed harder against St. John's temple. "Sally, are you all right?"

"I'm fine. My aunt's upstairs. He was taking me away, probably to kill me. He told my aunt that he wouldn't, but he's a miserable liar. James, he hit her and she's all ready to forgive him. What's wrong with her?"

"I'll get her," Thomas said. "Don t worry, Sally. I won't hurt her."

Sally got to her feet. She was sore, her scalp hurt, and she felt better than she'd ever felt in her life. "James," she said, "I'm so glad to see you. You, too, Corey. Amabel said the three of you were in that shed behind Doc Spiver's cottage."

"Yeah," Quinlan said, "but we're special agents. We got out. Well, actually, it's Corey who's the hero. You know, Sally, I noticed a gray hair. Let Corey untie your hands."

When she had feeling back in her wrists, she went and stood over the man who'd been her father for so many years, the man she'd hated for so long, the man who hated her. He was on the floor, at her feet.

She got down on her knees. She smiled. "Now it's my chance to tell you what I think of you. You're pathetic. You're nothing. You'll never have a hold over anybody again for as long as you live. I hate you. More than that, I despise you." She drew back her fist and slammed it into his nose.

"I've wanted to do that for such a long time." She rubbed her knuckles.

He was quivering with rage. His nose began to bleed. He quieted only when he felt the gun press still harder against his temple.

"You want to know something else? Noelle is ecstatic that you're gone. She hates you as much as I do. She's free of you. I'm free of you. Soon you'll be in a cage where you belong."

She stared down at him, at the blood seeping out of his nose, at the rage in his eyes. "God-awful bastard." She rose and kicked him in the ribs, then kicked him two more times.

"You crazy bitch. Hey, you're a cop. Don't let her beat me."

"I'll let her shoot you in the balls if she wants to," Quinlan said. "Sally? Would you like to shoot him?"

"No, not now. Well, just not this exact minute. You know what, old man? Noelle looks utterly beautiful. I'll bet she'll be going out again very soon. She'll have any man she wants."

"She won't dare. She knows I'd kill her if she even looked at another man. Yes, I'd kill both of them."

"You aren't going to kill anybody," Sally said, eyes mean and bright, joy in her voice. "You're going to jail for the rest of your miserable life." She patted his face. "You're an old man. Think of how much faster you'll sag and wrinkle in prison."

"I won't go to prison. I'm going to get you. I played with you for six months. I should have strangled you."

"Just try it, you old bastard." She smiled down at him, lifted her foot, and landed it square in his groin.

He screamed, clutching himself.

"Well done, Sally," Quinlan said. "You sure you don't want to shoot him?"

There was a shot from upstairs.

QUINLAN STRUCK Amory St. John hard on his jaw.

One down, he thought, as St. John's head lolled to the side. They had only one weapon—Quinlan's gun, taken off old Purn Davies, the one that Quinlan had pressed to Amory St. John's temple.

When Thomas had gone upstairs unarmed, Sally hadn't thought, hadn't imagined that her aunt could shoot someone.

Suddenly Corey moved like lightning, throwing herself into the shadowed recess just to the side at the base of the stairs.

They watched in silence as Thomas, his arm bleeding rivulets through his fingers, came down the stairs, Amabel behind him with a pistol to the back of his head.

"Throw that gun toward the living room, Mr. Quinlan."

Instead, Quinlan slid it across the highly polished oak floor right toward the spot where Corey was crouched.

"You don't have such a good aim, do you? No matter. Now, move away from him. That's right. Go stand by Sally.

"You, sir, keep moving or I'll shoot you in the back of your neck. You wouldn't like that, would you?"

"No," Thomas said, sounding dazed, "I wouldn't like that at all."

"You're bleeding all over my floor. Well, who cares? I doubt we'll ever come back here anyway. Now, Mr. Quinlan, you and Sally just take two more steps back. Good. Don't try anything. You're always bragging about FBI agents, but this one's just like you, Mr. Quinlan, he's just a man. Look at all that blood—and it's only a little wound in his arm. He's not whining, I'll say that for him. Now don't move." She looked down. "Amory, you can get up now."

There wasn't a sound from Amory.

"Amory!"

She waved the gun and screamed at Quinlan, "What did you do to him, you bastard?"

"I coldcocked him, Amabel. Real hard. I don't think he'll be coming around anytime soon."

"I should shoot you right now. You've been a pain ever since you set foot in this town, ever since you first saw Sally. No, Sally, just keep your mouth shut. My future is with him, and I intend to have it. I know the town will fall, but I won't. No one will catch us, not even your precious FBI."

She shoved Thomas to the bottom step. She must have sensed something because she quickly moved back up two steps. "You try to turn on me, boy, and I'll blow your head off."

"No, ma'am," Thomas said. "I won't do anything. Can I go on down and let Quinlan wrap a handkerchief around my arm? I don't want to bleed to death. I don't want to ruin your pretty floor and carpets."

"Go on, but try anything and you're dead."

Thomas was pale, his mouth drawn thin with pain. He was holding his arm tightly. Blood still dripped slowly between his fingers.

"Come here, Thomas," Quinlan said, motioning him forward with his hand. "You got a handkerchief?"

"Yeah, in my right coat pocket."

Quinlan pulled out a spiffy blue handkerchief with the initials TS in the corner and tied up his arm. "That should do it. Too bad you guys killed Doc Spiver, Amabel. Thomas could use his services right about now."

She had to come down those three remaining steps. She had to. Just three steps. Come on, Amabel, come on.

Sally said suddenly, her voice loud with shock, "There's blood coming from his mouth." She was pointing wildly at Amory St. John. "And something white, oh, my God, I think it's foam. He's foaming!"

"What?" Amabel came down the last three stairs, slowly, trying to keep her attention on the two agents and Sally and see what was wrong with Amory. "All of you, bunch together, there. Sit on the floor. Now."

They all sat.

Just a bit farther, Quinlan said to her silently. Just a bit farther. He saw Corey poised in the shadows, his SIG-Sauer at the ready in her hand.

Just then Amory St. John groaned. He jerked up, then fell back. He groaned again, then opened his eyes.

"Oh, God," Sally shrieked, "there's blood in his eyes. James, you hit him that hard?"

In those precious seconds when all of Amabel's attention was focused on Amory, Corey leaped from her left side, a lovely training move taught at Quantico, her right fist going right into Amabel's side, her left fist straight into her neck.

Amabel turned, but not in time. The gun went spinning out of her hand.

Corey said, "I'm sorry, Sally," then hit Amabel square in the jaw. She crumpled to the floor.

Amory St. John groaned again.

"Corey," Thomas said, "please say you'll marry me. Like a reformed smoker, I'm now a reformed sexist. I'll become a feminist."

Sally laughed from sheer relief. Quinlan told Thomas to stay where he was on the floor. He rose and shook hands with Corey and hugged Sally to his side. "Now we'll just wait for the cavalry to arrive."

"I smell smoke," Thomas said, stiffening as he sniffed the air. "Quinlan, there's smoke coming from under that door."

"It's the kitchen," Sally said, dashing to it.

"No, Sally, don't open it. It'll just suck the flames in here."

Amory St. John moaned again and lurched to his side.

"More flames," Corey said. "Someone's set us on fire. The old folks have set the place on fire!"

"I'll carry St. John. Corey, you get Amabel. Sally, can you help Thomas? Let's get out of here."

"Whoever set the fire will be waiting for us," Sally said. "You know it, James."

"I'd rather risk being shot than burn to death," he said. "Everyone agree? There's no other way out except through the kitchen, and the door's already burning. It's got to be the front door."

"Let's go," Corey said, as she shoved the SIG-Sauer in her belt. She heaved Amabel over her shoulder.

Quinlan, with St. John over his shoulder in a fireman's carry just like Corey's, kicked the cottage door open. The sun was just rising, the dawn sky streaked with pink. The air was crisp and clean, the sound of the ocean soft and rhythmic. It was a beautiful morning.

There were at least thirty people standing in front of the cottage, all of them armed.

Reverend Hal Vorhees shouted, "Throw down your gun, Mr. Quinlan, or we'll shoot the women."

Well, damn, Quinlan thought. At least the old folk hadn't automatically shot them down when they'd come out of Amabel's cottage. All the bravado about preferring a gunshot to a fire—was bullshit. Nobody wanted to die. Now they had some time—at least he prayed they did.

Quinlan nodded to Corey. She threw his SIG-Sauer right at Reverend Hal Vorhees. It landed close to his feet.

"Good, now lay that madman down, Amabel next to him. We don't care what happens to him. He's evil and a blight. He's nothing more than a filthy traitor. He made Amabel turn on us. Come on now, the four of you come with us."

"We're going to a church service, Reverend?"

"Just shut up, Mr. Quinlan," Hunker Dawson said.

"A helicopter will be arriving in just about five minutes, Hal," Quinlan said after he'd dropped St. John to the ground, landing him in the middle of Amabel's daffodils.

"We called the FBI office in Portland from Doc Spiver's cottage. Sheriff David Mountebank's deputies will be here soon as well."

Actually the deputies should have been here long ago. Where the devil were they?

"No, we took care of the deputies," Gus Eisner said. "Come now. We don't want to waste any more time. You're lying about that helicopter.

Besides, it don't make no difference. You'll be gone by the time the feds arrive."

"You'll never get away with this," Sally said. "Never. Don't you have any idea at all what you're dealing with?"

"Look at us, Sally," Sherry Vorhees said. "Just look at all these nice old people. We wouldn't even kill mosquitoes, now would we? Who would deal with us? Why, there's nothing to deal with. I'd invite them all in for some of the World's Greatest Ice Cream."

"It's gone far beyond that now," Sally said, stepping forward.

Reverend Hal Vorhees immediately raised his gun higher. "Listen to me," Sally went on. "Everyone knows that James and the other agents are here. They'll mow you down. Another thing, they'll dig up every grave in the cemetery and they'll find out those are all the missing people reported over the past three years. It's all over. Please, be reasonable about this. Give it up."

"Shut up, Sally," said Hunker Dawson. "All of you, enough of this bullshit. Let's go."

"Yes, sure thing, Hunker," Quinlan said. They had more time. How much more, he had no idea. But even one more minute meant hope.

They walked like condemned prisoners in front of the mob. He was aware of the unreality of the whole situation even as he felt fear seeping deep into him.

Quinlan said over his shoulder, "What will you preach on this Sunday, Hal? The rewards of evil? The spiritual high of mass murder? No, I've got it. It'll be the wages of trying to bring justice to people who were brutally murdered for the amount of cash they carried."

Quinlan staggered from the blow on his shoulder.

"That's enough," Gus Eisner said. "Just shut up. You're upsetting the ladies."

"I'm not upset," Corey said. "I'd like to pull out all your teeth and listen to you scream."

"I don't have any teeth," Hunker said. "That ain't a good punishment for this group."

What to say to that? Quinlan thought and winked at Corey. She looked furious. Thomas was walking on his own, but Corey was helping him. His arm wasn't bleeding so much now, but the blood loss was taking its toll, that and shock.

Sally was trudging along beside him, looking pale and very thoughtful. He said out of the side of his mouth, real low, so maybe all those old people wouldn't hear him, "Hold up, Sally. We'll figure out something. Hey, I can take at least a dozen of the old guys, no problem. Could you pound the old ladies?"

That made her smile. "Yeah, I could pound them into the dust. But I want to go back and get Amory St. John. They just left him and Amabel there, James, both of them. They'll get away. My aunt, well, I don't know, but she's not quite the aunt I'd hoped she was."

An understatement, Quinlan thought. Another blow for her, another person she'd believed she could trust had betrayed her. Thank God her mother had come through for her. He thought he just might come to like Noelle St. John a lot in the future. If he had a future.

Quinlan said, "Maybe the calvary will arrive before St. John and your aunt get their wits back together and can get away. But even if they do escape, we'll get them sooner or later."

To Quinlan's surprise, they were herded up the wide, beautifully painted white steps and into Thelma's Bed and Breakfast. He had thought they'd be taken to the Vorhees house.

"Would you look at that," Quinlan said as he got a poke with a rifle, shoving him into the large drawing room. There was Thelma Nettro, sitting on that chair of hers that looked for all the world like a throne. She was smiling at them. She was wearing a full mouth of false teeth and her pumpkin peach lipstick.

She said, "I wanted to join in the fun, but I just don't get around as well as I used to."

There was Purn Davies sitting on one of the sofas, looking white and shriveled. Good, Corey had whacked him hard.

"Why are we here?" Quinlan asked, turning to Reverend Hal Vorhees.

"You're here because I wanted you here. Because I ordered my people to bring you to me. Because, Mr. Quinlan, I'm going to tell you all what we're going to do with you."

They all stared at Martha as she moved from behind Thelma Nettro's chair. There was nothing soft and bosomy about her now. There were no pearls around her neck. Her voice was loud and clear, a commander's voice, not her gentle cook's voice announcing an incredible meal. Damn, Quinlan thought, what was going on here?

"Martha?" Sally said, bewildered. "Oh, no, not you too, Martha?"

"Don't look so surprised."

"I don't understand," Sally said. "You're a wonderful cook, Martha. You go out with poor Ed. You take grief from Thelma. You're nice, damn you. What's going on?"

Quinlan said slowly, "I knew there had to be a ringleader, one person with a vision, one person who could get all the others to fall in line. Aren't I right, Martha?"

"Exactly right, Mr. Quinlan."

"Why didn't you just let them elect you mayor?" Sally said. "Why murder innocent people?"

"I'll let that go, Sally," Martha said. "Oh, poor Mr. Shredder. You, Corey, set him down in that chair. Too bad Doc Spiver fell sick of cowardice and remorse. He drew the straw and had to kill that woman who'd overheard a meeting we were having. We caught her on the phone, dialing nine-one-one. Poor bitch. She was different. We didn't know what to do with her. She wasn't like those tourists who came into town for the World's Greatest Ice Cream. No, we wouldn't ever have picked her. She was too young; she had children. But then, we didn't know what to do with her either. We couldn't very well let her go.

"When she got loose that first night and screamed her head off— you heard her, Sally, Amabel told us the next day—we put a guard on her. But then two nights later she got loose again, and that time Amabel was forced to call Hal Vorhees over, because of you, Sally. There was no choice. Since it was Doc's fault that she got loose, since he'd been her guard, we all decided that she had to die. There was simply no other choice. We were sorry about it, but it had to be done, and Doc Spiver had to kill her. He just couldn't stomach it. He was going to call Sheriff Mountebank." She shrugged.

"Fair is fair. Yes, we've always been scrupulously fair. Helen Keaton drew the straw. She put the gun in his mouth and pulled the trigger. If it hadn't been for that sheriff and that medical examiner in Portland, it would have been declared an accident. Yes, that was a pity. Amazingly unfair."

It was remarkable, Quinlan was thinking, that every criminal he'd ever known had loved to talk, to brag about how great he was, how he was smarter than everyone else. Even a little old lady.

"Yeah," he said, "a real pity."

Martha was fiddling with her glasses, since she wasn't wearing her pearls, but her voice was calm and assured. "You don't appreciate what we've done, Mr. Quinlan. We turned a squalid little ghost town into a picture postcard village. Everything is so pristine. Everything is so beautifully planned. We leave nothing to chance. We discuss everything. We even have a gardening service for those who don't enjoy tending flowers. We have a painting service that comes in every week. Of course, we also have a chairperson for each service. We are an intelligent, loyal, industrious group of older citizens. Each of us has a responsibility, each has an assignment."

"Who selects the victims?" Corey asked. She was standing beside Thomas, her hand on his shoulder. He was still conscious, but his face was white as death. She'd wrapped a hand-crocheted afghan around him. It looked as if a grandmother had spent hours putting those soft pastel squares together.

Quinlan stared at that afghan. Then he stared at Martha. He'd be willing to wager that she had knitted the afghan. No accounting for grandmothers. Martha was a vicious cold-blooded killer.

Martha laughed softly. "Who? Why, all of us, Ms. Harper. Our four gentlemen who play gin rummy around their barrel? Yes, they look over everyone who drives in for refreshment at the World's Greatest Ice Cream Shop.

"Zeke down at the cafe eyes every tourist from his window in the kitchen. When he's too busy, then Nelda pays attention when folk take out their wallets to pay.

"Sherry and Della run the souvenir shop in that little cottage close to the ocean cliffs. They check out tourists there. As you can imagine, we must make decisions very quickly." She sighed. "Sometimes we've erred. A pity. One couple looked so very affluent, drove a Mercedes even, but we only found three hundred dollars, nothing else of any use. All we could do was send Gus to Portland with the car to sell it. It turned out it was leased. That was close. As I recall, Ralph refused to lay them out, didn't you, Ralph? Yes, that's right, you said they didn't deserve it. And we all agreed. They weren't honest with us. They lied."

"Exactly right," Ralph Keaton said. "I just wrapped them each in a cheap sheet, the dirty liars. Helen wanted the name Shylock on their grave marker, but we knew we couldn't be that obvious so we changed it to Smith, so nondescript it was like they'd never even existed."

"This is amazing," Sally said, looking at each one of those old faces. "Truly amazing. You're all mad. I wonder what they'll do with all of you. Put you all on trial as mass murderers? Or just chuck you into an insane asylum?"

"I hear a helicopter," Reverend Hal Vorhees said. "We've got to hurry, Martha."

"You're going to shoot us?" Corey asked, stepping away from Thomas. "You honest to God think you can get away with killing all of us?"

"Of course we can," Purn Davies said, rising from the sofa, looking a bit less pale. He picked up a shotgun from beside him and walked forward. "We've got nothing to lose. Nothing at all. Isn't that right, Martha?"

"Perfectly right, Purn."

"You're all senile and stupid!" Sally screamed.

In that instant, when most attention was focused on Sally, Quinlan grabbed Purn Davies's sawed-off shotgun and leaped at Martha. He took her down and rolled over her. He had his arm around her throat and the gun digging into the small of her back. His right hand was tangled in the chain that secured her glasses.

There was stunned silence. Thelma Nettro slowly turned around in her chair. "Let her go, Mr. Quinlan. If you don't, we'll just kill her along with the rest of you. You agree, don't you, Martha?"

There was no choice, none at all. Quinlan knew that. He knew he had to act quickly, with no hesitation. He had to make them believe. He had to scare them down to their old bones. It had to be shocking. It had to punch these old people back to reality, out of the insane world they'd created and inhabited. He had to show them they had no more control.

Quinlan raised the shotgun and shot Purn Davies in the chest. The blast knocked the old man off the floor, against an ancient piano. Blood spewed everywhere. The old man didn't make a sound, just slid onto the floor. There were a dozen screams, curses, and just plain horrified yells.

Quinlan shouted over the din, "I can get at least three more of you before you get me. Want to bet it's not going to be you? Come on, you old geezers, come and try it."

The shotgun was double-barreled. One of them would realize quickly enough that he had only one shot left.

"Corey, grab my gun, quick."

She had it in an instant. Reverend Hal Vorhees raised his pistol. Quinlan shot him cleanly through his right arm. Corey threw Quinlan his SIG-Sauer.

"Who else?" Quinlan said. "This gun is a semiautomatic. It can take you all down. Anybody else? It will make a bigger, bloodier mess than that wimpy little shotgun did on old Purn. It'll spew your ancient guts all over this room. I'll bet none of you has ever dispatched your victim with a semiautomatic. It ain't a pretty sight. Just look at Purn. Yeah, look at him. It could be you."

Silence. Dead silence. He heard someone vomiting. That was

amazing. One of them could actually throw up seeing Purn Davies after they'd killed sixty people?

Thelma Nettro said, "You all right, Martha?"

"Oh, yes," Martha said. She flexed her hands. She smiled. She kicked back against Quinlan's groin. He felt searing pain, felt his head swim with dizziness, felt the inevitable nausea. He took the SIG-Sauer and hit her on the temple.

He didn't know if she was dead. He didn't particularly care. He said between gritted teeth as the nausea began to get to him, "Sally, get me Gus's gun. Be sure to stay clear of any hands that could grab you. The rest of you, drop all your weapons. Ease those old bones of yours down to the floor. We're going to stay here nice and quiet until my guys arrive."

Thelma Nettro said, "Did you kill her, Mr. Quinlan?"

"I don't know," he said, the pain still roiling through his groin.

"Martha's like a daughter to me. Don't you remember? I told you that once." She raised a pistol from her lap and shot him.

In the next instant, the front door burst open. Sally, who was running to Quinlan, heard a man shout, "Nobody move! FBI!"

"MR. QUINLAN, can you hear me?"

"Yes," he said very clearly. "I can hear you, but I don't want to. Go away. I hurt and I want to hurt alone. My Boy Scout leader told me a long time ago that men didn't whine or moan, except in private."

"You're a trooper, Mr. Quinlan. Now, I'll make that hurt go away. How bad is it?"

"On a scale from one to ten, it's a thirteen. Go away. Let me groan in peace."

The nurse smiled over at Sally. "Is he always like this?"

"I don't know. This is the first time I've ever been around him when he's been shot."

"Hopefully that won't happen again."

"It won't," Sally said. "If he ever lets it happen again, I'll kill him."

The nurse injected morphine into his IV drip. "There," she said, lightly rubbing his arm above the elbow, "you won't hurt very soon now. As soon as you have your wits together, you can give yourself pain medication whenever you need it. Ah, here's Dr. Wiggs."

The surgeon was tall, skinny as a post, with the most beautiful black eyes Quinlan had ever seen. "I'm in Portland?"

"Yes, at OHSU, Oregon Health and Sciences University Hospital. I'm Dr. Wiggs. I took that bullet out of your chest. You're doing just fine, Mr. Quinlan. I hear you're a very brave man. It's a pleasure to save a brave man."

"I'm going to get even braver soon," Quinlan said, his voice a bit slurred from the morphine. He was feeling just fine now. In fact, if he weren't tied to this damned bed with all these hookups in every orifice of his body, he'd want to dance, maybe even play his saxophone. He'd like to call Ms. Lilly, maybe even tell Marvin the Bouncer a joke. He realized his mind wasn't quite on track. He had to remember to ask Fuzz the Bartender to get some decent white wine in stock for Sally.

"Why is that, Mr. Quinlan?" the nurse asked.

"Why is what?"

"Why are you going to get even braver?"

He frowned, then smiled as he remembered. He said, his voice as proud and happy as a man's could ever get, "I'm going to marry Sally."

He turned his head and gave her the silliest smile she'd ever seen. "We're going to spend our honeymoon at my cabin in Maryland. On Louise Lynn Lake. It's a beautiful place, with smells that make your senses melt and—"

He was out.

"Good," Dr. Wiggs said. "He needs lots of sleep. Don't worry, Ms. Brainerd. He'll be fine. I was a bit worried for a while in surgery, but he's strong and young and he's got a will to survive that's rare.

"Now, let me just check him over. Why don't you go outside? Mr. Shredder and Ms. Harper are in the waiting room. Oh, yes, there's a Mr. Marvin Brammer there too and a man who's sitting on the sofa with a computer on his lap."

"Mr. Brammer is James's boss. He's an assistant deputy director of the FBI. The guy with the computer—"

"The sexy one."

"Yes, that's Dillon Savich. He's also FBI."

"Mr. Brammer's got quite a twinkle in those eyes of his," Dr. Wiggs said. "As for Mr. Savich, no matter how gorgeous he is, I don't know if he's even aware of where he is. I heard him say, to no one in particular, 'Eureka!' but nothing else. Go out now, Ms. Brainerd, and leave me alone with my patient."

The waiting room was just down the hail. Sally ran into Marvin Brammer's arms. "He's all right," she said over and over. "He'll be just fine. He's already complaining. He was talking about his Boy Scout leader telling him that men never whine or moan except when they're alone. He'll be just fine. We're going to get married, and I'll make sure he never gets shot again."

"Good," Marvin Brammer said, hugged her tightly, then turned her over to Savich, who gave her a distracted hug and kiss on the cheek. "I've found them, Sally," he said. "I've found that damned jerk who isn't your father."

Marvin Brammer said, "Eureka?"

"That's it. I've got to get to the FBI office in Seattle. They're at Sea-Tac Airport. Yeah, the idiot bought two tickets to Budapest, via New York. He used a phony credit card and a phony passport."

"Then how did you get him?" Thomas Shredder said, walking over.

His arm was in a sling. He had good color in his cheeks again. He was no longer in shock. "He doesn't look like Amory St. John anymore."

"Not hard," Savich said, patting his laptop. "Me and MAX here and our modem can do anything. Sally's aunt used her own passport. Ain't that a kick? She had to, I guess. I suppose they just prayed that she'd get through. They should have laid low until they got a phony one for her too. Corey, you and Thomas must have really scared them. They couldn't wait to get out of the country."

"So," Sally said slowly, as Savich phoned the Seattle FBI office. "It's nearly over. What's going to happen to the town, Mr. Brammer?"

"Agents are all over the cemetery. Like the old folk said, they buried all the people they murdered with their identification, so there's been no problem determining who anybody is.

"Mass murder, nothing else to call it, all by a bunch of senior citizens." He shook his head. "I thought I'd seen just about everything, but this takes the cake.

"Evil," he added, stroking his chin. "Evil can sprout up just about anyplace. None of the seniors is saying a word. They're loyal to each other, I'll say that for them, even though it doesn't matter. That Martha Crittlan, she'll pull through, although I'll bet she'll wish she hadn't. Just imagine, that seemingly sweet old lady was the brains and resolution behind the town."

"She's the most wonderful cook," Corey Harper said and sighed. "That last dinner was the most delicious meal I've ever eaten in my life."

"Yeah," Thomas Shredder said, "and it could have been our last meal, since she drugged us."

"You'll survive," Marvin Brammer said. "Oh, yes, one of the agents found a slew of diaries that old Thelma Nettro kept throughout all her time in The Cove."

Sally said. "She always had one with her. Do you know that she had a black circle on her tongue from licking the end of the fountain pen before she wrote?"

"Knowing our people, they'll probably check for that. Old Thelma was very specific about how everything came about. It's probably the best proof and history anyone could have of the entire episode. I mean, she wrote everything, beginning back in the 1950s after she and her husband came to The Cove.

"It's all the attorney general's problem now. I'll wager they're hating every minute of it. You can't begin to imagine what the media are doing with all this. Well, maybe you can. It's nuts. At least Sheriff Mountebank came out of the coma this morning, that's one good thing. His three deputies are pulling through as well. They were drugged and tied up in that shed where you guys were."

"Amory St. John and my aunt Amabel," Sally said. "Mr. Brammer, what will happen to them when you nab them?"

"He'll be in jail three lifetimes. As for your aunt, Sally, I don't know if they'll toss her in with the other seniors or if they'll add kidnapping charges and conspiracy charges. We'll just have to see."

"Eureka again!"

Everyone turned to Savich. He looked up, grinning a bit sheepishly. "Well, I just wanted all of you to know that Sally's divorce will be final in six months. Let's make it the middle of October. I've booked Elm Street Presbyterian in D.C. for the fourteenth. Everything's set."

"Will you marry me, Corey?" Thomas Shredder said.

She gave him a sharp look. "You have to prove to me that you're no longer a sexist. That could take a good year, even if you try really hard. Don't forget, a condition is that I become the SAC of the Portland office."

"You could always shoot him in the other arm if he backslides," Brammer said. "As to special agent in charge, why, Ms. Harper, I'll do a great deal of thinking about that."

Sally just smiled at them all—all of them lifelong friends now—and walked back to James's room.

He would live. As to all the rest of it, well, she just wasn't going to think about it until she had to.

Life was all in your perspective, she'd decided during that helicopter ride to Portland, James white as death lying on that stretcher beside her, tubes sticking out of him. She was going to keep her perspective on James's face. A nice face, a sexy face. She couldn't wait for him to get well so they could go to the Bonhomie Club and he could play his saxophone.

THE NEXT MORNING, Quinlan opened the *Oregonian* that a nurse had brought him. The headline was:

ARMORY ST. JOHN KILLED WHILE FLEEING FBI

Like he didn't deserve it, he thought. "Yeah, poor bugger," he said aloud, and read on. Evidently Amory St. John had tried to run, but he hadn't made it. He'd left Amabel in a flash, jumped onto a baggage truck, knocked out the driver, and driven off, the FBI right behind him. He hadn't gotten far. He'd even been stupid enough to fire on the agents, refusing orders to stop and throw down his weapon.

He was dead. The bastard was finally dead. Sally wouldn't have to go through a trial. She wouldn't ever have to face him again.

What about Amabel?

Apparently the *Oregonian* hadn't known which headline to splash— The Cove murders or Amory St. John. Since The Cove had gotten the big print the day before, he supposed they decided it was Amory's turn.

Amabel Perdy, he read, had pleaded innocent of all charges, both with regard to Amory St. John and with regard to The Cove, saying she had no idea what was going on in either case. She was an artist, she maintained. She helped sell the World's Greatest Ice Cream. That was all she did.

Wait until the media found out about Thelma's diaries, he thought. That would nail her hide but good. All of the seniors' hides. He was tired, his chest hurt real bad, and so he pumped a small dose of morphine into his arm.

Soon, he knew, he would be sleeping like a baby, his mind free of all this crap. He just wished he could see Sally before he went under again.

When she appeared at his bedside, smiling down at him, he knew he must be dreaming.

"You look like an angel."

He heard a laugh and felt her mouth on his, all warm and soft.

"Nice," he said. "More."

"Go to sleep, buster," she said. "I'll be here when you wake up."

"Every morning?"

"Yes. Always."

Epilogue

SALLY ST. JOHN BRAINERD and James Railey Quinlan were married on the date Dillon Savich had set for them—October 14. Dillon Savich was Quinlan's best man and Sally's mother was her matron of honor. She attended her daughter's wedding with Senator Matt Montgomery from Iowa, a widower who'd taken one look at Noelle and fallen hard. She had worn a two-piece bathing suit that summer.

There were 150 special agents from the FBI, including two special agents from the Portland field office, one of them the newly appointed SAC, or special agent in charge. Every Railey and Quinlan within striking distance arrived at the Elm Street Presbyterian Church in Washington, D.C. Sally was simply enfolded into her new family.

Ms. Lilly, Marvin the Bouncer, and Fuzz the Bartender were in attendance, Ms. Lilly wearing white satin and Marvin announcing to everyone that the chicky looked gorgeous in her wedding dress. Fuzz brought a bottle of Chardonnay for a wedding present. It had a cork.

The media mobbed the wedding, which was expected since the trial of Dr. Beadermeyer—aka Norman Lipsy— had ended just the previous week and Sally had been one of the major prosecution witnesses. He'd been found guilty of conspiracy, murder, kidnapping, extortion, and income tax evasion, which, a TV news anchorwoman said, was the most serious of all the charges and would keep him in jail until the twenty-second century.

Scott Brainerd had plea-bargained to a charge of kidnapping and conspiracy, which the government finally agreed to, since the feds could find no solid proof of his activity in arms dealing. He was sentenced to ten years in jail. But Sally knew, she told Quinlan, that Scott would have the best behavior in the entire prison system. She'd just bet the little worm would be out in three years, curse him. Quinlan rubbed his hands together and said he couldn't wait.

In the previous June, Sally had become the senior aide to Senator Bob McCain. She had begun showing Quinlan a glitzy Washington, D.C., that was sleazy in a very different way from what he was used to. He said he wasn't certain which Washington was more fascinating. Sally was running every day, usually with James, and in July she began to sing in the shower again.

Amabel Perdy, it had been agreed to in late July, was going to be treated differently from the other fifty members of The Cove. Besides committing eight murders—four by stabbing—she'd also shot a special agent, kidnapped her niece, and aided and abetted the escape of a murder suspect, thus becoming an accessory. Her trial would be held at the end of the year. Neither Quinlan nor Sally was looking forward to it.

All the murders were detailed in Thelma Nettro's diaries—how they had been done, when, and by whom. Thelma Nettro wrote that there was little or no remorse among the townspeople after the twentieth victim had been dispatched. Poison was the favored method, she wrote, because Ralph Keaton didn't like mess when he laid the people out for burial.

She herself had murdered two people, an old couple from Arkansas, she wrote, who'd died quickly, smiling, because they'd eaten slices of Martha's New Jersey cheesecake and hadn't tasted the poison.

It came out that the last two murders of old people who'd had the misfortune to want to try the World's Greatest Ice Cream had occurred just two months before Sally Quinlan had arrived for the first time in The Cove to hide at her aunt Amabel's cottage. Reverend Hal Vorhees had drawn the highest number. He'd persuaded an affluent old couple to remain for a special evening spiritual revival service that had just been organized that very afternoon.

Thelma had written in her diary that it had been a very pleasant service, with many people rising to give thanks to God for what He'd done for them. There were punch and cookies after the service.

Revered Hal hadn't put enough arsenic in the cookies, and the old couple had had to be poisoned again, which distressed everyone, particularly Doc Spiver.

Three books were being written on The Cove, all with a different slant, the biggest best-seller presenting Reverend Hal Vorhees as a crazed messiah who had murdered children in Arizona, then come to The Cove and converted all the townspeople to a form of Satanism.

Since it was obvious that the murders would have continued until either all the townspeople died off or were caught, as was the case, the Justice Department and the lawyers agreed that the old people would be separated, each one sent to a different mental institution in a different state. The attorney general said simply in an interview after the formal sentencing, "We can't trust any two of them together. Look what happened before."

The ACLU objected, but not very strenuously, contending that the ingredients in the World's Greatest Ice Cream (the recipe remained a secret) had induced an irresponsible hysteria in the old people that led them to lose their sense of moral value and judgment. Thus they shouldn't be held answerable for their deeds. When the ACLU lawyer was asked if she would go to The Cove to buy ice cream, she allowed that she would only if she was wearing tattered blue jeans and driving a very old Volkswagen Beetle. Perhaps, one newspaper editorial said, it was a collective sugar high that drove them all to do it.

Thelma Nettro died peacefully in her sleep before the final disposition of her friends. Martha hanged herself in her cell when she was told by a matron in mid-July that young Ed had died of prostate cancer.

As for The Cove and the World's Greatest Ice Cream, both ceased to exist. The sign at the junction of highways 101 and 101A fell down some two years later and lay there until a memorabilia buff hauled it away to treasure it in his basement.

Hikers still visit The Cove now and again. Not much there now, but the view from the cliffs at sunset—with or without a martini—is spectacular.